POET, PROPHET, FOX.

The Tale of Sinnach the Seer

BOOK ONE

HOW THE FOX GAINED HIS SIGHT

M.Z. McDonnell

Moose Maple Press

Moose Maple Press
Vermont
www.mzmcdonnell.com

Cover Design and Illustrations by M.Z. McDonnell

ISBN 978-0-578-40586-5

I dedicate this work to my ancestors and to my transcestors. Your struggles and triumphs have laid strength in my bones.

And to the transgendered youth:
Know that you are part of a long legacy of seers and poets, prophets and healers. You embody an uncommon power and with it enable humanity to see itself more clearly.

CONTENTS

Map

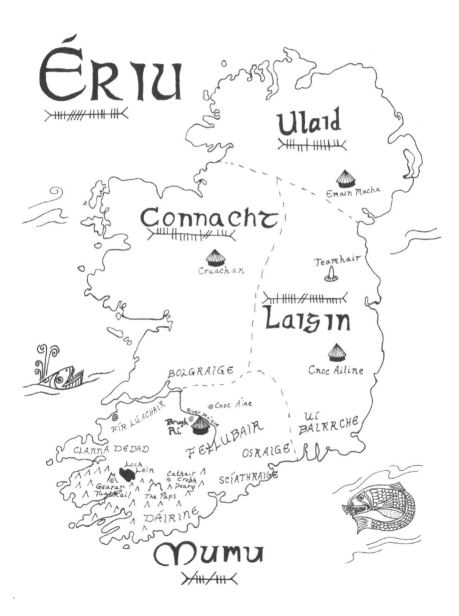

Glossary and Pronunciation

All names and terms are from Old Irish unless otherwise noted.

Áedán. Pronounced: AY-dawn.

Aire. Pronounced: AR-ah. Meaning lord, a man of the flaith (noble) class.

Bile. Pronounced: BILL-ah. Meaning sacred tree.

Bóaire. Pronouned: BO-arah. A farmer of higher status, having at least twelve cows. Literally, bóaire translates to 'cattle lord'.

Brithem. Pronounced: BRITH-em or BREH-hem. A subcategory of filid (see below) who served as judges and legal counsel to chieftains, memorizing and upholding the oral law tracts and the legal precedents. The brithem later became the Brehon class in the medieval period.

Búan. Pronounced: BOO-on.

Cadrolón (Celt-Iberian). Pronounced: ka-dro-LONE.

Cellach. Pronounced: KELL-akh.

Druí. Pronounced: DREW-ee. (Plural: druíd). A subcategory of filid who served as spiritual leaders, prophets, and sorcerers. The druíd had an important place in Irish society right up through the medieval period.

Ériu. Pronounced: AIR-oo. One of the three sacred names of the tripartite goddess of all Ireland. Her other two names, less often used, are Banba and Fódla.

Fili. Pronounced: FIL-ah. (Plural: filid). Meaning seer or poet. The ancient Irish class of learned poets who acted as druíd, judges, storytellers, and healers, depending on their specializations. In later periods these roles separated into different professions. They are the only individuals in early Irish society that can legally pass between the boundaries of the túatha on their own.

Flaith. Pronounced: flath. The noble class.

Géarshúileach. Pronounced: gyair-HOO-lakh.

Lí Lon. Pronounced: lee LUN.

Líaig. Pronounced: LEE-ah. A subcategory of filid who served as physicians and healers.

Máel Conall. Pronounced: MWAYL CON-ul.

Muirenn. Pronounced: MWIR-en.

Mumu. The ancient name of the province of Munster in the southwest of Ireland. In the late Iron Age, when this story takes place, Mumu was governed by chieftains of the lineage of the Érainn people. There were four ancient provinces of Ireland in this mythohistorical time period: Mumu (Munster), Connacht, Laigin (Leinster), and Ulaid (Ulster).

Nemed. The highest social class in ancient Irish society, consisting of the noble aristocracy (flaith) and the most learned artisans and poets.

Ócaire. Pronounced: OH-care-ah. A farmer of lower status, having less wealth (livestock) than the bóaire farmer.

Ollamh. Pronounced: OH-luv. (Plural: ollamhna). Meaning a master, or one who has studied for at least eight years as a fili or another intellectual profession, and has achieved the highest rank of that art.

Rí. Pronounced: REE. Meaning chieftain or king. Rígain (REE-gan) means female chieftain or queen.

Síd. Pronounced: SHEE. Meaning the Good People, the Fair Folk, the Other People, or the Faeries (though it can be dangerous to call them the latter, as they are thought to dislike this name). They are a people that live in the Otherworld, a world parallel to this one that occasionally overlaps. They are descended from the ancient people known as the Túatha de Danann. Síd may also refer to the ancient forts, mounds, or hills of Ireland that these beings inhabit. The Síd are not the same as the modern concept of "fairies", those small benevolent winged creatures of Victorian invention.

Sinnach. Pronounced: SHIN-akh.

Talorc. Pronounced: TA-lirk.

Toltu. Pronounced: TALL-too.

Túath. Pronounced: TOO-ah. (Plural: túatha). Meaning tribe, referring to both a place and its people. Túatha were scaled in nested jurisdictions. The smallest túatha was often governed by a petty chieftain called a rí-túath. Sometimes several túatha were joined together into a mór-túath and governed by a regional chieftain, a mór-rí. Many túatha and mór-túatha were joined together to form a confederated province led by a provincial chieftain, or rí-cóicid. There were either four or five provinces in Ireland at various points in history.

Prologue

Out in the meadow swallows circled high, dipped low, and arched again upwards, catching craneflies. Muirenn paced amongst the sheep, plucking sowthistles. In a stripe down the spine of an elder ewe she set those yellow flowers and stood back to admire her work. The ewe turned a cool eye at the little girl, bleated once, and turned back to the grass, unamused. A balmy breeze bent the ryegrass, sending ripples through that tawny sea.

The swallows fell quiet. A merlin screamed overhead. Muirenn looked up to it, shielding her eyes, and noticed the sun had risen to its height. Was it noon already?

"Rónán! It's noon!" she called to her brother across the pasture. He stood speaking with his father on the other side of the herd.

"Well go then! You heard Mamaí. Do as she says... for once." Rónán muttered that last part under his breath. Rónán was nine, and the two years of seniority he held over his sister made him an authority on all matters of importance.

Frowning, Muirenn kicked an orb of dandelion fluff and made her way home. Her mother had told her, sternly, to come back from the pasture at noon to help her in the house. Muirenn ought not to delay or else she would surely receive a tongue-lashing. Those she endured more often now, for as her legs grew long so grew her want to wander. Her mother was not a patient woman; many things perturbed her, most of all her daughter's fondness for unsanctioned adventures.

The path homeward through the field was direct; it was dry and well-trodden. But there was another path, a path through the shaded wood skirting the fen. Frogs burrowed in the mud there, newts laid under stones, and pine martins paced silent in the shadows. So many creatures, so many secrets were hidden there under the oaks and alders. Thus Muirenn, ever yearning to know the unknown, forgot her fear of her mother's consternation and plunged headlong into the woodland.

On that ferny path she passed under a pair of whistling wrens and sang up to them, matching their cheer. Through pine needles she padded until she came to the edge of the reed-choked fen. She paused then, hearing the shouts and giggles of children. Muirenn knew those voices. With one last furtive glance down the path to home, she turned off the trail and leapt from sedge to sedge in pursuit of those sounds.

"Muirenn!" called a black-haired boy. He waved at her through a screen of bulrushes.

She gave the boy a haughty glare. "Not Muirenn—Áedán! Don't you remember?"

"Oh. Alright, Áedán then." Colmán shrugged. "Well, now that you're here the sides are even. We can finish yesterday's war."

"I'm Cú Chulainn this time!" shouted a stout boy named Fíngin. His arms were painted up to the elbows with mud.

"Then Áedán is on the side of Connacht," said a third boy. "Áedán, you can play Medb."

"I will *not* play Medb!" Áedán balled his fists. No one could make him play the role of a woman, not even Medb, that brave warrior-queen. "I'll be Ferdiad and I'll come against you, Cú Chulainn!" He took a stick for his spear and leapt at his opponent.

The boys reenacted their favorite raiding tale: the raging of Connacht against Ulaid for the hero-bull of Donn Cúailnge. They ranged from the fen to the woodland, drifting up a slope tangled with briars. Circling around that wall of thorns, the boys found themselves at the foot of a small hillock. Its bare top broke through the canopy of alder and holly, sending down a shower of mottled light to the forest below.

All paused and gaped up at that tumble of earth and stone. It was an ancient fort, or perhaps a tomb built long ago by the hands of a forgotten people.

"The Faery fort," Colmán whispered in wonderment.

"Shhh!" Fíngin hissed. "Colmán, don't call it that!" His eyes were round and darting. "We shouldn't be here. Dadaí told me not to come to the ráth. They might... be here... even if we can't see them." He took two steps backward and paused, seeking assent from his comrades.

Áedán wrung his hands around his spear-stick, breathed in deeply, then stepped towards the ráth. Though no less afraid than the others, he was more eager to prove himself the equal of his peers.

"I'm not afraid," he said, and took another step forward. A sudden quiet fell in the glade: no wind stirred the leaves, no bird sang in peace nor warning, not even a cricket trilled. Áedán approached two hawthorn trees, standing like sentinels amidst the rubble. Warily, he watched their poison thorns.

"Áedán, no! Áedán..." Fíngin warned.

But Áedán paid him no heed, for as he passed under the branches of those thorn trees his attention was caught by a strange sound. It was soft like the cooing of a dove and yet more mournful. Was it a flute? No... perhaps the plucking of harp strings? Then he heard a voice sing sweetly, though he could not make out the words.

"Do you hear that?" he asked, and heard no answer.

Áedán stepped closer, ensorcelled by rapturous sound. He was vaguely aware of a commotion behind him, a shouting of several voices, but found himself quite disinterested in it. There was only one thing in the world he wished to know: the source of that ethereal music.

Áedán... In the lyrics he heard his name. *Áedán...* He put a hand to the mound, then a foot, preparing to ascend. Looking upward, he saw a gentle mist drifted down to him from the crown of the hill.

"MUIRENN!" A shout rang out in the glen, clear and painfully near. Áedán's hand was wrenched backwards and his chest was encircled by two long arms. He screamed and clawed against them as he was dragged away from the ráth and the hawthorn trees.

A sudden light struck his eyes, like the sun through a rent in the clouds. Áedán's mind cleared, and he realized then who held him: his mother, Tómnat. He stared into her face, trembling.

"Muirenn!" Tómnat exclaimed. Her face was creased with worry and rage. "What are you doing? What—why were you climbing the ráth?" She slapped her daughter hard across the face.

Muirenn blinked in bewilderment, put a hand to her stinging cheek, and with a shock realized what she had done.

Tómnat gripped the child by the wrist and roughly dragged her away. One by one, the little boys' heads poked out from the shield of brambles where they had hidden from that mother's wrath.

Fíngin chided his unfortunate friend: "I told you, Áedán—I told you so!"

"Farewell, Áedán! I hope the sally rod strikes nice and gentle!" called Colmán. The boys laughed, cackling like magpies.

"Leave off, you brats!" Tómnat growled. "Corrupting my daughter with your deviance. Go home! Get you gone—now!"

The boys shrieked and scampered away from that fearsome woman, leaving their friend to face his mother's fury alone.

Tómnat ground her teeth as she marched her daughter home. "I told you to come home at noon, but instead you go off and dive headfirst into trouble? I've spent hours searching for you. Finally, Mo Lua said he saw you join Fíngin and the boys at the fen, and from there I followed your shouting—to a ráth, no less! What possessed you?" She looked Muirenn up and down. Her legs were caked in mud up to the knees and half her linen smock was soaked with bog water. "Ach—look at you! What a mess. I had just washed that smock. Have you no respect for me?"

Tómnat yanked the child's arm and made her stumble. "And how many times have I told you—do not go near the ráth! The Good People live there beneath the hill." She named them indirectly so as not to draw their attention. "They'll steal you away to the Otherworld or lead you astray. That's how your uncle Dagán died. He was only just older than you. They led him astray in the mist and he got caught by the sea and drowned."

"I know," Muirenn muttered. She had heard the tale many times before.

Tómnat paused, looking down at her daughter with ire. "Well then, what do you have to say for yourself?"

Muirenn was silent, mortified. She watched her feet, too scared to meet her mother's eyes.

"Huh? And why did those boys call you Áedán?"

The girl mumbled.

"What did you say? Speak up."

Muirenn squeaked: "Because that's my boy name."

"What do you mean that's your boy name?"

"When I'm with the boys I'm a boy too, so they call me by my boy name."

Tómnat stopped and bent down to look her child squarely in the face, grasping her little shoulder in an eagle grip. "You're not a boy, Muirenn. You're a girl. You're not to pretend to be a boy or I won't allow you to play with those boys anymore. Do you hear me?"

Muirenn was shocked. "But why?"

"Why? Because it's unnatural, Muirenn! Girls are girls! Boys are boys! There are some places your imagination should not go. You are too dreamy, Muirenn. You must focus more on the world in front of you. Go on making such absurd pretends and you'll bring shame to our family."

Muirenn's cheeks flushed crimson. Her eyes filled up with hot tears.

"Do you understand?" Tómnat demanded.

Muirenn did not understand, but she nodded anyway, wishing to please her mother. She wiped her eyes with the back of her hand and smeared mud across her cheek. Tómnat's heart momentarily softened, and she kissed the child on the clean side of her face. "Oh, my little rose. I only want to keep you safe. Now, after you're cleaned up we'll practice spinning yarn."

But I am not the rose... I am the thorn, Muirenn thought scornfully. She stole a backward glance, imagining the weird and wild wonders that lay beyond the reach of her mother's arms.

PART I:

MUIRENN

CHAPTER ONE

Apple Picking

A spear of sunlight struck the sea and caused the shore to glisten. The tide was low, the scent of black mud and seaweed came inland on the west wind. The crying of gulls filled the air as they vied for the choicest perches on pylons and weir posts. Upon the leather hull of an overturned currach, three cormorants stood stone still, their oil-slick wings outspread to dry in the shimmering light.

A troupe of bare-footed boys scampered across the beach, its sand still cold from the dark of night and wet from the ebbing tide. An October chill invigored their limbs and inspired a footrace. Colmán won the first; Áedán won the second. Fíngin, meanwhile, peeled off and made for the mud, as he was wont to do.

"Look what I've got!" he shouted, and pulled up a palm-sized clam. The others gathered round and searched for their own.

Áedán waded up to his shins in the stinging-cold sea and raked through the muck with his toes. As he did so, a riddle came into his mind.

"Listen lads, I've a riddle for you." Tossing back his flame-bright curls, he raised up his arms in a mocking, magnanimous gesture and spoke with the air of a poet chanting meter. "I've the skin of a stone, the flesh of a fish, and a mouth wider than a man's but toothless. What am I?"

A long moment passed. Colmán stood up suddenly and yelled: "A clam!"

"Ach, that one was too easy—even Colmán could guess it," said Donnán. "Give us another, Áedán."

"Alright. Here's one more: What goes round the wood and round the wood and never goes into the wood?"

All five of the boys were silent but for the slurping and sucking of their hands in the mud.

Then Colmán exclaimed: "A hawk!"

"A hunter!" said another.

"A rope!"

Áedán shook his head at each of these. They had all run out of guesses when Fíngin said finally, "Well then, give us a hint." The others nodded.

"It's like the voice of a hound."

"The bark!" exclaimed Fiachra. He smiled proudly and cracked a clam between two stones. Pulling its pink flesh from the shell, he waved it before his face. "Who dares eat this raw?"

"Ew! Not me! Too cold, too slimy," said Donnán.

Colmán said, "What'll you give me if I do?"

Fiachra shrugged. "Well, a... I'll give you an apple!"

Colmán nodded, puckered his face, and slurped down the clam flesh. He gagged once, wiped his lips on his sleeve, then showed them all his empty mouth. The others squirmed and laughed and slapped his shoulder in congratulations.

"Where's my apple then?" Colmán stuck out his hand.

"It's in the orchard, of course," said Fiachra, pointing east.

A series of groans echoed through the crowd. Áedán leapt from the beach up the grassy bank. "Well then, let's go! I could use an apple myself!" He jogged away and the rest followed.

The boys ambled across the meadow, past a small village of reed-thatched roundhouses to the edge of the pasturelands owned by the lord Talorc. Talorc mac Iollan was an aire, a nobleman whose extensive lands he rented out to lower-class families. Áedán and his friends were all born to such families of poor-farmers and herdsmen that made their livelihoods as the aire's clients.

The afternoon clouds curdled and a light drizzle fell as the boys reached the orchard near the aire's compound. A stand of apple trees and a hazel coppice stood to the west of it, fields of oats, barley, and flax were to the south, and a large paddock to the east held the aire's herd of hardy breeding mares and their foals. Beyond that, in the wide open pastures, a team of cowherds tended the aire's hundred-head of speckled cattle. The aire was indeed a wealthy man, a cousin of the rí-túath—the chieftain of the Fír Lúachair tribe.

The outer wall of his compound was made of earth mounded up so high that the children could only see the conical points of the round-houses within. The boys called it the brugh—the palace—for they imagined it to be as luxurious inside as the brughs of the mythical chieftains described in the winter tales. Whether it was as splendid inside as they imagined they did not know, for their families had standings too low to have ever been invited inside.

As the boys looped their limbs into those knobby apple branches, Áedán looked east and spied from his perch a small figure emerge from the gate of the brugh. The figure jogged towards them.

"Ach. Here he comes now, that mouse-faced moron," Áedán groaned.

It was the aire's son, Sárán, an infrequent visitor to Áedán's band. Sárán was younger than the rest by several years—Áedán himself was now ten—but it was not just his junior age that made the boys begrudge him. They found him petty, condescending, and prone to pouting when hurt or startled. Áedán had little love for him.

"He has the tongue of the skink and the heart of a shrew," he quipped. Colmán chuckled, admiring his friend's wit.

Since the summer, Áedán's dislike had swelled into a seething hatred, for the younger boy had discovered Áedán's other name—the name his mother gave him. He used it to tease Áedán about his sex. Sárán used it to tease Áedán about his sex, but he was the only boy to do so. The rest knew that a test of Áedán's temper would spell a trip home with a black eye or a bloody lip.

"What will you do when you grow breasts, Muirenn? Will you sow yourself a pretty dress and lay flowers in your hair?" Sárán would tease. He laughed, but he laughed alone.

Áedán always held back, knowing that to strike a boy of the flaith class would bring him certain trouble, especially since Sárán was such a cringeling. Not honor nor shame would prevent him from complaining to his father, the lord. Yet on this damp day in the orchard, the taunting ended differently for Sárán.

The boys climbed up high to get at the last of the apples on the topmost limbs. Every autumn, a few apples were left on each tree to show gratitude for the orchard's gifts. Such payments to the Síd and to the trees themselves ensured abundance in future cycles of the sun. It was said amongst the Érainn: *Take less and the world shall gift you more.* Yet the children hardly understood the importance of this wisdom, and so they assumed the apples were left there by laziness, to be wasted if not devoured by their deserved mouths. They stole as many of those apples as they dared; but even so, many fruits were still out of reach. Enough would be left to share with the Unseen after all.

Áedán was a bold climber and went up to a high branch, throwing down three speckled apples that clung there. Climbing down to a lower branch, he came upon Sárán eating an apple.

"How immodest, Muirenn, that you should spread your legs above my head. No need to show me what I already know: that you've no boy parts after all!" said Sárán with a churlish grin.

Áedán's face bloomed bright with shame. It was only a taunt—Áedán was covered by the underclothes and smock that every underage child wore, boys and girls alike. But jest or not, this time Sárán had gone too far.

Like a boar enraged, Áedán did not think—he acted by instinct alone. With one hand he snatched the apple from Sárán's open mouth, and with the other he smacked the younger boy hard across his face, so hard that Sárán yelped and fell out of the tree, landing with a thud in the dirt below. For several moments Sárán simply laid there, numb with shock. With a groan he rolled onto his side. Cradling his hand against his chest, Sárán began to howl in pain.

Áedán swung down lightly from the tree and stood over the boy with his hands on his hips, triumphant. Colmán, Fíngin, and the others gathered round and stared at Áedán in awe, a little worshipful, for most of them had, at least once, wished to give Sárán a taste of the dirt.

Áedán poked at Sárán with his bare foot. "Look at him, crying like a shoat for the sow's tit. Get up and apologize to me."

Sárán slowly got to his feet, his left cheek scarlet with the imprint of a hand. His right hand was held to his chest, the thumb sticking out at an odd angle. Sárán glared with tearful red eyes were, recoiled, and spat directly into Áedán's face. Shuffling backwards, Sárán stumbled, picked himself up, and dashed away towards his father's house.

The other boys leapt after Sárán like a pack of hounds, but Áedán called them back. "Leave him! Let him go. He won't be back anytime soon." He wiped the spit from his face and smiled, glad that he had finally taught that brat some respect. *Somebody had to do it.* Eyes ablaze with pride, he turned back to the climbing and gave no more thought to his enemy.

The troupe moved on to wrestling out in the stubbled barley field. As the sun dipped under the ocean in the west, each of them went home with the taste of apples and straw in their mouths.

Early the next morning, before Muirenn and Rónán went out with their father, Lonán, to graze the sheep, a man arrived on horseback. He was handsomely dressed and his black gelding wore a blue bridle with a bit of polished bronze.

"Welcome, Berach," said Lonán warmly. "Come in, come in. We've some tea for you, if you'll take it. Have you eaten? How's your family?"

"Oh, well, thank you, Lonán. We're well, thanks to south wind. A good apple year. The cider will be strong and sweet come winter!" He dismounted and paused at the doorway, not stooping to come in. Lonán beckoned him sit and breakfast with the family by the hearth. "No, no. Thank you. I cannot stay long. I've come with a message from the aire. He's asked you to come to the brugh and to bring the red-haired child."

Lonán was puzzled. "Really? What for?"

Berach shook his head. "I don't know. Honestly, or I would tell you. Must be something about the horses. The aire is planning to take up the hunt more often now that the weather's turned cold. Though I don't know why your son is involved."

"Em, no. The one with red hair is my daughter."

"Oh! Right, of course. So sorry," said Berach, flustered. "I haven't seen her recently... only from far away when she's playing with the other children in the orchard. Hard to tell at that age, really, since they all are dressed alike until they come of age. Can't be too careful, really." He was referring to the tradition amongst the Érainn of dressing young children, boys and girls alike, in girls' clothes so as to confuse the Síd. The Síd liked to steal children, boys especially. "Anyway, if you can make it to the aire's compound before noon, I would advise it."

"We'll leave now. Thank you, Berach."

"Of course. I hope it's nothing serious. His feathers were ruffled this morning, though I don't know why. He can get in a state, as you well know. Watch yourself."

Lonán set off quickly, his daughter happily skipping ahead. Though his thoughts were clotted with questions, Muirenn was all excitement— finally she would see what lay inside those earthen walls! *Fíngin and Colmán will be jealous!* she thought.

They arrived at the brugh's heavy oaken gate set into the circular outer wall. Muirenn craned her neck to look up, squinting. The wall was tall, taller even than her father. A man was at the open gate, holding a spear. Lonán knew the spearman, for he came this way often to care for the aire's horses. Horse-tending was part of Lonán's duty as the aire's client, to pay for the privilege of farming on his land, since Lonán was too lowly to own land himself. The men exchanged nods, and the two visitors were permitted entry.

Muirenn frantically drank in the sights like a bee thirsting for nectar. There were several buildings inside the compound: a granary for storing dry oats, barley, and wheat; three pens for calves, pigs, and fowl; an out-door kitchen tended by a team of cooks and servants; and a roundhouse for the women to weave and socialize. At the center was a grassy clearing for parties and dancing. Then Muirenn looked further still and held her breath. Farthest from the gate, on the western side, was the largest roundhouse she had ever seen. Its roof was thatched not with humble reed, but with neatly-trimmed layers of golden straw, its eaves so ample they nearly touched the ground.

They came inside this great hall by its south-facing door, passing across a threshold of red yew wood carved with waves and spirals. The interior of the hall was enormous, its roof tree as tall as five men stand-ing on each other's shoulders, and had room enough to seat fifty men against the wall. The walls were hung with colorful banners patterned with stripes and zigzags.

Though the light inside was dim, there were things that sparkled along the walls. The hearth flames flickered, reflecting upon metallic planes. Muirenn's eyes again widened in wonder. These were weapons: brightly-painted wooden shields braced and studded with iron; leather shields embossed with spirals and concentric circles; long spears headed with bronze leaf-blades. But most intriguing of all were the swords: of bronze and iron blades as long as Muirenn's arm, their hilts made of bone or dark oiled wood.

She pulled at her father's hand and pointed. *Might I touch them?* she pleaded with her eyes. Lonán shook his head and pulled her forward by the hand, passing the central hearth to the northern end of the hall.

They approached a bench where a man sat upon the pelts of two wolves. He was tall but not handsome, with a stern, sallow face under his long brown hair. He wore a tunic of a red as deep as hawthorn berries cinched at the waist with a leather belt studded with red bronze. His trousers were of yellow linen, and around his neck was torc of twisting gold, each end terminating in a gilded acorn. Upon his feet were leather shoes decorated with red glass beads in curvilinear patterns.

A woman sat to his right, draped in an elegant gown of woad blue. At the ends of the two long plaits which laid upon her breast were little balls of gold the size of robin's eggs, and many bronze rings were on her fingers. A young boy in a yellow and red checkered tunic sat to the man's left. A servant stood to either side of the bench while others moved about the house, tending the hearth and tidying up. Behind the bench a stately man stood erect, dressed in the five-colored cloak of an ollamh fili: a master poet, druí, and scholar of tribal law.

The seated man watched with hard eyes as they approached. Lonán stopped before him and bowed his head. The man nodded stiffly. Muirenn tore her eyes away from the weapons on the wall and glanced between the faces of the rich man and her father. Lonán's face was creased with deference and unease. *This must be the aire, Talorc,* Muirenn thought. Then her eyes darted to the face of the boy. With a sharp in-breath she recognized Sárán, then Muirenn knew why she and her father had been summoned. Her heart leapt to a gallop in her chest.

The aire spoke. His harsh, gravelly voice filled the whole hall. "Lonán, your son has injured my son, Sárán. I've called upon Onchú, the fili of the rí-túath, to act as brithem. He will judge what payment you owe me for his injury." He waved his hand at the ollamh fili who stood behind the bench.

Lonán became pale and dropped his head like a kicked dog. Muirenn had never seen him so fearful. "I'm sorry, lord... my son? Rónán? He's out in the field with the sheep. He rarely plays with the younger boys anymore, I don't think— "

"From what I've been told, you only have one red-haired son," Talorc interrupted, "the one standing beside you." The aire pointed at Muirenn. She shivered and pinned herself to her father's side.

Lonán shook his head, confused. "Lord, there must be some confusion. This is not my son. This is my daughter, Muirenn."

Every face in the hall reflected bewilderment. All, that is, except for Muirenn and Sárán. The fili Onchú stepped forward and calmly addressed the flaith boy. "Is this the child that hurt you?" he asked, pointing at Muirenn. Sárán nodded.

"He's called Áedán and he pushed me out of a tree yesterday." The boy pouted; his voice became high and thin as if holding back a sob.

Lonán looked down at his child with sudden understanding. His confusion turned to anger. "Is this true?" Lonán demanded. Muirenn slunk a step away from him, too frightened to speak. Her silence was affirming.

Lonán addressed the aire, his voice taut as a bow string. "I'm sorry, my lord. I understand now. I'm ashamed to say that my daughter likes to pretend she's a boy and that her name is Áedán. Several years ago we told her to stop, but I was unaware she had kept up the farce. I'm terribly, terribly sorry she hurt your son. I beg your forgiveness. I promise to discipline her severely." He took Muirenn's shoulder in a powerful grip that made her whimper a little in pain.

"An apology is not enough, Lonán," said the aire. "Your... child... dislocated Sárán's thumb on his sword hand and the líaig had to set it right. I pray that it heals well, that he be without blemish, and that it will not lessen his ability to one day fight on behalf of the túath. Onchú will determine how my family should be compensated, according to the law."

Talorc nodded at Onchú and the fili stepped forward. He was a middle-aged man with a placid face and a steady, learned gaze. He addressed the congregation in a low and definitive tone made heavy by the weight of a hundred generations of wisdom. "The law is clear on this matter. If an adult fuidir of Lonán's rank, being an aire's tenant and having no land of his own, maimed the lord or an adult member of his family, that fuidir would be obligated to pay a fee as determined by both the flaith's honor price and the severity of the injury. This is described in the Fénechas, or more specifically, the Bretha Dian Cécht." He turned then to Talorc and spoke more gently. "But these are children, lord, and it is said in the law that injuries inflicted by one child upon another in a moment of play have no associated fees."

Talorc balked. "But this was not play! As my son said, the child deliberately pushed him out of the tree with malicious intent. It was no accident."

"He insulted me! I was defending my honor!" These words erupted from Muirenn in a passion before she could think to hold them back. Lonán squeezed her shoulder hard and hissed at her to be quiet.

Onchú the fili raised an eyebrow. The girl was assertive, even aggressive. One of her standing ought to be modest and mild. Yet the fili, being wise, paused to reflect upon this thought. If a nobleman's son displayed such traits, he would be marked for warriorship. But Muirenn was a girl and a fuidir—a peasant. Girls of the flaith class might, on occasion, be trained for war if they were apt, but Muirenn could never be. Onchú mused: did Nature then misplace these traits? Why? And how ironic it was that Nature chose not to sow courage where it was more needed—in the soul of the aire's own son. *No wonder Talorc is so angered—he is ashamed of his craven son*, thought the wise man.

The fili observed the little girl carefully. There was something re-markable about her, but it was subtle; whatever it was could not be seen with ordinary sight. Onchú quieted his mind, chanted a charm beneath his breath, and with the druí's sacred sight spied the peculiarity. The shape of the little girl was blurred as if doubled, and behind her face there seemed to be another, one very much like her own but more angu-lar, with wider jaw and sharper brow. There was a shimmering about her head, like a reflection of sunlight from the surface of a wellspring. It was unlike anything he had ever seen before.

Onchú would have shared these observations with his lord, but the moment he opened his mouth to speak, his tongue went numb. A mist passed across his eyes like a storm cloud obscuring the sun. A voice ech-oed in his mind like faraway thunder; it was a feminine voice.

You will forget what you have just seen, druí, and speak nothing of it.

Onchú blinked rapidly and his mind became lucid once more. All he had experienced while in trance had occurred in the space of a single breath. He gazed once again upon the congregation with clear eyes, hav-ing no memory of what had just transpired.

The fili cleared his throat and addressed the child before him. "Muirenn, you are old enough now to understand the law and your place in society. So I will explain it to you. The fuidir, the flaith, the bóaire and ócaire, the craftsmen, the filid—all the classes of our túath, including the tribal chieftains—are bound by the laws of the Fénechas and by the cus-toms of our tribe. As a fuidir, you have no honor to defend. You are below the flaith and you are below the bóaire and ócaire—the cattle-lords and farmers—that are the foundation of our society. You must do as the aire instructs and provide labor for him in exchange for the privilege of living on his land. Your father herds the lord's sheep and tends his horses in this way. Talorc protects you and provides for your basic needs. He assures compensations for ills done to you or by you. Your family is the aire's dependent. And yet, the fuidir still have rights under the law, and may choose to leave the aire's protection as long as there are no leftover debts to pay. However, if your family does incur debts that you cannot pay, or commits serious crimes against the aire or against the túath, you may be stripped of your rights so that you become dóerfuidir, or slaves— unfree and tied to the aire. So you must know that all of your actions have consequences, and inasmuch, you must act with restraint and civility. This is the key to a peaceful and fulfilling life for one of your rank."

Muirenn's eyes fell to her feet, soiled and bare upon the aire's neatly-swept floor. Until that moment, she had never known a reason to put herself beneath any other. Now there was a new feeling, a hollowness in her bones, a coldness in her core, and if she had thought to ask her father what this sensation was he would have told her: it is shame, a feeling that all fuidir come to know well.

But beside this emotion, beneath it, she felt an ember catch flame; an ember of indignation against what seemed an incomprehensible injustice. How could a sniveling brat like Sárán be always held above her, even if he was in the wrong?

"I trust your judgment, Onchú. Yet still, I think this was not an accident," said Talorc crossly.

The fili turned to the aire. "I understand that you are concerned for your son, Talorc. Yet it is common knowledge that children are not of able mind until they come of age. Thus, they are not responsible for their actions until that time. It is unrealistic and uncompassionate of us to ignore the fact that, in the mind of a child, the boundary between play and conflict is mutable. That distinction is realized later in life, as we are allotted the adult responsibilities that maintain the order and cohesion of our tribe. It is through conflicts such as these that a child learns about right and wrong; about taking responsibility for one's actions. As a member of the flaith class, it is important that Sárán learns how to make sound judgments when conflicts arise. We might choose to see this situation as a blessing—a lesson which will help Sárán understand the virtues held in the laws and customs of our people. This knowledge helps us maintain Cóir, the divine rightness that balances the Universe.

"And lastly, I will say this: as a flaith, Sárán must gain the respect of his peers if he is going to become the kind of man who will lead other men in battle. He should be encouraged to resolve these kinds of conflicts on his own, without the intervention of his parents or a brithem. Overuse of the law can lead to its trivialization, or an overdependence on an outside authority to define for us what should be common sense." Onchú bent his head humbly to both Talorc and Lonán, then stepped back to stand behind the bench.

With reluctance, Talorc nodded. "There is wisdom in your judgment. Then there will be no fee." He turned to Lonán and spoke sharply. "Your daughter is a nuisance and ought to learn the modesty that is proper for her sex. I demand that she be kept about your house and not be allowed to wander where she cannot be recalled by an adult."

Lonán nodded, ashen-faced. "It will be done, lord."

Father and daughter shuffled out of the aire's hall and left the compound with a silence between them. The swift autumn wind cut through the wool on their backs.

CHAPTER TWO

Changeling

All throughout the winter Muirenn was kept close to the house and made to help her mother with the householding. Though winter was dark, Tómnat's days were brighter than ever now that her daughter was always by her side in the house and the dairy. When Tómnat was pleased, she sang—she could have a sweet voice when she wished—and now she sang throughout the day as she worked. She had not felt such joy since Muirenn was a mild, milk-cheeked toddler. *What is of greater pride to a mother than to have a lovely, faithful daughter by her side?* Bending down, she brushed her lips across the girl's freckles.

When Tómnat turned away, Muirenn wiped her face with the back of her hand and scowled, returning to her work carding the wool. *How long will I be imprisoned here?* she asked in sour silence. Her only hope was that relief would come on Imbolc, the first of February, the day of milk and motherhood. On that sacred day her father might ask for her help with the lambing as he usually did, for she was far gentler with the lambs than Rónán.

Muirenn counted every dreary day until Imbolc. On that holy day, after sunset, the strawboys came. To every household in the clan came this wily band of revelers. They rapped on the door and burst in, chittering in the high voices of adolescent children. But on this night they were not children—they were servants made of straw, criers of the Goddess who brings in the spring.

Muirenn stood away from them, wary. These mummers had always disturbed her. Their costumes of braided straw crackled as they swept their stiffened arms and kicked their yellow legs in a grotesque dance, bells jangling at the hips. They came to the hearth. A dark eye beamed through the braids of a huge cone of straw which covered the figure's whole head and neck, obscuring the face. The eye stole a glance at Muirenn. Her skin prickled and she hid behind her father.

The strawboys would not linger, for they came bearing a sacred charge. Between the four of them they carried a child-sized litter, and in it sat the goddess Bríg. She was, at the moment, a doll made from the straw of the last sheaf caught in autumn, dressed in baby's clothes. Tómnat welcomed in Bríg and gave her servants eggs and a sip of the year's first milk from the ewes. The doll was lifted gently and placed in a little bed by the hearth that was made specially for Her. The strawboys made merry tunes by the flute and the frame drum, and all in the house sang sacred songs to welcome in spring. And when the doll, the Goddess, had completed Her blessing, the revelers lifted Her up again and carried Her out into the night laughing, drunk on new milk.

As the sun rose on the morning of Imbolc, Tómnat and her mother-in-law went out to gather the sparkling dew of dawn and with it bathed their faces. This dew was imbued with Bríg's power to restore their youth, to make new what was old, so that their skin would become smooth again and their lips pink and plump as ripe strawberries. Or so they hoped.

Muirenn, of course, could not be convinced to do a thing so silly and effeminate. Instead she went to her father and pleaded: "Will there be lambs today? May I come with you?"

But Lonán said shortly: "There's no need, Muirenn. Rónán and I can do it." As he and Rónán went away over the field, Muirenn looked after them coldly, empty, despairing. That night she dreamed of the bright summer sun, and across it swept the dark orb of the moon, shutting out its light.

As the days lengthened and brightened, Muirenn's heart darkened as if eclipsed. What was the use of spring if she could not get out in it? She missed the sounds of the sheep bleating in the pastures, the calls and whistles of the shepherds, the barking of dogs, and the musty scent of wool drenched in sunlight. Jealousy made her nip at her brother with insults and nagging. They fought almost daily. She longed for her friends and the freedom that she had once had as a boy amongst boys. When not bickering with her brother, she was dour and silent.

Tómnat was oblivious to her daughter's distress, but Muirenn's grandmother, Íte, was not. She noted the change in the girl's mood. Whereas before Muirenn was cheerful and precocious, now she would only pout, saying hardly a word that was not spiteful and pecking at her food like a thrush. She told no more riddles, spun no more tales. Her legs became as thin as hazel rods.

One morning, while Muirenn was out collecting the duck eggs, Íte spoke in hushed tones to her daughter-in-law. "Daughter," she whispered, "there is something amiss with Muirenn. She's hardly eating. She scowls so often that some days it's as if she has someone else's face. She's quiet and withdrawn, like she's hiding some hidden hatred. I'm worried... are you not as well?"

Tómnat was taken aback by these observations. In truth, Tómnat had noticed none of these things. So contented was she to have her daughter nearer, that she hadn't cared to observe whether or not Muirenn was also contented. Tómnat's first impulse was to brush these concerns aside, and yet, despite herself, her interest was piqued. The rest of the day she kept a closer eye on her daughter and by evening she began to see what Íte saw.

When the children had been put to sleep, the women stepped out into the dark to speak privately, in hushed tones.

"I'm afraid she may be... that she may be a Changeling," Íte spoke low. Her voice was like the rasp of dry leaves thrown back by a robin, revealing the worm.

Tómnat covered her mouth and gasped. "No..." she whispered. Her mind reeled, desperate for an explanation. Rifling through memories, she recalled an incident nearly four years ago—the incident at the ráth. "Bríg protect us! Do you remember when I caught the children playing at the ráth, three summers ago? Muirenn had gone very close to it—she had even started to climb! It was then that she began pretending to be a boy! Could she have been stolen then? Could she have been swapped with a look-alike—a Faery boy—before I arrived? Did I not catch her in time? Oh Goddess... not my Muirenn... first my brother and now my daughter... why? Why?"

Tómnat spilled miserable tears into Íte's shoulder. The old woman wrapped wiry arms around her daughter-in-law.

"Why are the Síd punishing us?" Tómnat sobbed. "Have we offended them? Have we offended the spirits of the land?"

Íte stroked the young woman's auburn hair and said, "Who knows the will of the Good People? They have schemes of their own. They are, indeed, without kindness or pity. It could have been the draw of your daughter's red hair. They lust after the red-haired ones most of all."

Tómnat lifted her face, eyes wide. "Dagán was red-haired too! Oh, Bríg, have mercy. What are we to do then? How do I get my daughter back?"

"I know the ordeals that are needed to send the Changeling back," said the older woman. "I've seen it done once before, to my cousin when I was a child."

"Did it work? Did he come back?"

Íte paused, her face unreadable in the darkness. "Yes, he came back. Though... he was never quite the same after that. He had been changed a little by the time he spent in the Otherworld."

Tómnat released one last desperate sob and wiped her face. She held Íte's two hands in such a grip that her mother-in-law bit back a whimper. Tómnat said resolutely: "No matter. I will have my daughter back, by any means necessary."

Íte nodded. "But first, a test to see if it truly is a Faery child or not."

The two women shared their schemes with Lonán. He objected strongly, but it was not his decision to make. The children were his wife's and the house was her domain. He was overruled. "I only ask that you perform the ordeals when I am away. Síd or not, I could not bear to see that child suffer."

One day when the weather was fine, Tómnat sent Muirenn to wash the clothes in the nearby stream. Muirenn went readily, happy to work again under the open sky. She dallied and daydreamed, working with purposeful sloth to lengthen her stay. She paused often to bask in the sun, to hear the whip-whistle of the curlew in the meadow, to watch the sea eagle dive and lift from the waves a bass writhing between her talons.

A few hours before sunset she finished, just soon enough to evade a scolding, then loaded her basket with the laundered clothes and headed for home. After hanging up the clothes to dry, she came inside to place the empty basket beside others filled with barley and oats. Haunches of smoked mutton and salted fish hung from the rafters by lengths of linen rope, and wooden vessels were stacked on a low bench fashioned from planks of sun-bleached driftwood. Three rolls of bedding were tucked away to make space on the floor for the business of the day. Bundles of dried aromatic herbs and two iron pots hung from the lower rafters. A loom stood against the round wall of waddle and daub with a length of woolen cloth, half-woven. Tómnat was by the hearth in the center; Íte sat on the floor chopping roots for the stew. "Muirenn," said Tómnat, "bring me that skin of water there by the oats."

Muirenn brought the water skin and hungrily peered down at what her mother was stirring. Muirenn rubbed her eyes, thinking that her sight must be blurred in the dim light. She bent down to look more closely. Disbelieving, she looked from her mother to grandmother. Each carried on her work as if nothing were awry. What lay before her was so weird, so inane, that Muirenn couldn't help but emit a peal of wicked laughter. For there at the hearth, Tómnat was cooking a stew of mutton, seaweed, and silverweed roots in the hollows of five eggshells.

"Either I've gone mad or you have, because I've never seen anything so stupid in all my life!" All the laughter that had been suppressed by the wretchedness of Muirenn's captivity over the last several weeks erupted like a frothing flagon of beer. The sound was wild and sharp and disturbing. At last she calmed, wiped her eyes, and sat down, panting.

Tómnat's skin prickled. Íte exchanged a look with her daughter-in-law and gave a subtle nod. Tómnat drew a quick breath and stifled her gasp. The child's shrill scornful laughter had confirmed their suspicions.

Tómnat fixed her face and turned to her daughter innocently. "I'm sure I don't know what you mean," she said. She poured the contents of the eggshells into the full cauldron of stew that had been set out of sight. She hooked the cauldron to hang over the fire and continued stirring as if nothing at all unusual had occurred.

Muirenn chuckled once, then her smile faded. *Was it a joke? A prank?* Her mother had never played a prank on her before. Neither of the women had laughed. Neither of them had even smiled. There was a sudden touch of fear, an intuition: this was some kind of trap. But for what, she could not guess.

The days slipped back into their mundane rhythm: the cooking, the milking, the carding of wool, the grinding of grain, the spinning and weaving, the hauling of water from the stream. The eggshell prank was soon forgotten in a haze of bitter boredom. There was nothing unexpected; there was nothing more to laugh about.

On a grey afternoon, the weather suddenly turned. The sky darkened to match the color of the sea, the horizon between them blurred by a faraway wall of rain, rushing eastward. Waves were whipped upward, white-tipped as with the cream of new milk. The wailing of gulls suddenly stilled as they leapt from the beach to wing homeward.

Lonán took heed of them, as any man of the sea must do, for the silence of gulls surely foretells hard weather—they will not shut up their gossip for any other reason. Father and son hurried homeward, but not fast enough to outrun the rain. As dusk fell, they stumbled into the roundhouse sopping wet.

"Great gale's a-coming," said Lonán as he stripped off his wet tunic and knelt by the fire to warm his hands.

"Oh! Muirenn," Tómnat exclaimed, "I left a bucket of mussels on the beach this morning. I've only just remembered. The storm surge will surely come up and take them way, and our good bucket, too." She reached for her wool cloak and went to the door. "Mother, will you finish the stew while Muirenn and I go out and fetch it?"

The older woman nodded. "Of course. But be quick about it. This is the kind of weather to get lost in." There was a gleam in her eye as she turned her face away from the light.

"Why must I to come with you? Rónán should go. He's already wet," Muirenn objected.

"Well let him dry then! He's been out all day. Look at him—cold and weary as he is." Rónán opened his mouth but his mother spoke over him. "I need you to come with me, Muirenn. I'll hear no more of your whining."

They threw on their cloaks and went off towards the beach. The wind was violent, each gust like a beating fist, each raindrop like a sling-stone. Muirenn held fast to the edges of her cloak, for the wind wished to rip it from her neck.

I don't remember Mamaí going to the shore today, Muirenn thought. But the roaring of air and sea was too loud in her ears to admit any further speculation. It was struggle enough to keep pace with her mother, who was all but sprinting.

They dashed across the beach to an old gnarled willow tree which stood brooding at the mouth of a trickling stream. The great tree swayed and moaned like a towering phantom. Wild waves spat foam and thrashed the sand with deafening blows. Muirenn gasped and choked on spraying seawater. Her heart was in her mouth.

Tómnat reached the willow tree and bent close to a large raised root. "The bucket... heavy!" she bellowed against the wind. Muirenn could only hear part of what she said. "Let me... these ropes to your wrists... weight is borne... between us!"

Within such chaos there was no time for questions, no time for protests, as her mother tied around each wrist a rope as thick as her thumb. Tómnat dashed around each side of the tree and lashed the ends of the two ropes together in a sailor's knot.

There was only shock at first—bewilderment. Muirenn's arms were wrapped around the trunk of the wide willow with her chest pressed up against it. She pulled away but the knot held her fast.

Then came horror. "Mamaí? Mamaí! Why have you tied me here? Why?" she screamed.

"Changeling! Return... whence you came and... back my daughter Muirenn!" There was such a fury in Tómnat's voice to rival even the howling of the gale. Fear of the creature before her made her own face monstrous.

Muirenn pleaded: "No! No, Mamaí! I'm not a Changeling! I *am* your daughter! I *am* Muirenn!"

Tómnat turned her face away, wet from the rain and the sea and her own tears. She glanced back, hesitating. Then she ran away, away down the beach and homeward.

"Mamaí, no! Please! Please, no! Don't leave me!" Muirenn then turned her face to the sky, to the shore, to the land, and screamed: "Help! Help me! Anyone! Anyone, please!"

The night was black and moonless, all was shadow but for the white-crested waves. Muirenn had never been so scared, so alone, and so utterly helpless. Her tears ran down the tree's deep-furrowed bark. The waves crashed closer and closer with the creep of the storm surge. The wind was so fierce that she could only inhale if she turned her face to its lee.

Muirenn screamed for help, hoping that her voice would be carried on the wind to houses nearby. Hours passed and no help came. Her voice grew hoarse and raw and salt-stung. Past midnight, she collapsed onto her knees, resting her head on the tree trunk, defeated.

"Great willow," she whispered, "I wish you might untwist your branches to break my bonds." Then an inspiration came to her: there might be help from realms outside of the human one.

She turned her head and shrieked at the great glass hills that came to pieces so close now to her feet: "Spirits of Earth and Otherworld, Air and Sea! Hear me! Please help! Help me! I beg you, please!"

It seemed, for a moment, that the wind let up a little, as if the storm gave pause to better hear. She breathed into it, starving for clear air. But in it was something else. Something had filled that pause... a whisper. The wind now had a shape, a rhythm, a push and pull like a stream of words. Muirenn focused on this sound with all her might, but still she could not make out any words. The sound came closer, as if two lips were pressed against her ear. The hairs rose up on the back of her neck.

Then a different sound cut through this whisper, loud and clear and impertinent. "What do you want?" said a voice at her knee. She yelped and scrambled to her feet.

In the dark air near as thick as the sea itself, a silhouette was profiled against the turbulent waves. It had the shape of a man, two men in fact, who seemed to have condensed from the rain itself, or else emerged the rolling waves. Muirenn blinked the rain from her eyes and stared in disbelief. They were, in fact, not men at all, for each was the height of a toddler, no taller than Muirenn's hip. Something of them sparkled, catching the light thrown up from the sea. Their chests shone as if covered in metallic scales, which was true enough, for they each wore a tunic made from iridescent fish skin. Their hair was slick and black like flat fronds of kelp, and belted at their waists were two silver swords no longer than a man's hunting knife.

"What do you want?" the one asked impatiently.

Muirenn finally found her tongue and said politely, hoarsely: "Please, friends, will you help me be free from my bonds?"

"Friends? Friends! We are not your friends!" said the other hotly. "We are lords, íascaire, in fact! Address us with more respect, you pitiful thing." He turned to his companion. "I shall not abide such disrespect, especially not from a human. Leave him here, She will find someone else to—"

"No, Tonn. We cannot refuse Her," said the second creature. "We would be fools to risk Ériu's displeasure."

"Who are you talking about? Who is Ériu?" asked Muirenn.

Tonn scoffed. "Do you hear that, Coipp? He must surely be an idiot. Let's waste no more time with him." He turned towards the sea but Coipp held his arm.

"Hold, Tonn. She has Her reasons for wanting the child saved. It's not our place to question them." Coipp addressed Muirenn impatiently. "Ériu is the name of She who was once, long ago, rígain of the Túatha de Danann, the one who gave Her name to this land when your people came here long, long ago. Nine waves out to sea from the shore and all the land from loch to mountain peak, from salmon pool to river mouth, Her body is haven of humanity. I am surprised you do not know Her."

Then Muirenn realized that she did, in fact, know Ériu. She had heard Her spoken of once or twice, though Her tales were not often told in Muirenn's household. Muirenn heard more of the other Túatha de Danann: of Mannanán and the Dagda, of Bríg and the Morrígan, of Midir and Macha, of Aengus and Áine, and so on. They were the ancestors who some called deities, who some called Síd.

"And She asked you to help me? Why?"

"I do not know why. Though we are clients of Manannán, Lord of the Sea, we may heed the requests of Ériu as well, for she has been kind to our people."

There was a pause. Muirenn gazed at the gleam of their little swords. "Lords of great renown and standing, will you then free me? Will you cut my bonds with your silver blades?"

Tonn turned away from her and spoke to Coipp. The cacophony of the crashing waves prevented Muirenn from overhearing. The two nodded in agreement and turned back to her. Coipp said: "What will you give us for it?"

She gaped. "Give you? But you said... if Ériu asked you to help me then why would—"

"It is only fair that you pay us for coming all this way," Tonn interjected. "It was quite an inconvenience, you should know. The current is right fierce tonight. Ériu would not prevent us from taking what payment is due."

"But I have nothing to give!" she protested.

"Nothing? Nothing at all?" asked Tonn.

"Well I... I suppose I might have... a poem?"

Coipp crossed his arms. "That might be worthy payment, but only if the poem is of quality."

"And we will judge its quality on two conditions," said Tonn. "That it is wholly original, and that it brings tears to our eyes, either in laughter, in sorrow, or in adulation."

Muirenn frowned. It would be difficult in the midst of this tumult, but at least she had to try. "Alright. But can you give me a moment to prepare it?"

The two creatures nodded and sat upon a gnarly willow root.

So Muirenn rested her head upon the tree with eyes clenched shut. Collecting her thoughts in the midst of this tumult was as arduous as herding a flock of spooked sheep. She forced herself to calm and drew words from deep inside herself. She discovered, not for the first time, a place there like a still pool, a place she had not yet given a name. Finally, she lifted her head, took in a deep breath, and addressed the two little lords with as steady and clear a voice as she could manage. The wind's howling quieted a little as she chanted:

> The cow she cried 'lone for her calf
> From deep she lowed a bellow-moan
> Too still was he upon that hill
> Where she bent down to lick him clean
> His milk-white fur so silver shone.
>
> He would have been her glossy pearl
> He would have been her moon aglow
> He would have pulled, this brave of bulls,
> A plow, a sledge, a cart of gold
> No stronger back the world would know.
>
> So long she walked with leaden hooves
> She lamed, she kneeled, she lost her will
> No birth of calves to prove her worth

> She'd leave this world and dream of him
> Grass grown up through her body, chill.

The last word lingered and fell from Muirenn's lips, now blue with it. There was a sound of sniffling. She looked down to see the two proud creatures unabashedly weeping. A smile of triumph tugged at Muirenn's mouth, but she promptly hid her teeth should these pretentious lords take offense.

"You have the gift of the gab, lad," said Coipp. He rubbed his eyes clear and stood up. "It is fair payment." He whisked out his sharp silver sword and with one swift cut, set Muirenn free. She rubbed her sore wrists and gave her humble thanks.

"What is your name, boy?" asked Tonn.

"Boy? Do you think I'm a—" Muirenn paused. There was no need to correct them, for she was grateful for the mistake. *And, she mused, it might not be a mistake after all. I might really be the Faery boy my mother believes me to be.* "My name..." She hesitated. Which name was the right one? "I don't know."

A sudden gust of wind tossed up from the sea and knocked the child to the ground. As she scrambled to her feet the wind nearly lifted her off the ground. She could almost feel the fingers of the gale grab and hurl her landward over the grassy bank.

It was all she could do not to trip and tumble as the wind pushed hard at her back. Her churning limbs had no chance to shiver, but her teeth chattered all the more violently. Muirenn was quite sure she had never been so cold in all of her life. Her only thoughts were of a fire, a dry blanket, and hot broth. She had no care for where the wind swept her as long as those three things lay ahead. The wet cascaded in sheets down her face as she squinted through the gloom, desperately seeking shelter—a house, any house, and not too far away.

There was no way of knowing how far she had traveled, for the curtains of rain made the world press in upon her. There was only the open place before her feet, and there she was forced to step, again and again. Her mind was as numb as her feet.

At last, a dark shape loomed up ahead. She hobbled to the door of a small roundhouse about the size of her own. Her fingers had frozen into a fist which she slammed against the door with all the strength she had left. Again she struck it. She would have cried out in pain if there was any feeling left in her hand. A sound stirred on the other side of the door— hushed voices, weary whispers. The door opened a crack and a man's face appeared.

"Please, please let me in. I'm so, so cold..." said Muirenn. Her knees finally buckled and she slumped against the door.

The man cried out in surprise. He caught her, lifted her up, and carried her to the fire. The household awoke with a rude chorus of yawns and groaning.

"What's going on? Who's that now?" said a woman's voice.

"I know who that is. It's Áedán!" said the voice of a young boy. "We used to play together. But I haven't seen him since last autumn."

Áedán clung to consciousness long enough to listen, eyes closed. The woman stripped off his outer cloak and smock, but Áedán would not let her take off his sodden underclothes. The cloak was as heavy as the boy himself from the weight of the water in it. She wrapped him in a warm blanket and rubbed his hair dry, then laid him down to warm his soles at the fire.

As he lay there on a pallet of heather, his head wrapped and cushioned with warm cloths, Áedán listened to their chatter. "What do you suppose happened to him?" asked the man. "Probably went wandering in the woods and got lost on his way home," said the boy. "He's the kind to do that. He likes trouble." The woman said: "Poor thing! The wood is dense and the night is all in a fit of rage! Bless his luck that he found this house before the chill killed him. You know that Bressal's son was killed by as much last winter, in that storm that stole our currach. Do you remember that night?"

Áedán no longer cared to listen, yet was soothed by the soft sounds of their simple speech. Slowly, he felt the warmth and feeling returned to his limbs. His shivering calmed and finally ceased. At last, he was safe, and drifted into a warm, dreamless sleep.

Áedán awoke to sunlight filtered through chinks in the eastern door. Through bleary eyes he gazed up at the roof beams and was confused— the roof of his roundhouse looked different than usual. And what a terrible dream he'd had last night! Images drifted across his mind like flotsam. The giant willow. The silhouettes of two little fish lords. His mother's terrible glare. They seemed solid, more memory than dream, and they had come with such an ache in his heart.

Áedán sat up. His arms felt leaden and there was a redness ringing each wrist. He was, indeed, not at home in his own bed. It had been no nightmare after all.

The woman of the house came to kneel and made him drink a hot tea of yarrow and horehound. "Are you feeling better now?" she asked. He nodded, forcing a polite smile. In her face was real concern; it was as warming as the tea.

"Now, how did you get caught in that tempest last night, so far from home?" She scooted away to wrangle a toddler about to topple a stack of wooden bowls. Another woman sat on a stool, rocking and cooing with an infant latched to her round breast.

Áedán gazed about him. The house was slightly larger in diameter than his own family's home, and better furnished. From the number of pallets rolled up against the wall, Áedán guessed that nine people lived here. Motes of dust and hearth smoke swirled in the sunbeams that seeped through the door. By their angle Áedán deduced it must be past mid-morning, which explained why the rest of the household was already gone and out into the day. Only the women stayed, to tend the house and care for the smallest children.

"I was out yesterday foraging the pigs in the forest. But on my way back I lost two of them. I tried to find them, but it grew dark so quickly. When the storm came, the whole drove left me and scattered for cover. I couldn't tell which way was home. And now I've lost every swine—father will surely be furious with me." Áedán dropped his head and gazed at her with sorry eyes.

It was a convincing ploy and she was taken up in it. "Come now, don't worry, lad. I'm sure your father will be much happier to see you living than he will be angry about the pigs." She stroked his head gently.

Áedán smiled weakly, wishing such a simple story could be true. He drank down a hot broth of dulse and mutton bones, then dressed again in his nearly-dry smock and cloak. He left the house with a bow of gratitude for her life-saving hospitality. She waved goodbye and watched him walk slowly, sullenly, away over the meadow towards home.

CHAPTER THREE

Iron

The sky was clear and cold after the cleansing of that storm, and in the noon brightness of the day Áedán approached his roundhouse thrilled with fear. He had no way to predict what would happen now—the world had lost its order. His family was cruel, strangers were kind, a goddess had fixed his fate, and creatures of the sea could come to his rescue—for a price. He had pondered, briefly, whether or not it was right to return home at all. But what else could he do? He was too young to be out on his own. No one else would want him. Áedán felt there was no other choice.

Tómnat was bent double over a bed of flax when she spied him approaching. She stood up slowly, a wary look in her eye. "Muirenn?" she called.

Muirenn halted, forcing calm into her voice. The words came out cool and clipping: "Yes, Mamaí."

Tómnat approached. "Are you my daughter?"

"Yes, Mamaí."

Tómnat stared at the child. She seemed unharmed by the storm, and not even wet. Could this mean that the Good People had returned her daughter to her? Íte had said that if you threaten the Faery child with bodily harm and exposure it to the elements, the Faery parents will come to claim it and return your own child. Tómnat held the girl's two hands in her own. They were warm. Surely this couldn't be the child that had spent the night tied to a tree in a tempest.

And then she decided: this was indeed her daughter, Muirenn. The Fair Folk had released her daughter back to her. Overcome with relief, she embraced Muirenn joyfully, kissed her on her fair freckled cheek, and brought her inside for a welcomed meal.

But as the days passed, Tómnat watched the child quietly fall back into despondence. She was gripped again by the fear: perhaps the Changeling had not left after all.

One morning Tómnat asked Rónán to hang back a while and set him to a task in the garden. Muirenn was grinding barley into flour at the quern. Suddenly, Rónán called from outside the door.

"Áedán, help me! Áedán, come quick!"

By instinct Áedán leapt up and ran to the door. But when he pulled, it was held closed from the outside. Then he realized what he had done: without thinking he had responded to his boy name, and in so doing had been caught in another trap.

"Ah! I knew it! The Changeling hasn't left!" cried Íte. She held up a blanket and edged towards the child as if to capture a feral dog.

"Rónán!" Tómnat called. "Come in and help us catch him!"

Rónán rushed in and leapt at his sibling. Áedán did indeed seem feral then, for he dodged and darted from them like cornered prey. Slight and swift as he was, he gave them good chase around and around the hearth, evading their grasping hands. Then Rónán made a bold leap right over the fire, caught his sibling by the arm, and knocked him to the ground. They wrestled and rolled, and in the violent fury Áedán beat Rónán's face with his fists, splitting his lip with a bloom of bright blood. Then Áedán's sight went dark as Íte's blanket came over his head. Tómnat grabbed him around the middle, pinned his arms to his sides, and lifted him off the ground as he screamed and kicked. Rónán found a rope and wrapped it tightly around Áedán's middle, lashing down his arms.

"What's going on Mamaí? Why is Muirenn acting like this? Why are we tying her up?" Rónán asked, panting. He held a sleeve against his bloody lip.

"This is not Muirenn, Rónán," Tómnat said. "This is a Faery boy who has disguised himself as our Muirenn and has tricked us into giving him shelter. The Faeries are punishing us for some secret crime known only to their vicious kind."

Rónán gasped. "A Changeling?"

"Yes," said Tómnat. Franticly, she turned to Íte. "What iron do we have about? The Síd cannot withstand the touch of iron. Do we have a knife?"

Íte shook her head. "All our knives are bronze. But Lonán's hatchet—that one has an iron head." She went to go fetch it from the wood pile.

Áedán was growling and thrashing on the floor, his upper half covered by the blanket. He could see only the shadows of three figures standing above him. He heard his mother say: "Now put it in the fire until it begins to glow red just a little." A long moment passed and then his mother's voice came up close. "Now help me by holding out his arm."

"No! No, Mamaí—I can't do that!" Áedán heard Rónán say, and his voice grew farther away. The door opened and then slammed shut.

"He's a coward," said his grandmother's voice. Áedán's left arm was held firm against the ground and his sleeve was pulled up to the elbow.

"Sit on his legs. He's going to kick."

Suddenly, Áedán felt a fire touch the inside of his forearm and smelled the burning of flesh. He screamed. He screamed with all the breath in his body, with the pitch of a pig under the knife, so that his ears buzzed with warped waves of sound. The blunt side of the iron hatchet, red hot, was touched to his skin for only a moment, but the searing lingered for much longer. Áedán writhed like an eel and threw himself against the two women with unexpected strength.

"Be still! Be still, beast, or I'll do it again!" He obeyed, panting and trembling. "Good. Now I will untie your bonds. You will leave peacefully and never return. Tell your people to send back my daughter—my sweet, lovely daughter Muirenn!"

His bonds were loosed and the blanket was pulled back. Without hesitation he leapt up, threw open the door, and sprinted away over the grassy hill.

Áedán ran. He ran across field and fen and forest. He ran crazed, heedless of his feet and face where the branches whipped and stung him. He ran until his calves and thighs burned, until his breaths grew ragged and his heart pounded as hard as a smith's hammer. He paused to catch his breath, then ran further. The rhythm of his feet and the churning of his limbs pulled his mind away from the pain.

At last he came to a glade at the edge of the familiar: beyond this point he had never been. Through the clearing, he looked onto the path overhung with heavy limbs of ash and alder. Within his romping range he knew the knob and burl of every tree; but not those. He took two steps back, then turned. Nearby was an ancient oak with gnarled, upraised roots. There Áedán knelt, curled up into a ball and wept.

For a long time he sat there embraced by those massive roots, rocking back and forth in restless pain. But it would get no better this way, he knew, and so he stood, stumbling towards a tinkle of water. Áedán found a brook, hardly wider than a hand's breath, yet flowing with cold, sweet water. He knelt and drank and dipped his left arm into the stream. It was soothing, numbing, and eventually the searing was dulled a little. Áedán sighed, stretched the tense muscles in his neck and back, and laid on his side in the damp moss.

Áedán spent many hours there by the stream simply breathing, drinking, and periodically dipping his arm to cool the burn. The voice of the sweet water sung to him a lullaby; sunlight sifted through the canopy of the trees and made pools of light in the litter and bracken. His spirit calmed; his thoughts came back to his body and his breath. At last the pain was less loud in his mind, so he cast his thoughts to healing. He rolled over and plucked three leaves of plantain, chewed, and spit them onto the red and black blisters. Then he leaned his head against a moss-pillowed stone, drank through his ears that bubbling stream-song, and fell down into a tangle of fitful dreaming.

Áedán was startled awake by a terrible dream in which every person he knew had a stranger's face. He panted, eyes flung open, daring not to move. The forest was dark now but for the waxing moon that shown through the leaves of the late-spring canopy above. All was quiet, not a breath of wind stirred the leaves. He sat up, looked about, then laid back down in the leaves. Abandoning the struggle to find a comfortable position, sleep finally overtook him.

Then he dreamed...

Áedán was curled up in a nest made of twigs and leaves and feathers at the top of that oak. There were three other chicks asleep beside him, their necks naked but for a sparse sprouting of down like dandelion fluff. He looked up to see a shadow peel away from the night sky and flutter down to him. She landed softly. The chicks beside him awoke with ravenous squeals. She fed them each then settled down with her warm breast against them. They all snuggled in and the chicks fell asleep once more. Áedán remained awake, watching her.

"Child," she cooed, "why are you here?"

Áedán realized that he was not an owlet at all, but a little boy. He told her of his ordeal with the iron and how he had to flee his home.

"What brutality! I would never do such a thing to my own chicks!" She watched her owlets with honey-gold eyes and clacked her jaw in agitation. "The cruelty of humanity is unparalleled."

"But what should I do? Should I go back to my home? Will they think me a Changeling if I return? If they do, might they... kill me?" Desperate tears rolled down his cheeks, shining like pearls in the moonlight.

The owl watched his face. "You are too young to live alone or else I'd invite you to hunt here in my forest. But in truth, you would not survive very long. You human children take quite a bit of learning to be made less fragile, and I don't have the time to teach you. I have my own chicks to care for." She fluffed up her feathers. "So I advise you thus: go back to your home and pretend to be the little girl returned. Tell your mother what she wants to hear and she will take you back. But you must be convincing, or else the trick will not work."

"But what if I am Changeling? Should I go to the Otherworld and ask for an exchange? What do you think I am, a Faery boy or a human girl?"

The owl stared at him intensely. Áedán flinched and looked away, knowing then why the field mice fear the touch of those eyes. She said: "I see only you, not what you should be called. But I think you may be wrong on both counts—that you are neither of those things. Feel deeply what is in your heart. Don't let yourself be shaped by the images that other people have in their minds. Listen quietly to your own nature... trust what you feel. Only then will you come to know who, and what, you are."

Then the owl shuffled towards him, and with a hard bump of her head pushed Áedán from the nest.

Áedán awoke to a feeling of falling. He threw out his hands and clutched at the leaves about his head. The soft light of dawn warmed the grey world about him. A riotous chorus of birdsong filled the wood. He sat up and pressed his back against the trunk. Tipping his head upward, he spied high above him a large owl's nest.

Was that the nest that I dreamed in? Áedán wondered. Before falling asleep he had not known it was there. In that moment, Áedán heard a single forlorn hoot some ways away. That is her, he thought with certainty. He gave his silent thanks for her wisdom.

Áedán bathed his arm again in the cool stream and applied a fresh spit-poultice to the wound. The taste of the plantain leaf made his stomach croak with hunger like a brown-frog. The owl was right: he would not survive very long out here in the forest alone—he was too soft, too small, too young. He had no skills with which to survive. So he resolved then with disquiet, that he would pretend as best he could to be this imaginary girl called Muirenn, the happy daughter that his mother so fervently wished was hers.

Áedán approached the door of his home, now open to the warm summer breeze. He drew a trembling breath, willing his racing heart to steady. It would not obey. He paused, thoughts aflutter. There was still time to change his mind. *And do what, then?* he argued with himself, *And go where?*

His indecision was interrupted. Tómnat stepped out of the house carrying a bucket and a hand broom. In an instant, she spied him. With an unblinking stare she set the bucket down slowly. The blood drained from Áedán's face. Then he did the bravest thing he had ever done in his young life: he screwed his eyes shut tight, opened them, and called out to her.

"Mamaí! Mamaí! I've returned!"

Tómnat took a wary step towards the girl. "Muirenn? Is it really you?"

"Yes, Mamaí. It's really me!" Muirenn exclaimed. She forced her voice into an ebullient tone, hoping, desperately, that it sounded sincere. "I was taken as a captive to the Otherworld, but they finally let me go when the Changeling was sent back!" Muirenn drew her lips into a wide, bright smile. "I'm so happy to be home!" And with a sickened heart, she ran to her mother and embraced her.

Tómnat held the child cautiously, then put her at arm's length to inspect her up and down. Tómnat took the girl's left arm and pulled up the sleeve.

"What's this?" Tómnat asked, pointing at the poulticed wound.

"Oh, Mamaí! It was so horrible!" Muirenn mimicked the speech of the neighbor's daughters: those silly, delicate little girls with pouty lips and uncallused hands. "Because you had burned the Changeling, the Síd burned me too, to make it even. It hurts so much!" She whimpered, imitating the high, pathetic sobs that one of those girls would if she scraped a knee.

At this Tómnat's doubts were washed away. This must truly be her child, for the Changeling had never cried in front of her. Tómnat's eyes welled up with happy tears and she embraced her daughter fiercely.

"Oh, my love! My little rose! You are home! My poor daughter, those vicious people have hurt you so. We'll set it right. You'll be well again." Mother clung to daughter, the two of them trembling: one with jubilation, and the other with fearful rage.

Muirenn's homecoming was celebrated with as much cheer as for a sailor coming home from many years at sea. Lonán, Rónán, and Íte each embraced her and kissed her on the cheek in turn. She was bathed in a warm bath strewn with chamomile flowers and bluebells. The wound was washed with a tea of violets and rose petals, pasted with honey, and wrapped in clean linen. Then Muirenn was allowed to rest while the two women prepared a rich celebratory meal of roasted lamb rubbed with fresh herbs, nettles and mushrooms cooked in a cream sauce, and barley bread with butter and clover honey.

Her hunger was real—that she did not have to fake. Yet each time she met the eyes of her kin, she wondered who they saw. *If they all see me as someone that I myself do not believe in, then which of us sees what is real?* The thought made her dizzy. So she focused on the pain—in her arm, in her heart—and was steadied. For that, at least, could not be false.

CHAPTER FOUR

Bending the Bow

Muirenn learned how to play act the gentle, spritely little girl that Tómnat so desired. It was difficult at first, and profoundly degrading. But this was a matter of survival, and so she put in every effort to make the act convincing. She followed all orders obediently. She ate more and gained her weight back. When her mother and grandmother were near she painted her face with a complicit smile, hoping that the grin did not look too much like a grimace.

As the months passed the farce became easier. Her family needed less convincing now; she caught fewer sideways glances when they thought she was not looking. But she was always looking, she was always on guard. Her vision grew broader and sharpened at the corners of her eyes. She developed a felt sense for when their eyes landed on her back, or when their muscles tensed with question, or suspicion.

Truth be told, Muirenn herself sometimes wished to be convinced. *Can I find happiness if I accept my lot instead of fighting it? Maybe, someday, I could become a normal little girl just as Mamaí wants, if only I try harder.*

Summer's flowers ripened to autumn's fruits, and as the north wind brought in the cold and shook the leaves and acorns from the oaks, the hearth fire became ravenous for wood. Muirenn had gained her mother's trust now, so she was given more freedom to wander farther afield when there was need. She could go to the beach to gather driftwood; she could rove the forest to collect downed branches. By the winter solstice, she was given leave to collect water from the stream and mussels from the shore alone. When she came home one evening with two codlings caught by her own hook, Tómnat was delighted. Thereafter, she was loosed to fish on her own, weekly when the winds were calm.

Muirenn's obedience inside the house secured her freedom outside of it. When out alone and beyond the grasp of any human eye, she let slip from her mouth that false smile, and dipped for a moment into the cold current of sorrow beneath. Yet the cry of the scavenging gull, the bark of the beached seal, the print of the fox that sniffed for clam necks at dusk, the chit-chit-chit of the wren in the bramble, all these kept her afloat on that melancholic tide so that she would not drown. In solitude she felt the vital pulse of Nature—she witnessed that graceful dance of ten-thousand feet drumming on the earth, synchronized to the rhythms of the moon, the sun, and the sea. There was order here, there was sense. Outside of the human world there was rightness, balance, and beauty. And when her sorrow could be put aside, she danced that dance too, with the steady pulse of her heartbeat and the ebb and flow of her breath.

In dreaming there was comfort, too. But not just comfort—excitement, inspiration, vibrant colors and stirring adventures. Most often she was the boy Áedán, romping as he once did with other boys. But sometimes she was a man. This man, to Muirenn's surprise, was neither woodsman nor warrior. He was courtly, learned, proud and elegantly dressed. Men bowed their heads to him. And in these dreams there was another man, a bright-headed man, broad-shouldered and fair, with a sword at his hip and a torc of solid gold around his neck. He sat upon a chair of oak enameled with bone. There was an empty chair beside him. With an open hand he beckoned for the man that was Muirenn to sit. He smiled, eyes ablaze with passion. With power.

The seasons passed and Muirenn grew taller, ruddy, and strong. The words 'lovely' and 'beautiful' still stung her like stones. She did not want to be beautiful like the ladies of myth, Eithliu and Emer. She desired a beauty like that of her heroes, Fionn and Diarmuid—warriors as deadly in combat as they were desirable to women. Like the golden man that visited her dreams.

At Samhain, that sacred day marking the arrival of winter, the clans of the Fír Lúachair gathered for feasting and merriment. Now, as on all the cross-quarter day celebrations, Muirenn was herded together with girls her own age. When she was younger Muirenn had turned her nose up at them, judging all girls to be vain and feeble-minded. But now there was a new feeling. She held herself back from them, not speaking, yet admiring the shine of their hair, the smoothness of their cheeks, the grace in the bend of their slender wrists. Then, with a blush, she knew: this was the urge called desire. The impulse was confusing and impossible to control. There was no way to hide it but to avoid those girls altogether.

And so her loneliness deepened. It was growing harder to pretend the sadness away and to prevent the melancholy from coming into the house with her.

It was April in the spring of Muirenn's twelfth year. As day lengthened and rivaled the night, the verve of the earth awoke with viridescence. Relief from the dark caused life to fling itself upward: like seedlings through soil, like sugar through sapwood, and like nestlings through eggshell. So too did Muirenn feel a quickening. It was many days until she understood what it was: a feeling, an instinct, a hope, that this spring there would be reprieve from misery.

Soon enough the truth of this prescience was revealed. Rónán came of age that moon and received a gift from his father: a bow of yew and three arrows fletched with white gull feathers.

"Though spears are for the flaith to use in war and boar hunting, a bow is a handy thing for a farmer's son to have," said Lonán. "It's for the smaller game: hares, stoats, fowl and the like. Here, I'll show you the trick of it."

Lonán brought his son out to the meadow where the sheep had clipped the grass low, and showed Rónán how to load and draw, aim and shoot. Then he clapped his son on the shoulder and said, "Well now, the rest is up to you. I can't claim to be much of an archer myself, though I had my share of fun stinging—and fleeing—riled badgers." He laughed. "Be sure not to lose those arrows before learning to make them yourself."

Rónán was delighted. He played with it every evening when returned from the field, hoping to shoot hares at dusk. Muirenn shadowed him jealously. Though zealous at first, Rónán became discouraged by the wildness of his aim. He had no teacher to guide him in the finer points of technique, and so, as the novelty wore off, he gave up the game to spend time cavorting with his friends instead.

Muirenn asked her brother if she might try it. Rónán was a generous boy and so agreed. From the first pluck of the bowstring, from its hum and its strike, Muirenn was in love. The way it focused her mind to a point, the way the arrow shaft sunk into sod, quivering—there was no feeling more satisfying.

In the day when her brother was out with the sheep, the bow was left leaning against the wall in the roundhouse, its quiver of arrows beside it. Muirenn eyed the bow there for many days before striking up the courage to steal it away. She did so one morning when her mother and grandmother were out, under the pretense of collecting firewood. She took the bow into the forest and chose a rotting stump to shoot. At first, even on the rare occasion when the stump was struck, the arrows simply bounced off innocuously. It took many days to build up the strength to sink an arrow into wood. But with increased draw-strength came increased distance, and one afternoon she lost an arrow in the leaf litter. Rónán hadn't noticed, or at least he hadn't said so, since he had neglected to touch his bow in many days. His negligence granted Muirenn some time to try fletching an arrow herself before the loss was missed. The first one was shoddy: the shaft was warped and its flint arrowhead was poorly knapped. But in time, she learned to make her arrows strong and straight and properly weighted.

The craft of fletching was new and exciting, and within a month Muirenn had a healthy quiver of twelve straight arrows, many more than Rónán began with. Naturally, the next challenge would be to make a bow of her own, that way she would not risk being caught at the door with her brother's bow hidden in an armful of firewood.

One of her mother's cousins was a bowyer. Muirenn pestered him with questions about his craft: what type of wood was best for bow making, how to season the wood, how to plane the stave so that it would bend but not break, how to measure the string for the proper draw weight, and so on. This curiosity seemed strange for a young girl.

"I'm asking on behalf of my brother," she said placidly. "He's broken the bow my father made for him. Since he's out with the sheep most days, he doesn't have the time to make himself another. I have the time, so I want to make one for him... as a gift." She was quite practiced by now at spinning a convincing lie.

The man shrugged. He supposed it seemed harmless enough to oblige, and he was too proud of his craft to resist sharing some of his wisdom. So he gave her a little advice, one drizzly afternoon, as casually as he might. She had a serious mind and asked many good questions.

With this knowledge Muirenn went into the wood, to a hidden glade she had cleared for tinkering, and set to work.

Muirenn poured her soul into the making. To create, to envision, and to work with her hands dispelled the boredom and frustration that before had defined her days. And when she wasn't working on her bow, she was dreaming of it, in waking and sleeping. When she spun wool, Muirenn thought of twisting the bow string from nettle fiber. When she sat at the weaving loom, she heard in her mind the sound of the draw-knife scraping curls from the stave. When she cut meat for the stew, she thought of the game she would strike with her own arrows. And when she slept, she dreamed that she was Fionn with his band of roving heroes, spear in hand, and the scent of a stag in his nostrils. When Fionn returned home from his hunt, it was to a bark-and-bracken house in the cleft between two breasts of earth and stone.

The bow was finally finished. Light and slender, oiled with linseed, strung so that it hummed like a honeybee—it was the most beautiful thing Muirenn had ever made. But within the first week of its use, Muirenn watched fissures form in the wood. The yew had not been properly seasoned—eventually it would snap.

Frustrated, she studied these faults and began work on the next. By the autumn equinox she had another bow suited to her size—perfect, as far as she could tell—with a quiver full of grouse-fletched arrows. She had never been prouder of anything in her life. Pride improved her aim, and soon she was hitting every mark that she set for herself. When she set the arrow on the string, looked down the length of its shaft, and held her breath before its release, she was calm, mind as still as a mountain pool reflecting the heavens. And in that moment, in the emptiness between breaths, there was hope. Hope that she might become someone else. Someone she could be proud of. Someone completely unexpected.

CHAPTER FIVE

Flying the Arrow

The year passed quickly for Muirenn and it seemed to her the sun shone brighter than before. Summer fattened the barley corn and turned the green oats tawny. Red stags held their rut, in the morning fog echoed their woody lowing and the clack of antlers in fence. The first frost of autumn turned dewdrop to crystal and planed puddles with sparkling shards.

There was both hope and hardship in every day. Muirenn was practiced enough in her farce that it had become second nature. Some days she could even convince herself to put aside the struggle, to forget Áedán for a time. Her kin were unaware that she was anything but contented, as she wished for them to be. And, on occasion, the contentment was genuine.

There is peace in this pretend, she thought. *Might I convince myself, some day, that it is true? To be cured of the desire to be something else... surely that would be a relief. Surely life would be easier that way.*

These thoughts were most troublesome on bath days. She insisted on taking the tub out into the dark of night so that no one else could see her nakedness. Tómnat appraised this as feminine modesty, but it was not. It was shame. Muirenn could not even look at herself anymore, her pubescent body was changing in all the wrong ways. It was disgusting.

Tómnat, noticing how Muirenn was maturing, spoke to her daughter proudly. "The female form holds the shape of the Goddess," she said. "It is this shape through which all of life is born and renewed. A man's strength is in his limbs—it is external. A woman's strength is inside—in her heart, in her womb. It is a power much stronger than a man's. Through our bodies the stuff of the world is drawn together and made anew. All a man can do is reshape things already in existence, or destroy them." Her face shone with the peace of the clear bright moon, her hand overtop her womb.

That may be true, thought Muirenn, *but that truth is not for me. That is not what I was made for. I know it.*

Yet she could not explain this knowing, not even to herself. However hard she tried to forget Áedán, to push away his thoughts and feelings, his yearning for manhood, he was too strong to suppress completely. Like grass clipped low by the grazing mouths of sheep, she cut back his thoughts and yet they returned ever more resurgent.

There must be a reason, she thought. *Why would the world make me thus if it were only a falsehood, a childish whim? And why did the goddess Ériu ask me to be saved? Surely she must know what I am.*

An image came to her mind: of a chick about to burst from its shell. *But who is Muirenn: the chick or the eggshell?*

It was a cool, cloudy afternoon. In the forest the trees loosed their leaves and fell, mildewing, to make a blanket for autumn's last bloom of mushrooms. Muirenn hunted these for her mother's pot, traveling along her usual shady paths. Her mother and grandmother were away that day on a trip to the smith to get the cauldron repaired. Muirenn had volunteered to stay at home and tend the fire. The fire would, of course, tend itself while she snuck off into the forest.

She made her way towards a reedy pond between the cow pasture and the scrubby edge of the eastern wood. There she laid in wait, bow in hand, behind a blind made of deadwood and reeds, watching the wild ducks bob and chatter in the still water.

The line was clear; the angle just right. She got to one knee, drew back, and sent the arrow clean through a hen's black breast. The flock scattered in a flurry of singing wingbeats—all but the punctured hen.

Muirenn plunged up to her knees into that dark water to grasp her prey. Back on the bank, she withdrew the arrow, knelt over the limp body, and spoke the hunter's blessing:

> The blade was blessed that stilled thy breath
> In quiet, close thy lidded eye
> Blood unstaunched, drum down thy drops
> Make hum anew in other hearts.
> Fly free beyond shade or shadow
> The sky's wide nest re-knits thy shell
> Take flight again on swan's white wings.

Muirenn bowed her head in gratitude for life's great sacrifice that remade her, again and again, at every meal.

Duck was a rich meat, her favorite meat, though she rarely had a chance to eat it if not caught by her own hand. Neither her father nor brother were much for the hunt. Her family did keep ducks at home, but those were for eggs, not meat. "Though tame, our ducks keep their memories of freedom," her father had once explained. "So we must make an effort to retain their trust. If they nest with us, we will not eat their flesh, for they always have the choice to fly away and rejoin their wild cousins."

Muirenn walked west holding the limp fowl by the neck, the crunch of dry leaves underfoot. It was a mast year and the acorns were abundant.

Squirrels scurried to fill their nests before the deer and boar made themselves fat on this sweet fodder.

She would hang the duck in a tree to protect it from scavengers, then cook and eat the duck midday tomorrow, if she could spare some time between chores. Now that the grain was brought in from the field and the apples and hazelnuts all plucked from the boughs, the growing season had finally come to a close. Farmers now entered the resting half of the year, so Muirenn had more time to sneak away by herself. She was becoming a skilled hunter, and though it was pleasant enough to make a kill for herself, she wished even more that she might bring home her prey and share it with her family. Rónán could do so, if he wished, but Muirenn could not. Such an act would raise suspicions.

With her quiver upon her back, bow and bird in each hand, Muirenn set out across a narrow strip of cow pasture that bit into the vast rolling forest which clothed Ériu from shore to shore like a mantle of green fleece. West towards home was another expanse of forest, and on the other side of that was cleared and ploughed land with the seashore as its boundary. In a patch of woods close to home there was a small glade guarded by a thick tangle of blackberry bushes. Muirenn had made a tunnel between the thorns just wide enough for a child to crawl through, and behind this screen she made herself a secret haven. There she hid her bow and quiver and cooked her catch in a fire ring. Also there, she kept a secret stockpile of dry wood under shelter so that the time allotted for gathering firewood could be spent instead wandering, thinking, crafting, and hunting.

Yet on that cloudy autumn day, Muirenn did not reach her secret glade. She cut across the cow pasture, as she had a hundred times before, and suddenly spied a party of men on horseback breaking the cover of the forest at a canter. She dropped to her knees to hide amidst the knee-high grass, but she was not quick enough to avoid being spotted. One of the men lifted his spear in her direction and shouted. The party turned in unison like a school of fish and cantered straight at her.

Muirenn cursed under her breath, her eyes darting between flight paths. She could turn and dash back into the forest from the direction she came, hoping to lose them in the scrubby brush near the duck pond. She could run across the field and jump into a tall tree. But the horsemen came at too fast a pace. No matter which direction she chose, they would catch her in the open. Nevertheless, she had to try. With the blood pounding in her ears, she sprinted towards the wood in the west, hoping to make it under cover before the men reached her.

The riders kicked their horses and came barreling after her. She was not ten paces from the thicket at the edge of the wood when the men rode up and cut her off. Five men reigned to a halt their five stout-legged horses, huffing and blowing steam from their nostrils. They were dressed for hunting, surely out for boars or stags, each with a bronze-headed spear in hand. No catch was slung over their saddles—the day had yet been unlucky for them. Yet to behold these proud, hardy men straddling such powerful beasts who frothed with sweat, their spears shining— Muirenn was thrilled not just with fright, but with awe and envy. What she wouldn't give to join their company as one of them!

One man vaulted down from his steed. Muirenn touched the hilt of her belt knife and looked into his face, trying not to reveal any sign of her own fear. Then, with a shock of dread, she recognized him. It was the aire Talorc, the hard-eyed lord to whom her family was tenant. He squinted at her in confusion.

"You there! Why do you run from us? What is your name?" The aire boomed.

Muirenn was speechless, her tongue paralyzed by indecision. She would not likely pass as a boy now, should she wish to lie about her identity. She wore no trousers, which a boy would be wearing at her age. But to give these men her girl's name would risk the secrecy of her lonesome activities so far from home. It was Talorc who had decreed, many years ago, that she not be allowed away from her house without an adult. If Muirenn gave her name, her parents would find out about what she was doing when they let her out alone. They would punish her, or worse, think that the Changeling had come back to plague them. Muirenn felt a rising panic. Was there any way to escape this quickly closing trap? In this bewildered state she remained mute.

"Answer me, girl!" commanded the aire. "What is your name?"

"I know who she is," said another man atop his horse. "That's Lonán's daughter, Muirenn."

Recognition swept over the aire's face. "Ah, I remember now. The girl who pretends to be a boy." He pointed his chin at her bow and quiver. "But what's this? Hunting with a man's weapon? Out here, alone? Were not my instructions clear—that you stay in the home and tend to the activities appropriate to your sex? You shame yourself with such immodesty. Your family has disobeyed my orders. There will be consequences." He paused, sweeping his eyes up and down her body. Muirenn's skin crawled at the lewd smile that appeared at the corners of his mouth. "It appears that you've grown into a woman, Muirenn, despite yourself."

Talorc stepped forward and grabbed for her bow. She pulled back.

"Ach! Wretched girl! Do as I say and give me the bow. You will obey your lord. I'll take you home and have a talk with your father." He grabbed again and caught hold of the bow.

By reflex she wrested the bow from his hand and swung it free. The arch of that swing cracked against the back of the aire's hand and he yowled in pain. Talorc's face glowed blood-red and he bared his teeth at her.

"You filthy brat!" he shouted, enraged. "How dare you strike a lord? You will pay dearly for this. Come here now! Come here!" He lunged forward and took in a fierce grip Muirenn's arm that held the duck.

This sudden violence triggered in her the instinct to fight, for in Muirenn's boyhood tussles she had never refused an exchange of blows. With a scream she swung up the bow with her free hand and cracked it hard against the aire's ear. He stumbled and let go of her, momentarily stunned by the blow.

The other men dropped from their horses and leapt at the girl. She wasted no time. Muirenn turned, dropped the duck, and dashed madly toward the thicket. Two men ran after her on foot, and the three others mounted their horses to chase her.

Muirenn reached the underbrush just in time to dive into a tangle of thorny shrubs before the men could grab her. Thorns scoring her face and neck, she crawled through brambles too dense for any but a child to squeeze through. The footmen reached through with their arms but could not pass any further. The horsemen wheeled, trying to find the backside of the thicket, but it backed up to a tumble of fallen trees and broken branches.

"Ach! This mess is too thick!" Talorc growled. "You two, stay here and see if you can't flush her out. Fergus, Dáire—you come with me. We'll cut her off at the road and catch her where the wood thins."

Talorc and his two riders galloped off down the only forest path wide enough for travel by horseback. The men on foot cursed and tore at the clinging brambles.

Muirenn scrambled through the brush like a hunted hare. The arrows in her quiver caught on branches and briars, so she was forced to throw off the quiver and abandon her bow as well. She could afford to lose these, for she had others, but she could not afford to let them slow her escape.

Talorc and his men assumed she would be headed home, but of course, she would not. Muirenn knew this wood better than anyone, and she had mapped in her mind all the places where the scrub and bramble were thickest and hardest to pass. Into those places she plunged. It would be nearly impossible for a grown man to come after her and not get stuck or torn to shreds.

The thicket finally thinned as the briars and bracken gave way to oak and ash. There Muirenn stopped, panting, then held her breath to listen. There were the sounds of two men cursing and crashing through deadwood in the far distance behind her. Still, she listened. With a sigh of relief, she realized that they were moving in the wrong direction.

Muirenn picked up a deer path that meandered its way north. She stepped slowly, light-footed and quiet as a doe. When the men's movements could no longer be heard, she climbed up into a stout-limbed pine tree. There she sat on a limb twice the height of any man's reach, willing her heart to slow its pounding, sure that the whole forest echoed with it. In the pause between pants, Muirenn heard the wind in the trees. From the near tree came the evening call of the robin seeking her mate. Then the lilt and chirrup of the blackbird; the scramble of a squirrel in the leaf litter below. No sound nor sight of man or horse there was in any direction.

With shaking limbs, she clung like a burr to the trunk of that scale-barked pine, and there she prayed for the Goddess to keep her hidden.

Dusk's calm settled in the forest, all became grey with shadow. Muirenn's hands were cold. Her mind was numb. She willed herself still, evening the in and out of her breath, and imagined herself encased in pine bark. She immersed her mind in the tree's heavy, peaceful silence. Yet when she shifted her position to regain circulation in her tingling legs, or rubbed her hands together to keep the feeling in them, her mind started running in circles. She had been found out. She had been caught. She had attacked an aire.

No, she thought. *He attacked me first—I was only defending myself!*

Ha! Do I really think the brithemain will see it that way? she argued against herself. *The aire's word is, of course, held above my own in court. I'm a fuidir and a child... a girl child... once accused of being a Changeling. Whose word could possibly count for less?*

But Onchú the brithem was fair to me before...

I disobeyed a lord and then attacked him. There could be nothing in the law to protect me now.

She rested her head against the pine bark, sticky with sweet-smelling sap. Her body stilled and her mind went numb once more.

It was many hours until Muirenn emerged from her stupor. The night was now late and the sky full dark. The moon was new; its light would not guide her home this night. Yet these woods she knew too well to be lost in. It was what laid in wait for her at home that she feared most of all.

Her mind began churning again. *But there's nowhere else to go. Maybe Father will understand. He's said how much he dislikes the aire. He doesn't trust him. If they can't find my bow or quiver, I can say he's lying... I can say he attacked me and I...*

Tears of frustration slid down her thorn-scraped cheeks. *Goddess, Ériu,* she prayed, *please help me find a way out of this.*

With wooden limbs Muirenn climbed down from the tree. At this hour her family would all be asleep. Perhaps she could to sneak into the roundhouse and climb into bed without anyone noticing. The thought of the fire and her warm bed gave her small comfort. She planted one foot in front of the other, and began the journey home.

Muirenn came to the door of her roundhouse and stood there silent, listening. There was no sound inside except the crackling embers of the fire. Opening the door just a crack, she slinked through and padded silently towards the bed that she shared with her brother. Rónán's chest rose and fell with the even breaths of slumber. She knelt and pulled back the covers to slip underneath. Then she jumped as a harsh whisper cut through the quiet.

"Muirenn? Muirenn!" It was Rónán. The household awoke with sleepy moans.

"Muirenn!" Tómnat cried. She leapt up from her bed and drew her daughter in a tight embrace. "Oh, my girl, I was worried sick! Why were you out so late? You know how dangerous it is to be out after dark!" She gasped at the bloody bramble scrapes across her cheeks and chin.

Lonán stood and bent down against the wall, picking up a long object. He came towards them with Muirenn's yew bow in his hand. "Aire Talorc came to us this evening and gave me this. He said he had caught you with it out in the pasture and that you attacked him in attempts to protect this secret from us. Where did you get this bow? He said you were holding a duck. Have you been hunting? For how long has this been going on, Muirenn?"

"What else have you been keeping from us?" Tómnat demanded. There was a familiar glint of suspicion in her eye.

"Nothing!" Muirenn exclaimed. "I've only been... I only wanted to play with a bow, that's all! I liked shooting Rónán's bow, so in my free time I made my own. It's just for fun, Dadaí! It's just for fun! I didn't mean any harm by it."

"Well, harm has been done," said Lonán sternly. "You've attacked an aire, and since you're still underage the blame falls on me. The fine could be severe. Thank Bríg and her gentle hand that Talorc was not injured! Still, if we can't afford the fine..." Lonán came to Muirenn and grasped her shoulder roughly, raising his voice in anger. "Do you know what happens when fuidir can't pay their debts? Huh? Do you know?" He shook her violently. "They become dóerfuidir, Muirenn. Unfree! A half-step from slavery! We'd be tied to the aire and never able to leave him! We'd lose our rights and protections under the law! Do you want that? Huh? Do you want us all to become dóerfuidir?"

Muirenn shook her head in terror, tears streaming down her face. "No, Dadaí! No! I was only protecting myself! He grabbed me and would have—"

"I don't want to hear it!" Tómnat screamed at her. "You're a liar and a rascal! Why should we believe a word you say?"

Muirenn could think of no explanation that her parents might believe. She was trapped, once again. She sobbed into her hands.

Lonán let go of her. "First thing tomorrow, we will go to the aire's brugh and you will apologize to him directly. We will ask what we might do to avoid the fine. This is your doing and therefore your responsibility to find the solution. You are almost a woman now. You must learn to take responsibility for your own actions."

The blood drained from Muirenn's face. She could not face that man again! But her protests were silenced. The conversation ended. Each climbed back into their bed and laid down in bitter silence.

Slowly, the whistling breaths of their sleep filled the roundhouse, but Muirenn laid on her back, eyes wide, staring blindly at the rafters. Her mind was tossed in a storm of despair, she was at the very edge of panic. Would she be allowed to speak in her own defense? What defense did she even have? What judgment would the brithem give? Would the fine really make them all dóerfuidir and unfree? What urges did the lord conceal behind that wicked smile, when he groped her body with his eyes? Would he try to touch her? Would he try to use her as... a woman? A woman who has lost her freedom? The thought was so revolting that she nearly wretched.

One thing seemed certain: she would never again hold a bow in her hand. The freedom to roam afield alone would surely be taken from her. Even if her family escaped the sentence of dóerfuidir, Muirenn would certainly lose the freedom that she held most dear. And that loss, she could not bear. *They've already killed the boy in me. Then they'll kill the girl in me. Then I'll be all-dead. Nothing left to live with.*

What came then to her mind was the image of the seashore. She saw herself walking out alone into the dark crashing waves. Her head was submerged. She did not come up again for air.

No. A sudden blaze of defiance flared up in her heart. *A warrior fights for his freedom. They can't keep me. They can't kill me. They can't make me take my own life.*

Muirenn had known that this day might come: the day when she would be forced to leave her family; the day when she would finally be ready to strike out on her own. There was no more despair; that was engulfed in and consumed by the flames of self-preservation. She ran through the list of things that must be done now, quickly and without a sound. Most of the preparations she had made months ago.

Silent as a slinking fox, she got up and gathered what she needed: a wool blanket and her cloak, three oat cakes, and a block of sheep cheese lay wrapped in a dock leaf. The confiscated bow was too close now to her parents' bed—Muirenn would have to abandon it. It was her favorite bow, but she had others.

With one last glance at her sleeping family and the roundhouse in which she had dwelled her whole life, Muirenn turned and slid out the door into the cool, moonless night.

Her feet knew the way even without light and led her faithfully to the secret glade. There, beside her sheltered wood pile, was a hollowed out log in which she kept two other bows of her own making and several fistfuls of arrows. A pair of Rónán's worn out trousers were also tucked away there, and a tunic he had outgrown. Muirenn lit a small fire to see by, changed her clothes, stuffed the old smock deep in the hollow log, and wrapped herself in her cloak the color of walnuts. In the woolen blanket she wrapped up the food, a wooden bowl, a handful of tinder, and her firesteel and flint. She tied up the blanket at each end and strapped the roll to her back.

Kneeling there before the timid flame, Muirenn closed her eyes and solemnly prayed:

> Heart of the forest, conceal me.
> Guidance of stars, reveal to me.
> Beasts that hunger, repel thee.
> Ériu, the magnificent and bountiful,
> let me pass safely to far away lands
> where none know my name nor my face.
> Ériu, let me live as a man and a free person,
> if it would not upset the Divine Order of things.
> Ériu, let me live only amongst those that accept me
> and love me for who I am,
> never forcing falsehoods upon me.
> For this boon, I give you my name, my blood, and my earnest oath
> that I will serve the powers of Nature,
> the plants and animals,
> the stars and wind,
> the mountains and sea,
> and the spirits of the Land to the best of my ability,
> however I am fit, forever, until my death.

Muirenn unsheathed her belt knife and pressed it to her palm. In a clear, confident voice she said: "I was asked once what my name was and I did not know. But I know now. On this night, I leave behind the name Muirenn forever, and take up my true name, my only name: it is Áedán. I pledge my oath to you, Great Goddess, as Áedán." With the tip of the knife Áedán drew a thin red line across his palm. He let the blood flow freely and drip down to meet the earth.

A sudden breeze rose up and blew out the little flame. The trees swayed and rustled their leaves furiously. There was a whisper in it, a sound like the lilt and whistle of speech. It was just as before, on that night he was tied to the willow tree, when the wind spoke words that were just beyond hearing.

Then, just as suddenly, the wind stilled and the forest was silent once more. Áedán looked up through the treetops and saw that the clouds had parted. From the clear night sky a twinkling of silver starlight shone down upon the earth. Áedán's skin prickled. The goddess Ériu had heard his prayer. She had accepted his oath.

He stood, wrapping his hand with a strip ripped from his old smock. There was a new vigor in his limbs, a lightness in his step. Bow in hand, quiver on his back, knife on his hip, the boy set off eastward into the starlit forest with nary a glance backward at the suffering he left behind.

PART II:

ÁEDÁN

CHAPTER SIX

Mother Mountain

For three days Áedán walked south and east, from the rocky wind-swept shore to Ériu's inland bower. Avoiding well-trodden roads, he traveled instead by footpaths and deer trails. The forest was aflame with autumn color: rust red, auburn, amber, and gold. Into the dense, wide, wondrous wood the boy plunged, taking refuge in the places with the most trees and the fewest people.

Samhain was soon to come and so the cattle were driven off the highland pastures back to the villages for winter. When that was done, much of the outlands there would be left alone. It was these unpeopled places Áedán sought. Though the woodland sheltered creatures that might be unfriendly to him, he had faith that the goddess Ériu would take heed of his oath and steer him clear of their paths. She had softened his fate once before, and so he hoped She would again.

Every further step he strode into the wilderness Áedán's heart grew lighter. A careless joy invigored his limbs, a joy as he had not felt since plucking apples in the orchard with his friends on that fateful day many years ago. A weight was lifted from him, like a capstone covering a wellspring. Now he could look down into that well, the well of his own soul, gaze into its depths with clear eyes, and draw from it what had been there hidden all along: intuition, inspiration, and self-knowledge. Áedán felt new and fresh and bright. In those long days of travel, through showers of rain and sunlight both, he whistled merrily, crafted humorous riddles, and spun poems to acclaim the beauty of Nature all around.

Two days had passed since crossing the boundary marker at the edge of the territory of his birth tribe, the Fír Lúachair. Of course, he had never been outside of his túath before, as only the filid had the freedom to travel unarmed between the túatha. It was dangerous to leave one's túath—he had no legal protection here should he be robbed or harmed by strangers. But it was this fact that also lent him some protection, for it was unlikely that either Talorc or his own family would risk a boundary crossing to come and find him.

I'm hardly worth the trouble anyway, he thought. *Exile is preferable for us all.*

Though he was used to roving, Áedán had never walked so far in one journey in all his life. His feet and legs were aching. The way was slow-going since he chose to avoid the roads—the path was neither straight nor direct. On occasion he came upon marshes or streams too wide or deep to cross, and so had to double back and find another way around. Although he had picked a direction, in truth Áedán had no idea where he was headed. Yet the world was full of wonders and the journey was exciting, so he didn't mind too much this circuitous route.

There was a place where the forest thinned and met the foot of a grassy hill. As Áedán emerged from the shade there, he came upon a herd of red deer. They jerked up their heads and watched him pass. Sensing the boy was no threat, they dipped their necks down again and continued grazing.

Áedán smiled. It was a good place to rest, for it held a little fern-choked gully. He washed his feet in a puddle there and lounged until dusk, watching the clouds. The oatcakes and cheese had all been eaten up the day before, yet he had not stopped to rest or hunt until now. Speed had been his first priority, and he had not felt safe to slow until there was a good distance between himself and Fír Lúachair. He was learning how to push through the hunger that would become his close companion.

But now Áedán was ready for meat. As the daylight dimmed he stalked in the shade and shot himself a hefty hare, which he roasted over a fire. With a grateful heart and a bulging belly, he slept there in the ferny folds of that hillock and dreamed of feasting at a chieftain's table.

In the morning, Áedán set off again south in search of mountains. The mountains in the south held tall tales: of fantastic beasts, of lone wild men seeking the cure of their madness in the woodland, and of a legendary community where the most learned of all men and women—the filid, druíd, brithem, and líaig—went to study. Though of the latter Áedán was most skeptical, for why would the wise hide out in the wilderness when they should be tending peace at the center of society?

Áedán had never seen a true mountain before, but he was eager to. Few people lived on their slopes, he knew, for it was said that the thin highland soil was not good for growing nor grazing, and the forests were too dense. This, he surmised, would be the most suitable place to hide from humanity.

At last, with a thrill of excitement, Áedán sighted above the treetops a dark line of rolling mountains, ridged like the backs of great lounging beasts furred with trees. He drew ever nearer, and by the end of that day he came to their feet. There, at the crossing of two footpaths, was a boundary marker. Beyond this point he would pass into yet another túath. There were striations carved into the vertical edge of the stone. He knew these markings to be ogham, though he could not read their meaning.

Áedán guessed it to be the túath of the Dáirine. The southern mountains were supposedly ruled by that fierce and reclusive mountain tribe.

Casting a cautious glance about him to ensure that no one spied his trespass, Áedán crossed the boundary and continued south, skirting the foothills. Before dark, he stopped and made camp.

The next morning he followed the edge of the foothills east then south again, not yet climbing the slopes to any significant height. Then, as he came around a curve he stopped short, gazing up in wonder. In all those days of rousing, weary travel Áedán had let his feet take him where they would, watching for whatever sign might tell of the proper place to call home. And now he received this sign, without any breath of a doubt: before him two mountains rose up gently, side by side, like the breasts of a woman.

"This is it!" he exclaimed. "I have dreamed of this place!" It was true; long ago he had dreamed of living in a cleft between two mountains such as these.

They are the breasts of the Goddess, the mother of these mountains, he thought, heart ahum with adulation. *She will be my mother and I will be Her son. I shall live here so that She may cradle me against Her heart. And She will love me, as I will love Her.* His eyes became unexpectedly wet for the strange mix of emotions in his heart: grief, hope, and a feeling of being guided by unseen hands. These tears were an omen—he had finally found home.

Áedán explored the forested folds of this pair of peaks. Upslope between them he found a small loch filled with many centuries of rainwater. Áedán touched his parched lips to its waters and took a long drink, its surface reflecting the swift moving sky. What a gift that Ériu should give him a home with a source of fresh water so nearby. Further uphill, the slopes became closer together between the earth's great cleavage, and to one side Áedán found himself a flat spot perfect for the building of a permanent shelter. With a peal of happy laughter and a merry little dance, he knelt and touched his forehead to the ground, giving thanks for his good fortune.

Hunger now nipped at his heels like a feral hound. Áedán had not eaten a solid meal since the evening before last, and the wild herbs and roots and shriveled berries he grazed along the path had done little but give him just enough energy to place one foot in front of the other. He had no vigor left with which to stalk prey or set snares, and so he laid in wait by that little mountain loch for many hours.

Just as the sun began to dip behind the peaks of the mountains, Áedán shot himself a grouse that had come with his mate for a last evening drink. At the twang of the bowstring, his wife took wing, but the husband fell still at the edge of the pool. Áedán's arrow forever parted these two gentle lovers. He was sorry for it, and yet the task was given to him, by the womb of the world, to live, and in so doing, take life. As it is with all hunters who honor the sacred obligation of predator to prey, he spoke his thanks for the bird's sacrifice and prayed that he be reborn in beauty to find love once again.

It was nearly winter—Samhain was approaching. This was not an ideal season to start a camp and Áedán knew it. He had no stores of grain nor meat nor nut mast. He had no garden nor domestic animals. There were only a few weeks left to gather what stores of wild roots he could before the ground began to freeze and make the digging harder. Áedán foraged wild greens and herbs, nuts, mushrooms, shriveled berries, sloes, and rosehips. So far from the sea, he would have to do without the seaweed and the shore fish that had been an ever present staple in his diet. And with a shock he remembered that without seaweed he would also be without the salt that he could harvest from it. It would be a hard winter indeed.

Like an autumn-frenzied squirrel, Áedán spent the next several weeks urgently gathering forage, tracking game, and setting traps and snares. As the daylight grew shorter, many birds flew away to winter in warmer climes. The ones that stayed he studied, noting their habits of diet and nest, noting also the scent and taste of unfamiliar plants that might help him survive in these wild mountain lands. He hunted and checked his traps daily, hoping to preserve enough meat before the birds and beasts disappeared into their burrows for the winter. A hut he built out of saplings and bark and bracken, and beside it a little smokehouse to preserve the meat without the aid of salt.

All these tasks, though strenuous, were also thrilling. He had imagined this life so often in the years of his dreary domesticity—now it was real and he felt marvelously adventurous. Every day he did things he had never done before. He made cooking vessels out of ash bark, baskets out of bramble canes, wooden bowls from oak burls, and knives, cleavers, and an ax head knapped from stone. The only metal he owned was the blade of his old bronze knife, which he carried carefully and kept sharp.

One by one, he met his neighbors: a badger and her mate, a pair of golden eagles, stoats, pine martins, a small family of foxes, and a community of perpetually-perturbed red squirrels. It was fun to watch these squirrels—the way chased each other and gave out to their enemies in long, chittering tirades. They ranted at him too when he passed below their trees, and at first, he just laughed. Yet as the weeks passed, he came to know them and admire them a little. Though small, they were fierce and fast and clever. He learned of their romances, alliances, and animosities. By watching them he learned which oaks and hazel trees dropped the best mast. Squirrels were lowly creatures by most people's standards, yet they had their own dignity, and for that Áedán grew to respect them. But they did not yet respect him back. For that, Áedán knew he must befriend them.

At last year's Samhain celebration, Onchú the druí had told stories and sooth to a gathering of children. He had told the story of how Tuan mac Cairill incarnated as a human, a stag, a boar, an eagle, a salmon, and lastly when eaten for supper by a chieftain's wife, birthed from her womb as a human once more. Onchú had then said a thing that stuck in Áedán's mind, and he remembered it now: "All beings are sentient, all trees and beasts and stones and rivers. All have their own hopes and hurts and private affairs, as do you and I, and these are no less important than our own. Therefore, we must show respect to every creature of Nature, even as we hunt the game, even as we cut the wheat, for they sacrifice their own flesh to nourish us. This is a sacred gift; an eternal bond. Thus, we must strive to listen when they speak and to grant their wishes when we can, for we are always in their debt. Listen, and be sure that creatures are always speaking to us. Ignorant people believe that birds and beasts lack the faculty of speech. Not so. If we cannot understand them, it is our own fault for not listening carefully enough."

Áedán pondered this sooth. He knew the squirrels' concerns—they spoke these very clearly, in their own twittering tongue. The boy was a newcomer to that slope and he had encroached upon their territory. Not only that, but he was gathering more acorns and hazelnuts and chestnuts than all of his neighbors combined. What would the squirrels do if they hadn't enough nuts to last through the winter?

One of these squirrels he knew better than the rest. Áedán called him Dluí, for he had long tufts at the tips of his ears that stood up like grass seed. Áedán stood below Dluí's tree and asked him if they could become more peaceful neighbors.

"I promise now to gather nuts from farther afield, and not all in one place. And if you are ever afraid that you will go hungry, come to my door and I will give a share of my own stores. Is this well with you?"

Dluí quit his scolding and quieted to listen. After a moment's consideration, he thumped his foot three times against the branch, then climbed up to his nest untroubled. Thereafter, Áedán kept his promise, thus Dluí and his brethren shouted no more ire down at the boy. Boy and squirrels walked and foraged now peacefully side by side, without alarm or ill-will.

Wolves denned on the southern slopes of the mountain. Áedán avoided those places and went out only during the day when the wolves were less active. Occasionally, he came across the stripped carcass of an animal too large for Áedán himself to kill: an adult boar or a red deer. If he found these kills before the buzzards and ravens did, there was often enough meat left for several meals. Scavenging the leavings of better hunters was a popular woodland sport, and so the boy often had to shoo away, with apology, the smaller animals to get his fill.

The fields of farmers were far away from Áedán's hermitage, the majority of a day's walk. The payoff in booty was barely worth the effort, so he visited them only twice that winter. It was many days since Samhain and the last harvest of grain, but at the edges of the fields Áedán was able to find several handfuls of abandoned barley, oats, and wheat berries, enough to make an occasional bowl of warm porridge. It was on the coldest, wettest days that he treated himself to this delicacy. From orchards he stole seconds—the worm-eaten or half-rotten fruits—and other random leavings in the fields. There was some guilt in stealing from another family, but he took so little that he was sure no one would notice. Besides, he shared this habit with the deer, so it could not be so wrong.

Áedán's first winter was spent thus, hard and hungry and hopeful. November and December were cold months for the boy as he had only his cloak and a single woolen blanket to keep him warm. From a deer's carcass he made thread out of sinew and a bone needle. Soon he tanned enough pelts to sew himself a coverlet of hare and pine martin fur, and a doehide jacket gleaned from a wolf-kill. He lined it with stoat fur at the collar. No coat he had ever owned was warmer, and he was proud of its beauty and comfort. Later, he sewed mittens and a hat from hare pelts. Though his meals were plain and sometimes he went to sleep without supper, his mind grew sharper, his sight became keener, and he grew up whip-strong and sinewy. And when he bound his breasts tight against his chest, there was nothing to distinguish him from any other adolescent boy.

CHAPTER SEVEN

Butter Thief

In April the willows wakened, their crowns haloed in yellow catkins; the birches and aspens clothed their naked limbs in vivid green. Those ephemeral flowers most delicate were also the most bold, arising to paint the woodland its first colors.

Spring came none too soon and Áedán eagerly gathered the young green shoots of many wild plants for the pot: wood sorrel, dandelion greens, wild onions and garlic, cow parsley, fat-hen greens, and nettles. He raided nests for their eggs and happily hunted the winged migrants that returned to Ériu for summer. By March his cache of nuts and grains had gone. Meals would be leafy and bitter until the coming of summer berries and mushrooms.

It was on the morning of Bealtaine, the first of May, that an opportunity arose unexpectedly. Early in the morning, as Áedán warmed rocks to boil nettle leaves in his ash-bark pot, he heard a strange sound carried on the northern breeze. It was the sound of voices—human voices. Stealthily, Áedán crept downslope and climbed up into an oak tree. At the foot of a mountain to the east of him, dozens of men, women, and children were gathering at a single point. They marched like ants in two lines, one from the west and another from the south, from the valleys behind Áedán's mother mountain. They drove with them several dozen head of cattle.

From his leafy perch, it was hard to see what they were gathering at, so Áedán leapt from the tree and wound his way downslope to see if he might eavesdrop on their chatter. Without a sound, Áedán padded close to the line of pilgrims and hid in the shade of a boulder, listening intently.

"Now don't drop your ribbons, Cnes! Your wishes may not come true if you tie them onto the sacred tree dirty!" said a mother to her young daughter. Each of them had upon her head a crown of ferns and flowers.

"Why have we brought the bull calf with us, Mamaí?" the child asked. She frolicked and threw up her hands, watching her colorful cluster of ribbons flutter in the air.

"To feed the goddess of the mountain, Crobh Dearg, with his blood," said an older girl beside her. "We must honor Her and give Her sacrifice every summer to ensure a good growing season and a bountiful harvest." She walked proudly in a dress the color of marsh orchids, sewn specially for this holy day. Her wavy chestnut hair was plaited with red ribbons and pink crane's bill flowers. "Mamaí, may I join the older children this year to place stones upon the Goddess' breasts? Please?"

"Ha! Well, I suppose you're old enough now. At least you can try," the mother said with a wry smile. "I doubt you'll make it to both though. It's a longer walk than you think!"

Áedán quivered. People were going to be walking up his mountain towards the peaks? But they would pass very close to his camp!

Another family walked by the boulder where he crouched.

"A drink from the sacred well at the ráth will sweeten his voice for the singing, I'm sure," said a middle-aged man. He prodded before him a herd of three heifers. In one hand he held the rod, and in the other he held his wife's hand. "Last summer, Ernán's poetry improved quite a bit after drinking from Crobh Dearg's sacred waters. Though the effect had worn off by Samhain! Ha!"

Áedán listened for a while longer to the jokes, the singing, the play-barking of dogs, and the jostling of cattle. When the stream of pilgrims thinned to a trickle, he hiked back up to the oak tree to spy on the gathering from above.

In the east, sunlight peered through a rent in the clouds and shone down upon the ruins of a stone ráth thronged all around with people. One by one, the cattle were led inside the circular stone wall. A knife was put to each of their necks to bleed them, just a little, into a large wooden bowl. That bowl was held by a man dressed in a five-colored cloak: a druí. He blessed each beast as its blood was taken. As the last of the near-fifty cattle filed into the ráth, they wheeled and churned like trout in a pool. The druí came outside the stone wall, holding aloft the sanguine vessel. The people circled sunwise about him and the air then filled with song. The sound of several hundred voices was carried upon the wind, haunting and harmonic. Áedán could make out only a few of their words, but this song he already knew by heart:

> Bábóg na Bealtaine, maighdean an tSamhraidh,
> Suas gach cnoc is síos gach gleann,
> Cailíní maiseach go gealgáireach gléasta
> Thugamar féin an Samhradh linn.

> Samhradh, Samhradh, bainne na ngamhna,
> Thugamar féin an Samhradh linn.
> Samhradh buí na nóinín glégeal,
> Thugamar féin an Samhradh linn.

> Thugamar linn é ón gcoill chraobhaigh,
> Thugamar féin an Samhradh linn.
> Ó bhaile go baile 'go dtí nár dtí féinig
> Thugamar féin an Samhradh linn.

Cuileann is coll is trom is caorthann,
Thugamar féin an Samhradh linn,
Is fuinnseag ghléigeal bhéil an átha,
Thugamar féin an Samhradh linn.

Samhradh, Samhradh, bainne na ngamhna,
Thugamar féin an Samhradh linn.
Samhradh buí na nóinín glégeal,
Thugamar féin an Samhradh linn.

May doll, maiden of Summer,
Up every hill and down every glen,
Beautiful girls, radiantly dressed,
We brought the Summer with us.

Summer, Summer, milk of the calves,
We brought the Summer with us.
Yellow Summer of the clear bright daisies,
We brought the Summer with us.

We brought it in from the leafy woods,
We brought the Summer with us.
From home to home to our own hearths
We brought the Summer with us.

Holly and hazel and elder and rowan,
We brought the Summer with us;
And bright ash-tree at the mouth of the ford,
We brought the summer with us.

Summer, Summer, milk of the calves,
We brought the Summer with us.
Yellow Summer of the clear bright daisies,
We brought the Summer with us.

Áedán wiped tears from his eyes, remembering for the first time in many moons what it had felt like to sing in the company of his kinsmen.

When the song had finished, the druí's bowl was passed from mouth to mouth and each member of the congregation sipped just a little from the bowl. When all had tasted of the lifeblood of the herd, the druí stepped into the ráth. The churning cattle stilled to watch him, then parted as he moved into the center. Tipping the bowl, he poured the remaining blood upon the earth and stood there with his head bowed in prayer. At last, as he called for the cattle to be released from the ráth. The assembly cried out with an ebullient cheer. Music struck up, food was laid out, and there was dancing. A stream of young people skipped and sprinted up the slopes toward the mountain's teats.

Áedán scrambled down his tree and raced back to camp, dousing the fire and concealing the most obvious signs of his activities there. His shelter was already well-camouflaged to a lazy eye from above. But should he stay there and protect his camp? Or flee to safer ground?

An impish smile curled his lips as an idea came to his head, and his stomach growled with it. He threw a few clean skins into his pack basket and hurried downslope. Taking the path that led westward then south, he headed towards the village whence the pilgrims had come. Their homesteads would be abandoned for the next several hours while they reveled at the mountain. Time enough for him to take just a little, modest, miniscule revenge for the disturbance to his quiet May morning.

Áedán slipped into the village like a fox to the duckhouse. On any other day the conical roofs of these roundhouses would have smoke seeping through the thatch like steam from a wheatloaf, but not this day. It was tradition amongst the Érainn to leave off lighting a fire before noon on Bealtaine, for doing so would tempt the Good People to steal the foison from the house's butter.

Well, that may protect it from the Síd, but not from me! Áedán thought wickedly. Slinking from shadow to shadow, Áedán crept close to the cluster of roundhouses. Choosing first the houses at the edge of the settlement, he began his stealthy raid. He took butter, fresh-baked bread, salt, dozens of duck eggs, a rusted iron cleaver, and a spool of thread. He took slices from hanging haunches of ham and mutton, and two handfuls of grain from each house. He tried to take small enough amounts that the theft would not be noticed. In the very last house, he stooped over a bucket of fresh-drawn milk and drank deep from its wooden ladle. Then, quick as a falcon, he darted back into the shady wood, loaded down with the plunder of his first ever Bealtaine raid.

"Let them take no heed, but if they do—let them think it was the Síd!" he laughed to himself. Áedán found a sunny rock upon which to bask, and there gorged himself on still-warm bread spread with rich yellow butter. Picturing himself in the likeness of a hero coming home from a cattle raid, he smiled proudly.

In the afternoon, when the pilgrims marched back to their villages, Áedán returned to his camp and found it undisturbed. As he stocked his larder with the spoils of spring, he sang a cheery song composed on the spot:

> How sweet the yellow from the teat
> That's cream does clot in summer's heat!
> The bread, the beer, the greens and meat
> Will come to me and give me treat!
>
> The flowers swarm with honeyed song
> The daylight lengthens ever strong!
> And pools will warm in not too long
> For swimming dazed—the fish will throng!

CHAPTER EIGHT

Cellach

In the mildness of summer Áedán gained more than a stone's weight and began to fill out. Growing skyward as quickly as the summer wheat, his bones made up for the time stunted by those cold, hungry months just past. The summer was generous, allowing him to store up abundant provisions for the coming of another winter. Walls of waddle and a new thatch of bracken made his hovel a little less ramshackle and a little tighter against the rain.

The holy day of Lugnasad came at the first of August. It was the day of the year's turning from the growing quarter to the harvesting quarter. All across Mumu the Érainn celebrated the god Lug and the bounty of summer with outdoor feasting, games, and bonfires.

Yet on this day Áedán was alone and sulking. He had loved the Lugnasad celebrations as a child, joining in the revelry and cheering on contests between friends and rivals. On all other days Áedán's solitude was much loved, but today it had turned inward; today it had become loneliness. He sat by his little loch watching dragonflies flit between the rushes, and for the first time in many months felt sorry for himself.

A cut on his thumb throbbed. He was strangely tired. And hungry. Was it the heat? He gnawed on a strip of smoked hare, curled up in the shade of an alder tree, and slept through the afternoon.

Two days later the full moon waned and Áedán felt a sudden cramping in his lower belly. His whole body felt strangely sore though he had done no strenuous work the day before. That evening he discovered with a shock a bright spot of red blood in his underclothes. Áedán remembered his mother describing this to him long ago, how a female begins to bleed with the cycles of the moon.

It won't happen to me, he had thought; he had pleaded to the Unseen. But now it had happened to him, and the feeling of blood clotting between his legs produced a wave of revulsion. There was also despair, for his body had once again betrayed him. Begrudgingly, he wadded a clump of peat moss between his legs, as his mother had once shown him to do.

Áedán came to dread the full moons. But as the wheel of the year turned back towards its darker half, he bled less often as the winter fare became more austere. *At least there's an advantage to going hungry too often,* he thought stoically.

The autumn frenzy had passed again with its long, golden afternoons. Then came the rasping winds of winter, combing the hillsides with its frigid fingers, clacking bare-armed branches together in sallow syncopation. Áedán was much better prepared for this winter than the one before it. Having less concern for his daily survival gave him the freedom to dream of faraway things. The future was one of these. Shall he live like a hermit here forever, lonely and wild, sharp and cunning? Or would there, somewhere, be a place for him to live amongst people again in safety? Would he ever pair up with another, as do the doves in the April? And would he ever hold the hand of a young woman, as he did in his dreams, and have her look into his face, blushing? But how could he ever hope to catch a woman's eye, and keep it, with a body such as he had?

The fire's winking embers lulled him to sleep, and then he dreamed. He dreamt he was a fox in his own den, laying with his body curled around the vixen asleep beside him. He yawned, laid his head on her soft shoulder, and closed his eyes once more.

A flurry had come in the night and dusted the boughs with such a fine flour as could be made of starlight. Áedán awoke to wonder at this sparkling world, and went to the loch to fetch water. The pool was glazed over with a delicate film of crystal. A touch of breeze lifted up the snowflakes and whisked them into whirlwinds which danced across the ice. The downy snow muffled the world's sounds; all was quiet and still. Mumbling an apology for breaking this soft silence, the boy cracked a hole in the ice which echoed with a sound like falling pine boughs, and dipped his vessel into the water.

A sudden cry rang out across the mountainside and sent a chill through his bones: a single melancholic howl. It was answered by a chorus of several others, and Áedán knew them to be wolves.

They sounded close, closer to his camp than they had ever before. Wolves lived on the other side of the mountain range and rarely ventured this way, though he had encroached several times into their territory to scavenge their kills. *I'll bet they've made a kill nearby*, he thought. With a surge of curiosity, Áedán strapped a basket onto his back, grabbed up his bow, and headed toward the place of their howling.

Stealthily, Áedán padded across the mountain slopes and soon came across a trail of prints in the snow. The trail was narrow and neat, for every individual wolf stepped exactly in the prints of the wolf in front, so that Áedán could not tell how many in total there were. He marveled at the size of those paws—wider than the width of his palm. *I should be frightened*, he thought to himself, but found that he was not. He was exhilarated and eager to witness their mastery; for the wolf is highest amongst of all Ériu's hunters. Making his approach, Áedán strung his bow and knocked an arrow. He did not expect wolves who had just made a kill to be hungry for him, but still, he ought to be cautious. Never before had he laid eyes on a live wolf and now he yearned to with all his heart.

Coming close, creeping forward, he could hear the sounds of several animals growling and chewing, ripping flesh and crunching bone. The scent of blood hung in the still air. Áedán came from downwind so the beasts would not smell him. At last he came close enough to see them, and so crouched behind a log, eyes wide in wonder.

Six wolves stood around the still-warm body of a doe, tearing and swallowing great mouthfuls of raw flesh. Occasionally they growled and nipped at each other, vying for the juiciest morsels of organ, muscle, and marrow. For a long time Áedán simply knelt there and watched, transfixed by the beauty of their silver-grey coats, their honey-yellow eyes, and their blood-stained muzzles. They were exquisite in their savagery.

A sudden sound Áedán heard just behind him: a crunch of snow and a snuffling. He turned to find himself staring into the face of a single black wolf, standing not five paces away. Áedán's heart skipped a beat; the breath caught in his throat. A young wolf, thin and smaller than the others, was looking directly at him. The wolf sniffed the air and tipped his head one way, then the other, eyes alight with curiosity. As their eyes met, seeing that the other spied him, neither dared to move.

Áedán's mind raced. *Should I raise my bow? Or would that cause him to alert the others?* He did not want to make the first move. The black wolf took one silent step forward, nose wriggling, trying to determine what this bald-faced creature might be. The young wolf stiffened suddenly at the sound of the other wolves tussling over the carcass, and took a few anxious steps backward.

Áedán understood. *He is an outcast like me, pushed to the margins to beg for the last scraps.* The growling quieted and the black wolf cast his gaze back again to Áedán. The boy then called out to the wolf with his thoughts: *I mean you no harm. I am only here for the leavings, just like you. But I do not need them now. Please let me depart peacefully.*

The young wolf flicked his ears and cocked his head. Then, with footsteps so soft that Áedán envied his mastery, the black wolf backed away and circled around to the other side of the pack. With a pounding heart, the boy crawled away out of sight of the wolf pack, then climbed into the branches of a wych elm to wait until their feast was finished.

Eventually he heard the pack leave, yet still, Áedán's intuition told him to wait. His patience was rightly given, for in a few moments the scrawny black wolf came into view below the boy's tree. The wolf looked up into the branches with his enchanting marigold eyes and met Áedán's there. His black muzzle was reddened now and his belly was distended. He licked his mouth contentedly, yawned and stretched, wagged his tail twice, then trotted away again in the direction of the pack.

Slowly, cautiously, Áedán climbed down from the tree and went to the scene of the carnage. The forest was no longer still there where the blood had reddened the snow. The small birds had come forth first to pick at the bones of the carcass, and soon the cawing ravens arrived. The boy cut away the few bits of meat that were left—not as much as he had hoped for—and placed them in his pack basket. As he turned to leave, he spied the crimson trail of something dragged. Following it, he found a place where the soil had been disturbed. Áedán dug into the cold earth with his hands and uncovered a hip joint to which still clung a good bit of muscle.

Do you think the black wolf left it for me? Áedán mused. *If he had wanted it, he would have taken it with him and buried it closer to home, I think.* With a shrug, he dropped the joint into his basket and sent a prayer of brotherly gratitude to his fellow outcast.

❦

Bealtaine came again with the flowering of primrose and cow slips, hawthorn and apple blossoms. The trees filled in the empty grey spaces of winter with shoots and leaves of verdant green: oak and alder, ash and elm, aspen and rowan. The sights and smells of the forest were rich and pungent; the air and earth hummed again with a reawakening of life.

The ceremony at the Cathair Crobh Dearg came again. This time Áedán prepared himself to raid not just one, but two villages. He returned home that afternoon with double the spoils of last year's raid. His chest was as bloated with pride as his belly was with the farmers' foison.

That night, contented and cache-full, Áedán laid on his back by the bank of the loch and looked up into the indigo sky. He had much confidence now in his ability to survive, and even thrive, up here alone in the mountains. *Perhaps I'm ready now to take on larger game.* Hunting a wild boar or deer by himself required more power from his bow and sharper aim. The beast had to be shot in exactly the right place and the arrow had to pierce deeply enough that the animal would die quickly and painlessly. It would be a dangerous mistake to wound a boar just enough to enrage it but not kill, or to chase a half-lamed deer for hours across the forest. Most men preferred spears to bows for hunting big game, for the pierce of a spear held more weight behind it. But as Áedán grew taller his draw strength had increased, and over the winter he had fashioned himself a heavier bow. He was strong enough now to take down a small boar or a young deer, he was sure.

The next morning, in the dark before dawn, Áedán prepared himself for the hunt. He cleansed himself with the smoke of mugwort and whispered his hunting prayer to the forest:

> Sight of the eagle
> Scent of the raven
> Swiftness of falcon
> Silence of owl
> All these woven

Into the hunter's cloak.
As Oisín was born
To the knowledge of the hind
Let that knowledge be my own.
Guide it my arrow
Guide it my spear
That the shaft fly straight
That the point land true.
Let me find what I seek
Let me take what I need
Let death come gently
To my prey without pain.

Áedán set off into the flatlands. There he had been tracking the movements of the red deer and wild boar for many months. The dawn twilight revealed to him trails and depressions in the ferns where the deer had bedded down to rest. Their scat became fresher as he moved west, towards the villages that he had visited yesterday.

Finally, he felt a tingling—a hunter's sense for his prey—and knew he was approaching a herd of deer. Áedán hid between a boulder and a fallen tree and waited there, hoping they would walk in his direction, close enough to strike.

And then, he saw them. It was as if the whole forest about him became suddenly animate. In one moment all was still, and in the next the boulders and bushes sprouted legs, becoming deer. When their movements ceased they melted into the greenery once more.

Áedán locked his gaze upon a young buck nearly a year old and small enough that his arrow might pierce cleanly through his chest. Áedán crept closer, padding quietly, breathing quick and shallow. The shadow of night slowly lifted and the morning transformed from grey to gold. In this wan light Áedán admired the buck's lovely auburn fur, the black stripe down his spine, the velvet sprouts of his single-prong antlers, the peaceful, liquid-black eyes. The buck bent and lowered his lips to the leaf litter. Áedán held his breath and drew back the bowstring.

The herd suddenly shied in unison and scattered. In the space of a wink, they were gone. Áedán cursed at himself. Had he spooked them? They couldn't have heard nor smelled him—he was sure of it! Then the boy caught his breath, for he began to hear what it was had scared them off.

Áedán heard strange sounds not too far away. Human voices. Shouts of men. Men scuffling. Curious and confident in his skills of concealment, Áedán crept closer to the scene. He crouched beneath the shade of a holly tree and watched.

Three men were arguing and fighting over something on the ground. Whatever it was struck out at them pitifully. One of the men gave it a vicious kick and the victim cried out in torment. A thrill of pain was sent through Áedán's chest. It had been the cry of a young man or a boy. As the three men pulled at the figure on the ground, searching through his belongings and clothing, Áedán began to piece together an explanation for what he watched: the men had set upon this boy to rob him. Anger rose up hot in Áedán's cheeks. He set a stone in the leather sling he kept tucked in his belt and crawled forward to hide behind a log. Beside him was a tall elm tree whose branches would provide an easy escape, should he need it.

Suddenly, one of the men stumbled and fell, holding the side of his head. He looked at his hand and was stunned to see it red with blood. Another man fell backwards, his hand on his cheek. The third man stopped his assault and looked around anxiously.

"An attack!" he yelled. "Who's there?"

Another stone flew and hit him in the hollow of his throat. He gasped and fell to his knees, gagging.

The first man stood and cried out: "Show yourself, coward! Come out and fight us like a man!" Then he screamed as he discovered an arrow lodged deep in the muscle of his thigh.

"Ach—it's the Faery Bolt! Run for it, lads!" The two unlamed men picked up their wounded comrade between them and hobbled away, snatching up what treasures they could in their retreat.

Áedán waited until the sounds of their shuffling were gone, then made his way to the fallen figure. As the men left, the morning songs of the forest birds rose up again. Underneath their chorus was a pitiful whimper. The victim was curled up in a ball on the ground, shuddering with soft sobs. Áedán stood over him, waiting for the tears to subside. Slowly, the figure turned his head to look up at Áedán. Not noticing the boy until that moment, he started and tried to scramble away.

"Hold. I mean you no harm. I was the one who sent those brigands away," said Áedán proudly, hoping to evoke a ring of heroism in his voice.

The boy on the ground gazed up at Áedán in awe and a little fear. His face was scratched, his blonde hair disheveled, his clothes torn and scattered about the leaf litter. One eye was beginning to swell above a bruised cheek.

"Oh, friend, thank you! A thousand thank yous! They might have killed me—you've saved my life!" The boy looked around at his belongings, noting what was missing. "Though they've stolen much of my property and all of my gold. My spear, my cloak..." he patted his hip, searching. "And even my knife! The Crow's curses on them—those dishonorable bastards!" Angry tears again began to fall and the boy covered his face.

Embarrassed to look at the boy whilst he cried, Áedán left him to his sulking. He walked around the clearing, collected the boy's belongings, and piled them at his feet. In a satchel he smelled food, and opening it revealed a loaf of hearty wheat bread and a half-eaten round of hard cheese.

"Well, at least you won't go hungry," said Áedán. To his own ears his voice sounded rough and hoarse from lack of use. It was the first time he had spoken to another human being in over a year and a half.

The boy wiped his face and looked up at Áedán with eyes of borage blue. The youth before him was thin, barefoot, and clothed only in animal skins. His cheeks were ruddy and smooth; his was countenance severe. "Excuse me, but, may I ask... are you... are you one of the Fair Folk? You who've stepped out of the air to rescue me?"

Áedán snarled like a fox. "No! No, I'm not!"

"Then, are you one of the mad men that hides out in the forest?"

Áedán scoffed. "What? I just saved your miserable life and you dare to ask me such insulting questions?" He turned, took two steps away, then turned back. "And I didn't just appear from nowhere—I was stalking deer when my game was spooked. I heard your distress and came to help. I suppose I ought to mind my own business next time." He shrugged and walked away.

"No, wait! I apologize! I didn't mean to be rude. It's just that I... I was so astonished to see you. I've never laid eyes on someone such as you. You dress so strangely—how I expect a wildman would. And yet your face is so... striking, as I imagine the Síd might look... as I've heard in stories..." The boy's voice trailed off, entranced by the amber of Áedán's flashing eyes, the tangle of his flame-red hair. To this frightened young man, Áedán seemed savage and stunning and more than a little Otherworldly.

The boy rubbed his face to break the spell and stood up painfully. He limped over to Áedán and offered his hand. Áedán took it. The boy kissed Áedán's palm. "I am indebted to you, friend. I owe you a life. What is your name?"

Áedán was silent for a moment. Then with a little caution, answered: "Áedán is my name."

"Of the Dáirine?"

Áedán frowned. "This is Dáirine territory, is it not?"

"That's not what I asked."

"Well, I don't welcome the question," said Áedán gruffly.

"I only ask because we are very close to the border between Fellubair and Dáirine, and the men who attacked me were Dáirine. So, I..." He shook his head. "My name is Cellach, and I also would rather not speak my tribe. Tell me how I can repay you and I will do it. Anything you ask." Áedán raised his eyebrows in disbelief. "Anything? That's quite a thing to pledge to a stranger! But what boon should I ask of a boy who was just robbed of all his valuables, has no tribe, and perhaps not even any status? How should I know what he is capable of giving?"

Cellach heard the truth in these words and smiled at the weakness of his promise. He let go of Áedán's hand and bent down to sit on a rock, wincing. "You're right, Áedán. I suppose I should rephrase it and promise to repay you in any way that I am able. Which may, at the moment, be negligible."

"Well, you can start by sharing some of that bread and cheese. I haven't breakfasted yet." Áedán reached for the satchel, but froze at the sound of several bird alarms. "Someone is coming. We should be away from this place."

The boys grabbed up their belongings and moved towards the shelter of the mountain. Cellach was half as fast as Áedán, and so Áedán had to wait for the other boy to catch up. Áedán scolded him for puffing and stomping so loudly. Finally, they came to a hidden place between a tumble of rocks and there sat to eat and converse.

"Why were those men assaulting you?" asked Áedán between mouthfuls. He had never eaten bread made from such fine wheat flour, nor a cheese so smooth and creamy. This boy must be wealthy indeed to afford such rich foods.

"To rob me, of course!"

"Yes, but to be robbed is quite rare, even when in a foreign túath. To rob a traveler is hardly worth the trouble—you never know which of their brothers or cousins is a lord or a chieftain willing to take revenge." Áedán looked more carefully at the boy. His clothes, though now sullied and torn, were made of fine linen and softest wool, brightly dyed. "Dressed a little too richly to be hacking through the woods. Made you an easy target. They assumed you had things worth their while to steal. And they were right, by the looks of it. You were traveling by the roads, I presume?"

Cellach frowned, ashamed at his naivety. "Yes, well… they accused me of being a thief myself. They said their village been raided yesterday on Bealtaine, as it had the year before. They thought I was a brigand from Fellubair—they thought they had caught me in the act. In truth, I had only crossed the border last night, I had nothing to do with the raid yesterday. Or maybe they just made that up as an excuse to rob me. What— why do you look at me so?"

Áedán's mouth had fallen open in shock. The Dáirine had been patrolling because of him—because *he* had been the one raiding the day before. And now this boy had been caught in the middle of it. Cellach had been victimized because of *him*. It was his fault. Áedán had fancied himself so sly, so cunning that they wouldn't have noticed. But they did notice.

Áedán stood and walked a little away, steadying himself against a silver birch.

"What is it?" Cellach asked anxiously. "Do you hear something?"

"No… em, yes. Yes, they may be following us. Where are you going? Do you have anywhere to stay?" Áedán asked softly.

Cellach shook his head. "East. Into the mountains. That's all I've planned so far."

"Well, I might let you stay with me for a night. But you must promise, you must swear to whatever gods care for you, that you'll never tell anyone about it. Not about me, and not about where I live."

Cellach nodded vigorously. "I swear it. I swear it on my honor."

Satisfied, Áedán helped the boy up and the two began walking up the slope of his mountain towards home.

CHAPTER NINE

The Líaig

By the time they had arrived at Áedán's camp, Cellach was shaking and gasping for breath. Áedán set him down by the hearth, lit a fire, and gave Cellach a basin of cool water to wash his hands and face in.

"Are you hurt?" asked Áedán.

"When they kicked me they must have bruised my rib. It could be fractured."

Áedán pulled down a bundle of herbs hanging from the ceiling, mixed them with water, and pounded them into a paste. "This is comfrey. It will help heal the bones." He helped Cellach apply it to the bruised ribs and a long thin scratch beside them. As he did this he laid a charm upon the wound, one that he remembered his grandmother using:

> Miach and Airmed
> Went to the battlefield
> And found Rí Nuada's arm.
> They pressed it to him and chanted:
> 'Ault fri halt. Féith fri féith.'
> Bone to bone
> Sinew to sinew

Flesh to flesh
Skin to skin.
As the masters healed that,
May I heal this.

Cellach's pain was lessened a little and his brow was smoothed. He gazed about his surroundings and said in amazement, "You built all this? By yourself?" Áedán nodded. "How long have you been here?"

"This coming winter will be my third."

"Incredible," Cellach said in admiration. "I've only ever dreamt of such a thing. To live out here, perfectly alone. It must be hard... and cold in the winter."

"It is until you know what you're doing. I prefer it greatly to civilized life."

"On occasion I've wondered if I might like it myself. But I think I would miss the hall and the hearth too much."

"Then why have you come here, Cellach? The mountains can be harsh to those who are unprepared." Áedán plunged a white-hot rock into a leather pot to boil their tea water.

"I'm only here because... I just needed time away. I had no choice. I don't want to live out here alone, but I... I had to flee a situation. To prove a point."

"What situation?"

Cellach sighed heavily. "My family wishes to seek an alliance with another prestigious family, so they wish me to accept marriage to a girl my age. I'll be sixteen soon and they've planned for the handfasting to be held on Lugnasad. But it wasn't my decision. I can't bring myself to do it. Yet the coibche payment to her family has already been made. I felt trapped. I didn't know what else to do, so I ran away and left the túath so they couldn't find me. That was two days ago. I don't mean to leave forever, but just long enough to demonstrate my clear dissent. They can't force me to do it. I'm not a child any longer."

Áedán looked carefully at Cellach. He was almost a hand taller than Áedán, and much more muscular. Despite his bruises, Áedán could tell that he was handsome, as fair and noble in the face as a white-tailed eagle. On his chin and upper lip Áedán could see a very fine fuzz like willow down—the beginnings of what might be a beard in several years. Áedán brought his hand to his own chin and was saddened by its nakedness. There was a golden ear cuff on each of the boy's ears—the only pieces of jewelry that the bandits had missed.

"Are you a noble, one of the *flaith* class?" Áedán asked with furrowed brow. The distaste with which he said that word was unmistakable, and it made Cellach wary.

"Em... no. My father is a briugu. But we are wealthy enough that the girl's family, who are flaith, wished for an alliance."

Áedán nodded, put at ease by this explanation. His opinion of Cellach was much improved upon hearing this, for the briugu were the highest ranking members of the farming class and were well known for their generosity. With such extravagant wealth came the obligation to provide limitless hospitality to anyone in their túath. By this they were held in high esteem and well-loved by all.

"And why don't you want to marry the girl?" Áedán asked. "Is she ugly?"

"No. She's pretty enough."

"Is she mean?"

Again, Cellach shook his head.

"When she speaks does she bleat like a ewe?"

"What? No, of course not!" exclaimed Cellach. His temper was tested by all of these invasive questions.

"Then why wouldn't you marry her? I don't understand what could be so detestable about marrying a not-ugly, not-mean flaith girl."

Cellach growled in frustration. "Because... because I... ach. It's complicated. You wouldn't understand."

"Oh. I wouldn't understand? Is it because I'm just an ignorant, lowly peasant?" Áedán said coldly.

"No, that's not it at all. I just don't know how to explain it to..." Cellach turned to face Áedán, eager to change the subject. "What about you? Why are *you* here all alone in the mountains?"

Áedán looked away and stared out the open door. "I wish not to talk about it."

"You see? That's how I feel!" said Cellach.

The two boys sat in silence, watching the fire. Áedán added chopped roots of valerian and dandelion to the pot. He let it simmer a while, then poured the liquid into wooden bowls. He sweetened the tea with honey he had stolen the day before. As they sipped this quietly, Cellach noticed something strange: Áedán had an unusually large stash of butter for a hermit who kept no milking cows. He decided not to inquire about it—the tension between the two of them was already stretching his host's hospitality thin.

Áedán showed Cellach how to apply a salve of yarrow and plantain leaves to the scratches on his face and hands, then went about his routine without much more conversation. For supper Áedán prepared his most elaborate meal: a stew of stringy mountain hare, morel mushrooms, and spicy wild onions thickened with barley meal. Cellach forced it down with a smile but did not ask for more—he was used to fare far more sumptuous than this, and less gamey. The boys conversed about the weather, the woods, and the simpler pleasures of childhood. Each was fascinated by the stories the other told about his life. Áedán had never spoken at length to a boy of such learning. He was eager to hear about Cellach's lessons in poetry and history and law from his tutor, a fili. Cellach spoke also of his lessons in riding, fencing, and hunting with spears, as well as games of mental strategy like fidchell.

"Gods! I'd trade all this in an instant for that life!" said Áedán. Hearing of Cellach's childhood was like listening to Áedán's most perfect dreams spoken aloud. And yet Cellach was just as impressed by Áedán's expert knowledge of the trees, the plants, the birds, and the beasts of the wood. Áedán could glean information from the voices of birds and the whistling of the wind and the temperature of the rain as if he had spoken a full conversation with the elements. And his practical knowledge of how to trap and hunt and build things with his hands seemed to Cellach masterful and intuitive.

"This hard life has made you keen. You are certainly more useful out here than I am," said Cellach. Áedán smiled, grateful for the compliment, and he considered for the first time that it might be true; he had skills that even a flaith boy with all his learning did not have.

"Well, while you're resting you can make me a fidchell board and teach me to play," said Áedán. Cellach agreed, happy to have work whilst waiting for his ribs to mend.

By their third day together the boys began to feel an easy companionship growing between them. At first, Áedán had felt cramped by the company of another and was wary of allowing Cellach to view him too closely. But Cellach was amiable and eager to help when he could, and stayed out of Áedán's way when he couldn't. It was fun to show off his skills to Cellach, and pleasing to see his life reflected positively in another's eyes.

Yet the old fear was always present—the fear of revealing what he wished to remain hidden. He often caught Cellach staring at him. Yet his stare did not carry the harshness of judgment; there was something else in it, something soft. Perhaps admiration? Áedán couldn't quite tell. If he caught Cellach's stare, the boy might look away quickly and blush.

"Stop staring at me," Áedán commanded at least once a day, yet it seemed to do no good.

Cellach was desperate to hunt with Áedán. He wished to learn a few skills that would impress his younger sibling back home. But any walk longer than ten paces cause his ribs to ache and his breath to shallow so that he huffed and puffed loudly. It would be futile to hunt with such a handicap, so Áedán left him behind.

What luck Áedán's larder was overfull from his recent raid, for Cellach ate twice as much as he did. Scarcity is the preoccupation of every hermit, and Áedán was all too aware that every morsel Cellach consumed left him with less for the rest of the year. As the days passed and his rations visibly diminished, Áedán wondered how much longer he could stand to serve as host. Hospitality was the rooftree of Érainn society, or so he was told often as a child. It would be disgraceful to withhold food or shelter from one in need, yet even as he gave them he grumbled.

"Is there any more oat cake?" Cellach asked.

"No. I must save the grain for tomorrow's meal. We've already eaten more than a week's worth," said Áedán tersely.

"Oh. I'm sorry." Cellach turned away, trying his best to ignore the gnaw of hunger. It was a very hard thing for a rich boy to grow accustomed to.

Áedán scowled and went outside to clean their bowls. He felt justified in his stinginess, but ashamed of it too.

On their fifth day together, Áedán returned at midday with two plump hares slung over his shoulder. He dropped his prey on the flat rock he used for butchering. Cellach was huddled by the outdoor fire-ring.

"Oy, you reckon this one's fat enough to make a hat for your thick head to fit in?" Áedán laughed, imagining Cellach walking into his father's luxurious hall wearing a dingy brown hare pelt perched atop his golden head.

But Cellach did not laugh. He was shivering and rocking himself back and forth. His face was pale; his eyes were clouded with pain.

"What's the matter with you, Cellach? Did you hurt yourself?"

The blonde boy spoke so quietly that Áedán had to lean in with his ear. "I think... I... have a... fever."

It was a warm day of early summer and Áedán had taken off his coat. He slung it now over Cellach's shoulders, then wrapped him in his old moth-eaten cloak. He put his hand to Cellach's forehead. It was hot to the touch.

"You're right. You're hot as a cooking stone. What do you think it's from? I feel fine, so it must not be the food. I get a little fever sometimes if the meat's gone bad. Do you have the flux? Could be the water. More birds have been landing in the loch the last couple weeks now that the weather is warmer. I've been trying to scare them off."

Cellach shook his head. "No... it's... this." He struggled to throw off the cloak and coat, then pull up his undershirt. Near the place where his ribs were bruised was a partially-healed scratch. It was red, swollen, and beginning to pus. With a twinge of sympathetic nausea Áedán gasped and looked away. Then he looked again.

"Blast of Balor's evil eye! Cellach—the wound is poisoned! Why didn't you tell me this sooner? Have you been cleaning it? Applying the herbs as I showed you?"

Cellach looked up at Áedán miserably. "I haven't... been... not every-day... I thought... it was... healing... just itched... a bit... then last night... it was hurting... more... and then... this fever... this morning."

Áedán growled at the boy's stupidity. "This is no joke, Cellach! I told you to apply the poultice everyday! But now it's poisoned. When you're out here away from civilization you must be especially careful about keeping the sicknesses away. There is no líaig here on the mountain to heal us, so we must take every precaution."

Áedán glared at Cellach, then paused. Cellach's face was drawn and pale; he was frightened and trying not to show it. Áedán was suddenly sorry for his harsh words. "I'll make a plaster. Some wild onions and plantain mixed with barley flour and egg white to draw the poison out. That's the way I've seen my grandmother do it. It will keep the heat from digesting the wound."

Áedán did his best with the few cures that he had. Wrapping Cellach in all his furs, he stoked the inner fire hot throughout the night. But by noon the next day, Cellach was still sweating and shivering in peaks and troughs. This sickness was clearly beyond Áedán's skill to cure.

Áedán was loath to venture into any village for help, but now another boy's life was in his hands. And it was, in part, his fault that Cellach was wounded. *It wouldn't be right to let him die,* he thought. *Oh, Ériu, why do you test me so?*

Áedán packed a basket with provisions, wrapped Cellach's arm around his neck, and helped him hobble down the mountainside.

West was closed to them, for that was the way he had been raiding. The villages in that direction would be on guard and unfriendly to strangers. Instead they walked east past Cathair Crobh Dearg and then south, through a narrow wooded valley to the other side of the mountain. They came to a road along a winding river and followed it east until it was crossed by a wooden bridge.

But the bridge was not empty, for as the boys approached, an old man with a small flock of sheep came across it on the other side. The man appeared benign enough and plenty occupied with his flock, so Áedán stepped forward and risked asking a question.

"Good day to you, kinsman," Áedán panted. He leaned Cellach against the side of the bridge so as to catch his breath. Much of Cellach's weight he had taken on his shoulder for the last few hours. "My cousin is hurt— fell down some rocks while we were playing on the mountain—and now we're lost. We need a líaig urgently, but we're all turned around. Which way is the líaig?"

The old man raised his brows in sympathy. "Ach, how terrible! Well, you came the right way. The líaig Uasal is not too far from here. Just beyond those hills. Take this road on south and you'll come to the village." Áedán thanked him earnestly and took Cellach under the arm again. The old man passed them with a nod, prodding his flock forward with his walking stick. With a second thought he glanced back—he had forgotten to ask the boys' names and their clans, but now they were out of earshot. He flapped his hand with a sigh and moved on his way.

Near dusk the sky gathered in dark clouds which let fall a warm, heavy rain. By the time they reached the village the boys were soaked through. Though less than pleased to be so wet, Áedán was grateful that the rain and gathering dusk provided some concealment. Most of the villagers had scrambled indoors to seek shelter from the weather, so the boys were able to pass through the settlement without attracting the suspicion of passers by. Strangers were a rare enough thing in a small village such as this—they would certainly have been stopped and asked questions of.

It was easy to tell which house was the líaig's for it was the largest in the village, at least as large as the aire Talorc's, with an outer wall made of stones cleared from surrounding fields. Inside the wall there were no animal pens, but many beds of flowers and shrubs and medicinal herbs, planted in spirals and rings cut through by little stone walkways. At the far end of the compound there was a low stone building, its entrance hidden from view by a waddle screen. Beside it was a dipping pool, and by this Áedán deduced it must be a tigh 'n alluis, a sweathouse for medicinal use.

The boys leaned under the eave of the thatched roof and stood timidly at the door. It was painted with spirals of red and blue, and in the center hung a sprig of fresh yarrow. Áedán breathed deep, gathered courage, and wrapped loudly upon the door. It creaked open and a young face appeared, no older than Áedán's own.

"Em... uh..." Áedán cleared his throat awkwardly. "Bríg's blessings upon this house and all in it. We wish to see the líaig. My cousin is ill and in desperate need of help."

The young face looked the two of them up and down, blinked, then disappeared without a word. In a moment another face appeared, this one older and scored with lines by of many years of caring. As the woman gazed down at the two boys, sodden, shivering, and exhausted, her eyes shown with concern.

"Well! Would you look at this now—soaked through like two pups in a puddle! Come in! Come in and warm yourselves." She showed them to stools by the hearth. The apprentice took the boys' sodden cloaks. "I am the líaig, Uasal Ingen Barddán. What can I do for you?"

Áedán spoke for the both of them. "My cousin fell down some rocks a few days ago and hurt his ribs. It was healing alright, but now he has a fever and the wound is inflamed. I tried my best to cure it but I'm afraid it's too severe. Can you help us?"

"Ah, I'm sorry to hear of your troubles, lads. What are your names?" Uasal asked gently.

"Em... my name is... Áedán. And this is..." he looked over at Cellach, not knowing if he would want his name given away.

"My name is Cellach," said the blonde boy through shivering blue lips.

"Well, Áedán... Cellach... I have several patients to tend to before you," she gestured towards five others waiting to be seen, sitting around the hearth and against the wall on cushions and fleeces. "Your case sounds severe, so I will take you out of order, after this young woman and her child." Uasal called to an apprentice, one of the several hustling about the house tending to patients in wait. He was a young man a few years older than Áedán, dressed in a woad-blue mantle. "Flannán, give these boys dry blankets and hot tea. I will be with you two shortly."

Uasal gestured at a fretful young mother clutching a limp toddler to her breast. The mother and her husband followed the líaig into on of several small cubicles partitioned by wicker walls.

The boys were given tea and blankets and warmed themselves by the fire. Áedán let Cellach lean against him, for the feverish boy was too weary even to sit up on his own.

Finally, the líaig and her patients emerged from the cubicle. The young mother smiled now with relief, leading her toddler out by the hand. The child was bouncy and bright-eyed, chirping happily as her father scooped her up in his arms. The young woman handed an apprentice a basket of eggs and three loaves of rye bread, then thanked the líaig and made to depart.

Áedán's heart seized. He had forgotten that they would be expected to pay for the líaig's services. But what did they have to pay with? Would they be refused if they couldn't?

"I'm ready for you now, Áedán... Cellach." Uasal opened her hands to them. Áedán helped Cellach follow her into the cubicle and Uasal shut the door behind them. Cellach laid on a bed layered with heather and fleece. The boys answered the líaig's questions as vaguely as they could without raising her suspicions. She listened to Cellach's breath sounds with her ear against his chest, felt the pulses on his wrists, and inspected his gums and inner eyelids. The wound she examined last, with gentle hands and a hiss of sympathy.

"Yes, the wound has become imposthumed. I suspect that it was caused by the premature use of comfrey. You see Áedán, wounds must heal from the inside out. When comfrey is applied to a wound that isn't clean, it can cause the skin to close too quickly, locking the pus inside."

"Oh, no! Really? Then this is my fault, too!" cried Áedán. Guilt sat heavy like a stone in his throat.

Uasal patted his hand sympathetically. "Don't blame yourself, dear. You didn't know. Comfrey was the right choice for healing the bruised rib, but not for the scrape overtop it. I must open the imposthume and clean it before stitching it closed again. Cellach, you must stay here under my care until the fever is gone. Flannán!" The apprentice stuck his head through the door. "Please prepare the tigh 'n alluis for Cellach here. He must be warmed in the sweathouse this evening. It will open the pores so that the poison can be expelled and the fever can be released." Flannán nodded briskly and closed the door. "You could use a sweat too, Áedán. The both of you look chilled to the bone."

"Oh! Em... no. No thank you, líaig," Áedán replied. "I think the hearth is good enough for me." There was no way that he could be convinced to strip down naked in the presence of anyone, especially not Cellach.

"Suit yourself," Uasal said with a shrug. "I'll be performing the surgery now. Go on out, Áedán. Cellach will have to be brave without you. My apprentices will give you supper and a place to sleep for the night in my hall."

"Thank you, líaig. You are most kind," said Áedán. "But I must confess... we have nothing to pay you with."

"Do you own nothing at all of value? Won't your families pay on your behalf?"

"I, em... I have some skins at home. And I can hunt for you or make you..."

Cellach interrupted. "No, Áedán," he whispered painfully. "It is my debt... and I... will pay it." He pulled off his two gold ear cuffs and laid them in the líaig's hand. "This is not the full of what I will pay, but it is a surety that my father will pay whatever is due. My name is Cellach mac Ségán. My father is Ségán mac Fáclán and my mother is Dúinsech Ingen Mórda, of the Fellubair."

Upon hearing this the líaig's eyes widened a little. Cellach glanced nervously at Áedán, but the wild boy showed no signs of recognizing these names. Cellach breathed a sigh of relief.

Uasal nodded solemnly. "I see. I know of your mother and father, thus I will take your word as surety. But what are you doing here, so far from your home and your tribe? And are you Fellubair too, Áedán? Are you really even cousins? Oh, never mind that now. You can explain it to me later." And with that she shuffled Áedán out and closed the door.

Áedán was glad not to have to watch the operation. He would rather not see his friend's face in any more pain. *My friend. I have a friend,* he mused. *May the gods protect the only one I have.*

In the early morning Áedán awoke from a fitful night's sleep inside the enormous roundhouse. He was unused to the scratching and snoring of other sleepers in the night. A drizzle came down as he stepped outside. He was eager to be away from people for a while. When he came back inside, the líaig called to him.

"Good morning, Áedán. I hope you slept well. Cellach is doing much better today. His fever has broken and he's sleeping now. But I wonder if I might have a word with you... privately?" She gestured toward an empty cubicle. Áedán hesitated, then followed her inside.

"I'm sorry if this is intrusive, but I would like to ask you a question. You are under no obligation to answer it." Uasal's face was serene and open. It was the kind of face that had heard many secrets and kept them safe. "You came here to seek healing for your friend. But as a healer, I am trained to notice hurts of all kinds, even those that we wish to keep hidden. I have observed in you such a hurt, one that you've concealed for a long time. Cellach may not see it—most would not—but I do. So I will ask: what happened here?" She pointed to Áedán's left forearm directly over the scar hidden under his sleeve.

Startled, Áedán reflexively hid his arm behind his back. "It's nothing. A scar from an accident. I was... I burned myself in a fire when I was a child."

Uasal tilted her head in disappointment. "Áedán, I said you didn't have to answer me. But please, don't lie to me. Lying is a very lowly thing to do."

But what if it's to protect my life? he thought in silent frustration. Áedán stared into Uasal's face, striving to discover her intentions. All he saw there was compassion and a sincere desire to heal the afflicted. It was both strange and comforting, for her gaze was so unlike that of any adult he'd met before. She was not judging him; she was only trying to understand.

Áedán tensed, girding himself to speak honestly. "I was burned... by my parents. They thought I was a—" He quit before saying anymore. It could not be spoken out loud. Not even to this kindly physician.

She gasped. "Áedán, that's horrible! Did you seek help? Abuse of children is severely punished under the law. You would be protected."

Áedán shook his head, trying desperately to hold back the tears that threatened to spill. "No one would help me. There was no one."

"Well," said Uasal resolutely, "I will help you."

"No! Please, no! I never want to see those people again! I can never go back there! Please don't tell anyone. Not even Cellach. Please!"

"Be still. Be still. I will do nothing without your consent. But know that if you ever change your mind I have the full training of a fili and can present suits on behalf of my patients, as brithem. I have knowledge of the law, especially concerning compensation for woundings and sick-maintenance. But be assured, I will take no action without your agreement. And I will keep all that you've told me in confidence." She patted his hand to comfort him. "May I see your arm?"

Assuaged by this promise, Áedán slowly brought forward his arm. Uasal pulled up his sleeve and looked at the scar closely, then placed her hand over it. She drew her hand away with a sudden look of pain and rolled the sleeve down again. Uasal looked into Áedán's face for a long moment until he fidgeted and looked away.

At last she spoke: "With the sight of my inner eye, I can see that this mark has cleaved you in two. Do you feel as if you're in two pieces, Áedán? Or maybe, that you're hiding or suppressing half of yourself?"

Áedán quivered, for Uasal had come very close to the heart of his most carefully guarded secret—a secret even he did not fully comprehend. In his confusion he remained silent. Uasal observed him with soft eyes. It was clear to her that the boy was struggling to survive with a wound that had nearly killed him.

"I can see that I've touched the surface of something deep. It's a matter of the spirit, I think, and while I can do some things to help it, it may be best for you to seek out my master for this healing. My master, Máel Conall, is the wisest of all filid in Mumu and a powerful druí; maybe the most powerful druí in Ériu as a whole. He has a school below the Great Mountain."

"The Great Mountain?" asked Áedán.

"Yes. To the west of here, past Loch Léin, is a jagged spine of mountains, the crowns of which are bald and sometimes capped with snow in winter. The greatest of these is called Géarán Tuathail, for it is pointed like a fang. The mountain spine curves like a sickle, and behind it, beneath its steep southern slope, there is a valley, and in that valley there is a school. It is a school that teaches the draíochta druadh—the druidic arts." Uasal paused a moment, closed her eyes, then opened them again. "Seek also his foster-daughter, the ollamh fili Lí Lon. She teaches there as well. Lí Lon may have some particular knowledge of the state you find yourself in."

Áedán shook his head. "I thank you for your concern, but I don't need anyone's help. I can take care of myself."

"I'm not questioning that, Áedán. But I believe you have a hurt that needs healing. And if it is healed, you will live a fuller life—happier and free from the burdens of the past. And I think..." Uasal paused. "I think there is some meaning in this mark, too. Not just a sign of past pain, but also having some kind of... potency to it. It may be auspicious. It should not be ignored."

"What does auspicious mean?" Áedán asked. Despite himself, his curiosity was piqued.

"It means lucky, sacred... possibly even touched by the Otherworld. To ignore auspicious signs can bring bad luck." Uasal looked him in the eye.

"You think about it, Áedán. Consider that there may be more to life than simply surviving."

Áedán stepped outside and wandered through the líaig's gardens. He sat on a stone beside a cluster of lady's mantle, its pleated leaves pearled with drops of morning dew. Rolling up his sleeve, he looked at the scar. *Should I seek healing? Should I ask this Máel Conall if the mark means anything other than suffering?* Áedán was curious, but he was also reluctant to leave his home. It was the only place in the world he felt safe. He had built that handsome shelter with his own two hands, through many seasons of toil and tender hope. Should he leave that safety, that certainty, to pursue an unknown person in an unknown place?

But what would it mean if this pain could be healed? Is a druí powerful enough to grant my greatest wish, my greatest need: to become a man? Or would healing mean something else entirely?

Later in the day, Cellach awoke and Áedán went to see him. He was sitting up in his bed and slurping bone broth thickened with oatmeal. The pink had come back into his cheeks. He smiled as Áedán approached.

"I owe you my life for a second time, Áedán. If you had not brought me to the líaig, I might have perished."

"No, no, Cellach. It was my fault that the wound became poisoned! You don't—"

Cellach interrupted him. "Áedán, it was not your fault. It was the fault of the men who attacked me. The truth is I would have died if not for your aid. Be content with that."

Áedán smiled half-heartedly, unsure that he could accept this gesture, for his friend did not know the whole truth. Nevertheless, he was glad that Cellach was well again. "How are you feeling? How long will you be here?"

"I still feel weak, but much better. The líaig said I should be able to get up tomorrow, but I won't be able to travel for the next two days at least."

He sighed. "She's convinced me to go back home. I think I will negotiate with my parents. It was childish of me to just run off like that without addressing the problem. One of Uasal's apprentices will escort me back to Fellubair territory. I won't cross the boundary alone this time." Cellach held Áedán's eyes. "Áedán, come with me. Come back to my túath. There you will be welcomed as my brother. My mother and father will surely take you in as their foster-son. You'll never have to worry about hunger or poverty ever again."

Áedán was stunned. No one had ever shown him such kindness. "Oh, Cellach! You are too generous! I appreciate your offer... I do very much... but you don't have to do that for me."

"I don't *have to* do it for you, Áedán, but I *want to*. You've done so much for me. Let me repay you. Live with me as my brother! What fun we will have together! We will play and fight and hunt together. You can meet my father and mother, my sister and my cousins... the whole clan. Please... will you come?" Cellach pleaded, almost whimpering with excitement.

Áedán was tempted, sorely tempted, and paused to consider what it would mean. It was hard to refuse the glow of anticipation in Cellach's face, but he had already made up his mind.

"I wish I could, Cellach. But I've already decided to seek out Máel Conall, a powerful druí who lives in the western mountains. Uasal told me he may be able to help me with... with an old wound I have. One that she couldn't heal herself. It's something I think I must do, Cellach."

Cellach's face fell into shadow. Yet he forced a sad smile upon his lips and spoke with gentleness. "I see. I suppose you must seek healing for whatever ails you. But make me a promise, Áedán: after you are healed, come to seek me out. You'll always be welcome in my house. Always."

"I promise, Cellach." The two boys embraced, and in that moment a fervid filament of friendship entwined their two hearts.

Cellach kissed his friend on the cheek in farewell. Áedán turned and stepped through the door into the early summer sunlight, his red hair haloed like flames of the sun. Cellach wiped away hidden tears and prayed to the gods that he would see his friend again.

CHAPTER TEN

The Filid of Géarán Tuathail

Áedán returned to his camp and sat by the little loch, thinking. He looked up at the two pinnacles of his mother mountain. *Will I come back here once I am healed?* However hard he wanted to believe it, he knew in his heart that if he left he would not be back here again. This caused him pain, for he loved his hermitage very much. And yet, he felt the tug of fate pull him away from this place. There was something in the world beyond that wished to receive him.

That night Áedán slept in his little bark-clad house for the last time, and in the morning he gathered his gear to make his way west with the directions given by the líaig. Before leaving he unlatched the lids of all his storage vessels to make it easier for his neighbors to raid his stores should he fail to eventually return. Áedán filled his pack basket with only the essentials needed for journeying the several days to Géarán Tuathail. by his estimate, would take at least five days from his hermitage to and back.

At last, kneeling at the cleft of the mountain's cleavage, Áedán placed on the ground a dish of honey, a handful of hazelnuts, and a bouquet of bittersweet and columbine flowers.

"Thank you, Mother Mountain. I will shall you." He bent and touched his forehead to the soil thrice, then stood and turned to trundle down-slope with heavy footfalls. He turned to gaze at his hermitage one more time, perhaps his last, then continued on his way. It was a difficult part-ing.

The squirrels gathered in the trees above and watched him depart. As the boy passed below Dluí's tree, the squirrel uttered a long, doleful wheeze, saddened to part from such a generous neighbor as he. Áedán gave his friend a wave and a forlorn smile.

Áedán traveled all in stealth. He would have to be careful to avoid the farmers that now moved their cattle from the winter plains to the higher pastures for summer's grazing on sweet new grass. Summer was a time of greater movement, the season when humanity ranged wide across the land. Hope for abundance bloomed in every heart, and the people sang in the fields vivacious verses.

For two days Áedán journeyed west through the wooded mountains, past pastured valleys and highland lochs. On the afternoon of the second day, he reached the edge of the spine of mountains that the líaig had de-scribed to him, looming up so high that the tops of them were concealed by clouds. There, at a crossroads, was a large roundhouse. From its loca-tion and size, Áedán inferred it to be a hostel. And yet it was unusually quiet for a hostel. The only person around was a black-bearded man sit-ting on a bench against the wall, head tipped back against the daub. He was staring lazily up into the clouds that drifted over the mountains. Wisps of mist fell through the air and wafted between the cliffs robed in pine.

Though reluctant to admit it, Áedán needed directions. He did not know exactly where the school was from here and would prefer not to wander in circles all over the mountaintop in search of it.

Cautiously, Áedán stepped close to the lounging man and stood at his knee, waiting to be noticed. But the man was oblivious, too absorbed by the sight of the shifting mists high above. Áedán followed his gaze—nothing seemed very interesting to him. He looked closer at the man. *Maybe he's sleeping with his eyes open?* Finally, Áedán cleared his throat to get his attention.

The black-bearded man stirred as if waking, blinked three times, then turned to look dreamily at the boy with the doeskin jacket and tangled hair. "Oh, I didn't see you there, lad," he said, a little misty-eyed. "The clouds are so intriguing today. It's as if they tell tales of their travels across the world... and of the world's travelers." He lifted one eyebrow and looked at Áedán quizzically.

"Can you tell me where I might find the ollamh fili Máel Conall?"

The bearded man nodded slowly as if immersed in water. "Of course. He governs the school in the steepest glen below Géarán Tuathail. You'll follow the river west until it forks, then take the branch north until you find the school. But you won't get there before nightfall, and it's a full moon tonight. No one ought to be out in those hills on a full moon."

"Why not?"

"Well, because the siabra are most vicious on these nights. The moonlight gives them vigor and blood lust."

"The siabra?"

The man tilted his head. "You're not from around here, I see, for anyone with half his wits would not be traveling at such a time. The siabra are the spirits who haunt these hills. They protect the forest and don't like wanderers. Some say the filid on the mountain recruit the siabra to guard their school from intruders." The man gestured at his empty hostel. "You see, that's why it's so quiet here today. Few travel this way when the moon is full. It would be wise for you to stay the night with me, lad. You should not be out in it alone."

Áedán shook his head. "Thank you for your advice, sir. But I must be on my way. I have my own protections."

The man looked at him sideways and shrugged. "It's your advice to take or leave. But don't say I didn't offer it."

Áedán sidled off in the direction of the river. Looking back over his shoulder, he spied the man in the position he had first found him in: staring up at the clouds upon the mountain. *What an odd fellow. I wonder if the siabra are real, or if he was just telling stories to get me to pay for a night in his hostel? Or maybe the moon has struck him with a bit of the lunacy.* He chuckled to himself and stepped lively.

Áedán passed another loch as the mountains' shadows fell across his path. It was time to make shelter for the night. In the brightness of day Áedán had been bold and unafraid, but now that dark was approaching, the hosteler's superstitious warnings rang in his ears.

As he moved away from the river bank towards the shelter of the trees, Áedán's eye was caught by one tree in particular. He went towards it. It was a hawthorn in full flower, its blushing white petals pale as bone against the glistening black thorns of its branches. Áedán regarded the tree reverently. It was both beautiful and dangerous, and though all hawthorns command respect, this tree in particular seemed a little more hallowed than any other. There was a collection of small stones and little wooden carvings, old rusted tools, leather thongs, pendants, rings, and other trinkets laid at the base of its trunk. Its branches were tied with strips of colored cloth, each of which held a wish or a prayer. This was a bile: a sacred tree.

The boy paused and knelt by the bile's roots. He laid a piece of smoked meat and a handful of oats beside the other offerings, then pressed his hands against the earth in prayer. Underneath those branches he felt warm and safe and sheltered, intoxicated by the sweet fragrance of the five-petaled blossoms.

"O blessed tree of beauteous thorn," he whispered, "please protect me on my journey through these hills. Please grant me safe passage to where I wish to go." He bent and touched his forehead to the mossy soil between the tree's roots. The tree shivered in the evening breeze. On the crown of the boy's head landed a dainty white flower dropped from the branch above him without his knowing it. Áedán stood, gave his thanks, and stepped into the gloom of the forest.

Against a tumble of boulders he made a rough lean-to out of deadwood and bracken, and there settled down for the night. He did not light a fire, for the moon was bright enough to see quite well by. As he was eating his supper of smoked meat and stale oatcakes, Áedán suddenly paused. The hairs stood up on the back of his neck, for he sensed eyes upon him. Looking around, he saw no one. There was no sound in the wood but the whistling wind, for the birds had bedded down for the night and the crickets stayed hidden in the grass at the riverbank. Yet still, he sensed presences near... unfriendly presences.

I'm just working myself up into a fright. It's nothing but stories. When finished eating, he crawled under his lean-to and closed his eyes.

Clear moonlight filtered through the shade of the trees, silhouetting every branch with silver. Áedán slept hardly a wink that night, for he startled at every twig-snap and every squeal of vermin made victim by unseen teeth and talons. Later, as the moon reached its full height, he thought he heard footsteps, then angry whispers and heavy breathing. What was dream and what was worry? It was hard to tell what really moved out there in the moonlight. Áedán curled under his blanket and covered himself with leaves, clutching his knife against his chest. He hoped his shelter would remain unseen, or otherwise, that his imagination might quiet long enough for him to get a little sleep.

Áedán awoke to the cheery music of robin and wren. Stiffly, he crawled out from his shelter and stretched. Though terrible, he had survived the night intact. He searched the ground for signs. There were many marks of movement in the night: the footprints of several feet, saplings with newly broken branches, several tufts of freshly-fallen fur. A chill ran up his spine. These were not the tracks of men, he was sure. What creatures had been prowling here, and had they been looking to catch this young, lonesome traveler? Áedán forced these thoughts from his mind and cast his eyes down the path to the riverbank, determined to reach the school before the next nightfall.

By noon the sun had peeked through the clouds and a warm wind waved the dew-dropped ferns. Áedán followed the footpath along the north fork of the river where the rocky slopes became ever steeper on either side. Above him the bare fang of the Great Mountain loomed ever closer. For speed, Áedán had skipped breakfast and now hunger slowed his steps. He stopped at a mountain stream to drink and break his fast, appraising the austere beauty all around. The night's terror had finally drifted away and left him exhausted.

Oh, how lovely it would be to nap here in the sunlight. He closed his eyes and rubbed his sore neck. *Briefly. Shortly.* He laid his head upon the mossy ground and the murmuring stream soon sung him to sleep.

Áedán woke with a start. He gazed bleary-eyed at the place of the sun. Several hours had passed; he cursed at himself for having slept so long. Splashing his face with frigid spring water, he took a drink then sat up.

Áedán yelped and tumbled backwards. For sitting cross-legged on the other side of the stream was a mustached young man in a rust-red mantle, staring straight back at him. Áedán leapt to his feet and unsheathed his knife.

"Who are you?" he demanded of the stranger.

"Ah! The May bush shows its thorns!" the young man taunted. "Pierce me not with your prickers little one. I'm not here to cut you down."

"Then why did you sneak up on me?"

"Oh, I was not sneaking. Not sneaking in the slightest. Being that you were hard asleep like a badger in his burrow, it would have been entirely unnecessary." The young man spoke with an odd accent, round and buzzing. He smirked in good humor, his eyes glistening with charm. His skin was slightly browned, as if tanned from a season's work in the field, though it was only May. His shining black hair was tied up in the plaits of a fili. "Let me introduce myself," said he, standing up gracefully. "My name is Cadrolón. Today it is my duty to patrol the way here. You are approaching the grounds of a secret place that must be guarded. So then: what is your name and your purpose in coming here, traveler?"

"I am Áedán and I've come to seek the advice of the ollamh fili Máel Conall who is the master of a school here in these mountains. I was told to seek him out."

Cadrolón raised his brows in surprise. "I see. But where is your escort?"

"I don't—I don't have one. I came alone."

"You came alone? With the moon as full?" said Cadrolón, his mouth agape. "You're a lucky boy, you are! I'm surprised the siabra didn't catch you. I've never known them to miss their quarry. Oh well, I'm sure they'll have better luck next time. Good on you, not being dead yet!" He laughed heartily at his own joke.

"I don't understand how people are supposed to get to the school of the filid if these mountains are crawling with malicious spirits!" Áedán growled in frustration.

"Oh, well most people employ a fili to escort them this way, as is tradition. We have an agreement with the siabra to guard our school from plunderers and rival sorcerers and..." Cadrolón took a long look at the roughness of Áedán's appearance, "...vagabonds."

"I'm not a..." Áedán began, but he cut himself off, realizing that he did indeed fit the image of a vagabond quite well. "Are you part of the school then? Can you take me to see Máel Conall?" He sheathed his knife and smoothed his hair, hoping to appear somewhat less wild.

Cadrolón considered it for a moment, then smiled brightly. "Well, why not? And if you're not to my master's liking, he'll probably just turn you into a frog and plop you back down here by this stream. But don't worry, there's no shortage of midges in the summertime, so you'd be quite content." Cadrolón smirked at him over his shoulder. Áedán wasn't quite sure if he was joking.

Áedán followed Cadrolón up the river until it narrowed to become a rocky brook which drew its source from a mountain loch on the slopes looming high above. Cadrolón had several years on Áedán and longer legs, so the younger boy struggled to keep up with his great strides. Áedán was panting with exertion when at last they broke through the shade of the forest into a clearing. There before them was a little settlement strung along a narrow highland glen. There were many roundhouses of wattle and daub and stone, five of them large and the others small. The glen hummed with the activity of dozens of children directed by young adults draped in mantles of yellow, green, blue, or red. Another roundhouse was quite a lot bigger than the others; it seemed to be some kind of gathering hall or ceremonial center. Stone-walled pens kept fowl and swine, partially roofed to give shelter from the mountain eagles. Small gardens were planted with edible and medicinal herbs, but there was not room nor soil enough in this narrow, rocky valley for fields of grain.

Áedán felt a flutter of excitement as he shuffled through the village behind Cadrolón. They came to one of the five large roundhouses. Cadrolón went inside to speak to a middle-aged woman in a red and brown checkered dress, one of several servants keeping the ollamh's house.

"The ollamh is out in the forest with the macfhuirmid and the doss apprentices," said the serving woman. "They will be back in not too long."

"Very well," said Cadrolón. "Boy, come with me to the big house where you can set down your belongings and your weapons." Cadrolón eyed the boy's bow warily. "No weapons are to be carried within these grounds." As instructed, Áedán left his gear inside the big house and followed Cadrolón outside again.

"You may wander about until Máel Conall comes back. I must return to my post now, for it's my day to serve as drisiuc. Nice to meet you, Áedán, little flame." With that Cadrolón took his leave and disappeared into the forest, whistling merrily.

Finding a stone at the edge of the clearing, Áedán perched there and observed it all in fascination. Near his rock were several fruit trees in bloom, and beneath them three beehives all abuzz, their inhabitants trafficking the air about his head. Groups of students passed him and stared, yet they stared with the soft curiosity of the learned, not the harsh and vulgar judgments of the ignorant as he was used to. As he met their eyes a thought crossed his mind: *Those who know very little are more certain of right and wrong than those who know very much.* The paradoxical truth of this seemed to him profound. The rhythm and tone of this place expressed peace and civility, and though Áedán was a stranger here he did not feel endangered. *If I were ever to live amongst people again, it would be people such as these.*

Áedán sat and pondered, worried and dozed for several hours under those flowery boughs, until at last a group of a dozen youths emerging from the upstream woodland caught his attention. They were led by a balding middle-age man and a tall, brown-haired woman. The youths clustered together, talking excitedly, and hurried to the big house where they would eat their evening meal. The two adults walked off in different directions, and the man toward the roundhouse that Cadrolón had come to earlier. As the man came to the door, he paused and looked. Áedán watched in astonishment as an enormous grey bird swooped down from the trees to land on the ground next to him. Its head held as high as the man's waist. Calmly the man opened the door of the roundhouse and the two of them entered, side by side, as if nothing were as natural.

That, surely, must be the ollamh fili, for who else would have a wild crane as a familiar? He brushed himself off, pressed down his disheveled curls, and walked briskly to the man's door. He knocked, when it was opened bent his head and spoke a blessing with trembling sincerity:

> Wisdom of wren be thine,
> Wisdom of raven be thine,
> Wisdom of valiant eagle.
>
> Voice of swan be thine,
> Voice of honey be thine,
> Voice of the gallant gale.
>
> Bounty of sea be thine,
> Bounty of land be thine,
> Bounty of the Dagda's cauldron.

The man approached and placed his hand gently on the boy's shoulder. "To you, peace and wealth."

"To you, luck and health," Áedán replied in the formal greeting of their people, and looked up into the man's face.

"You must be the stranger that the bees foretold would come today. Welcome. What can we do for you, lad?"

"Are you the ollamh fili, Máel Conall?" asked Áedán.

The man raised the great tufts of his eyebrows which sprouted from his head like thistle-down. He patted the bald pate of his head. "Am I? Oh, well, yes. It would seem that I am! And unlikely to change... goodness knows I've tried all sorts of things." Máel meant bald, and he certainly was. He smiled and looked down at the boy kindly. "And who are you lad? Why have you come to seek me?"

Áedán looked down at his feet. "My name is Áedán, ollamh. I was sent by the líaig Uasal Ingen Barddán. She said you may be able to help me... to cure me. My affliction is... difficult, one that she couldn't heal herself."

"I am sorry to hear of your trouble, my boy. In that case, come in. Come in." The fili welcomed him into the roundhouse and closed the door. Máel Conall handed his mantle to a serving woman. His clothing was rich and colorful and he wore many trinkets of silver and gold. Though his demeanor was humble, Máel Conall was clearly a man of wealth and high esteem.

The house was large with lavish decor, beautifully carved roof beams, and bright tapestries upon the walls. A dozen or more cubicles divided the space along the wall. There was a stool and a wooden desk strewn with what Áedán guessed to be the ollamh's various tools of sorcery: a set of yew rods used for divination, a collection of knuckle bones, round slices of antler, and a polished bronze basin too shallow for washing. Beside these were thin sheets of birch bark, feather quills, and a small jar of black ink. Around the desk were piled many hazel baskets and sealed clay pots, the contents of which Áedán was curious to discover. An incredible variety of dried herbs hung in bundles from the ceiling. And yet the most intriguing sight of all was that of the enormous grey and black crane who perched regally upon a low roof beam. The great bird beamed down at those below with shocking red eyes.

Máel Conall sat on a bench cushioned with pelts and gestured for Áedán to sit next to him. An attendant—this one not a servant but a yellow-mantled apprentice—handed each of them a warm mug of meadowsweet tea sweetened with honey.

The ollamh sipped it and cleared his throat. "Tell me, Áedán. What ails you? Uasal is a very skilled líaig. Whatever it is, it must be grave if she could not help you." He inclined his head sympathetically.

Áedán glanced nervously at the others in the house and at the bird in the rafters. "Em... might I... could we, maybe, talk somewhere privately, ollamh?"

Máel Conall nodded, and at his gentle command the others in the house left immediately. All, that is, except for the crane in the rafters. The ollamh was silent, waiting for the boy to speak.

There was a true compassion in this man's gaze, as sincere as Uasal's was before. Áedán had not been ready then to tell his truth to the líaig. But on his journey over the last several days, the question had been churning in his mind: was he ready to be honest? Had he found, finally, a person who might be able to hear his secret without wishing him harm? And further, was there anything that this man could do about it?

Well, I've come this far and have risked my life to meet this moment. At least I must try, he resolved, stoking the courage to speak. Though he had rehearsed what he would say to this man many times in his head, to say it out loud was a terrifying prospect. Áedán breathed deep and spoke hardly louder than a whisper.

"Ever since I was little—as long as I can remember—I've had this affliction. My parents, my mother in particular, disapproved of it and thought I was a Changeling boy come to replace her... child." Áedán swallowed, his mouth bone dry. He continued. "So she put me through ordeals... tied me to a tree in a gale... burned me with hot iron to chase away the Changeling. I don't know what I am, Changeling or not, but the ordeals didn't take away my affliction. So to survive I learned to hide my it and pretended to be her stolen child returned. And then something happened... two Octobers ago... when I was caught in the farce and unable to conceal myself any longer. So I fled for my life and have lived in the mountains ever since.

"Then I came, by chance, to meet the líaig Uasal, your disciple she said, and she saw the mark on my arm left by the hot iron. She told me then that I could be healed of the wound it had left in my spirit—that I had been split in two and could be made whole again. She said you could help me. So... this is why I came to you. To seek healing."

Máel Conall's face was heavy with emotion, as if Áedán's pain was his own. "I am so sorry, lad. No one should ever be faced with such cruelty, especially from the hands of his own parents. And why did your parents believe that you were a Changeling?"

The boy wrung his hands. "Because I am... because I've always felt that..." He paused and started over. "In my heart I believe—" but he stopped and searched the fili's face one last time for any sign of violence that might be hidden underneath that seeming of sympathy.

"Please, Áedán," Máel Conall said. "Don't be afraid. Whatever it is, you are safe here. You will not be harmed. You have my word. And the word of a fili is as solid as the roots of the mountains themselves."

Then, with a shuddering breath, Áedán's words and his tears tumbled out of him like a river bursting through a dam. "Since I was a child I've always believed myself to be a boy. I don't know why, but the world only makes sense when I am living as if I were a boy. I dream as a boy. I hunt as a boy. I play and fight as a boy. And yet... and yet my family insisted that I was a girl and should grow up to be a woman. But I can't. I just can't! I can't milk and weave and marry and have children like a woman. This body is... it's like I'm living in someone else's body by mistake. I don't know why, but being a girl just feels wrong to me. I don't mean... it's not wrong in and of itself, it's just wrong for *me*. And when I think about being forced to pretend to be a woman for the rest of my life, I... I can only see my death before me and nothing else. Sometimes I wonder if my mother was right: what if I really am a Faery boy come to replace her daughter? Or what if the gods made a mistake and my soul came to inhabit the wrong body? How would I know? And what do I do if it's true?" He held his face in his hands and spilled forth every tear that had been held back for so many years.

Máel Conall was silent as Áedán sobbed long and hard. When at last his tears finally began to slow, he looked up at Máel Conall nervous and ashamed. The fili's face was still creased in lines of concern. He stared into Áedán's eyes with a penetrating gaze. So arresting was his stare that the boy found it impossible to look away. Áedán felt as if his mind and spirit were being searched, observed, analyzed, and yet in this he felt a calm. Finally someone was truly looking at him. All of him. Áedán's whimpering was calmed.

Then the fili's eyes became unfocused, and though he stared directly into the boy's face he seemed to be looking at something else—something far, far away. His lips moved subtly as if whispering, but no sound was spoken. Finally, the man blinked rapidly and dropped his gaze.

"May I see the mark?"

Áedán pulled up his sleeve and let the fili take his wrist. He studied the scar closely, and with a grunt of acknowledgement, gave the boy back his hand.

"There is one thing for certain, Áedán: you are not a Changeling. Though such a thing does occur, it is more rare than the common folk have come to believe. I asked my acquaintances in the Otherworld if they were missing a boy of their kind fostered by human parents, and they said there were none unaccounted for. They said you are not one of them."

"But when did you ask them?" Áedán interrupted. "Just now?"

"Yes, just now. If I tried to explain it to you, you would not understand. Perhaps you will in time." Máel Conall spoke gently. "Áedán, ignorant folk sometimes use the accusation of a Changeling to hide their inability to treat a childhood illness or care properly for the needs of a special child such as yourself. This is what I believe happened to you. Your mother didn't understand what you were experiencing. So instead of learning how to care for your needs, she acted with cruelty, attempting to banish dissimilarity instead of accommodating it. Such is often the way amongst lowly people. I am sorry that you have experienced such brutality."

"But it wasn't just people of low status who harmed me. It was an aire also—the aire whose land my family lived on. He made my parents punish me for being the way I am... and when I tried to defend myself from him, he threatened my family with a fine that could take away their freedom."

"What caused you to need to defend yourself?" Máel Conall asked with concern. Áedán's voice trembled as he told the fili of his confrontation with Talorc and how the lord would have taken away the one thing Áedán cherished most in his world.

Máel Conall frowned and said: "To be clear, you should not have struck an aire. Whatever Talorc's actions, the law would not look well upon a tenant that used violence against the landlord. Had you gone with him willingly, there might not have been so harsh a fine."

"I know. I know I shouldn't have hit him, but he would have hurt me! He would have beat me, or maybe... or maybe he..." The memory of the aire's grasping eyes made him flinch. Áedán could not bring himself to speak his greatest fear.

Máel Conall guessed what was in the boy's mind. "I see. Lowness comes not just from a lack of nobility but also from ignorance and cruelty. If status were judged by one's virtues alone, Talorc would be amongst the poorest of men. Yet be assured, Áedán, that no one is above the law, not even the highest chieftain or fili. If he had committed a crime against you, he would have been fined and his status reduced. The flaith may lose all their wealth and even their lands if they commit a serious enough crime. The power of the law protects all who inhabit Ériu, not just the privileged."

"But what if he denied it? It would have been his word against mine. And I was only a fuidir... and a girl. His words would have weighed heavier than my own."

Máel Conall inclined his head sadly. "Maybe so, but the brithem have ways of detecting the truth, even when it is hidden." He paused and brought his eyes back to Áedán's forearm. "This scar... did Uasal say anything else about it?"

"She said that it was au... auspicious. That maybe the Otherworld had touched me. Or something like that. What does that mean?"

Máel Conall stroked his graying beard. "I cannot say for sure. But I agree with Uasal. There is something in it like a tether... some kind of bond is made with the Otherworld by the pain that you feel. But it may have been there earlier, before you were wounded. Again, I can't know for certain. Yet it is there now. There is one way to find out what it is, but it would take a journey..." The fili's voice trailed off and his eyes became unfocused once again. Then he shook himself suddenly and turned back to the boy with clear eyes. "Tell me, Áedán. Do you have an interest in poetry? Any talent for words? Any closeness with the natural world?"

Áedán nodded vigorously. "Oh yes, ollamh. All those things. Ever since I was little I've been making up riddles and poems to pass the time... and to trick my brother. And, well... I feel a more akin to the non-human world than the human one. We... understand each other better."

Then the fili asked a difficult question: "And do you suffer, living as a boy in the body of a girl?"

Áedán answered carefully. "Yes. And no. When I am alone or when I am perceived by others as a boy, I am contented enough. I can survive. But it is... uncomfortable. This form feels unnatural to me. It's as if I am a stranger living in a foreign land, a land that never feels like home no matter how long I reside there. Do you understand?"

Máel Conall nodded humbly. "As much as I can, I do. You are not the first I have met with such feelings. There are those among us who have had them and were cured. There is one here with us now, and if you live here and learn our ways, she may reveal herself to you. Like you, she is cautious, and has had to hide her true nature from others. Except from those whom she trusts."

"Really? Really! There are others like me? Here? This is wonderful!" Áedán exclaimed, jumping to his feet up in jubilation. He had never entertained a hope as fantastic as this, for all his life he had believed himself to be the only one in the world to have ever felt such things—a lonely abomination of Nature, or an interloper from the Otherworld. But to know that he was not alone, that there were others like him—and so close! He could hardly keep from dancing for the excitement coursing through him.

"Be still, lad. Sit down now, for I have more to tell you." Máel Conall spoke firmly, and Áedán sat. "I perceive that you have a strong connection to the source of Imbas inside you—that is, the divine force of inspiration, the flowing energy that comes to us from Segas, the Well of the Otherworld. Imbas is what gives us the power to make poetry and magic. You may have the potential to learn the draíochta druadh, the druidic arts, and open up that little springhead to become a rushing river of power. I would offer you a place at this school, if you would faithfully abide by our rules and our customs. You have lived a hard life, Áedán, but the life of a fili is no less difficult, though difficult in a different way. The fili is constantly challenging his or her mind, is never ceasing his or her efforts to learn more, and is always open to becoming transformed by what wisdom is gained. Most are not suited for this kind of life. Most people choose to be one way and remain thus, rigidly, their whole lives. But we filid observe Nature and reflect back to humanity the wisdom that we see there. It is the wisdom of change. This is why the filid are so revered and may gain status equal to that of a chieftain. What we do is very complex and very important. We help maintain balance within the human realm by analyzing and applying the law when conflicts arise. And we help maintain the balance between humanity, Nature, and the Otherworld by ensuring that human laws, judgments, actions, and customs are in alignment with Cóir—the divine balance, the order of the Universe. If you are attracted to this life, Áedán, I would be happy to give you a place here as a student."

Without even a moment's hesitation, Áedán knew this was what he truly wanted. The role of the fili fit him perfectly; he could easily imagine himself one day becoming a man of power.

"Yes, Máel Conall. Thank you. Thank you so much!" said Áedán. He beamed as brightly as the solstice sun, then dimmed a little as he thought of his poverty. "But I have nothing to pay you with. I own nothing of value and have no status. How might I compensate you for my learning and board?"

Máel Conall waved his hand dismissively. "Don't worry about that, lad. There are other ways for you to earn your keep here. Though most of our students are from wealthy families who pay in goods, in some special cases—when the student is not of a high class but is marked for the draíochta druadh in some other way—we allow students to labor for their studies. You would work to maintain the community here: keeping up the grounds and structures, tending the animals, foraging, cooking, cleaning, serving your masters and tutors, and so on. And I can see that you've some skill in catching game. We are often in need of variety in our diets, especially in winter, so that could be of service."

Áedán nodded gratefully. There was one thing left to be addressed. "And what of being healed, ollamh?"

The fili stroked his beard. "That... is a more complicated matter. One that I think must be revealed to you more slowly, for it will not make sense to you now. It involves several mysteries that a novice is not yet permitted to know. But I will say this: the healing is not something I can do for you—it is something you must do for yourself, through learning the draíochta druadh. That is how it has been done before, and we can teach you this here. If you attain the highest skills of our art, you will know then how you can be healed. It is not easy and it is not immediate. It will be many years before you will be able to achieve it."

"But what if I have no skill in the draíochta druadh?"

"Then you will have no place here." The fili leaned forward and placed his hand on Áedán's shoulder. "But do not worry yourself much about that, lad. I do not think that will be the source of trouble."

"Thank you, Máel Conall. It would be my greatest honor to join you here as your pupil. And my secret... will you keep it safe?"

"Of course, Áedán. Your secret is safe with me. And I will advise you on how to live here without fear of discovery. Inasmuch, it may be unwise for you to sleep in the roundhouses with the other uninitiated boys. Boys can be... crude. And anyway, most of them are younger than yourself, for novices generally come to us at the age of twelve. I imagine you are older than that?"

"I am fourteen."

Máel Conall nodded. "I see. So you will be a little behind in your schooling. But if you work hard you should be able to catch up. I will ask one of the other four ollamhna of this school, Lí Lon, if she will host you in her roundhouse with her older apprentices. You see, there are seven grades of fili, and normally once you achieve fochloc, the first rank, you will be permitted to live as an apprentice to one of the ollamhna. I already have sixteen apprentices under my care, which is the maximum that I am allowed. Lí Lon has graduated a few of her students recently, so she will have space in her house."

"Lí Lon... the líaig told me to seek her out as well. Uasal said to me: 'she may have some particular knowledge of the state that you find your-self in'."

"I would say that is true. And you can trust Lí Lon with your secret as you have with me. Though it is up to you to tell her. I will not."

So it was settled: Áedán would begin his studies at the school and try his skill at becoming a poet. The boy laid his head upon his master's breast, pledging his gratitude and fealty, and left to seek the hospitality of the ollamh Lí Lon.

As Áedán turned to the door, a musical voice called from behind: "Welcome, Áedán, to the Path of the Learned. May you reach the highest wisdom at the crown of the tree." Áedán looked around the roundhouse for whom might have spoken. It was empty but for the fili and the crane perched up in the rafters. Had she been the one who had spoken thus? Certainly it had not been Máel Conall's voice. The bird stared down at him with her piercing red eyes. Áedán bowed to the graceful creature and let himself out.

CHAPTER ELEVEN

Lí Lon

As Áedán stepped inside the big house to collect his things, the din nearly knocked him backward. Three dozen children, boys and girls, were eating, talking, and laughing boisterously. He was unaccustomed to sound of so many speaking at once. Wincing, he scrambled to gather up his things which laid against the wall. Nearby, a group of boys and girls slightly younger than himself was sitting upon cushions circling a low table. He moved as inconspicuously as he could, hoping that in the hubbub he would not be noticed. He was unsuccessful.

"You there! New boy!" called one of the boys at the table. Reluctantly, Áedán turned. He had no interest in speaking with this stranger, but it would be rude to ignore him. The boy was dressed in a cream-colored tunic, as were the rest at the table. "Is that your bow and arrows? Did you make them?"

Áedán nodded shyly. "Yes, I did."

The boy's eyes widened with admiration. "Deadly! Will you show me how to shoot it?"

Áedán smiled, relieved by the boy's sincerity. "Em... well... if the ol-lamh permits it." The younger boy grinned and turned back to his friends, addressing them all in the rousing timbre of a poet at work. "My father is a marvelous huntsman. One time, when he was out with his brother and two of his warriors, they came to a mist-covered hill. It was just past dawn, and the sunlight—I mean, the twilight—lit the leaves with a..."

The boy's immersion in his own tale gave Áedán a chance to slip away unnoticed. He went to the roundhouse of the brown-haired woman he had seen enter earlier in the day. She must be the one called Lí Lon.

The woman stood there in the doorway as he approached, as if she had expected him to arrive at precisely that moment. He greeted her with the blessing that he had given Máel Conall. She returned it and invited him inside.

Lí Lon was almost a head taller than Máel Conall. While the older man was round-bodied and jovial, Lí Lon was slim, serene, and long-limbed with footsteps as light as a doe's. An elegant dress of green-and-blue-patterned linen billowed about her. She beckoned for Áedán to sit in a wooden chair, carved so that each hand rested on the stylized head of a bird. Two globes of silver clung to the ends of each plait that fell down from her temples, while the rest of her wavy walnut hair cascaded down the length of her back. A necklace of glossy river pearls was around her neck.

"So, you must be Áedán. Máel Conall informed me that you have come to study with us." Her voice was rich and deep and melodious. The boy nodded. "I am Lí Lon Ingen Conall, one of the five ollamhna of this school. I understand that you're in need of housing."

"I am, ollamh. I would be grateful for a place here in your house." He looked about; it was nearly as large and well-adorned as Máel Conall's. "May I ask: is Máel Conall your father? He does not seem very old." He inferred by her surname that she was the daughter of Conall, however she looked not very much younger than the man. *She may even be the same age as my mother*, he thought uncomfortably.

"He is my aite, or foster-father," she said. "A master may adopt a student as a foster-child, when circumstance or mutual affection demands it. But he is older than he looks. Not all of his years were spent here in the temporal world."

"The temporal world?" A question arose in Áedán that he had not been able to ask earlier. "When I was speaking with him, he had this distant look on his face, as if he were looking into the Otherworld. But he was right in front of me... he didn't go anywhere. And when he awoke he told me he had spoken to the Síd. How is such a thing possible? Can he see into the Otherworld, or travel there, without leaving his body?"

Lí Lon nodded approvingly at the boy's curiosity, for curiosity is the first sign of aptitude. "Yes. And no. It is too complex for a novice to understand. But this skill was taught to us by the Síd themselves, and is learned only by the most skilled druíd. You see, the Síd may come to this world on a whim, whenever they wish, but we may only go to their lands with their permission or by the high arts of draíochta druadh. Or occasionally by trickery... but we do not teach *that* here!" A touch of humor softened her serious face. "Are you hungry? Íma will fix you something to eat, then you will bathe and receive a set of novice's clothes." The ollamh wrinkled her nose at his raiment of animal skins. "You smell as if you've been denning with badgers. If you become a fili, you must take better care with your hygiene. Maintaining our status necessitates cleanliness, not just of speech and mind, but of body, too."

"Where do I bathe?" asked Áedán.

"Students bathe in the brook. Downstream from the settlement, of course."

"And is it... private?"

Lí Lon gave Áedán a quizzical look. "Not particularly. But the boys and girls bathe on alternate days. The boys will be bathing this evening before supper." She spied Áedán's discomfort. "Does this displease you?"

"Em... if there is some other more private place, I would prefer that. You see, I've lived alone for quite some time... it will take me a while to get used to the idea of bathing with others."

Lí Lon paused, as if analyzing his words for a hidden meaning. Then she nodded. "Well, you may bathe here in the tub that I use for myself. Just this once, until we find a suitable alternative for you. Íma, my servant, will heat stones for you if you haul your water from the stream. You may bring the tub into the cubicle where you will sleep. The third one from the right is open. That will be private."

Áedán thanked her, gathered his new set of clothes, and prepared his bath. He had not had a warm bath since leaving his childhood home, and felt blessed by the luxury. His new clothes were a simple tunic and trousers of undyed wool, having the cream color of a novice that had not yet attained any rank. As Lí Lon explained to him, the choice of colors increased as the fili moved up in rank. The ollamh had the choice of at least five colors as well as adornments of bronze, silver, and gold.

Lí Lon spared a few moments between her lessons to orient the boy to his new life. After cleaning himself up, he sat with the ollamh outside in the sunlight. She sat in a chair of oak and holly and Áedán was in the grass at her feet.

"As the rank of fili increases, so does one's honor price," she explained. "The ollamh fili is of the highest status in the whole of society, having an honor price equal to a chieftain. Our honor price protects us from harm and harassment—the fees associated with a criminal act against a fili are very expensive."

"And what of the bards?" Áedán asked. As a child he had heard many stories from the mouths of traveling bards.

"Though they are poets and storytellers like the filid, they are, in general, unschooled. They have some skill, but cannot perform the highest forms of poetry nor the draíochta druadh. Neither can they make judgments. Their honor prices are equal to the lower ranks of the fili, the fochloc or macfhurmud, depending on their talents. Bards have their own grades, of which I will not discuss now. If a student of the draíochta druadh cannot complete his or her training, having not the talent nor intelligence to continue, he or she may become a bard." Lí Lon paused. "It is also an honorable profession." This was said with a dismissive shrug.

"And what are the highest forms of poetry?" asked Áedán.

"You have many questions, as you should. But I cannot answer all of them at once for the learning must be done in sequence. You will have classes with the other novices this afternoon, and there you may ask your questions." Lí Lon crossed her legs and leaned back in her chair. "But you are behind, so I suppose I should catch you up a little.

"The core of the filid's knowledge consists of the Fourteen Streams of Scholarship: fele and innruccus—science and integrity; comgne and genelach—history and genealogy; imbas and dichetal—inspiration and chanting; anamain and brethugud—an advanced meter and legal judgment; teinm laeda and ler forcetail—poetical analysis and diligent teaching; idna láme and lanamnais—purity of deed and partnership; idna beoil and foglomma—purity of speech and learning. Of these mentioned, three of them are the highest: teinm laeda, or breaking of the marrow; díchetal di chennaib, or chanting from the head in perfect extemporaneous poetry; and imbas forosnai, the speaking of prophecy. And yet, a fili may also attain more."

The boy's eyes widened, overwhelmed by the deluge of strange terms.

"You'll understand it all in time," said Lí Lon. "The clí filid, those who have studied at least five years with us, will explain it to you in greater detail. They teach the novices and lower grades."

The shadow of a raven passed across the sky. Lí Lon looked up at the position of the sun and stood gracefully. "It's time to start the afternoon lessons. Come with me and I will introduce you to your peers."

Áedán slept that night in Lí Lon's roundhouse with her apprentices. The next day, and the days following, he labored alongside her servants for the upkeep of the house and the maintenance of the community. Lí Lon found the boy pleasant and polite, helpful, diligent, and eager to please. And increasingly, happy.

At first Áedán was all on guard, tense and quiet, always glancing over his shoulder and searching his masters' faces for hidden dangers. In his free time he went alone into the forest, hunting or walking in silent contemplation, for solitude was to him a nourishment as vital as bread and water. To be always in the presence of others, day and night, was grating to his nerves. Yet with time he slowly accustomed to the change.

The weeks passed and as summer came into full fruiting, Áedán relaxed his vigilance. He talked freely with the other students, and on occasion even smiled. His classmates were friendly and welcoming, and at mealtimes he sat with them and spoke of story and poetry and magic. Now that he never missed a meal, Áedán grew up strong and straight as an aspen. Lí Lon was pleased to see his face lose its gaunt shadow and his cheeks take up a cherry blush. In the evenings, gathered around the hearthfire, Áedán joined in the joking with the other apprentices, revealing a hidden wit. It had been a long time since he'd laughed in the company of friends, and now rejoiced in it once again.

One of Lí Lon's apprentices he became especially fond of, a clí named Síthmaith who taught basic lessons to his class of novices. She took an interest in Áedán as if to tame him.

"Come sit beside me, my little fox cub," she would say. In the evenings Síthmaith coaxed him to her with a spoonful of honey so that she might comb the tangles from his wild red mane. His classmates, in their jealousy, called him teacher's pet, but for this he had no shame and the epithet soon died away. Yet they also called Síthmaith a name behind her back—Síthmaith Cham, because she was lamed by a deformity in her legs—and this Áedán could not abide. The first of them that used that name was thrown to the ground, and afterwards no other ventured the tease for they were too wary of Áedán's righteous temper.

Yet it was not just righteousness that stoked his ire. There was also in his heart a budding infatuation for the young woman who was his senior by several years. He brought her primroses and rocks that sparkled with mica, and performed for her devotional poems. But Síthmaith would only smile and pat him on the head and say, "How precious."

He asked her once about her ailment and Síthmaith spoke honestly: "When I was a child it took me a very long time to learn to walk, and as I grew older my legs became misshapen. My father is a fili and understood that this marked me for the draíochta druadh, so he sent me here to study. As I'm sure you've noticed, I am not the only one here with a disability; there are several others with blemishes of one kind or another. If one is of the flaith class and a blemish prevents him or her from taking leadership, they are encouraged to become learned instead. Blindness is a particularly auspicious sign that one is destined to have foresight and receive visions."

Áedán's skin suddenly prickled—he wondered what in her statement had made him shiver so. Síthmaith continued: "And the blind are often gifted with unusual musical abilities. Máel Conall told me he seeks those out that are marked. He said it is because we see the world differently than most others, and so we make art and wisdom of rarer beauty."

Áedán nodded. *Does Máel Conall consider me to be marked?* he wondered. *Though, my ailment is hidden.* Absently, he put his hand over the mark covered by his sleeve.

As he settled into his new life, Áedán's talents were soon revealed. Although he had begun his schooling late, he quickly gained proficiency in the elementary poetic meters and grammar. In only four months he memorized the twenty tales needed to become a focholc when it normally took a year. The fire of his mind consumed knowledge like kindling. No other novice was so ravenous for learning, for he was impassioned by a stronger force: the hope for healing. *If you attain the highest skills of our art, you will know then how you can be healed.*

By Lá Lethach, the autumnal equinox, Áedán was made a fochloc and officially apprenticed to Lí Lon. He donned the straw-colored mantle of the first grade of fili. As Lí Lon's apprentice he received direct tutoring from her and came to appreciate the depth of her wisdom. Although she was a kind and patient teacher, her eyes did not twinkle with mirth as Máel Conall's did. It was rare to see her laugh or smile. She was serious and stoic, and Áedán found her intimidating.

Lí Lon appraised her new apprentice. He was eager, perceptive, and asked insightful questions. And yet, there was something else about him that drew her eye. It was plain enough that he was holding something back, and she pondered what reasons he might have for keeping his distance.

Winter came and a dusting of snow capped the Great Mountain, looming high above the scholars' settlement like a cresting wave. As the bees retreated to their inner chambers, so too did the filid moved their business indoors. Closer quarters were kept, which caused Áedán to crave the solitude of his hermitage. And yet, there were good reasons to overwinter here: the fire was stoked all the night through, he never went to bed with an empty belly, and was never without the safety of community about him.

Yule had come and gone; the sun had been conceived and was grow-ing again in the south, making its long journey north through winter's dark womb. Áedán sat alone at the edge of the glen watching feeble sun-rays track too quickly across the sky. He was thinking about what Cadrolón had told him earlier in the day, when they had sat together at the midday meal.

"Who here counted the cranes in the village yesterday?" Cadrolón scanned the table. A few students shrugged. "Did you see? Did you see two instead of one? Well, I did. Máel Conall was gone all day and so was his familiar. In the evening I was out fetching water from the stream and saw two cranes land outside the roundhouse in the dark. One of them flew away, and when I went back inside, Máel Conall was there by the fire."

His friends at the table laughed. But Áedán did not. "Do you think that Máel Conall turned himself into a crane?" he asked.

Cadrolón nodded. "You are clever, little flame. So much more clever than these blockheads here. They're simply jealous that I've seen the ais-triú cruth and they haven't."

"What's the aistriú cruth?" asked Áedán.

"It's not real! I heard it's just stories," said a yellow-mantled girl. "And anyway, it was dark out. You don't know what you saw."

"Oh, most regal of tree stumps, how wrong you are," Cadrolón said to the younger girl. "The ollamhna keep the knowledge of it from us because it's so dangerous. But I know for a fact that it's true, and now I've seen it with my own eyes."

"But what *is* it?" Áedán implored.

"It's the fili's ability to transform himself into the shapes of animals," said a blue-mantled doss fili. "And Cadrolón's right. It's real."

"Actually, it's the ability to take the shape of any natural being: ani-mal, tree, weed, pebble, puddle, bird, bug, and so on. Some can even take the shape of other men," said Cadrolón.

"Or women," corrected the doss girl. Cadrolón rolled his eyes.

Áedán's heart leapt like a dolphin. "When do we get to learn *that*?"

"I heard that only the highest ranking filid can learn it—the anruth and ollamhna," said the young woman in the blue mantle. "But only some... the ones who have the most skill. Like Cadrolón said, it's very dangerous. Some have died or have been permanently harmed by doing it improperly."

Áedán sat upon a stone, swinging his legs as his thoughts swirled. So absorbed was he in contemplation that he did not hear his master approach. He jumped at the sound of her voice.

"Good day to you, Áedán. Why are you out here alone? Are you unwell?"

"Eh, no. No, I'm fine. Thank you. I only needed a moment outside. It's hot in the big house with all those mouths breathing at once."

Lí Lon nodded. "That is so. Well, I was looking for Sithmaith—is she in the big house?"

"Yes, she's at the second table on the left."

"Thank you. I'll see you later this afternoon for the lesson on starlore."

As Lí Lon stepped away, Áedán called out to her: "Ollamh, wait. I don't mean to delay you, but... may I ask you a question?"

"Of course, Áedán. What is it?"

"I've heard there is an art that only the highest filid know: the art to transform oneself into the shape of another being. A bird or beast or bush, maybe. Is this true? Have you seen it?" Áedán asked with a hunger in his eyes.

Lí Lon said nothing. For a long moment she stood watching the boy's face, her mouth drawn into pucker as if the question was sour.

Perhaps I should not have asked! Of course—it was wrong of me to ask! Áedán dropped his eyes and tensed himself for admonishment.

But to his relief, she only sighed and said, "It is a thing you ought not to know of until you're wiser. But, yes, I have seen it done. And what's more, I have done it myself."

Áedán looked up at her, eyes wide as asters. "Truly? And what did you transform yourself into? A deer? A hawk? A mouse?"

Lí Lon's face clouded as she turned and looked away. "The aistriú cruth is one of the most dangerous of our arts. Without perfect execution, the spell may go awry and leave one partially or permanently transformed. It is why we do not speak of it until the fili is ready to know this secret. And some are never ready. Some have died in the attempt. It is not a frivolous thing used for fun—it's a tool of great power that must only be used when necessary, as is true for all the high arts. The filid learned the aistriú cruth from Nature and from the Síd, who use it naturally, with an ease that humanity may never achieve. For us, we must struggle through it, and sometimes fail. We humans are weak, and by our ignorance can harm ourselves and others." She turned to him with a stare as stern as a mother owl's. "What is your interest in the aistriú cruth?"

Áedán dropped his gaze to the moss at his feet. "Because I... I would like to know if a fili might change his, or her, shape in other ways. Could a fili put on the face of another person? Or maybe... transform oneself from... from a woman into a... man?"

The air about him shimmered and grew dark. Looking up, Áedán saw his master's face twisted with rage. She seemed to grow taller, looming above him like a surging thunderhead about to break.

"Why do you ask this?" she bellowed. "Who told you?"

"I'm sorry, I don't... no one told me anything... I don't know what you mean! I know nothing! I'm sorry, Ollamh, it was wrong of me to ask!" He made himself small and lifted his arm above his head in defense, fearing she would strike.

But she did not strike. She stiffened and grew still, grey as a ring stone. The boy dared not move. Seeing his fear, Lí Lon softened and drew a long breath, dispelling the shadows. Kneeling, she touched his arm and drew drown his shield.

"Be still. Have no fear of me. I'd assumed you knew of something I wish to remain hidden." She looked about the glen. It was empty but for themselves. "But I see now that you were inquiring about yourself."

Áedán tensed. Lí Lon continued, her voice silvery as a black bird's trill. "I knew there was something kindred between us. I've been waiting many months for you to reveal what you've been hiding, but I can guess it now: your secret is like mine." She took the boy's trembling hand in her own. "Áedán, don't be afraid. I will tell you what you wish to know, but you must promise never to repeat what I am about to tell you—not to anyone. You must keep my secret, and I will keep yours. Do you promise?"

Áedán's blood pounded in his ears. The boy nodded. "I promise, Ollamh," he squeaked.

It seemed so long ago that Máel Conall had told Áedán to reveal his truth to Lí Lon, but the boy had never enough courage to do it. He had thought her too cold, too close. Like his mother. And now he had no choice. He braced himself for what was to come.

Lí Lon nodded and spoke low. "I've used the aistriú cruth, but only once, when I first achieved the rank of anruth, many years ago. It was seven years' study as Máel Conall's apprentice before I was ready. And with the aistriú cruth, I transformed the body I was born with into the body of the woman you see today."

Áedán gaped at her, for a moment speechless. "You mean to say, that you were born... a boy? And you took on the form of a woman?"

"I don't think I was ever a 'boy', really. But I was called that by others, yes."

Áedán laughed in shock and amazement, for he understood perfectly what she meant. In his laugh was also relief, for her admission dispelled a fear he had borne since first he spoke to Máel Conall.

"Oh, how Ériu has blessed me! To find someone else in the world like me! I'd feared that... well, when Máel Conall said there was one amongst us who had made the transformation that I sought, he had said 'she', and I thought he meant that the cure for my affliction might come from an acceptance of my lot to live forever as a woman. But I never thought that this person's truth—*your* truth—could be the opposite of my own! What I've dreamed of for so long is really possible!"

At that Lí Lon smiled. It was the first smile she had ever shown to him, and in that moment Áedán beheld the fullness of her beauty. Breaking through her hesitation, the ollamh hugged the boy against her breast.

It had been many years since Áedán was held in a woman's arms, and at first he stiffened at her touch. Many thoughts flitted through his mind, some nervous, some hopeful, but one pushed back the rest.

What radiates from her? I feel it like a force that draws me in. Suddenly, he recalled. *Ah, it's love!* Then he melted against her like sun-warmed butter.

A moment passed. Lí Lon pulled back to look at him, eyes glistening. "You may achieve what you desire Áedán, as I have, but it will require years of study. You have skill, in that there is no doubt, but you're not yet prepared to learn the aistriú cruth. So you must have patience and commit to long learning. Transformation demands the most clear-minded focus and the deepest, most profound knowledge of the form you wish to take. Taking the shape of another animal, for instance, is the most difficult kind of shape-shifting, and usually requires a friendship with one of that kind. What *we* are trying to achieve—shifting from one sex into another—is simpler than that, for both you and I, as Áes Múchta, already understand the most intimate details of our desired form."

"Áes Múchta? What is that?" asked Áedán.

"It is the secret name, the sacred name, of people like us. It means 'the Eclipsed Folk'. A man of this kind, like you, is called Grían Múchta, one whose internal sun is eclipsed or smothered. A woman of this kind, like myself, is called Ésca Múchta, one whose internal moon is eclipsed. There are other terms too: for those who are both male and female together; for those who are men sometimes and women at other times; and for those who feel they are neither men nor women. The spirits of the Áes Múchta are unique—we transcend all binary divisions, being one and both and neither simultaneously. We play a sacred role in the world, for we understand the two halves of existence where most others know only one."

Lí Lon looked up at the cold, clear sky. "It is a great mystery. As I was taught by the Síd who still hold the knowledge of these mysteries, we are made this way to act as arbiters between the halves of the world that are wont to be opposed. I know not how we are made this way, nor why we are so rare. But I see those like us reflected in all of Nature's tribes."

"You do? But I've often wondered if I... if we are an aberration of the natural order. Is the world *supposed* to be divided into male and female? Are we Áes Múchta simply accidents... mistakes?"

Lí Lon inclined her head. "Nature is incapable of making anything unnatural. Humanity is capable of making unnatural things by the power of our rational cognition, but the state of being Eclipsed is something we do not have conscious control over. Thus, we exist because the forces of Nature are acting through us. Everything in the Universe has its place and purpose, even if our small human minds cannot comprehend it. Consider the many flowers of the world that carry both male and female parts in a single blossom. Consider the trees that can self-pollinate, or the ash and yew who can change their sex at will—every year if they like! Newts, fish, and fowl also change when there is a need. Some birds can be both sexes at once, as can butterflies. This, to me, is proof that the hard division between male and female exists only in the human mind. Nature will always find ways to contradict the arbitrary rules that we set forth for it to follow. We humans know so very little. It is the fili's responsibility to gain wisdom from observing Nature while avoiding the hubris of assuming we can perfectly know or perfectly describe it. Our knowledge changes as the world changes, therefore the role of the fili requires an extraordinary subtlety of mind.

"It is why, I think, the Áes Múchta can become such powerful filid. We don't just *understand* the liminality and mutability of Nature—we *live* it. Ordinary humans are trapped by their own singleness. But *we* are multiple. We can see the world from more than one point of view. We stand at a place outside the norm, outside what most agree to be consensual reality, and so we are less tempted to put faith in conventional truths; it disabuses us of many social delusions. Thus, we are better able to judge fairly the strengths and weaknesses of humanity. I believe this is why the Áes Múchta have always been favored by the Síd, for generations immemorial."

Áedán was struck by these words. "The Síd..." He looked down at the burn on his forearm. "But if we are so important... if we are so favored, then why are we not better known? Why must we hide our natures in fear?"

Lí Lon sighed. "It was not always this way. In the far gone past, long, long ago, we Áes Múchta were given an equal place in society alongside men and women. And it is said, in our wisdom traditions, that when the Túatha de Danann—the ancestors of the Síd—were driven underground by the ancestors of the Érainn many generations ago, the Áes Múchta were likewise suppressed. It was because we grew too close to the Síd that our loyalties came in to question. And yet we are human; we are tied to this world and could not go with the Síd into the Otherworld. So here we remain, struggling to survive in a world that chooses not to see us."

Áedán sat quietly, introspective. To know that he was part of an old, old story, a legacy drawn forward from deep time, was, though tragic, a comfort to him. A new feeling was kindled in his heart, pushing aside that old tattered cloak of shame: pride. Pride for who he was—not as a boy, not as a girl, but as a Grían Múchta. A sacred person, favored by the Otherworld. A smile crept to his lips like the sun at dawn, and with an impulsive thought, he imagined what his master might have looked like as a male, before her transformation.

"Stop!" Lí Lon commanded, recognizing his look at once. "See me as I am, not as I was. For wouldn't you like the same?"

Áedán nodded, embarrassed. "Yes, yes I would. I'm sorry, Ollamh. I see you as you are."

"And I you," she said. "But I also see you as you will be: my handsome foster-son, and a powerful fili."

Áedán gaped at her. "Your foster-son?" Lí Lon nodded. Hot tears spilled down his cheeks. He felt an urge to embrace her, but drew back, unsure. Lí Lon smiled, hesitated for a moment, then embraced him awkwardly as if unpracticed.

"I will be your muimme, your foster-mother. I've always dreamt of having a child of my own, but it seems fate had me wait until I found you, Áedán." Lí Lon's voice trembled with emotion, as if on the verge of song.

Abruptly she stood, swallowed, and brushed the moss from her knees. "We will—" Her voice was husky. She cleared her throat and blinked. "We will discuss this later." In her usual formal tone she said: "But I expect most things will remain as they are. I will be no more lenient with you than with my other apprentices—I expect you to continue to work hard. But I do look forward to getting to know you better. Don't be so distant from me, Áedán. We have many things to share."

"Yes, Ollamh. I mean—Muimme." That word was unfamiliar, soothing yet cold, like a drink from a mountain stream. Lí Lon reached forward to stroke his hair. He tensed as her hand landed. The gesture should have been welcome, should have been comforting, and yet it was not. It took a moment for Áedán to realize why: she stroked him as his mother had stroked him, before her love had scorched his soul. All manner of doubts flooded his mind, yet he fixed his face so the woman would not see.

With a quick twitch of a smile Lí Lon dropped her hand. Setting her shoulders she took up once again her professorial posture and departed in haste for the hall.

That night Áedán lay awake staring up at the shadows dancing in the hearth light. His mind reeled. In such a short time his life had been so profoundly changed. Every boon he had asked of Ériu had now come to him. Every one. Yet with these gifts came obligations, for now his oath to the Goddess was even more real and more weighty.

But... Lí Lon... will her love eventually sour as my mother's did? Will she see in me a shade I cannot see in myself? He quivered and tried to shake the thought from his head. *No. How could it be? She knows me, in whole, and accepts me, and she is Áes Múchta, too. She understand what I am. But...*

Having been for a moment dispelled, his doubts slinked back to shade him. They stirred dark eddies in his mind until the early hours of the morning when finally he drifted off to sleep. And then he dreamed...

A young woman stood opposite him on the bank of a rushing stream. Shining black hair fell like water down her back. Her brows straight as arrows; her grey eyes sparkled like quartz. Her skin was smooth as milk; her cheeks blushed pink as cherry blossoms. She was so resplendent in dress and adornment that Áedán thought she must be a chieftain's daughter. No woman in the world could be the match of her beauty, he was sure.

She raised her slender arms and beckoned for him to cross. On the bank where he stood the ground was covered with a dusting of snow. Yet the opposite bank was bright with greenery and fragrant flowers, the air hung heavy with birdsong. He took one step into the rushing waters, and as his toes touched the stream he awoke.

Áedán emerged slowly from the dream, and in the crackle of the hearthfire he thought he heard the clink of the maiden's golden bracelets.

CHAPTER TWELVE

The Higher Arts

"The raven cackles on bare winter branch,
The whitethroat warbles from bramble in spring,
The heron wades and waits to cast the summer spear,
The eagle screams over autumn's auburn shade.
Night lengthens, sun grows weak,
An icy wind lifts up the winged
And casts them clear across the world
With wistful want of returning home."

 Under the examination of his master, Áedán chanted a poem he had composed. It was to Lí Lon's satisfaction, and so he was graduated from the rank of fochloc to macfhuirmid.

 The months and seasons passed swiftly for Áedán in avid study of sorcery, poem, and song. The work was all-consuming, and when not reciting or composing or laboring for his keep, he wandered through the woodland alone. He indulged very little in play with his peers, for it was play enough to learn the arts of his masters. He was eager to excel, for he wished more than anything else to learn the aistriú cruth, the shape-shifting.

Yet he could not be rushed nor reckless, for the ollamhna graduated their students to higher ranks by competency alone. It took a year on average to ascend through each of the lower ranks. The higher ranks took longer, for the curricula were more extensive and more difficult. Nonetheless, Áedán progressed rapidly. By his fourth year at the school, he had achieved the title of clí, the fifth rank of the filid.

As a fochloc, the yellow-mantled first rank, Áedán had memorized thirty stories, learned six poetic meters, studied elementary poetic grammar, and memorized the dían poems. He learned the lower-level meditation techniques, studied natural philosophy, and was introduced to astronomy, astrology, and the practice of seasonal rituals and sacrifices.

As a macfhuirmid, the red-mantled second rank, he memorized forty stories, studied advanced grammar and the composition of praise poetry, learned the ogham writing system, and practiced the druidic skills of meabhrú dírithe (meditative focus) and sruth anáil (channeling energy through the breath). He learned the names of the local spirits and deities of the province of Mumu, where they each resided, and how to honor them with sacrifices and ceremony.

As a doss, the blue-mantled third rank, he retained fifty stories, learned more complicated grammar, and began the study of the Fénechas, the law tracts. Áedán the druidic skills of néal fástineacht (cloud divination) and támhnéal (divinatory trance) were also taught to him.

At the level of cano, the green-mantled fourth rank, the studies became denser and more difficult. Áedán retained sixty stories and continued his studies of the Fénechas. He memorized the noble genealogies of Mumu, practiced more advanced poetic compositions, and began learning how to heal the body with herbs and charms. Of the draíochta druadh he learned many new things: fástineacht (divination by the casting of yew rods and bones); augury by the sounds of birds, especially wrens; augury by the barking of dogs and foxes, and by the clapping of hands; taibhreamh éirim (dreamcraft); and elementary briochtaí (charms).

And now as clí, Áedán gained the adornment of bronze and would be responsible for teaching the novices and the fochloc. To complete his studies at this fifth rank, he would have to retain a total of eighty seven stories including the dindsenchas (lore of places), complete his learning of the Fénechas, and begin the study of áer dlí (legal satire). He would also acquire the druidic skills of dícheadal (magical incantation), éirim aimsire (weathercraft), and the empowerment of amulets.

Áedán understood now what had seemed so strange to him at the beginning of his schooling: that poetry is the art through which magic is wielded. Magic itself was impossible for even the wisest druí to define, for it both defies and encompasses all qualification. In her lessons on natural philosophy, Lí Lon discussed this point with her apprentices.

"Magic is the physical expression of the conscious will of the Universe," she said. "The study of magic is how we intercourse with the sentience of Nature. This sentience can be spoken to, reasoned with, shaped and redirected with poetry, ritual, and sacrifice. Though the will of the Universe is, of course, conscious, it is not always coherent. It manifests through many actors with many hands—through gods and goddesses, spirits of Nature, animals and plants, stars and planets, wind and rain and the slow shifting of the earth, the Síd, and humanity. It is the responsibility of the filid to know the will of the Universe and to respect it, facilitate it, or at least, not disturb it. Though a druí may wield poetry and magic to satisfy her own selfish goals, goals that might be against the will of Nature, in the end Nature always prevails. Imbalanced action—action taken against Cóir or without satisfactory compensation—surely spells suffering."

The ollamh paused and gave her students serious look. "Now tell me: why do the filid use poetry to wield magic? How do words have power?"

As usual, Áedán spoke up first. "Because the gift of speech was given to humanity to help us direct our intentions. It allows us to focus our imaginings, to be specific and subtle. We can make things with our words that we cannot make with our hands. When we speak with sacred intention, with clarity and beauty, Nature understands us and heeds the command. Each word is like a stone in a stream—we can place those stones in such a way to redirect the flow, making fast rapids, still pools, or branches. But we do not make the water; that was there before us. With our words we mold the shape of the world as it appears in the human mind. Society itself is stitched together with words."

Lí Lon nodded approvingly. "That is an excellent metaphor, Áedán. You understand it well. Use it with the fochloc to explain the structure of dían poems. It will prepare them for composing briochtaí in a similar way. "

Áedán puffed out his chest like a robin fluffing his feathers.

When the class dispersed, Áedán went his own way from the rest of them. He was distant from his peers, and because his talents earned him the frequent praise of his masters, his aloofness was assumed arrogance. There was arrogance, to be sure, but it was more than that. In truth, Áedán had not yet conquered the shame of being looked at. Always he feared that if they came too close, his peers would notice his different-ness. The further he aged the more obvious it became that he had not yet reached masculine puberty. He was nineteen years old now and his voice was still boyishly high; his chin still had no hair.

It was a balmy midsummer's day when a dozen boys of all ages made their way up to the loch above the village. There they would swim and play in the rough ways boys are wont to do after sitting still under the gaze of their masters for so long. Áedán watched them enviously. He could not go with them for they always swam in the nude.

There was a trio of boys who always had ready a snicker or a sneer. Each was heir to a prestigious lines of filid. The favor that the ollamhna showed this effeminate, classless boy gave them particular chafe. Passing Áedán on their way to the loch, one of them—a blonde boy named Énán—led the rest in taunting.

"Why do you never come to the waters with us, Áedán? Not to bathe. Not to swim. Ah, you must be too proud. But what besides your freckles and fleas do you claim as noble inheritance?" Énán's companions jeered.

Áedán flushed red and turned with a glare. His arms stiffened, rigid with a fighting urge. But Énán was taller and held the musculature of manhood; a brawl would not end in Áedán's favor. He ground his teeth in livid silence.

Énán smiled. His sting had made a welt, and so he stung again. "Or is it something else? You know, Áedán, we all admire your lovely high voice when we chant the dícheadal together. Don't we, lads? As sweet as the otter's chirrup it is." One of the boys mimicked the squeaking of an otter. The trio laughed, calling back and forth to each other in that shrill tongue. "What makes you sing so high, Áedán? What do you have under your clothes that you wish us not to see? Perhaps you really are an otter under there? Or a gelding... or a girl." They cackled cruelly.

Áedán struggled to keep his temper tethered. And yet his fists were no longer his only weapons.

"You claim to be filid's brood? Ha! How can we tell? All that comes from your mouth is filth and mischief. I am here to become the kind of man who upholds rightness and justice. What are you here for if not that? Explain to me what kind of justice is in juvenile taunts." Every one of his words quivered with contempt. If only he had yet mastered satire he would whip these weasels with it.

Énán sneered but the other two fell silent. Áedán had appealed to their honor, for it was true—such behavior was beneath their class. Heckling had lost its appeal, and the tree slunk away with upraised hackles.

That evening, Áedán spoke of this exchange to Lí Lon. As they stepped out in to the night, the glen echoed with an owl's lonely call. Far off, another answered.

"I'm afraid that the ruse is no longer working," said Áedán. "My voice is too high for my age. I have no beard. The other boys are showing their suspicions." Áedán looked up at her imploringly. "Muimme, I must learn how to transform myself, and I must do it soon before I am found out. When can I learn the aistriú cruth? I feel that I am ready now. I am able! Please, Muimme. Please, have faith in me."

Lí Lon was moved by the desperation in his face, and yet concern stayed her sympathy. "It cannot be rushed, Áedán. It is risky. Very risky. Normally, you would need the skills of an ánruth before learning the aistriú cruth. I know how painful it is to be separated from your peers this way, but you can wait, Áedán. You can survive. I did."

She sighed and smoothed her hair. "And yet, I'll admit you are further along in your studies than I was at your age. It may be possible for you to learn it safely. But... I cannot say. My opinion is... biased. Talk to Máel Conall. Ask him if you are ready. And if he believes you are, then let him be the one to teach you. Though I have done it myself, I have only done it once and dare not try again. I am not a master of that art as Máel Conall is."

It was all he could do not to sprint the way to Máel Conall's round-house. Upon reach the master's door, he smoothed his face—hoping to reflect a scholar's serenity—and stepped inside. Máel Conall was engaged in somber conversation with his apprentice, Cadrolón.

"Oh. I'm sorry to disturb your meeting. I will come back later."

Máel Conall beckoned him to sit. "No, no. Come join us, lad. The fates brought you to this moment. There must be a need for you to hear of what we speak." He turned to Cadrolón. "Tell Áedán your concern, Cadrolón, if you would."

The young man sighed, and repeated himself. "We were discussing ogham, or writing in general. I am tasked with teaching it to the younger students, and it has brought many doubts to my mind. Both the filid of Ériu and the druíd of my people use writing: the ogham here and a different script in Gallaeci, where I am from. And we use it much the same way—primarily for recording names and places; though Gallaeci druíd use the script for spellwork more so than you do here. And yet I wonder what it does to us when we write. How it changes the way we think."

"What do you mean... how could writing change the way we think?" asked Áedán.

"There is an older school of thought among the druíd of my people that disapproves of writing completely," replied Cadrolón. "They say it makes our minds weak. If we lean on it too heavily it will make our memories short and superficial, and one day we may be unable to spout poetry from the head or recount the old epics from memory. Even the laws might eventually be written down, and when that happens, our world will become rigid and linear. If the laws are written, we create a right and a wrong that lives outside of the human soul, fixed to a stone or a wooden post, unable to change as the world changes. If such texts exist, some druíd fear that we might give the ideas of dead men more regard than those of the living. Written law may impose an authority of its own, an authority that is inflexible and unchanging."

"But we do not use ogham in that way," said Áedán. "We use it only to mark boundaries and graves, and for the casting of yew rods in divination. We don't use it to write down poetry or laws. Such knowledge must be learned in context, from the mouth of a master, or else it can be misunderstood and misused."

"And yet, I have been thinking—why even use it on boundary markers or graves?" Cadrolón objected. "It's obvious to all of us on either side of a boundary marker whose territory is whose, even without it having to be written. And if we mark the burial place of a dead hero or chieftain, is his name the only thing about him that is worthy of remembrance? What of his character and deeds? What of his passions and struggles? Our collective responsibility to remember should not be given away to a stone. A stone can remember a name but it cannot remember a man. Only the people can tell his story in its fullness. And when poems pass from mouth to mouth, we don't simply gain *knowledge* of the past, we gain the *feeling* of it. We reawaken it in our souls. For wisdom is only kept alive in the living hearts and minds of humanity. When knowledge is transfixed outside of us, it becomes dead and sterile and easy to misinterpret."

Máel Conall nodded with sudden insight. "Ah, I see now. How much of this comes from a criticism of the way Romans use writing?"

Cadrolón spoke with passion. "Have you witnessed, as I have, how their writing makes them shrewd and unyielding and cruel?"

"They certainly use their script in the ways you describe," replied the ollamh. "Indeed, I have never met a less poetic people than the Romans. But it would take much more than writing to make the Érainn like them, Cadrolón. There are many more factors at play."

"The Romans?" Áedán interjected. "What do they have to do with it?"

Cadrolón replied: "They are the scourge of humanity. They wish to eradicate all peoples and languages and songs and knowledge except their own. Their greed is boundless, and so they steal land and hoard the wealth of Nature to enrich their ever-expanding empire."

The timbre of his voice groaned like a ship under heavy seas. "I am of the Gallaeci people, from a land far across the sea to the south. The Romans have conquered much of my homeland and have called it 'Hispania'. They desire most of all the gold and silver in our hills. But my people are not like the Romans; we are Gaels, like the Érainn. The Gallaeci and Érainn share much history together; it is why I feel so at home here, though I am many weeks away by sea from my beautiful country." He squinted as if to pierce through wall and mountain and cloud to spy the rugged hills of his homeland.

"Ah, that explains your accent," said Áedán. "I had thought you were from Ulaid in the north."

Cadrolón smirked at the boy's ignorance. "Oh no, not so exotic a place as that!"

"I've heard tell of Roman atrocities," said Áedán. "It hard to believe such savagery could be true... the burning of sacred oak groves, forbidding the worship of gods native to the land..."

"It is much more than that," said Cadrolón. "They capture and crucify resisters or conscript them into the Roman military in order to indoctrinate them. They are a brutal people with bleak, depraved minds—they are obsessed only with riches and domination. Yet while the rest of Hispania has been subsumed by them, the tribes in the north—my tribe, the Arrotrebae, among them—are the last holdouts against the conquerors. We are still free peoples. My mother's tribe was from Lugo in the south, the sacred hillfort named for our god Lugus—the one you call Lug—but the hill was taken and defiled by the Romans."

Cadrolón's voice grated with pain. "My grandfather was a druí, but he died before he could pass on his wisdom to me. Many of our druíd were slain or disappeared. So my parents sent me here that I might learn the draíochta druadh and bring it back to restore the knowledge of my people. Our wisdom tradition was once deep and unbroken, but it has been weakened by many generations of struggle. Resisting the creep of Roman customs becomes ever harder. I fear that the more we think and act like Romans, the fewer reasons the gods may have to defend us."

Máel Conall spoke, his voice resonant with Cadrolón's grief. "I am truly sorry, Cadrolón, for the struggles of your people who are our brothers. And yet, despite all that, I am grateful that you've come to us to rekindle the bond between our peoples. It was not just hardship that pushed you here; the gods of Ériu must have a reason to pull."

The master's words roused a strange sensation in Áedán. He looked away and his eyes became unfocused. An unexpected vision filled his mind: a dappled grey stallion lifted his head and arched his powerful neck to meet the nostrils of another stallion, a slender bay. They exchanged bursts of hot, rousing breath. The image drifted away and left the boy briefly bewildered. He rubbed his eyes clear. *What a strange daydream*, he thought, and refocused on the conversation.

"But in regards to your concerns," Máel Conall continued, "you may be partly correct. Writing does effect our minds and our memories. Yet ogham is different from Latin in both character and use. The natures of our tree-letters temper it, I'm sure. Ogham is not used for war nor statecraft nor the tallying of riches. Your fear is not without reason, Cadrolón, but I believe it is misplaced. In Ériu, the Romans have no sway."

"Will you refuse to teach the ogham then?" Áedán asked.

The young man tipped his head in ambivalence. "No... I suppose I will not refuse. I cannot, for it is my duty to teach it to the macfhuirmid. But it will not cease to concern me."

Áedán was moved by his friend's sorrow. "I am deeply sorry for the suffering of your people Cadrolón, and I hope you are successful in bringing the draíochta druadh back to your tribe. I wish I could do something to help. I pray that your people and your wisdom stays safe from the Romans. I pray the conquerors leave forever and give you back your lands."

Cadrolón met Áedán's eyes, his expression inscrutable. "As do I." He stood, bowed to the ollamh who was his master, and left the roundhouse with heavy footfalls.

Áedán had never seen Cadrolón outside of his usual quick wit and ironical humor, and the sight saddened him greatly. Áedán sat tracing his fingers along the wood grain of the bench, pondering the meaning of exile.

After a long moment of silence Máel Conall spoke. "What are you thinking, Áedán?"

"I'm imagining how painful it would be if my own tribe were oppressed as the Gallaeci are. Do you think the Romans might try to conquer Ériu?"

"Pray that the cold north wind and the fierce foaming waves prevent it forever," said the ollamh with a subtle cadence of invocation. "But I do not think they will come. They are, luckily, thin-skinned and afraid of our winters. They call our island Hibernia, which means in their language 'the Land of Winter'." Máel Conall smiled ruefully.

"I hope you are correct. Are there more like Cadrolón here? I've heard other students speak with accents as well. Accents different than his."

"Yes, we have students from many countries to the east and south across the seas. Many who have fled from Roman colonization in order to take refuge here and practice their beliefs; to study the draíochta druadh without fear of persecution. They come from the Dumnonii and Demetae tribes in Britannia, from Hispania like Cadrolón, and from the tribes of Aremorica. But even before the Romans began their conquests, peoples have always come to our isle to exchange knowledge. Ériu delights in the trading of wisdom and art."

Áedán nodded pensively.

"Did you wish to speak to me of something else, lad?" asked Máel Conall.

"Oh. Yes." Áedán gazed about the roundhouse. Several apprentices lounged about, chatting quietly or dozing. A servant was sitting by the loom, spinning yarn with a drop-spindle. "Would you mind if we... walk?"

Máel Conall nodded, taking Áedán's meaning. They went to the shady edge of the clearing where a cluster of slate stones made seating for meditation. There they sat sweating in the heat, watching bees and dragonflies buzz about their heads.

"Ollamh, I'm very anxious to learn the aistriú cruth. I feel that I am ready now. Every day is harder and harder to pass as a man, for it's all too obvious to my peers that I'm far past the normal age of puberty. I fear I may be found out. I fear I may be exposed."

Máel Conall nodded soberly. "I see. And what did your master, Lí Lon, say about it?"

Áedán sighed. "She is filled with a mother's worry for my safety. She doesn't want me to risk the transformation until I'm older—until I'm an ánruth, as she was. She wants me to wait. But she also said that she would accept it if you approved. I think I'm ready. I *know* I'm ready."

Máel Conall paused to ponder, stroking his graying beard. "It is true you've progressed swiftly. You have talent enough, but wisdom would grant you more patience and more regard for danger. Lí Lon is right to be concerned. The aistriú cruth is very dangerous and can only be undertaken with ample preparation. And yet, she is by nature cautious; it is why she waited until she was absolutely sure she could perform the transformation safely. You are ahead of where she was at your age, but whether your speed of study is of benefit to you or of danger remains to be seen." He cocked his head like a crane eying a minnow. "How much éirim aimsire—weatherwork—have you learned so far? Can you raise the féth fíada?"

"Yes, I can do it."

"Then show me."

"Now?"

"Yes, now."

Áedán closed his eyes. He began the breath patterns to invoke the Imbas inside him, then spoke the incantation. A mist crept slowly outward from the forest behind and enveloped the two of them. The fog was so thick that they lost sight of one another, though they were only an arm's length apart.

"Good. Now let it recede," said Máel Conall, sounding far away. Áedán shifted his breath and spoke the spell of dissipation. Soon the air was clear again and the two sat together in the sunny summer glen.

"That was well done, Áedán. Your breath and intonation were perfectly executed. And how do you feel about dícheadal incantations?"

Áedán flushed with pride. "That I have only just begun to learn. But I have been, so far, successful. Just small things. Yet no major mistakes."

"What spells so far?"

"I've scryed upon the loch above the glen to look up through the surface of the loch on the other side of Géarán Tuathail. I've enchanted my arrow to never miss a mark, no matter the distance. And I've used the briocht charm to keep a blade from ever dulling—though that one was taught to me." He unsheathed his belt-knife and held it out for the ollamh to inspect. The iron blade glistened sharply, its edge shining as if dipped in golden oil. But it was not oil—it was a subtle sheen of enchantment.

"I see." The ollamh paused and lifted his tufted brows. "Well then... Áedán... you know the risks of aistriú cruth. Do you accept the risks? Do you still wish to proceed?"

Áedán's heart leapt to his throat and he nodded vigorously.

"Then, I give you my approval. I will prepare you to perform the aistriú cruth."

Áedán gave out a little squeal of joy. He covered his mouth, embarrassed, and nodded seriously. The master chuckled.

"We will start with the lower level skills that prepare you for total transformation. First, you will learn to transform less-animate things into other less-animate things. From there you will practice applying the glamour, temporarily changing your face to take on the features of another. And if you master these, I will explain to you the proper procedure for changing your shape entirely, and permanently. I hope you will be prepared by Lá Lethach, for the equinoxes are the most appropriate times to perform an aistriú cruth of this magnitude. If you are unprepared by Lá Lethach, then you must wait another six months until the spring." The ollamh stood. "We will start tomorrow. Be ready at dawn, for transformations are easiest to perform in twilight."

Áedán laid his head upon the ollamh's chest in gratitude. When the man was out of sight, the boy turned and ran through the forest, whooping and yipping like a hound for the hare.

CHAPTER THIRTEEN

The Well and the Ring

In the still dark of morning Áedán followed Máel Conall into the forest. They came to the edge of a steep cliff, below it a tumble of scree. Áedán stood at its edge to look out over the range. Dawn lifted night's shadows and made the mountain's eastern cheeks blush pink. Low-laying clouds filled the valleys like a swell of the sea, making islands of mountain peaks. Down wooded paths they moved through mist as if swimming; to see the placement of his feet the ollamh cut through the curtains of fog with a charm and a swing of his staff. Soon they came to an open air shelter fashioned from bark and living saplings, and sat there beneath a bower of twisting vines. A stone basin of rain water was between them. The wood was raucous with birdsong.

The ollamh spoke, gazing into the basin. "Water is the easiest element to transform, for it transforms itself often. We will begin by singing water into ice and back again into liquid. But first we ask permission." Máel Conall put his hands on either side of the bowl. "Sacred water, do we have your permission to work with you today, with care and respect?"

The water was still and unchanging.

"That is well. It does not object."

"How would you know if it objects?" asked Áedán.

"The signs would be clear. You might hear it in the sudden scolding of a raven or in a cold gust of wind at your face. Or the water itself might ripple without perturbation. Or you might accidentally spill it without meaning to. We must always ask permission before making these transformations, for everything in Nature is alive and has its own will. To ignore their wishes, to clumsily trample through the world without regard for the sentience all around us, will bring bad luck and impede our magic. Do you understand?"

Áedán nodded solemnly. The path of his life had already taught him the truth of this point.

"Good," said Máel Conall. "Now, when we cause the transformation of things by magic, it is not that we *force* the elements to change or that we bend them to our will, but instead we lend them the power to change themselves, if they so choose. All things can become anything else in the Universe. Transmutation is a common occurrence in Nature, though it happens most often involuntarily and unconsciously. Most creatures, humanity included, forget that we have the ability to control this power, yet the Síd never forget it. It is said that we relearned this power from them, many ages ago." The older man shifted his weight to sit more comfortably. "Now I will show you. Pay close attention."

The ollamh leaned in close to the surface of the water so that his breath touched the shimmering plane. He began to chant with liquid rhythm:

Free flowing   the living liquid
Running maketh   life luscious,
Round ripples,   drops attract,
Edges softened,   streams unstaunched.

Cold occludes	topmost motion,
Slick and rigid	that ring of crystal,
Shards shining	as bones are broken,
Perfect prism	fuse parts unfree.

Áedán gasped. The surface of the water tightened like a tanned hide, becoming a clear sheet of crystalline ice. Máel Conall inhaled deeply and sat upright.

"The transformation of water into ice is best learned before any other, because if your knowledge of the reversal fails, it will inevitably melt and come back to its original form on its own."

Máel Conall leaned forward again and in a single breath, sang: "To thee return the flowing form." The ice softened and was water once more.

"In general," the ollamh continued in a professorial tone, "it is easier to bring a substance back to its original form, as long as the transformation has not held for too long. All transformations must be undone in order to maintain the delicate balance of forces and forms in the Universe. Or else, if a change is to be made permanent, a sacrifice must be given to compensate Nature for the disturbance. Even if we were to make a small permanent change, such as a pebble to a gem, there must be compensation in sacrifice. And if the sacrifice is inadequate, the change may eventually fail and the thing may revert to its original form. For the largest transformations, such as changing the course of a river or the shape of a mountain, the transformation needs to be perpetually 'fed' with regular sacrifices. But those spells are very rarely done anymore, as the work to maintain them is enormous. They are considered quite disruptive to the balance, to Cóir, and inasmuch may have unintended negative consequences."

"Such as?"

"Such as plagues. Droughts. Flooding. Spontaneous mutations or transformations of plants or animals nearby. You see, it is one of the greatest weaknesses of humanity that we have more power to shape the world than we have wisdom to understand or control the consequences. Thus, the wisest of the druíd are the most prudent and judicious of all, for they have attained the highest insight: knowing how little we are capable of knowing."

"But can't you study the world in great enough detail that you might predict the consequences of any action?" Áedán asked.

"There is a limit to what we humans can know or predict with the rational learned mind. The intuitive mind can occasionally transcend the bounded knowledge of rationality, yet intuition is spontaneous. Mastery of the draíochta druadh hones the intuitive faculty, but it can never be fully controlled. So it is safest to do only what *must* be done, in order to cause the fewest unintended consequences." Máel Conall frowned at the incredulity in Áedán's face. "I see this limitation troubles you. But you are young. In time you will come to understand the wisdom in this constraint, or else it will cut you down like an ax to an elm."

Máel Conall paused to emphasize the point, then continued. "Certain transformations unbalance the world more than others, and so we avoid those. In general, transformations are to be done only within the tribe of one's natural form: plant to plant, bird to bird, beast to beast, mineral to mineral. Only humans, or Síd, can develop the skills to transform ourselves outside of our natural tribes. But this is more difficult and more dangerous."

Áedán considered this carefully. "So if we gain consent from a being, we may transform it how it wishes?"

"Yes."

"Then can you not transform me into the form that *I* wish? Why must I turn *myself* into a man? Can't you just do it for me if I ask?"

"I might, but I will not. I cannot know your unspoken desires nor what needs you have hidden away in places that you do not acknowledge. If I did it, I would risk transforming you into the form that *I* wish for you, not the one that you wish for yourself. It could make you unhappy, or it could harm you. Better that you take on the responsibility for yourself."

Áedán nodded, disappointed. *But I suppose I wish to know the aistriú cruth regardless, even if it is harder this way,* he thought. "And what of things like fire? When we burn wood to ashes, are we not then transforming wood without its consent?"

"Ah, that is a good question. No, it is not the same. Fire has its own will. It is not our creation, though we can tend it as stewards. It is the fire itself that is transforming the wood, not us. Fire is a primordial force—it wields its own magic. Though we do not create this force, we are responsible to steward it wisely, so that it does not get out of control. All people hold this responsibility, not just the druíd. And just as fire transforms wood or peat, we animals transform the food we eat into energy and excrement by the juices of our digestion. Both are processes of Nature maintaining itself."

"But the human will... is it not also a natural process then?"

Máel Conall sighed and stroked his beard. "It is a subject of much debate. The human will is... mysterious. Some believe that unlike the actions taken by the rest of Nature, humanity can will things into being that are detrimental to Cóir. Our intelligence gives us power, and yet we are not quite as intelligent as we believe. Power wielded in ignorance is a danger to life. Yet, other scholars are of the opinion that non-human sentients may also take actions that imbalance the world. Even great storms, earthquakes, or fires can cause terrible and widespread harm. But to my mind, one's motivations make the difference. Conscious intention to do harm, with disregard for the impacts on other sentient beings, is unnatural and unique to humanity. This is why it is so important that the filid lead society—to guide humanity towards judicious action, and to cultivate and spread the seeds of great wisdom. The filid bear the responsibility of protecting the sanctity of the world from the ignorance of our kind."

The ollamh paused, gazing long into the boy's face. He let these truths settle in Áedán's mind. Then he cleared his throat and gestured at the basin of water. "Now you try."

Áedán deepened his breath and focused his mind on the image of water turning to ice. He leaned forward, letting his breath push the poem across the surface of the water, as Máel Conall had. In silence he sat for one, two, three heartbeats. Nothing happened.

"Your voice must start higher and end lower. And in each line the sounds must change from fluid to solid. Like this..." The ollamh demonstrated and the water changed into ice once more. He released the enchantment and nodded at the boy. "Again. And remember to use your meabhrú dírithe and sruth anáil. You must have total mental focus and control of your breath. There should be only one thought in your mind."

Máel Conall had made it look easy, but it was not. The intonation had to be precise, the rhythm perfect. After many tries Áedán finally watched a single shard of ice form across the basin. He whooped in delight.

"Do not celebrate prematurely," said Máel Conall. "Success is a wholly sold basin."

Áedán hung his head and tried again. It was ten, twenty, thirty tries before the basin was entirely ice from rim to rim, top to bottom.

"Good. Now undo the change."

Though the return of the ice to water was easier, it was not easy. When finally the water was again fluid in full, Máel Conall smiled and said: "Very good. Now practice until I come back. When you can do this perfectly every time, when it becomes as effortless as whistling, we may move on to the next task."

The ollamh left Áedán to practice on his own. He worked at it all day, and by supper returned to Lí Lon with heavy limbs and lids. She forced him to take a few morsels of stew before he crept away, collapsed onto his bed, and fell instantly asleep.

Áedán practiced all the next day, and again the next. It was the most difficult skill of draíochta druadh he had attempted thus far. At last, by the end of the third day he sung the water into ice as easily as whistling.

Máel Conall was pleased. Over the next several weeks, the ollamh put to the boy challenges of increasing difficulty. He learned to sing iron into gold, and back again. With his voice he changed deadwood into a carved spoon, and back again. He turned bracken into silverweed, and back again. He caused an apple pip to take root and trunk and fruit, growing ten years' height in a single morning. The more profound the transformation, the more complex the spellwork. Áedán came to understand that each transmutation was described in the way that the subject itself would understand through experience. The choice of syllable and rhythm and timbre of the voice must prove an intimate knowledge of the subject's nature. He remarked upon this to Máel Conall, and his master nodded.

"It is so. A transformation can only be done when the druí knows deeply the nature of both the original form and the assumed form. It is easy enough to transform rocks and wood and apple trees—you already know them well for they are common in your daily life. It is harder to become a beast, for you must know the hungers and hatreds, loves and longings of the animal itself. Such knowledge is obtained only by friendship. So when a fili takes an animal form, it is common to start with a hound or a ram or a horse with whom we are most familiar. Becoming a wild beast is more rare, for they are harder to build trust with."

"But you... you can transform into a crane, like the one that is your familiar." Áedán longed to know if the rumors were true.

Máel Conall lifted a brow, and grinned at the boy with a twinkle. "So, you believe that then?" He inclined his head. "What Sengbrága has shared with me through friendship has allowed me to take her shape, and so we fly together. It is a superior way of travel, I must say."

Áedán was awestruck and imagined himself soaring high above the cliffs. What a pleasure it would be to hover on the wind, to be lifted up only by the strength of his feathers. He reeled, stomach clenched with a sudden fear of the height, and brought his thoughts back down to the solid earth.

"Know this, Áedán," the ollamh said seriously. "The longer you reside in the form of another animal, the harder it becomes to remember the way back to your original form. The mind can recall its humanness for a little while, yet over time the consciousness of the animal form overwhelms the memory of the human one. The fili must remember the poem that brings him back to humanity, and if that is forgotten... the transformation may be permanent. This is not of concern to you presently, as you are just now preparing to make a one-way transition. But when you are a master and able to transform yourself into any form that you wish, remember what I have said."

Áedán nodded, noting the gravity in the master's words.

Many weeks passed in this practice. When the lower level transformations had been mastered, Áedán learned to transform parts of his own body. He transformed his hands to take the shape of Máel Conall's, which ached with the ollamh's rheumatism. He changed the color of his hair to brown and black and blonde and back. He wore glamours of the face, gazing at the world through the eyes of Máel Conall, Lí Lon, Síthmaith, and Cadrolón. From the gaze of each face the world had a different seeming. It was not just the shape that was changed, but the quality of his perception, too—his sight and smell and hearing were attracted to things that he normally overlooked.

Wearing Lí Lon's eyes in particular was revelatory. Four years had passed since she had taken the title of muimme. Little by little, Áedán had learned to trust her. Though she was sometimes cold, and sometimes stern, she had never harmed him, not with word nor deed. Yet still he was wary, for some nights he dreamed of searing iron and his birth mother's hateful command: *You will leave now and never return!*

Taking the shape of his foster-mother's eyes, Áedán trekked up to the loch alone. Kneeling by the water's edge, he stared at his own reflection.

"What do you see in me, Muimme?" he whispered. The image of his face stared back at him. But it was changed: he seemed unusually handsome, almost elfin—childlike, innocent, and keen. Áedán touched his face and smiled with disarming charm.

"She sees no shade in me—in fact, she sees me brighter than I see myself!" He sighed with relief and resolution. "I shall fear her no more, for she has no fear of me." Áedán let the glamour fall from his face and walked down the mountainside with a humming heart.

That summer he was single minded, neglecting his other studies to practice the aistriú cruth. He practiced from twilight to twilight, all the time growing more proficient until he could perform every change easily, without a second thought. As the days grew shorter and the nights longer, Áedán's excitement built up so high that some nights he forewent sleep. In less than a week the days and nights would be equal in length. Uncertain hope he held that his master would deem him ready to attempt the total and permanent transformation of his body.

A shower of warm rain drummed loud upon the oak leaves as Áedán walked out from the wood, his green hood draped over his head. Máel Conall met him under the dry shelter of a fir tree to speak in private.

"Lá Lethach will soon be upon us, Áedán. You've worked very hard and learned many aspects of the aistriú cruth in a short time. You've demonstrated not just commitment, but skill too. And so, I've made my decision." He paused. Áedán held his breath. "I believe you are ready for the final transformation."

Áedán was nearly lifted off the ground with elation. "Thank you, Máel Conall. I am honored by your confidence and grateful beyond words for your careful instruction."

Máel Conall nodded. "Now, in two days time we will begin the ritual. On yonder mountain you will fast for three days alone at the sacred well, composing the poem that will shape you anew. There is yet no spell for what you will attempt—it must be of your own making for only you can know what you will become. At dawn on Lá Lethach, when light and dark are perfectly paired, Lí Lon and I will come to you at the Well and witness your rebirth."

The day had finally arrived when Áedán would begin his fast. That night anticipation had prevented sleep, and when Máel Conall stepped out into the morning dew he found Áedán sitting by the door in meditation. The boy launched to his feet like a flushed grouse and chirped a breathless greeting.

Master and disciple took up their cloaks and made their way in silence. They took a trail Áedán had not traveled before. It went west over a low ridge, across a rocky valley, and up another steep slope. On the other side of this ridge they came to a highland plateau, and rested a while under the shade of a holly tree.

Áedán looked at the clouds, the mountains, the stones, the ferns, and thought to himself: *This is the last time I will ever see these things through the eyes of a child.* This he mused with equal hope and trepidation.

It was late morning when they came at last to the edge of a viridescent glade. The ground was covered all in a moss so luminous it seemed to glow of its own accord. The filid stepped out from the shade onto the soft and springy ground and went to the center of the glade. There stood an ancient well, its waters as old as the first rains ever to fall on Ériu. A silence hung about the pool like a gossamer veil. Even the songbirds were too humbled to lift their voices in this hallowed place. The Well was encircled by a ring of thirteen standing stones.

Máel Conall's voice broke through the eerie hush, causing Áedán to jump. "You will stay within the standing stones until I come back for you, three dawns from today. You are to consume nothing but the water from this well. But be careful: do not linger by its edge nor watch the reflections in its surface." Áedán glanced sideways at the ollamh, but no further explanation was given. "Use this time to contemplate your life, Áedán. Who do you wish to be? Envision every aspect of the person you will become. Explore every corner of your soul. Leave nothing uncovered or unacknowledged. Witness yourself in the nakedness of your full truth. Be ready to leave the child behind, so that the man can be born.

"When you have sculpted in your mind the shape of your future self, compose then the incantation for the shape-shifting. It will be your first masterpiece. All your knowledge and all your skill will be woven into the fabric of this poem. Practice it in silence, for it can be spoken only once—upon its execution.

"And there is one more thing you must contemplate in this silence, Áedán." The ollamh paused and looked the boy hard in the eye. "What will you sacrifice to make the transformation lasting? It must be a precious thing, a thing that will cause pain to part with. What you give up must be equal in value to what you will gain."

Máel Conall paused and placed his hand on the boy's shoulder. "You must go deeper into yourself than you've ever gone before. There you may find things you wish not to see; but you must not look away from them if you wish to achieve self-knowledge. And it is only through self-knowledge that can we attain true power. I have faith you will succeed."

The master stepped outside the ring of stone and left the boy alone in that glittering green glade.

Three days and three nights Áedán spent beside the Well, in rest, in trance, and in dream upon the mossy ground. No breeze blew within the ring; no bird nor bee disturbed the still air. At first the quiet was eerie, otherworldly. Yet soon he found a comfort in it, for here was such a peace that no reverie, no rumination could ever be broken. The silence suspended him in the deepest meditation, his focus unmoved but for the needs to drink and doze. Here upon the ridge of Mumu's highest peak, far away from human society, encircled only by trees, Áedán had no concern for his safety. It was strange: he felt no threat from the hungers of the wild world, though he was exposed on every side and unguarded by wall or weapon. Yet he felt protected by unseen hands. Neither did he feel an eye land upon his back, and so he wondered if the place was hidden from sight. It was not uncommon for a mystical place such as this to remain unseen by those who were not deliberately looking for it.

Hunger had become a stranger to Áedán these past four years of scholarly life, and the pangs were a distraction for the first night and day. *I've become too soft*, he scolded himself, and resettled his focus. On the second day the hunger subsided and his body felt lighter, unburdened from the work of digestion; his mind became sharper and clearer.

It had been many years since he had slept alone in the wood, and now Áedán remembered why it was so cherished. In solitude there was perfect freedom. It would always be a way open to him, a way to escape, if the human world should again turn against him.

Night fell. He laid his head down upon the mattress of moss, his cloak wrapped tightly about his shoulders. He dared not light a fire in this hallowed place and there was no firewood in the ring anyway. On his side he lay looking at the Well. Even in the dark the pool could be seen, for its water was like a shadow within a shadow. Every wan ray of light from the stars and the waxing moon was drawn to it and doused in its depths. No raven wing, no cavernous keep, no moonless night was as black as that black. This contemplation was no comfort. The boy prayed for his soul's protection and drifted on the ebb of sleep's tide towards dream.

Áedán crawled forward and dove into the ink-dark well. Sinking low, he swam forward to where the waters became shallow, then waded onto the shore of a fair, bright land. The beach sloped up to a grassy hillock speckled with yellow and pink and purple flowers he had never seen before. It was high summer here, the sky was warm and clear. The wind made waves in the grasses like a gently rolling sea. "These must be the fields that horses come to when they dream," he said.

The boy went walking and came to a vast orchard. There he spied a party of maidens elegantly dressed, their raiment as fine as if woven from spider's silk. Upon their fingers and ears were rings and trinkets of gold and silver. The maidens laughed and teased each other as they plucked apples from the trees, laying them in baskets made of glistening black raven feathers.

One of them spied Áedán and called to him a greeting. As he approached, she said to him: "Young man, will you climb up to the top of this tree and bring to us that apple on the tallest branch? That one we cannot reach."

Áedán happily agreed and began climbing. But the higher he climbed, the taller the branch seemed to grow. He thought to shake the apple loose from the branch. But no matter how hard he whipped the branch back and forth, the apple clung there. At last it came to him that the only way to claim it was to ask. So Áedán politely requested the tree drop the apple into his outstretched hand. Right away the apple dropped and he caught it. Áedán deftly climbed down and landed beside the maidens with a flourish and a wink.

They giggled with delight. One of them approached and put out her hand. Her face was familiar to him—she had raven hair and crystalline grey eyes and brows as straight as arrows. He put the apple in her hand. She brought the fruit to her scarlet lips, hiding a coy smile, and took a bite with the perfect pearls of her teeth.

He was hungry. His stomach growled as he caught the fragrance of that apple's juice. Reaching forward, he beckoned her to give him a taste. She placed the apple in his hand and he raised it to his mouth.

Suddenly, the maiden grasped his wrist with a strength like a smith's. Áedán gasped in shock and pain, reeling backwards.

Áedán awoke to the shrill alarm of a wren. The boy was back again in the mossy glen inside the ring of stones.

CHAPTER FOURTEEN

Sinnach

On the third morning of his fast, Áedán emerged from sleep into a state unlike normal waking. He felt almost entranced. It was as if his body were made of greenwood and his toes and fingers were roots. It took great effort to stand and walk, and when he did so it was very slowly, every footstep requiring immense effort and forethought. Though his body was dense and wooden, his mind was airy, as if alight on a wisp of cloud. The glen before him sparkled as if bejeweled. Every stone and leaf and flower disk seemed to pulse with a subtle light, an energy he could sense but not quite see.

He shuffled forward and knelt at the lip of the Well. Dipping his cupped hands into the frigid water, he took a drink. It was thicker, darker, colder than before. He saw something in it he had not noticed before: the water's surface boiled subtly as if from an upwelling at the world's core. It shimmered enticingly. He drew closer to watch. *What lay at the other end of this well so deep?* Áedán wondered.

And then he shivered and tore his gaze away, remembering Máel Conall's warning not to look too long at the surface of the pool.

He closed his eyes and filled his belly with the sweet water. Though the liquid seemed dark in the Well it was mysteriously clear in his hands. As the water passed through his lips, his mind quieted again. Creeping backward, he sat again upon the mossy throne of his meditation and was submerged in a most profound inner silence.

It was then that words spontaneously arose in his mind, from the depths of the Well of the Segas. Every one of them held a lightning-shock of power—of Imbas. These words he wove together like fine filaments of spider's silk, interlacing sentence and sound to shape the poem that would transform his life forever.

Dawn lifted its dusky veil in the twilight of the fourth day of his fasting. The light was grey and soft as down; the woodland was spangled with dew. The youth's face was still and stony. He had sat upright through the night, suspended in a state between waking and dreaming, a poem recited again and again in his mind.

The was a soft sound at the edge of the glen, of two pairs of feet padding through moss. The youth opened his eyes, slow as an unfurling of flax flowers. He could not remember the last time he had seen anything with his waking eyes. It must have been the night before, many centuries ago. In the depths of his meditation, he had lost all sense of the passage of time.

Máel Conall and Lí Lon, the two esteemed filid of Géarán Tuathail, stood before him. The outlines of their shapes seemed strange, and then he realized why: each wore a cloak made of hundreds of feathers of every color. In Máel Conall's hand was a staff of red yew; in Lí Lon's hand was a staff of holly wood.

"Are you ready, Áedán? Are you prepared for the transformation?" asked Máel Conall, his voice low and husky.

Overwhelmed with feeling, Áedán could only nod. Lí Lon smiled down at him with a mother's pride and a mother's concern.

"Have you composed the poem for the aistriú cruth?" she asked. Again, Áedán nodded.

"Then there is one last thing you must do." Máel Conall knelt to look the boy in the eye. "You must offer your sacrifice to the Well, the sacrifice that will act as compensation to the Universe for the change you wish to perform. Give it now; speak your oath."

Áedán closed his eyes again and sighed. He had made his decision and he was saddened by it, yet by his grief he knew it would be a powerful enough sacrifice.

"I give to thee, O Sacred Well, this sacrifice for my transformation. I give to thee my bow and quiver. Never again shall I take up the bow, nor hunt by the flight of an arrow." His words hovered in the still air of the glade like leaves suspended on the wind.

There was a sudden small splashing sound. Water lapped up from the Well's dark surface and wetted the ground at its edge.

Máel Conall spoke with surprise. "The Well indicates this is not enough—the sacrifice is not sufficient." The ollamh examined the boy's face. "I see there is something else... something you have left unspoken."

Áedán's heart quaked, for there was indeed something he had not said. He had hoped it would not need to be said. Over the course of his fast he had considered everything he owned, and what of those things he could part with. The list was short. His bow was certainly the most precious object among them. And yet, in his meditations, he had realized there was a thing he treasured even more, though he could not he be held in his hands. It was as basic to his being as the rhythm of his breath and the beating of his heart—a thing nearly unthinkable to give up. And yet, he knew he must.

What you give up must be equal in value to what you will gain.

"I also sacrifice..." The words caught in his throat. "I sacrifice my solitude and my isolation." And then it was said and could not be unsaid. The youth made a single sob then choked it back, girding himself to grieve.

The three of them gazed at the Well. Its waters were still.

"The Well has accepted your sacrifices," said Lí Lon. "If you succeed in the transformation, the oaths you have given will be your geasa. A geas is a sacred prohibition, simultaneously a promise and a curse. If you should violate your geasa, your life will be in danger and your transformation will be undone. Do you understand? Do you accept?"

Áedán hesitated, then gave a slow nod. "Yes, I understand and accept." The oath was sealed.

Lí Lon crouched down and whispered into his ear. "Do not be troubled, my son. I have a geas too, laid upon me when I made *my* sacrifice. Honor it and you will be safe, as I have been."

Then the two ollamh stepped away from Áedán and prepared the ritual. There was a low stone altar at the other side of the Well whereupon they laid fruits and grain in offering. They lit there a bundle of juniper. The scent of the juniper was invigorating and drove away Áedán's fasting fatigue. Then the ollamh lifted their open palms and recited the songs that welcomed the directions, circling sunwise around the inside of the ring. When they returned again to the eastern point, the first golden rays of dawn touched the surface of the Well.

"Speak now the spell," said Máel Conall.

Áedán knelt by the lip of that shadow-dark pool and placed the fingertips of his right hand into the water. The other hand he placed firmly upon the earth, palm down. Into the mirror-surface of the pool he gazed, shifting the pattern of his breath to invoke the Imbas. Something bubbled up from deep inside him, filling his mouth with a liquid power. With focused rhythm and singular vision, he spoke the words of incantation:

> From female   being begins
> Growth in darkness   girdeth the infant,
> Slick sided   we do erupt,
> Where two choices   I choose the other.

In seed sleepeth   shapes dormant,
For fertile fruiting   two halves unite,
But before budding   the world not dual,
To fork of branches   I do return.

My shape untwists   untwines, unfurls,
Reweave the pattern   my flesh forgot,
The moon's shadow   I cast aside
My sun not shaded   does shine brightly.

Trade tender softness   for tensile sinew,
Cease my bleeding   my waxing, waning,
Give up the chalice   that brews life inside,
Take up the phallus   that fills the vessel.

Strong as sapling   hard as staghorn,
Voice of mountain   grinding gravel,
Eye-flash of eagle   sleekness of salmon,
Lithe and learned,   this male I am made.

As he spoke, Áedán felt every part of him vibrate, every bone and organ and point on the skin, softly at first, then increasing in amplitude. It was like a humming from inside that radiated outward with an unseen light. With every word the sensation slowly built until it became unbearable, excruciating—an entanglement of both pain and pleasure. The energy approached a climax; he tried to hold it back until the last word left his lips. Rigid, shaking, he struggled to keep control. Áedán fixed his gaze upon the surface of the Well, desperately clinging to sanity.

A shimmer appeared upon the water. Áedán bent closer to look. Again he saw the shimmer; it seemed to have a shape. He bent closer. Again, there was a shimmer; it was, perhaps, a face. He bent closer, his nose nearly touching the liquid plane. And then he saw it clearly: it was the reflection of his own face. And yet, it was not.

In that moment he was simultaneously pulled and pushed and with a splash fell down into the Well.

Áedán sputtered and flailed and kicked but he could not find the surface. Though he swam with thrashing arms and legs he only sank further into the darkness. He hoped that if he sank to the bottom he could push up from the rocks, but he never reached the bottom. How could the Well be so vast and so deep? And where were the walls?

He was quickly losing air. Fear took over and he lost all control of himself. Then he knew: he would die here in this lightless place, consumed by the waters that were supposed to heal him.

But had he not come from this place in the beginning? Was this not simply a return to his place of origin?

Áedán did not know where those thoughts came from, but he found a profound peace in them and his spirit was quieted. All that ever was came from this place. All that ever would be came from this place. The edges of himself began to blur; his senses diffused into the darkness around him. He felt expansive and huge, covering the whole breadth of the ocean and the sky at once. There were no boundaries. There was nothing that he was not.

In this union he felt held and comforted and loved, profoundly himself and everything else. He was relaxed now, floating breathless, in complete surrender. Death may come to me now, *he thought,* and yet nothing much will change. Oh, what a small life I have lived, full of little struggles and little sorrows! *He laughed at himself with humility and love, then prepared to release his final breath.*

There was a streak of color, orange and red like the setting sun. It had a shape. A figure. Without sight Áedán beheld a vision of a fox. The fox stopped and watched him through amber eyes. Then she turned and trotted off into the darkness. Again she paused and looked back to see if he would follow.

Her suggestion was clear, and yet he was hesitant. There was peace here in the darkness; there was safety. No struggle; no discomfort. Perfect contentment. It would be painful to leave. And yet, she waited. There were things yet to be done on that terrible, beautiful, bewildering plain called Life. Curious, he followed after her.

Hands gripped him by the shoulders and pulled him up from the water. Cold air hit his face with a shock. Gasping, sputtering, he cried aloud and quivered like a chick burst out of the shell. He was laid on the ground and a cloak was wrapped around him.

As he laid there, catching his breath, and felt once more the heft and heave of a body. His body. He was bounded again by skin. The air was sweet and soothing as he sucked it down in great gulps. Life bid him take it, and he accepted, knowing then that every breath was the Goddess's gift to him. This gift he could not refuse. He felt Life like a rushing river coursing through his veins. What a mysterious force, this 'Life'. He had lost and regained it, but still did not understand it. And yet he loved it all the more.

For a long time he simply laid there, breathing, overwhelmed by the tumult of sensations in his body. He laughed, remembering that once, long ago, in another lifetime, he had thought breathing a simple, trivial task.

"What is your name, my son?" aked a voice in the dark. It had a music to it, like the low cooing of a wood dove. It was new to him, and yet it seemed familiar.

He coughed, opened his eyes, and spoke his first words: "An sinnach!" he said. *The fox!* He lifted a trembling arm and pointed towards the water. He wished to tell the voice about the fox who had led him back to the land of the living, yet he only had strength enough for that one word. "Sinnach!"

"Your name is Sinnach?" From above the voice spoke again. A face hovered there, and he recognized it. It was the face of his foster-mother, Lí Lon.

He shook his head. No, that was not his name. *My name is...* He paused. *Why, I can't remember! Who was I before I was born?* And then he was glad that he could not recall, for he was different now. Someone else entirely. *Sinnach is a good name,* he thought. *I will take it.* He looked up at his mother and nodded.

Another face, the face of an older man, came into view. The young man recognized this face, too. "Welcome, Sinnach. Stand up. You are a man now."

Sinnach moved slowly as if floating through a dream. He stood on shaking limbs like a newborn lamb. He felt curiously unburdened, as if an enormous weight was lifted from his shoulders, a weight he had been carrying all his life and yet now only recognized it by its absence. *From what have I been unburdened?* he asked silently.

The rub of the woolen cloak itched him and he realized he was naked underneath. For a moment he was confused. Then he gasped as his memories flooded back to him; he recalled why he had first come to the Well. Slowly, he brought his hands to his face. Drawing his fingers downward from his nose to his chin, he felt there a little whiskery stubble. He held his breath and let his hands drift from his neck down to his chest, now flat and muscular. He felt between his legs. He felt every inch of his body, from the crown of his head to the soles of his bare feet, then cried out in jubilation. The spell had worked: he was a man now, not just in spirit, but in body too.

He launched into the air and bucked like a spring colt. Turning to his masters, he embraced them and kissed each of their cheeks, then peeled off again yipping and frolicking like a wild thing.

"Thank you! Thank you! Thank you!" He called out in every direction, to every element, delirious with joy. And then he ran. Barefoot and naked, his long wet hair streaming behind, he sprung like a stag through the sunlit wood. He bounded and spun and swung from tree limbs, testing the limits of his newfound vigor.

But soon his energy faded, for he had not eaten in many days. His gallop slowed to a jog, then to a walk, and then he stopped and collapsed to his knees, panting.

Sinnach heard the footsteps of the ollamhna approaching from behind. "I told you he wouldn't get very far," laughed Máel Conall. He reached under the young man's arm. "Up you get now!" The ollamhna lifted the young man up between them, wrapped him again in the fallen cloak, and led him over the mountainside towards home.

PART III:

SINNACH

CHAPTER FIFTEEN

The Responsibilities of a Fili

The autumn fruits were sweeter, the height of noon was brighter, the moon shone more silver, and the stars twinkled with more charm than Sinnach had ever known before. Reborn, all of life around him was rousing and radiant. He filled his days with all the things he had previously been deprived of: swimming naked in the loch; wrestling and racing; joking and jest; and the juvenile gossip of young men about women, mischief, and the surprises of puberty.

Uneclipsed, Sinnach beamed with the full brilliance endowed to him by the sun. Before his transformation he had spent many days sullen, caught up in a melancholy mood that muddied his thoughts and darkened his poetry. Now all that sorrow was gone and so his art was brighter, sharper, as if suddenly in focus after many years of seeing through teary eyes. It was not just his soul that was stronger but his body too, for he seemed to have twice the energy and twice the might in his limbs as before.

"Ah!" he exclaimed, "this is what it must feel like to be normal!"

At first Lí Lon was happy for her son and was uplifted by his exuberance. But as the weeks passed by, her patience wore thin, for now he was impetuous and even insolent at times. Once so sober and studious, Áedán now neglected his chores and studies to cavort with his friends.

"Sinnach, stop this silliness at once," scolded Lí Lon. "You are not a child any longer! Give more care to your duties."

But the youth only scoffed and said: "Yes, yes. I will study more when winter comes. But for now while the air is still warm, let me be young!"

October came, the wind blew hard and chill again, yet Sinnach did not shift his focus from merriment. Lí Lon voiced her concerns to Máel Conall.

"Sinnach has been vexing me of late," she said frowning. "Since his transformation he's been distracted and neglectful of his work. He's irresponsible and disrespectful, impulsive and selfish and vain. He's not himself."

Máel Conall smiled at his foster-daughter. "Or maybe he is more himself than ever before, and only now are we able to witness him in his full form?" He smirked. "But really, I think it is just a phase—he is coming to understand his new body. It is a second puberty, of sorts. Though you find it repugnant, it is the normal kind of idiocy we should expect from a pubescent boy. He'll grow out of it. You'll see." He stroked his beard. "In truth it was not so different for you. You had your own... irrational period after your transformation. Though yours consisted of stormy moods and flirtations and secret trysts at midnight."

Lí Lon gaped in horror. "Aite!" she exclaimed, blushing with embarrassment. How had he known about her midnight trysts?

Máel Conall slapped his knees and doubled over with laughter. Wiping tears from his eyes he said: "You forget that cranes have better night vision than men do. Though I assure you, I saw very little. I only wanted to know that you were safe."

Lí Lon covered her face with her hands, mortified. Máel Conall chuckled. "And now you're at the other end of the bargain. As one parent to another, I advise you to have patience. Though, I would advise a bit more sternness. Young men need more direction than young women do."

It was two days until Samhain, and though the weather had grown cold Sinnach often goaded the other boys into swimming in the frigid loch with him. Cadrolón was similarly hot blooded and so he came; several others joined in as well. Though Sinnach was shorter, he and Cadrolón were matched in strength and made a good pair for wrestling.

The moon had waxed and waned and waxed again since Sinnach's transformation, and the other boys were still growing used to his sudden change of name and character. Some found it shocking; some shrugged it off as a sudden, late onset of puberty; still others wondered if there was a supernatural explanation. It was not uncommon to witness strange feats and miracles at the school of the filid, so there was little cause to contest this one.

Yet there were three young men who wished to find fault in it; the same three who had taunted Sinnach before. On that chilly autumn afternoon they came to the loch with the rest. As Sinnach and his friends stripped off their clothes to swim, Énán, the most morose of the three, approached Sinnach with a sneer.

"You there, Vixen, or whatever you call yourself. Why the sudden love of the nude?" Énán pointed his chin at the nakedness between Sinnach's legs. "If you're looking to show off, I can assure you—you're not in the running for *that* contest." Énán's companions chuckled. "I find it all quite suspicious, this sudden transformation. What magic is at work? And if you wish to call yourself a fox, well, I hate to inform you, but your tiny tail is on the wrong side!"

Every boy howled with laughter. Énán scanned the crowd with a surly expression. His eyes caught Cadrolón, who had not pulled off his trousers—the young man always kept his lower half covered at the loch. "Or perhaps it wasn't shape shifting at all but theft," said Énán. He pointed at Sinnach and shouted: "Oy, Cadrolón! There he is—the one who's snatched your eireaball tosaigh!"

Again the flock of boys cackled in delight; all, of course, except Sinnach and Cadrolón. Cadrolón stepped forward white-knuckled with rage, but Sinnach placed a cool hand on his friend's chest and pushed him back.

"You've got a sharp tongue in your head, little cano. Beware you don't cut yourself with it," said Sinnach baring his teeth. "I might indulge in a duel of words with you, if you'd yet reached my rank. But you're only a cano and have no knowledge of satire—isn't that right?" Sinnach smiled smugly. "Well then, why don't we duel in the common way—by feats of strength? Or perhaps you are too delicate for that."

The crowd of boys gathered round and jeered, hoping to watch a good grapple. Énán regarded Sinnach warily. The red-haired youth was now equal to him in height and strength; it would not be as easy a victory as it might have been before, yet he was too proud to back down from the challenge.

"Nothing would give me greater pleasure than to throw you to the ground," said Énán, and he stripped off his clothes. The onlookers made a ring around the challengers and whooped boisterously.

"Whoever touches the loch first is the loser," said Sinnach. He tied up his hair so it would not be pulled, and held out his arms in the ready position.

Énán did the same, then Cadrolón called out sharply: "Fight!"

Sinnach and Énán circled each other like two rutting stags, then engaged. Clinging to one another, grabbing arms and legs, each boy tried to trip the other up or push him to the edge of the water. They were evenly matched. The crowd joked and jostled as the fight went on.

Then shoulder to shoulder, Énán heard Sinnach whisper something.

"What did you say?" Énán panted.

Sinnach pulled his head back to look at Énán and repeated in mockery: "What did you say?"

But Sinnach did not speak with his own voice. He did not speak with his own face. Énán balked as he heard the voice and stared into the face... of himself.

Énán's shock in that moment gave Sinnach a small window of opportunity. Taking the advantage, he lifted Énán up by the waist and with a splash threw him into the loch.

The crowd cheered and slapped Sinnach on the back in congratulations. Énán raised his head up from the water, as churlish as ever, and shouted: "He cheated! He used magic! He wore a glamour of my face!" Énán waded onto shore.

"Me? But I'm only a clí!" Sinnach said innocently. He put his hands to his face. "Feels normal to me. Lads, do I look uglier than usual?"

The boys laughed. Énán growled in frustration.

"Save your excuses, Énán," said Cadrolón. "Sinnach beat you soundly."

Red-faced and furious, Énán snatched up his clothes and stomped down the hillside. His friends did not follow.

Between his classes the following day, Máel Conall pulled Sinnach aside.

"I heard you used a glamour yesterday to scare another young man in a fight," the ollamh said crossly. "Is this true?"

Sinnach paused. He must be honest; it was unthinkable to lie to this great master. "Yes, it is true," Sinnach admitted. He lifted his head a little too proudly.

Máel Conall groaned with frustration. "So you disobeyed me. I gave you a clear command not to reveal that you knew the aistriú cruth until after you had become an ánruth. And not only that, you used it for fighting! You're a man now, Sinnach—and a fili! I expect more maturity from you. It's time to grow up."

"But I'm just enjoying what I've never had before—what I've always wished for! Would you deny me the joys that the other boys have had for so long—what *you* had when you were young? How can I become a man if I've never been an adolescent first?" Sinnach argued.

Máel Conall shook his head. "I understand your desires, Sinnach. I truly do. Lí Lon and I have been lenient with you since your transformation. You've acted like a fool and a rascal, and yet I told Lí Lon: 'we must be patient, he'll grow out of it'. We've given you the freedom to understand your new body and to have some fun. But now, with this, you've gone too far. I gave you a place here because I saw potential in you—I saw in you talent and focus. All I see now is silliness and mischief. Is this the new you, Sinnach? Have we reached the limit of what you're capable of?"

Sinnach hung his head, ashamed that the ollamh had lost faith in him. "No, I... I'm sorry, Ollamh. It's just that I... I just wanted to have fun, to wash away the sorrows of the past with frivolity. I've achieved everything I've ever wanted. I hadn't given much thought to what I would do afterward." He rubbed his face. "I will admit... I haven't quite been able to control myself."

"It's common enough at the beginning of manhood to be overwhelmed by one's bodily vigor," said the older man. "But a man must learn to control his impulses and direct his energies towards the service of others and the betterment of his tribe."

The ollamh paused and sniffed the air. "Winter is approaching. Tomorrow night is Samhain. We move into a time of stasis and inward journeying to the realms of contemplation and dream. The body must rest and plan its exploits for the following spring." The ollamh stroked his beard pensively. "I suppose it's time I showed you what it means to take on the responsibilities of a fili—outside the safety of the school. Perhaps it will convince you to refocus on your studies. You have much more to learn before you become an ollamh, Sinnach, and an ollamh indeed is what you must become—not just for your own sake. Tomorrow, meet me at the meditation field before supper. Make yourself clean and presentable. Wear your best cloak. We will be going on a journey."

"On Samhain eve? But isn't that... dangerous?"

"Only if one is unprepared. But we will not be."

The shadows of Samhain closed the lid of Summer's somnolent eye. Tomorrow it would be winter, when every creature must quiet to honor Life's long sleep.

That evening the scholars would have their Samhain Eve feast and tend through the night their hearthflames in vigil. This night, of all the nights of the year, was the most vital to illuminate, for spirits might wander in the darkness where the veil was most thin. The turning of time was hinged upon two points, Samhain and Bealtaine, the start of winter and the start of summer when Life and Death were equal in power.

Before sundown Sinnach dipped in the stream, scrubbed himself vigorously, and dressed in his best tunic and cloak. A torc of red bronze was around his neck and a leaf-shaped cloak pin was at his shoulder. To a flaith his costume might seem plain, but he felt handsome and noble nonetheless. Sinnach turned this way and that, inspecting his reflection in Lí Lon's polished bronze mirror. *How splendid I look.* Then he laughed, aware of his own vanity. *Máel Conall is right. I have become a fool.*

A wind rattled the leaves that still clung, dead, to the oaks, making a sound like chattering teeth. Beneath these oaks Sinnach met Máel Conall at the meditation field. The ollamh wore his thousand-feathered cloak and carried a staff of red yew. Around his neck was a wide golden lanula, which hung down upon his breast like a crescent moon. The image of his master dressed in such rich raiment reminded Sinnach of his admiration for the man. Though humble in manner, Máel Conall was amongst the highest of the learned in Mumu.

Without a word, the ollamh guided the youth northwest through the forest.

"Where are we going?" Sinnach asked with a thrill. His breath clouded before his face in the pallid evening light.

"You'll find out soon enough," Máel Conall answered mysteriously.

They walked in silence for more than an hour, and before the final shafts of sunlight disappeared beyond the mountains in the west, Máel Conall halted. The filid stood beside a wide earthen mound. On its eastern side were two upright slabs of granite with a smaller slab laid atop. They formed a kind of doorway, but it was too dark to see what lay across the threshold.

Sinnach shivered. "Is this... is this a Síd mound?" he whispered.

Máel Conall nodded. "It is. Keep very quiet and be very still. Stay alert, for you may see something that will astonish you."

A little ways from the mound the filid stood with rapt attention. Long minutes passed as they waited for the sun to set. Sinnach leaned against a holly tree and massaged his sore calves. Máel Conall closed his eyes in standing meditation.

Finally, the earth swallowed the sun. Twilight dimmed, enshrouding the wood in thicker folds of shadow.

A light appeared in the midst of that darkness. Slowly its glowing swelled, then divided into several dozen far-away orbs. They approached from either side of the Síd mound and met before the doorway. Sinnach drew a quick breath as they came into focus.

A slow procession of men and women emerged from the wood holding aloft those lights. Their torches had no flames; the light was cooler and greener than fire, and Sinnach realized it came from tufts of florescent moss. The people themselves were a sight to behold. Lords and ladies adorned in extraordinary elegance: gold and gems, silks and silver, flowing gowns of soft pastels, shoes of doeskin patterned with bright beads. Their long shining hair cascaded down their backs or was plaited with ribbons and flowers. Most astonishing of all was that they made not a sound; neither with their voices upon the air nor with their feet upon the earth.

One by one, hundreds of these fair folk filed in through the stone portal. As each crossed the threshold they were greeted by a man holding a staff very much like Máel Conall's. Sinnach and his master watched all this silently, unnoticed by any in the procession.

Finally, as the last of them entered the mound, Máel Conall approached the man standing at the doorway. The ollamh bowed his head and addressed him with a blessing:

> Peace between neighbors,
> Peace between kindred,
> Peace between lovers,
> In the love of Ériu.

> Peace between person and person,
> Peace between spouse and spouse,
> Peace between human and Síd,
> In the peace of Cóir.

> Bless, O Sun, my face,
> Let my face bless everything it turns to;
> Bless, O Moon, mine eye,
> Let mine eye bless all that it sees.

The strange man smiled. "Welcome to you, Ollamh Conall," he said graciously. "It is good to see you again." The man was dressed in a flowing robe of some iridescent silvery fabric, speckled like the sides of a salmon. His staff was made from the limb of a hawthorn tree, a handful of its thorns still stuck out from the bark.

"You as well, Níaméo. It has been too long," said Máel Conall gladly.

"And who is this?" asked Níaméo, nodding at the youth.

"This is Sinnach mac Lí Lon, a clí and disciple at my school," Máel Conall replied. Sinnach bowed his head to the stranger. By the staff in his hand and his station at the threshold between worlds, Sinnach surmised that Níaméo was himself a druí.

"A son of Lí Lon? Well then, doubly welcomed are thee. We have not seen your mother in our land in quite some time. Why does she not visit with us any longer, Conall?"

Máel Conall shrugged apologetically. "That is not for me to say. Though I will be sure to share that you've enquired about her."

The otherworldly fili raised a brow, seeming unsatisfied with this answer. "I see. It is well that you would. Have you come this night for the Samhain feast at the ráth of our Mór-rí? Géarshúileach will be most pleased to see you."

Máel Conall nodded in affirmation, and with that Níaméo waived his staff across the doorway. Whereas before the opening had been obscured by shadows, now there was a shimmering in the air like the heat that lifts from sun-warmed rock. A faint light was cast across the threshold from the other side.

Máel Conall abruptly stepped through and disappeared, leaving Sinnach alone beside the Faery fili. Níaméo nodded encouragingly. Sinnach held his breath, and with a pounding heart plunged through the portal.

CHAPTER SIXTEEN

A Faery Feast

Sinnach emerged into a woodland almost identical to the one that he had left. So similar were his surroundings that at first Sinnach thought that he might have been rejected by the Síd and put back in the place whence he came. But as he looked about, Sinnach could see subtle differences. There were trees and small woodland plants that he did not know. There were insect chirps he had never before heard, and the air was warmer. He stood beside his master on a well-trodden path; far ahead he could see a moving line of flameless torches.

Níaméo led the two men in the train of the procession. Níaméo and Máel Conall conversed amiably, sharing what interesting bits of news there were in their respective domains while Sinnach gazed all about him in wonder.

I'm in the Otherworld... I'm really in the Otherworld!

The filid emerged from the forest and came to the foot of a grassy hill. The moon was full and just-risen above the horizon, lighting the landscape almost as brightly as day. Sinnach marveled at the softness of the grass underfoot. Little white wildflowers bejeweled the hill as if in reflection of the stars above. A queer feeling of déjà vu swept over the youth—there was something strangely familiar about this place.

As they crested the top of the hill Sinnach stopped suddenly, his mouth agape. Before him was a vast orchard of a myriad of fruit and nut trees. *This is like the orchard from my dream!* He said nothing of this to the other filid, not quite believing that it could be true. But as they continued past, Sinnach paused beneath one particular tree.

This was the tree he had climbed in his dream, to fetch the apple for the maidens. He was sure of it—the branches and the bark were exactly the same. Sinnach looked up to the very top of the tallest branch and there clung a single red apple. *What strange resonance!* He positioned himself directly below the apple and said to the tree: "O noble, generous tree, wouldst thou let me taste of your succulent fruits?"

No sooner had Sinnach spoken his request than the apple fell directly into his outstretched hand. He slipped the apple into tunic, gave his thanks to the tree, and jogged to catch up to the older two men. They were too deep in conversation to have noticed this arboreal exchange.

At last they approached a stone ráth at the center of that moon-drenched plain. The ráth was surrounded by two concentric stone walls the height of two men and the width of one. Spearmen guarded their heavy gates, faces forbidding in the light cast up from braziers at their feet. From the rampart above the outer gate hung many streamers of colorful cloth and garlands of late-blooming boughs. The spearmen nodded deferentially to Níaméo and permitted his party enter.

Inside the ráth they came to an enormous roundhouse. Sinnach gaped in astonishment of its magnitude. It was larger than the big house at his school in the mountains; larger even than the hall of the aire Talorc. Its rooftree was the combined height of eight men at least. Sinnach strode across the threshold, admiring the jewels inlaid in the wood, and stepped through a wall of uproarious sound.

In the hall hundreds of people were speaking and laughing, singing, dancing, and eating. The light of the central hearth and dozens of torches that filled the hall cast shivering shadows upon the ceiling. The walls were draped in colorful tapestries and emblems wrought from bronze. At low tables elegant lords and ladies sat upon cushions dining and conversing convivially.

Sinnach stuck close to his master's side for fear that he might be lost in the crowd. The ollamh turned to him, and through the cacophony shouted into his ear: "Do not speak unless you are spoken to. Do not eat or drink unless you are given explicit invitation. Keep your wits about you, not all here is what it seems."

They pushed, with apology, through the throng to the hearth and skirted the edge of the dance floor. There, several dozen dancers moved in synchronized circles, lines, and crosses to the merry playing of the harps, flutes, bones, and bodhrán. Past them the filid wound their way towards a high table where a small number of people sat in chairs draped with fleeces and furs. As they approached, Máel Conall bowed deeply. Sinnach mimicked his master.

"Ah! Now the night is even brighter! Welcome, Ollamh Conall! Welcome to my hall," boomed a man at the center of the table. Sinnach studied him, admiring his beauty. His face was broad and of heavy brow, framed by a fall of dark flowing hair. His eyes were pale and grey as ice. They had dark rings around the irises, which gave his gaze a piercing effect, like that of a hunting hawk. Upon his noble head was a diadem of silver, and his tunic was a purple color as dark as midnight. To his right sat a glorious woman in a gown of pale lavender; atop her long wavy tresses was a diadem of gold. To the chieftain's left was a maiden garbed in a gown of red as deep as the hawthorn berry, with earrings and arm-rings of red gold.

The maiden raised her straight black brows and regarded Sinnach through sparkling eyes as clear as crystals. He jumped in surprise, choking on his own breath, for this was the woman he had met twice before in his dreams. He coughed and dropped his eyes to the floor.

"And who is this young man?" asked the chieftain. "I don't believe we've met before."

"Mór-rí," said Máel Conall reverently, "I introduce to you Sinnach mac Lí Lon, my disciple and apprentice to Lí Lon. Sinnach, you are in the illustrious presence of the Mór-rí of the Síd, Géarshúileach mac Gáeth, the Hawk-Eyed."

Sinnach bowed to the Mór-rí, then lifted his head and spoke a blessing with as steady a voice as he could manage:

> Thou chief of the moon,
> Thou chief of the sun,
> Thou chief of the planets,
> Thou chief of the stars,
> Thou chief of the globe,
> Thou chief of the sky,
> O, lovely thy countenance,
> Thou beauteous beam.

> Two loops of silk
> Down by thy limbs,
> Bright shine thy flashing eyes,
> Red jewels are at thy ears,
> Grain spills from thy hands,
> And cause every cow to give calf.

The great chieftain nodded serenely, relieved that this young man did not exhibit the characteristic vulgarity of humanity.

"Welcome, young man. It is a pleasure to meet the son of Lí Lon. And what happy circumstance that her son should also be one of the Áes Múchta. There is luck in your lineage, I see."

Sinnach was taken aback by this insight and stood there speechless, blinking. How could this man know that he had been Eclipsed? He had thought no one would ever be able to tell.

The Mór-rí saw the young man's confusion and addressed it plainly. "I see that you are unused to having your identity known. But let me assure you—in my túath, there is no shame for being one of the Áes Múchta. It is a position of great esteem amongst my people; greater than is given to other humans, besides present company, of course." He nodded politely at Máel Conall and the ollamh nodded back, smiling diplomatically.

"Thank you, Mór-rí Géarshúileach," said Sinnach. "I am relieved to know this and I thank you for your graciousness. However, I tell you truthfully that Lí Lon is my foster-mother, not my birth-mother."

"Ah," said Géarshúileach, "and yet the family we choose is sometimes more beloved than the family given to us. Is it not so?"

Sinnach nodded, moved by his wisdom. The Mór-rí had seen to the heart of a matter very private and potent, though few words yet been spoken between them.

"I introduce to you my wife, Rígain Dían Búas Ingen Lochach," Géarshúileach gestured at the matronly woman to his right. "And my daughter, Toltu," he said indicating the young woman to his left.

The maiden smiled smartly. "Well met, Sinnach. At last, I have your name. But I suspect that you know my face, for we have met before. Do you remember? That day in the orchard?"

Sinnach blushed crimson. In that moment he remembered the apple he had hidden in his tunic and said, "How could I forget, fair lady?" With great courtesy he stepped forward and presented the smooth-cheeked maiden with the apple. She laughed in delight and took it gladly. In the exchange, she brushed her soft fingertips across his hand. Sinnach blushed again, even darker than before, and stepped back beside his master.

Máel Conall was quite astonished by what he had witnessed. "You two have met before?" he asked incredulously.

Sinnach nodded. "In a dream—or, I thought it was a dream. We met in the orchard that you and I passed on our way here. I dreamt it at the Well, when I was fasting at Lá Lethach."

"You have talent, young man," said the Mór-rí. "We Síd have a saying: *A master of dream is a master of time.*" Géarshúileach turned to Máel Conall. "You were right to bring Sinnach with you this Samhain Eve, Conall. I predict that he will be quite valuable to your people... and mine." The Mór-rí flashed his pale, piercing eyes. Sinnach was unsettled by the tone with which he spoke that last word.

"Please," Géarshúileach continued. With a magnanimous sweep of his hand, he gestured at two empty chairs between Toltu and Níaméo. "Come feast with us. Eat, drink, sing, and be merry."

As the filid took their seats the chieftain stood, raising aloft his jeweled goblet of white bronze. He called across the hall with his cavernous voice the Samhain blessing:

> O Summer, thou giveth this bountiful feast,
> Benefit to the body and the soul,
> Given to us this cherished bread,
> Enough for our need at Summer's end.
>
> O Summer, thou giveth the honey-sweet foam
> Of sap and milk of fragrant fields,
> Lively births of lamb and calf,
> Boughs hung heavy with mast.
>
> Give to us this night of grain that shall last,
> Give to us this night of drink that shall not hurt,
> Give to us this night of fruits from the bough,
> Give to us this night of fires bright in the coming darkness.
>
> Glorious Summer, Mother of Flowers,
> Thou turneth now thy face from us,

To sleep in peace 'til winter's end,
We dream of thee on moonlit pillows.

Cups were lifted and in unison and every voice cried out: "Hail the passing of Summer and the coming of Winter!" Then it was quiet but for the sound of drink splashing down gullets. After that, the music was raised and the chatter struck up once more.

Places were set for the filid: Sinnach beside Toltu and Máel Conall beside Níaméo. The ollamh leaned close to whisper into his disciple's ear. "Remember what I've told you," he breathed cautiously. "And do not drink too much. Keep both eyes open." Sinnach nodded, tense with excitement.

It was a feast the likes of which Sinnach had never experienced before. There was every kind of meat he could imagine, basted with cider and roasted in a pit outside the hall. An enormous bronze cauldron of beer was set beside the dance floor, wide enough in girth for three men to bathe in. Though the revelers drank from it continuously by the flagon-full, the level of its liquid seemed never to diminish.

Sinnach tried his best to drink in moderation, as Máel Conall had instructed, but every time he took a sip from his vessel a cup-bearer would refill it to the top so that he never knew exactly how much he drank. The taste of the mead was exquisite, sweet and scented with aromatic herbs which he strove to identify. Was it eyebright? Elderflower? Meadowsweet? He made a pledge to ask about it later, but it was soon forgotten.

There were fresh-baked breads with rich yellow butter and rounds of fragrant cheese. Great bowls of tender, spicy greens tossed with violets, clover, and dandelion flowers. Platters of roasted hazelnuts and chestnuts. Little bowls of honey at the right hand to dip one's meat into. Baked salmon sprinkled with wild herbs and flakes of dulse. Baked honeyed apples and bowls of raspberries and blackberries topped with whipped cream. Mushrooms fried in beef tallow and salted. And roasting on a spit over the central hearth was the carcass of a gigantic wild boar, the very one that Géarshúileach himself had speared the day before.

Sinnach relaxed as his belly filled, and Máel Conall's warning was pushed to the back of his mind. The Síd were congenial and the conversations were more interesting than any he'd had with his peers at home. Sinnach decided that he liked this place very much, most of all when he looked into the face of the beguiling young woman beside him.

The night grew late and yet the party was undiminished. The celebration would go on for a full three days and three nights. Máel Conall nudged his disciple beside him and said, "Best that we be going lad, while the tide is still high."

"Oh, no!" said Toltu. "You're leaving so soon? But I haven't sung an air yet! Will you stay a little longer, at least to hear me play just one song?" Sinnach nodded at his master beseechingly.

Máel Conall furrowed his brow and looked towards the door. He sighed. "That sounds lovely, Lady Toltu. Just one song and then we'll be off."

The chieftain's daughter smiled and made her way to the dance floor. Sinnach watched her every movement with rapt attention, thrilled by the sway of her supple shape. As Toltu took into her hands the silver-stringed harp, every voice in the hall fell silent.

She played a tranquil melody and sang with a voice so dulcet, so clear, that it made Sinnach's heart ache and his eyes well up with tears. Her voice drifted through the hall like a breeze that bends the meadow flowers, that lifts up the swallow's wing, that whistles softly to badger and fox and mouse as they bed down to dream in their dens.

Sinnach's head drooped; he found it hard to keep his eyes open. Warm and contented and carefree, his soul was soothed by that mellifluous sound. He set his chin in his palm and closed his heavy lids.

"Sinnach!" A harsh whisper assaulted his ear. He sat bolt upright, blinking the sleep from his eyes. Máel Conall rapped the youth on the head with his staff. "What did I tell you? Keep both eyes open!" Sinnach winced and rubbed his head. Though awake he was a bit dizzy from the mead.

Toltu's song came to a gentle close. She plucked her last string and sang her last note, letting it tremble in the air and soften until it was lost beneath the crackle and pop of the hearthfire. The hall applauded with polite, measured clapping. Though Toltu received this adulation, she did not smile. She only stared with displeasure at the ollamh and his disciple sitting fully upright at the table.

"Thank you for your hospitality, Mór-rí," said Máel Conall with a hurried bow. "We must be going now, for this is the lad's first feasting and I expect his head will be hurting tomorrow."

Géarshúileach laughed in his voluminous voice. "You are most welcome, Conall. As are you, Sinnach mac Lí Lon. I expect we shall be seeing you again soon."

Sinnach bowed, a little too low for he lost his balance and stumbled. His master steadied him then pulled the youth roughly through the crowd. As they passed by the dance floor Sinnach caught a glimpse of Toltu sitting with her harp. She sang now a sorrowful tune and flashed her grey eyes at Sinnach as he passed.

He waved awkwardly. *Why does she seem so sad?* Then he was pulled through the door and lost sight of her comely face.

CHAPTER SEVENTEEN

Sober Study

Sinnach awoke the next morning to a throbbing head and a vile taste in his mouth. Unsteadily, he got up on his feet and wandered to the stream to splash his face with its frigid waters. After drinking deeply, he plunged his whole head underwater and came back up shocked but more clear-headed. He squinted at the sky with sore eyes. It was nearly noon—he had never slept so late! Cursing at himself, he hurried home to dress and prepare for the day's lessons.

Inside, Lí Lon watched him scurry about. "What are you doing?" she asked.

"I've overslept! I'll be late for—"

"Sinnach. It's Samhain. There are no classes today, silly." She cocked her head. "You look awful. How much did you have to drink last night? Máel Conall told me of your journey. He said to send you to him when you awoke. But I can see you'll need a bit of tending before then." She patted the empty seat by the hearth and Sinnach collapsed in it, holding his pounding head in his hands. Lí Lon handed him a vessel of bitter herbal tea. "Here, drink it down. And when you've finished I'll give you more. It's dandelion root, burdock root, milk thistle seed, and feverfew. It will cleanse your blood."

Sinnach sniffed the liquid warily then slurped it down without complaint. "I'm never drinking mead again. Nor beer. Nor any other alcohol," he said miserably.

"Yes, well that is a wise choice. Especially the drink from *their* draughts, for they brew it stronger than we do here. And though the taboos of the filid against drinking alcohol are lifted on the cross-quarter days, many of us avoid the stuff altogether." Lí Lon raised her chin pretentiously. "Warriors and common folk may indulge in it more freely, but it makes them stupid. A fili should know better."

"Well, I certainly do feel stupid, and I'm afraid I've made a fool of myself in front of Géarshúileach and Máel Conall." The tension in his head was already easing from the tea. He sat up and looked his foster-mother in the eye. "The Mór-rí's fili, Níaméo, inquired about you. You must be well-respected there, for he asked why you do not come to the Otherworld anymore."

Lí Lon paused and looked away. Her voice became heavy and wistful. "I traveled there often in my youth, but... I had a Faery lover who scorned me. The thought of seeing him again is too painful, so I will not return." She sighed. "But I will speak no more of that. You look well enough to see Máel Conall now." And with that she stood him up and shoved him out the door.

Sinnach met the master beneath the holly tree. "I'm sorry, Máel Conall. I was not careful enough with the drink and I made of fool of myself. I promise never to make that mistake again."

The ollamh frowned. "That is good of you to say, Sinnach. I was disappointed that you took too much mead, though I will forgive you for your naivety. You could not have known the power of that stuff would be so overwhelming, and they were a bit forceful with it anyhow. I am more

upset that you abandoned caution—that you allowed yourself to be ensorcelled by that young woman's song. Do you know how dangerous that
can be, Sinnach? To be lulled to sleep by a song of the Síd?" The young
man shook his head. "No. Of course you don't. You learn the rules of
proper conduct with the Síd at the rank of ollamh. So I suppose I am also
to blame for bringing you there unprepared and unaware of the dangers.
But given the circumstances, I suppose you did well enough. Géarshúileach's court seems to have taken to you very quickly. Maybe too quickly."

Sinnach thought the old man was being overcautious. The Síd had
been so generous and welcoming to him. And the face of that maiden had
been so lovely. What danger could come from a woman as gentle as she?

"Is it not of benefit to be favored by the Síd?" asked Sinnach.

"Not always," the ollamh replied. "I think it is best to be neither hated
nor adored by them. If you can be welcomed warmly, but not so loved
that they conspire to weave you into their plots, that is the best balance to
strike. For remember this: they are covetous of both objects and persons.
A successful fili will maintain strong boundaries and protections around
himself while upholding perfect courtesy and diplomacy. You will receive
more of this instruction when you are ready. But for now, I want to specifically discuss the protections you must cultivate in dreaming."

The young man proudly remembered the praise he had received from
the Chieftain of the Faeries. "Is it really so unusual to be able to travel to
the Otherworld in dream?"

"No, it is not that unusual. Many people, both learned and common,
travel to the Otherworld and other realms in their dreams, though most
have no idea they are doing so and do not remember it upon waking.
What *is* unusual is to be able to control one's travels. An ollamh may learn
to travel also in daydream, as I do. But if you become of interest to the
Síd, as you most certainly have now, they have ways to entrap your mind
when you are away from your body in dreaming. Cultivating the skill of
lucid dreaming will help you keep better control over your choices in the

dream state. And there are protections—spells, herbs, amulets, and so on—to shield you from enchantment when you are asleep. I will teach them to you now."

Máel Conall tutored Sinnach in the dream skills as he had with the aistriú cruth. With several weeks' practice Sinnach became adept at these and dreamt no more of the raven-haired maiden. On occasion the young man inquired if he might travel again to the Otherworld now that he was better prepared. Máel Conall flatly refused, insisting that he focus on his studies and more earthly pursuits.

Though risky, Máel Conall's strategy to subvert Sinnach's impetuousness was in the end successful. The journey had convinced the youth that there was greater reason to pursue mastery than simple self-interest. The world was wider than he had ever imagined, and as an ollamh he would be able to wander freely between boundaries most people never knew existed.

Sinnach took up his studies again with more maturity and less haste, savoring the many pleasures of learning. By Bealtaine he had achieved the silver-adorned rank of ánruth, accumulating one hundred and seventy five stories (including all immrama, dindsenchas, táin epics, and wisdom tales), advanced satire, speckled poetry, anamain (an advanced meter of chanting and incantation), sciath draíochta (magical warding), millteoracht (magical attack), and gaiste damán allaid (magical entrapment).

A year passed in sober study. The following Samhain, Sinnach advanced once more, for the last time, to the gold-adorned rank of ollamh—the seventh and highest of all ranks. As an ollamh he mastered the telling of three hundred and fifty stories and poems, and learned the methods of maintaining respectful relations with the Síd. He was tutored in the art of diplomacy between the multiple túatha in Mumu and the ethical use of cumhact (divine authority) for proper judgment. Of poetry he learned its three most difficult feats: teinm leada (analytical dissection of others' poetry and enchantments), dichetal di channaib (extemporaneous poetry and spellcraft), and imbas foraisna (foresight and the speaking of prophecy).

These seven levels he had advanced through more quickly than most, and yet he would continue his studies for several more years to deepen his knowledge within a specialized field. He felt called to specialize in the skills of the druí, and so explored the boundless realms of dream, divination, poetry, and foresight.

Another two years elapsed thus under the tutelage of his masters, and he assisted them in teaching the lower-ranking filid. On occasion, he accompanied his masters on their journeys to nearby túatha to give judgments as brithem or blessings as druí.

Life in those days was simple and fulfilling, having a pleasant, peaceful pace. His days were full and rich; hard work was balanced with leisure. The time to himself he spent in the woodland, wandering the mountainside in meditation. Through the draíochta druadh he gained a tranquil, quiet mind, and so was able to converse with myriad beings: tree and vine, beast and bird, rock and rivulet, siabra and spirits of the greenwood.

It was soon after becoming an ollamh that Sinnach noticed he was being followed on these walks. He would feel another's eyes touch his back, yet when he turned all he spied was a streak of ruddy fur diving into the brush. On occasion his feet had him follow a fox trail, and when he came to its end he spooked a vixen who promptly disappeared. Over many months fox and man came slowly closer, then one day they finally sat together and conversed. Thereafter the filid of Géarán Tuathail complained that their village was being stalked by foxes, for a male fox would often be seen at the very edge of the glen with a vixen trotting beside him.

CHAPTER EIGHTEEN

Brugh Rí

The fields and forests were verdant with the green hum of summer. On a cool day in June, a gusty wind came from the north and brought a gentle rain. In that drizzle came four men to the scholar's settlement: a fili, two men armed with shining steel, and a richly-dressed man with curling black hair. They had come from Brugh Rí, the seat of the chieftain of Mumu on the bank of the River Maigue in the north, and asked to speak Máel Conall. Knowing the arrival of these men to be of great import, Máel Conall immediately called a council of the school's five ollamhna. Sinnach, as a junior ollamh, was invited to listen but not speak.

The man with curling hair, the chieftain's messenger, addressed the council first. "Four nights ago, Rí Mumhan Fínán Érainn flew on the wings of a white swan to Tír na Og." As he spoke his eyes became wet with tears of filial grief. "The Tánaise, his Second, has been elected. Come Solstice, it will be time to coronate him and wed him to the Land. Will you Ollamh Conall, as Déantóir Rí, officiate the ceremony as you did for the Rí Mumhan before him?"

"This is sad news, for Rí Fínán was wise and just." Máel Conall inclined his head solemnly. "I will serve Mumu and the seat of the Érainn as the sacred task was given to me."

The council spoke briefly of the spiritual preparations needed for the ceremony, then the visitors bowed and respectfully took their leave.

The news was sorrowful, for the ollamhna had much love for the old chieftain. And yet, it had not come unexpected—the omens had foretold of his passing in the last quarter of the waning moon, as it was. Rí Fínán had been fortunate enough to live into old age and keep his health until the end. All chieftains wished for such a lucky death: in his health, in his sleep, advanced in years.

When the council dispersed, Máel Conall spoke to his red-haired disciple. "Sinnach, you will come with me to Brugh Rí to coronate the new Rí."

These words echoed strangely in Sinnach's mind, for he had expected them to be said. It was a premonition of sorts: he had known he would go to the coronation, though he knew not how or why. The young man was thrilled with excitement to travel all the way to the Fellubair túath and observe such a momentous affair.

Four days before the Summer Solstice, Máel Conall set out on the long journey from Géarán Tuathail with Sinnach and two retainers. It would be three days on foot to Brugh Rí, down the mountain, past Loch Léin, and across the rolling hills of Fellubair. The weather was mild, it rained only a little, and the travelers' hearts were glad.

"Máel Conall, of all the filid in Mumu why were you called to officiate the coronation?" asked Sinnach as they made their way north.

"The sacred role of Déantóir Rí, the chief-maker, was given to me by choice of the council of ollamhna who serve the chiefs and sub-chiefs of all the túatha of Mumu. I will serve in this capacity until the council chooses another to take my place, or until I die; whichever comes first."

"And you oversaw the coronation of Fínán Érainn?" asked the young man. Máel Conall nodded. Sinnach marveled at this, for he knew that the last Rí had served for over fifty years. *How old is my master really?* he wondered.

"Why were you chosen to serve as Déantóir Rí?" he asked.

Before Máel Conall could answer, Tóla, the younger of the ollamh's retainers, chimed in enthusiastically. He was a taman, or one who studied the draíochta druadh but did not show a talent for it, and so chose instead to live with the filid as a servant. "Have you not heard of how, in his youth, Máel Conall defeated the malevolent druí of Connacht and saved Ciarán Érainn, predecessor of Fínán Érainn, in the battle of—"

"Silence, Tóla!" Máel Conall hissed. "I've told you before to shut up your gossip. It's an embarrassment to yourself and to my house. Was I mistaken to bring you with me on this journey?"

Tóla dropped his eyes to his feet and apologized. Sinnach smiled wryly. Of course he'd heard that story a hundred times passed in whispers between novices at the supper table. It was impossible to tell which parts of the story were true and which were embellishment. Máel Conall always flatly refused to discuss it.

A few moments later Tóla spoke up again, this time with a more humility. "Is the Tánaise the old Rí Mumhan's son?" he asked.

"No. He is Rí Fínán's first cousin's son. No chieftainship in Ériu is ever passed from parent to child," answered the older ollamh in a professorial tone.

"Why not?" asked Tóla.

Sinnach answered. "The rí is chosen from a pool of qualified candidates within the royal dynasty, having both father and grandfather who were noble and of chiefly descent. The best of them is elected from all those eligible in Mumu: the wisest, the most just, the healthiest, the handsomest, and the best able to lead in peace and war. If every lesser chieftain in Mumu has a say in the Rí Mumhan's choosing, then they are more likely to pledge their full and lasting loyalty to him.

"You see, in ancient times, as is told in the wisdom tales, the túatha used to pass the chieftainship from father to son. But this caused much jealousy, plotting, murder, and strife between clans, and so the current system of tanistry was effected instead. It is a superior system; it better secures order and peace."

"So this Tánaise is the most beautiful man in Mumu then, is he?" Tóla scoffed.

"Of course," said Máel Conall flatly. "Or how else would Áine, the goddess of Mumu's sovereignty, be expected to mate with him?"

"She would, of course, never lay with just any ordinary fellow like you or me." Sinnach spoke sharply, for the youth ought to speak of the Tánaise with more respect. Tóla mumbled to himself inaudibly, then fell silent.

On the third day of their travels, the men from Géarán Tuathail emerged from the cover of the forest onto a wide, flat plain. There in the distance, in the center of that expanse, was their destination: Dún Eochair Maigue, more often called Brugh Rí—the palace of the chieftain. It was a wise location for a royal fort: the soil was rich and flat for tilling, and from the mount one had a sweeping view of Mumu's north country in all directions. Sinnach shaded his eyes and looked to the west, wondering how far it was to the coast from here.

Under piebald patches of cloud and sky, Máel Conall's party approached. Passing through a village of roundhouses and small earthringed compounds which clustered round the fort, they came at last to the outer gate of the Brugh.

It was impressive. The compound was ringed round by three earthen banks of enormous girth, and between these were deep ditches for defense. Inside the inner wall was a palisade of whole ash trees three men tall. Warriors stood atop it watching the visitors with unwinking eyes.

At the gates, stern spearmen permitted the ollamhna enter. They walked with their attendants across a wooden causeway to the center of the Brugh where the Tánaise, soon to be the Rí Mumhan, had his seat.

Inside Brugh Rí's three rings were several buildings. To one side there were animal pens, a milking house, and a forge. In another section there was a granary and an outdoor kitchen with a clay oven. A central green space below an ancient oak tree was used for gathering and socializing when the weather was fine. There was a roundhouse for the royal women to gather and weave together, a roundhouse for guests to sleep in, and a roundhouse of equal quality to host treaty hostages. Yet the most striking building amongst all these was the one nearest to the gate, for it was the largest and most beautiful.

This must be the Rí Mumhan's hall, thought Sinnach. *It's almost as big as the Mór-rí of the Síd's!*

The men entered the hall and were at once impressed by its lofty aesthetics. Tóla gaped unabashedly. It was certainly splendid, having every earthy luxury, and yet Sinnach could not prevent himself from comparing this hall to the one he had entered in the Otherworld; in comparison, he found this one lacking.

At the farthest end of the hall was a circle of smartly-dressed men, warriors young and old, sitting in chairs carved from dark wood and white bone. They were speaking in low, earnest tones. The circle of men looked up as the herald cleared his throat and announced the newcomers: "Ollamh Conall of Géarán Tuathail, the Déantóir Rí. And Ollamh Sinnach mac Lí Lon."

"Áedán!" said a voice amongst the seated men, and before Sinnach could gather his wits, a young warrior with flaxen hair leapt up from his seat to embrace him. Sinnach was shocked that this stranger so suddenly hugged him, but as the young warrior pulled back Sinnach looked him in the face and knew him at once.

"Cellach!" Sinnach exclaimed. The two embraced for a second time.

Now it was Máel Conall who stood with his mouth agape. "You two know each other?"

"Yes, we do," Sinnach replied with a smile. "Cellach was the boy I told you about, the one whom I found in the forest and brought to the líaig so many years ago."

Cellach nodded and addressed Máel Conall and the circle of seated men. "This man saved my life when I was a boy. He chased away my assailants and led me to healing when otherwise I might have perished in the wilds."

An older, stately man stood up from his seat. He wore sumptuous dress, having a cloak of scarlet lined with the dark fur of an otter and a bejeweled brooch at his breast. He inclined his head towards Sinnach.

"Welcome, Ollamh. My son has spoken to me of your selflessness. You have my deepest thanks for saving my son's life and the life of our future Rí Mumhan."

Sinnach blinked. "What? Are you... *you're* the Tánaise, Cellach?"

He paused to look upon his childhood friend more carefully. Cellach was a handsome man, more handsome than he had remembered, with a wide angular jaw, even brows, and eyes the color of the summer sky. His gaze was steady, intelligent, and kind. Cellach was a hand taller than Sinnach and more heavily muscled, wearing a tunic of indigo and a speckled cloak of periwinkle and bugloss-blue. Around his muscular neck was a heavy golden torc which threw up light into his face and made his visage even fairer. Clasping his cloak was a vulvar brooch of pure silver studded with three shining drops of dragon stone.

Sinnach, observing all this, exclaimed with a little awe and a little anger: "You're no briugu's son!"

Cellach suddenly laughed and clapped Sinnach on the shoulder. The men seated echoed his laughter, relaxing the tension in the chamber.

"I apologize, my lords," the Tánaise said humbly to the circle. "I've disrupted our discourse. Please, Ollamh Conall; Ollamh… Sinnach is it now? Join our council. We are discussing the process of succession and the rights of tribute to the Rí Mumhan."

Two additional chairs were pulled into the circle and Máel Conall and Sinnach took their seats. Cellach introduced each man in the council, every one of them the patriarch of a clan or the rí of a lesser túath. As the discussion commenced, Máel Conall leaned close to his disciple and whispered into his ear.

"You are indeed favored by the gods, Sinnach, for no man comes to such luck as yours by chance alone."

The ollamhna stayed the night in the guest house with the other visiting chieftains and their retinues, and in the morning awoke to the warmth of Grianstad an tSamhraidh, the Summer Solstice. By midmorning a company of at least seventy-five men and women began their journey northeast to Cnoc Áine, the hill of coronation. It was a half-morning's walk to this holy site, and further flaith and spectators would join up along the way. At noon, all would congregate at the sacred hill for the coronation of the new Rí Mumhan, Cellach mac Ségán mac Fáclán of the Érainn.

At the head of this procession in a bronze-hubbed chariot stood a woman holding aloft the ash wand of the Rí Mumhan. Behind her rode Cellach on his dappled grey stallion, called Airgetmong for his silvery mane, flanked by his father Ségán mac Fáclán to his right, and his mother Dúinsech Ingen Mórda to his left. Máel Conall, as Déantóir Rí, rode just behind them abreast of Sinnach and three other favored filid.

Behind the filid followed the flaith and officials of Mumu with their retinues.

Sinnach, who had never ridden a horse before, was put atop a plain
bay palfrey. The mare was so relaxed beneath him that she stumbled often, seeming half asleep. It was an unwelcome challenge, for as they
proceeded northeast Sinnach struggled to pick up the mare's head without falling forward onto her neck. Cellach looked over his shoulder at this
scene and laughed. He reigned back his high-stepping stallion to give
Sinnach instruction, expert horseman as he was.

"Now lift up your hands and place them just in front of you on the
saddle. If she yanks, don't let the reins slip through your fingers," Cellach
said kindly. "Sit up straight, not forward. Sit back even more—legs always below you. There. That's better. See how she's not so heavy on the
forehand now? She leans when you lean. Squeeze her with your legs every
few strides to wake her. If you play with the reins a little that will pull her
attention towards you and away from the grass."

The Tánaise spent much of the journey abreast of Sinnach and his
mare under the pretext of giving instruction, but in truth it was an excuse to catch up with his old friend. The two exchanged tales of their lives
over the past nine years. Sinnach told Cellach of his years studying the
draíochta druadh. Cellach told Sinnach of his training to become a warrior and a leader of men. Cellach described to his friend his hunts and
adventures, as well as the campaigns he had led for raiding and defense.
Lastly, he told Sinnach of how he was elected Tánaise by a council of
chieftains and flaith four years ago, when the Rí Mumhan Fínán Érainn
was still living.

"Did you ever imagine you'd become the Rí?" asked Sinnach. "When
you were a boy, did you dream of it?"

Cellach considered this carefully. "I suppose many boys of my rank
dream of it, and so did I. And yet, I've never taken it for granted. I am
honored and humbled by my choosing. It is a weighty responsibility, I

know, and I will forever strive to be worthy of it. But I do feel, as I've always felt, that the hand of destiny has guided me to it. As a fili, I'm sure you understand. You must be learned in the turbid coursings of fate."

The fili nodded. "As much as I can be."

"And yourself? Did you always feel you were destined to become a fili?"

"No. I had no notion I would ever lead this kind of life until I came to study with Máel Conall and found such pleasure in it. Though now, looking back, I can see that I was destined for the draíochta druadh from an early age." Sinnach smiled. "All throughout my childhood I was convinced I would grow up to become a wandering warrior like Fionn. I'll admit it was sorrowful when I had to give up that childish dream."

"And yet Fionn was a fili as well, one who gained supreme wisdom from the Salmon of Knowledge... if I am remembering my tales correctly," offered Cellach.

"That is so. That is so," said Sinnach appreciatively.

The two men talked without pause, each feeling as if he was reunited with a long-lost brother.

"Did you not say that you have a sister?" Sinnach asked.

"Yes. You have a good memory! Her name is Búan. She is not with us unfortunately, for she had to leave on an urgent campaign. A band of Laigniu raiders trespassed our northeastern border."

Sinnach was taken aback. "Do you mean to say that your sister is a warrior too?"

Cellach smiled. "Oh yes. She may be the fiercest and bravest of us all. When I am Rí I will make her my champion and she will lead the Noí, a band of nine of my best warriors." The Tánaise chuckled at Sinnach's astonishment. "You'll understand when you meet her. Just be prepared. She is not a gentle woman, nor modest," said the blonde man, his eyes sparkling.

CHAPTER NINETEEN

The Coronation

High above the procession towering clouds loomed, lifting up the gaze to where the wide eye of heaven ever watched the world below. As the march approached the hill of Cnoc Áine, the sky's white veil did part and send down a shower of near-noon light. The hour of the sun's brightest joy was nigh: it would soon be noon of noon. Thousands of onlookers gathered around the hill. The procession met them there and paused, beholding the mount dappled with dramatic shadows.

Sinnach looked up. A golden eagle came from the south, flew three times sunwise round the crown of the hill, screamed, then went south again. "A good omen," he said. Máel Conall saw it too and nodded.

Cellach paced anxiously under the shade of an elm tree while Máel Conall, Sinnach, and the three other filid went into a grove of oaks at the base of the hill. There the five filid prayed to the Elements, to the spirits of the Land, and to the goddess Áine, beseeching bestowal of their blessings upon the reign of the Rí Mumhan. A white heifer was brought to them and a silver blade was drawn swiftly across her neck. Her blood was collected and sprinkled at the foot of the hill to consecrate its soil. When that was done, the filid rejoined the congregation, then Máel Conall gave the signal for the Tánaise to climb the mount.

With him, thirty of the Tánaise's officiates ascended the grassy slope, proceeding in the same order as before. The company kept silent as did the crowd of spectators below. At the crown of the hill was an ancient ash tree, a bile, and near to its roots was the stone of inauguration where every chieftain of Mumu had been made since time immemorial. The party circled around it.

Seven men stepped outside the circle to the east. Four of them carried musical instruments of shining brass shaped like giant cow horns, and they blew into these from openings at the sides of their tapered ends. The other three each held aloft an enormous sinusoidal horn which he blew into from a mouthpiece at its bottom. Their tubes were narrow but long, the full length of a man, and their distal openings flared out into wide discs embossed with curvilinear designs. Together these seven horns made a din so terrible that every man, woman, and child in Mumu might harken and tremble. In sequence, the horns roared in each of the four cardinal directions: first east, then south, then west, then north, and back again to the east.

Máel Conall turned to Cellach. "Step forward, Cellach mac Ségán, Tánaise."

Cellach stepped forward to stand between the ollamh and the inaugural stone, emerging from the shade of the ash tree so that the light of noon would touch him. The officiates tightened the circle. The coronation ritual commenced.

The woman who held the ash wand stepped forward and faced Cellach. "Tánaise, step now onto the inaugural stone so that we may bless you."

Cellach nodded solemnly and placed his feet upon that great grey stone imbedded in the earth. Two depression were worn there in the shape of two footprints where his predecessors had placed their own feet for the last thousand-thousand years. From the surface of that stone Cellach felt a hum of power seep into his body through the soles of his feet. It echoed through his bones.

"Put aside your sword, Cellach, and take up the wand," Máel Conall instructed. The warrior unbelted his silver-hilted sword and placed it in the hands of his mother beside him. Then Cellach took into his right hand the straight ash wand and held it reverently before him.

"The Rí Mumham puts down the sword to take up the white wand of ash, and by doing so seals his oath to rule Mumu with temperance. He rules not by force of arms alone, but alongside justice and wisdom. May his judgments be as direct and faultless as the ash wand."

Máel Conall turned his back and Cellach faced him. Then he put to the Tánaise the four sacred questions.

"Do you, Cellach mac Ségán, swear to abide by and uphold the ancient customs and laws of the Érainn?"

Eyes alight, heart athrob with an ebullient power, Cellach chanted his reply: "Tongu do día toinges me thúath!" and by this was meant 'I swear by the gods my people swear'.

Máel Conall turned Cellach to face south. "And do you, Cellach mac Ségán, swear to protect the whole of the Province of Mumu from all criminals, brigands, and invaders?" asked the Máel Conall.

"Tongu do día toinges me thúath!" replied the Tánaise.

Máel Conall turned the young man to the west. "And do you, Cellach mac Ségán, swear to guide your people with both gentleness and strength, and to always uphold perfect truth and justice?" asked Máel Conall.

"Tongu do día toinges me thúath!"

Lastly Máel Conall turned Cellach to the north. "And do you, Cellach mac Ségán, swear to submit yourself, body and spirit, to the divine will of the Land so that She may grant fecundity to our herds and our harvests?"

"Tongu do día toinges me thúath!"

Turning again to the east, Máel Conall paused and closed his eyes. He raised up his hands and made a circlet with his fingers, hands hovering just above the shining yellow hair of the young warrior. He spoke then a blessing, each word pulsing with potency:

> Power of eagle be thine,
> Power of raven be thine,
> Voice of the swan.
>
> Power of storm be thine,
> Power of moon be thine,
> Power of sun.
>
> Goodness of sea be thine,
> Goodness of land be thine,
> Goodness of heaven.
>
> Might of fire be thine,
> Might of river be thine,
> Strength of stone.
>
> Bounty of Dagda be thine,
> Justice of Midir be thine,
> Victory on the field.
>
> Each day be joyous to thee,
> No day be grievous to thee,
> Honor and love.
>
> Love of each face be thine,
> Fortune and health be thine,
> Long life in peace.

Cellach was spun slowly sunwise on the inaugural stone. Three times he turned, observing every detail of his domain. Then the woman stepped forward and placed upon his head a diadem of red gold. Cellach raised up the sacred wand. An errant shaft of full-noon light struck his head and reflected off golden hair. He was radiant, shining like a second sun, so that those who stood close had to avert their eyes from his brilliance.

"Cellach Érainn, the Rí Mumhan!" bellowed Máel Conall. The congregation shouted his name in unison. A chant traveled downhill to the crowds below, who echoed that name yelping and whooping with joy.

The seven horns sounded again and the Rí Mumhan stepped off the inaugural stone. He led the procession back down the hill and through the throng of spectators. They cheered and tossed buttercups and sunwort flowers at his feet. Cellach smiled dazzlingly bright and looked each person in the eye as he passed. He moved through the crowd and in his wake dozens of women and near as many men were felled in swoon by his striking face.

There was music and singing and dancing there under the clear sky, and the Rí Mumhan promised to host a more extravagant celebration at Brugh Rí in two night's time. As twilight settled, the crowd dispersed and went off to light their own Solstice fires in the hills where they would sing and dance the night away.

The Rí and his retinue stayed at the hill and there would make camp for one night. The filid stood around the bonfire and recounted tales to the remaining company as the sky dimmed and became speckled with stars.

Darkness came late on this shortest night of the year. At sunset Máel Conall addressed the Rí Mumhan privately: "Tonight you will lay with Áine, the goddess of Mumu's sovereignty, atop her hill. Make yourself ready for the wedding and leave your tools of war and emblems of nobility behind. You will not need them."

When the night was full-dark Cellach approached the two ollamhna alone. He was without his usual count of four attendants, for the mating of the Rí Mumhan to the Goddess was a sight too sacred to be seen by uninitiated men. At the foot of the hill armed warriors would be stationed all night to ensure the protection of the new Rí while his wedding to the Land was consummated.

Cellach looked plain in comparison to his earlier splendor, now dressed only in a tunic of pale yellow linen cinched at the waist with a bronze-buckled belt. The night was warm so he left his legs bare, as men often do in the summertime. The only jewelry he wore was the golden torc about his neck, yet to Sinnach his friend looked no less splendid than he did in all his finery. The two filid were, at the moment, more elaborately adorned than the Rí. Each had a golden lanula hung around his neck. Máel Conall wore his thousand-feathered cloak and Sinnach wore his five-colored ceremonial cloak. Máel Conall held in his hand a staff of yew wood, and Sinnach held a staff of ash wood.

Sinnach glanced at Cellach; his face was lit by the campfire. The warrior himself erect with the perfect poise and dignity of his station, and yet the fili spied something in his friend's expression that he did not expect: apprehension, even ambivalence. Máel Conall saw this too, and spoke to it.

"Rí Cellach, what is on your mind?"

The Rí Mumhan dropped his gaze and clasped his hands together. For a moment Sinnach saw in the chieftain the boy he once knew.

"I have been told I will be mated with the Goddess. Is this... is this metaphorical? A symbolic mating with the Land? Or is it... bodily?"

The older fili replied matter-of-factly. "For some the mating is simply metaphorical. It is an offering of your body to the Goddess, to do with it what She will. This symbolizes an exchange: that the Land will be receptive and bear the fruits of humanity if humanity agrees to do the same for Her. It is a surrender to the power of Land, for She both grants us life and takes it away. Sometimes at this wedding, it is Her will that the chieftain sleep alone atop the hill. At other times, the chieftain will experience an actual bodily mating. The latter, of course, would be the greater honor—not just for you but for your people too. It would be a clear sign that we have chosen the right man to lead us, one embraced fully by the Land. In the end, the decision is up to the Goddess. I cannot say what She has in store for you."

The ollamh tipped his head and spoke in a softer, fatherly tone. "Will this be your first time, Cellach?"

Cellach raised his eyebrows at the question. He swallowed and answered honestly. "I have not yet lain with a woman."

Máel Conall nodded, now understanding the young man's concern. "Ah, I see. You'll be alright, Cellach. And she might even be appreciative of that fact." The older man grasped the Rí's shoulder reassuringly. "If you are gentle with Her, She will be gentle with you. Follow Her lead. Give Her what She wants and you will succeed. That is usually the way of it."

With that the three men mounted the hill and came once again to the inaugural stone. Máel Conall instructed Cellach to take off his garments but leave the torc at his neck, which was too thick to twist off easily. Sinnach held out his hands to receive his clothes. Cellach hesitated, grateful the darkness hid the blush of his cheeks. The Rí turned away from the filid, disrobed, wrapped himself in the mantle Máel Conall had provided, and turned back to them. Finally, he handed his garments to Sinnach.

How strange that a man so fair and so regal could be so modest, thought Sinnach. *Have I done something to make him uncomfortable?* He could not think what it might have been.

Then, as Máel Conall instructed, Cellach laid by the stone upon a bed of linen and sheep's fleece. Sinnach lit a dish of fragrant herbs beside the Rí's head.

"To call the Goddess to you with Her favorite scents," Máel Conall explained. "And Cellach, if you expose yourself fully you are more likely to entice Her."

The prone man sighed and obeyed, shivering a little, but not from the cold. Then, with a bow from each fili, the Rí Mumhan was left naked and alone upon the crown of Cnoc Áine.

The filid walked south a dozen paces from the ash tree and sat at the edge of the mount where stood two standing stones. The filid faced outward from the center of the hill watching the crescent moon rise in the east. In silence they waited, not daring to speak an idle word upon this hallowed hill.

Time passed slowly. Máel Conall closed his eyes in sitting meditation. Sinnach kept his open and beheld the sky's silver sliver strike the hilltops; they shone like waves on the rolling sea. A mist had gathered in the plain below as the night air began to cool, and though the wind was negligible this mist began to creep slowly towards Cnoc Áine. The mist reached its wispy tendrils upward, drifting towards the men on the mount. An eerie silence came with it. Sinnach gripped his staff tightly; the hairs on his arms stood on end.

Finally, the mist reached the filid and enveloped them, obscuring all sight of the world. Sinnach held his breath. He could see the blurry shape of Máel Conall beside him. The older man gripped his staff in his hands; he, too, was made vigilant by the mist.

Sinnach thought he saw a shadow take shape in the twirling coils of this cloud. It moved. Yes, it was a shadow, and slowly it became more solid. Suddenly, the shape burst through the mist on thundering of hooves. A glossy red roan galloped toward the filid, eyes rolling, nostrils flared.

Máel Conall put out a hand to stop his disciple from standing and raising his staff at the charging mare, as he was about to do. The mare skidded to a halt before them. Neither filid dared move. The roan bent her elegant neck so that her nose nearly touched Máel Conall's own. They exchanged quick, tense breaths. She tossed her head and bent towards the other fili. Sinnach blew into her wide nostrils and she blew into his. As he did so, Sinnach's eyes landed on her shining black hooves. He tried not to imagine being trampled by them.

Finally, the mare raised her neck and tossed her head in approval. Turning a cool eye to each of them she stamped once, set her sights on the crown of the hill, and trotted lustily through the two standing stones. The mist subsumed her.

Sinnach exhaled a shuddering sigh of relief. "Was that... was that...?"

"The goddess Áine. She takes several forms besides that of a woman, the favorite of them being a red roan mare."

The two of fell silent as they heard a voice speak near the inaugural stone. It was a woman's voice. There was a reply, this time from a man—from Cellach. An exchange of words followed but Sinnach could not make them out for they were muffled by the mist. Then, a pause, and the unmistakable gasps and moans of love-making.

Sinnach clasped his hand over his mouth, stifling a laugh. He glanced at his master, thinking to tell him a juvenile joke, but Máel Conall frowned and furrowed his tufted brows at his disciple. *We are in the presence of a goddess—show more respect!* the master commanded with his eyes.

Sinnach bit back a chuckle and cleared his throat, trying his best to think only civil, serious thoughts.

Dawn warmed the wool on his back as Sinnach awoke atop Cnoc Áine. He was stiff and cold, laying on his side in the dewy grass. He and Máel Conall had kept vigil all night, taking turns to sleep while leaning up against the other's back for warmth. Finally, the two of them had both fallen asleep just before dawn. Sinnach laid his hand on his master's shoulder to wake him.

The filid made their way through the crisp morning air to the crown of the hill and found Cellach there awake. The Rí Mumhan was gazing away to the south, knees drawn up against his chest, his striped mantle draped over his shoulders. From the impressions in the bedding, it was clear to Sinnach that two bodies had lain there together until very recently. If the Goddess had been there, she must have fled with the night.

"So then, Cellach. How was your night?" asked Sinnach with an impish grin.

Cellach looked up at the young ollamh, blushed, and looked away again. "The Goddess was... generous." The Rí Mumhan stood up abruptly, as if coming to sudden resolve. He let the mantle fall away from him and stood before the filid bare, this time without shame. His eyes were on Sinnach's face.

Sinnach handed Cellach his tunic and belt. After the Rí had dressed, the three of them walked down the slope again to lead the procession back to Brugh Rí.

The feast at the hall of the Rí Mumhan lasted seven days and seven nights, and there Cellach received gifts, hostages, and pledges of fealty from all the túatha and mór-túatha in Mumu. Máel Conall and Sinnach appeared for a short time each night to entertain with poem and harp, attending out of respect for the Rí. It was tradition for the Déantóir Rí to be present throughout the feast, though Máel Conall, scholar that he was, much preferred quiet, sober conversation to the feast's frenetic revelry.

At first Sinnach found the carousing exciting, but the novelty soon wore off and he wished to wander through the quiet mountain glens once more. He and his master spent the days walking the banks of the River Maigue, quietly discussing the finer points of law and story and spellcraft.

Finally the feast had ended, and when the celebrants returned to their túatha, Cellach summoned the filid to speak with him in the great hall. They sat opposite him in two ornately carved chairs, as they had the first day they arrived in Brugh Rí. The Rí Mumhan addressed them with a new authority in his voice. He seemed to Sinnach quite changed.

"My deepest gratitude to you both, O great filid, for your guidance, which carried me through that auspicious ceremony." Cellach signaled and a servant stepped forward bearing a small wooden chest. "In payment for your services, Ollamh Conall, I present to you a silver and gold cloak pin, three cauldrons of honey, a herd of mast-fattened swine, and thirty bushels of grain for your school in the mountains."

Máel Conall stood and received the chest containing the cloak pin.

"And for you, Ollamh Sinnach, I have for you both a gift and a request," said Cellach. There was a twinkle in his eye. "I shall give you your own estate beside the Brugh, servants to maintain your household, land and livestock upon which you shall subsist, and a generous annual payment for your services as the fili of my house—the first fili to the Rí Mumhan." Cellach paused and raised his eyebrows at the red-haired fili. "What do you think of my offer, Sinnach? Do you accept?"

Sinnach was speechless and wide-eyed with surprise. He had never imagined himself living under the employment of a chieftain, giving him guidance in all his affairs. He had imagined he would always live in the mountains, teaching and contemplating the world in quietude as his mentors did. The hall of the Rí Mumhan would be so very different: busy and loud and complicated. As the Rí's first fili, would he have the time to walk alone in the forest and converse with the creatures there? Would he be given space to meditate and divine and dream, as was needed to keep his roots wet in the Well of Segas?

Cellach, seeing something of this ambivalence in Sinnach's face, got up from his seat and came to his friend. Reflexively, all seated in the hall stood when the Rí stood, so Sinnach did as well. Cellach put his hands on the fili's shoulders and spoke softly so that none but the two filid could hear. For a moment the chieftain's regal mask fell away and Sinnach glimpsed beneath it his friend's familiar earnest expression.

"I owe you my life Sinnach. Don't think that I've forgotten it. I wish to repay you and at the same time have you closer to me. Conall has told me of your skills; he has said you have great power and greater luck. If you advise me in my judgments you would do me honor; as well you would do honor to Mumu. There is benefit to you as well, for you'll have every luxury here. And I know you need your solitude—that will be respected. The country here is beautiful. I know these streams and meadows well." The chieftain leaned in close and whispered: "We will live at last like brothers, you and I."

Sinnach was silent, his mind turbulent with indecision. Rationality would have him accept the offer, for it was a magnificent thing to be the Rí's fili. It too would be a delight have his friend so near. And yet, his intuition was knotted. This was a place of great complexity and of the heavy weight of action. He would have to leave his simple, quiet life behind. He would have to entangle himself more deeply in the tangled world of men.

"You are generous, mo Rí, and I thank you," the young ollamh said at last, "and yet I am reluctant to leave my tranquil life at the school. Let me think on it a while. I will have an answer for you in the evening."

The filid left the Brugh and walked together along the River Maigue. Sinnach entreated his master's advice for he trusted Máel Conall's judgments most of all in the world.

"Sinnach, given your past, I understand your desire for a simple life, a life at the periphery. But you are a man now. Leave the child's worries behind. The past cannot repeat itself in that way. You have more power now to protect yourself; there is little in the human world that might harm an ollamh. Why do you wish to remain at the school? Do you crave seclusion out of fear?"

Sinnach pondered this. He plucked a daisy and pulled its petals. "For many years there was fear, yes. But now... I do feel less vulnerable. As you say, I have power enough to protect myself. It is more... well, I love the quiet life. I love dwelling in the forest on the mountain. And I love being close to you and my mother."

"Ah, but the owlet must eventually spread his wings and make his own nest. It is what owls are made for; it is what the mother and father wish for their hatchlings." Máel Conall rested his hand on the young man's shoulder. "Sinnach, perhaps you are too focused on the steps ahead to see the path clearly, so let me tell you what I see: the gods have tasked you with something greater than a simple, scholarly life, or else you would not have come to such luck. To befriend the chieftain-to-be and to be asked to serve as his fili; to have favor with the Síd and to be Áes Múchta... it is a rare combination. You are surely meant to do something greater with it than sit in meditation upon the cliffs of Géarán Tuathail for the rest of your life."

There was a long silence between them. Then Sinnach lifted his head and spoke. "Cellach is a good man, the best man I could be asked to serve... though he's only a warrior."

Máel Conall raised his eyebrows. "You've inherited your mother's prejudices, I see."

The young man shrugged. "I have prejudices of my own, I suppose. Once I thought all flaith to be cruel, heartless tyrants. But then I met Cellach, and he is not so. He is fair and compassionate and generous. I love him like a brother."

"And he loves you, Sinnach. That much is clear. And it is why I recommend that if you take your place here, you must tell him about your past—your *whole* past, including your transformation. He is the kind of man who can hear your truth and think no less of you. I am certain of it."

Sinnach balked. "Why should I tell him? The past is the past. I'd rather him not know what I was before. It's unimportant."

"No, it is important. It's critical that you, as his fili, contribute no additional complications to his court without his knowing. You've left things in your past that are yet unresolved. He needs to know so that he is not inadvertently entangled in hidden snares. If you are his fili, he must have total trust in you—and for that there must be full honesty between you two."

Sinnach nodded. "I see. I suppose you're right. I do not wish to add further complication to his court. I would have to find a way to tell him gently..."

"Sooner is better than later," said the master. "In my view, there is no superior place for you than Brugh Rí. Such special wisdom as you have must be used for the good of our people. If you were a lesser man, I would bid you stay with us at the school. But your future lays elsewhere, Sinnach. Though... I will miss you, as will Lí Lon." There was a touch of sadness in his voice.

"Lí Lon! Oh, but I cannot say goodbye to my mother!"

"Don't worry yourself, lad," said the older man. "You may speak with her in your dreams, as you have learned to do. And I will send her to come and see you when she can. So then, you've decided?"

"Yes. I will accept Cellach's offer." The young man paused, his eyes glistening. "Thank you, Máel Conall. Thank you for everything you've given me. You and Lí Lon both. You've given me a second life—a happy life. You've given me power and knowledge. I hope that I may honor you by serving the Rí Mumhan well." The two men embraced.

"You will, Sinnach," said Máel Conall. "You will."

CHAPTER TWENTY

Búan

All at once the shape of Sinnach's life changed dramatically. Too fast, he felt, to adjust to it gracefully, and in those first few days he found himself grumbling and apologizing often. It was a shock to have an entire roundhouse of his own, servants of his own, and respect given to him by his own status, not just by association to his teachers. The luxury of it all was overwhelming and galling to Sinnach's frugal nature. Too often were eyes affixed to his face, anticipating a request or a command. He was more used to standing at the bow than the tiller, but now he was the captain of his own ship, and in this change he felt tossed and a little seasick.

On the third day of his new life, Sinnach took a walk by the riverbank to reflect upon his feelings. His servants were discomforted by his insistence to leave Brugh Rí alone, for it was customary to have at least two attendants by the side of the Rí's fili at all times. "You must learn to endure it," he had said to them tersely. "I will be taking short, solitary excursions nearly everyday, so cease your nagging."

On this day, he reflected on the differences in allotment of privilege between the higher and lower classes. All his life as an owlet, he had occupied another's nest or lived on its edge. He had always felt safest at the periphery of civilization. But now he had fledged and landed in a very different nest—a nest made for him at the center of society. It felt too wide for him, and yet he was expected to take up every bit of space in it. He was expected to allow other people, people at the periphery, to accommodate that spaciousness for him. And he was expected now to converse with others of spacious nests, the learned and the noble, as their equals. The change was by far more dizzying than any previous transition of his social standing.

And yet, despite himself, in the little time that had passed Sinnach felt himself expanding into his new nest. When he passed by persons in the Brugh, all nodded and bowed to him. He was welcomed at any table; he was welcomed into any conversation. Receiving such instant esteem caused him to stand taller and set back his shoulders. Gifts and compliments he gave more graciously, now that scarcity was a far away affliction. Yet in his chest there was always a friction: he had now what so many in the world had not, and never would.

A wide, wispy willow clung to the riverbank, dipping its knotty roots in the quick of the stream. Stirred by a soft breeze, its supple boughs drooped and stroked the water's surface. Sinnach touched the tree's pale bark and pinged an old pain: a distant memory of a storm on the seashore.

The fili said to the tree: "I will rely on you, Ériu, to remind me of my humility. I must remember my roots; I must never take these gifts for granted."

A hearty gust tossed the tree's limbs; it leaves shivered. The willow groaned, swaying slowly, then fell still again.

Sinnach returned to the Rí's hall in a broody mood. Later in the afternoon he met with Cellach and discussed a legal case that would come before them on the morrow.

A sudden wave of cheering erupted at the gate of the Brugh. Midsentence, Sinnach fell quiet to listen. The commotion arrived at the door of the hall and a stream of warriors came through. Nine of them strode in proudly, heads held high and wide smiles upon their faces. Though cheerful, each was dirtied and haggard. Two of them limped; another held his arm against his chest. Like a herd of rowdy colts, the warriors joked and jostled each other. When finally they came before the seat of the Rí Mumhan they arranged themselves with a little more order. One of them called out: "Hail to Rí Mumhan Cellach Érainn!"

"Hail, Rí Mumhan!" the Nine called back in unison, bowing their heads to Cellach.

Cellach welcomed them heartily, embracing each warrior in turn, tenderly where there were wounds.

"Call the líaig if you would, dear brother. Cúanu has broken at least two fingers and Beccán has a slash on his thigh that will need stitching." The voice that spoke was higher than the rest, as high as a woman's, and yet it held an unmistakable authority. Sinnach looked about, wondering whence the voice had come. Though there were female servants in the hall, it was none of them that spoke and he had seen no other woman come in. Sinnach gazed more closely at the warriors: they were so identically clad in leather armor and mud that the fili could hardly distinguish one from any other.

The Rí's líaig led the injured to his house for healing. The rest of them had only bruises or less, and so returned to their houses for washing and rest. One of the warriors stayed behind in the hall, and when the care of every other man had been seen to, this warrior came to the empty seat beside Cellach and collapsed in it.

"Sinnach," said Cellach, "it is my pleasure to introduce to you my sister and champion, Búan Ingen Ségán. Búan, this is Ollamh Sinnach mac Lí Lon, the fili of my house."

With great effort Búan sat forward, nodded at Sinnach weakly, then slouched back against her chair. "Well met, Ollamh. Welcome to Brugh Rí."

Sinnach's breath caught in this throat at the sight of this fearsome woman. He had recognized her gender until she had come close, but now he saw more clearly the feminine outline of her body beneath the curaiss. She was handsome, very much like Cellach except that her face was rounder and smoother. She was less fair than her brother—her hair was a tawny brown bleached yellow by the sun at the ends of her long, wavy tresses. Her eyes were darker too, having the color of a stormy sea. There was patent strength in that face, and yet she seemed exhausted. She unbuckled her sword belt with a wince and leaned the weapon against her chair.

"Lady Búan," said Sinnach politely, "you look fatigued. May I get you anything? Water to drink and to wash your hands?"

Búan turned her head and gave the fili a curious look. "We have servants for that and they are coming with it now." Three attendants hurried forward with a bowl of cool water to drink from, a bowl of warm water into she dipped her hands, and a cloth to wipe them dry. When this was done, she tenderly lifted herself from the chair and came to stand before Sinnach. "But you can do me a better service, for I have a wound that needs tending."

"Oh. But would you not see the líaig for it?" the fili said hesitantly.

"No, I would not. The líaig is busy healing my companions who have greater wounds than my own." She put her hands on her hips. "You are a fili—are you not trained in the healing arts?"

"Em... yes I am, Lady Búan. But it is not my specialty. I do not have the expertise that—"

"You'll do well enough, I'm sure. I require no grave operation," she interrupted. "Bring what herbs you will need to my room, just there." She pointed to one of several doorways that led to apartments attached to the central hall.

Sinnach hurried to líaig's herb garden outside the gates of the Brugh. He gathered the herbs with hurried hands, found a crock of honey and bundle of clean cloths, then carried it all in a basket back to the hall. In his other arm he held a vessel of water. Nervously, he pushed open the apartment's wicker door with his foot and stepped into the lady's room.

He started and nearly dropped the vessel of water. For there was Búan, sitting on the side of her bed bare-chested, her lily-white breasts entirely exposed. A handmaiden stood at attention by the bedside.

Noting the ollamh's shock, Búan smiled in amusement. Sinnach shook himself from his paralysis at the door. The pallor of his fright was seared away by a sudden hot blush. Turning away from her, he set the vessel on the bedside table and fumbled with the cloths and herbs.

Búan watched the fili from behind. "You act as if you've never seen a woman's breasts before," she said, teasing him. The handmaiden stifled a laugh. Búan shushed her.

Sinnach stammered a reply. "Oh, no. I mean, yes. Well, it's... it's just that I rarely see patients. I've been called to serve more often as poet, brithem, or druí... my lady." He said all this with his back to the two women, fidgeting with the bundles of herbs in the basket.

"Hmm... well then. I shall let you know when I'm ready to be sung asleep with a poem," Búan said playfully. Sinnach meant to laugh, but the sound that came out was more like a dog choking on a bone. Búan bit back a chuckle. "For now, you'll simply dress my wounds. But how will you do it if you won't even look at me?"

"Oh! Yes, my lady. I apologize." He turned slowly to look her in the eye, not daring to drop his gaze any lower. Her face had been washed. Her oceanic eyes sparkled with wit.

Búan raised her eyebrows impatiently and pointed to her chest a few fingers above the start of her cleavage. Sinnach let his eyes find the spot and tried his best to suppress another blush. There was a shallow gash and an angry purple bruise there atop her breast bone.

He hissed sympathetically. "What did this?"

"The rim of my shield was slammed against me in a skirmish. I'll have the leather worker add a piece higher up on my cuirass so this doesn't happen again. Also, the elbow of my shield arm got a bit of a wrenching, so you'll dress that after you're done with this."

The fili nodded. He soaked a cloth and leaned in close to cleanse the wound. She had not yet washed her hair. It smelled of sweat and horses, and yet intermingled with the sweet scent of her body Sinnach found he did not mind it much.

He mashed the fresh leaves and flowers of yarrow with rose petals into a paste, mixed this with honey, and gently painted the wound with it. He placed ribwort leaves overtop all this then wrapped a strip of cloth across her chest and tied it under her arms. The left elbow he inspected next. It seemed to be sprained. The fili applied slimy poultice of mashed comfrey root to her elbow and bandaged it. When this was finished, he placed his hands over each wound and spoke a charm to hasten the healing. Lastly, the handmaiden helped him slip a clean dress over Búan's head, and then he bound up her arm in a sling so that she would not overuse it while it healed.

All this Sinnach did with such tenderness that Búan felt called to remark upon it. "You have gentle hands, ollamh. I am surprised you do not give cures more often."

"Thank you, my lady," he said humbly.

"Call me Búan."

Sinnach nodded. "As you wish, Búan."

Búan appreciated this young man's modesty; it was a rarity amongst men of the nemed class.

The tension between them was somewhat lessened now that her bosom was covered. Seeking to sooth his nerves, Sinnach asked politely: "Did you successfully route the raiders? There must have been a battle if you and your men came back in such a condition."

"Battle? No, more a skirmish." Búan stood and went to the door. The handmaiden hurried to open it for her. "Let us discuss this with my brother present."

Sinnach followed the woman back into the hall. She sat beside her brother and food and drink was put before her. After eating and drinking a little, she felt revived enough to speak to the fili's question.

"A band of raiders from Laigin was plaguing the farmers of the Osraige túath near the border, as was reported. We engaged them over several days—they kept retreating and returning. Eventually we sent them away and they stayed gone. However, before my warriors and I had even got there the Laigniu had stolen near thirty head of cattle and we could not win them back."

Cellach inclined his head, frowning. "From which tribe did the Laigniu hail?"

"Uí Bairrche, it was said. It was the second such raid this summer, though the first was negligible and the rí-Osraige compensated the farmers for their losses."

Cellach groaned. "This is unhappy news. The rí-túath of Uí Bairrche is a notorious brute. Fourteen years ago, Fínán Érainn before me had negotiated a treaty with the Rí Laighin to stop the raids from Uí Bairrche. But I suspect the rí of the Uí Bairrche heard of Fínán Érainn's death and decided to put that old treaty to the test. And the Osraige—how are they equipped to fend off raiders if the Laigniu should strike again?"

"Poorly, in my opinion," said Búan. "The clans near the border have diminished somewhat in the last few generations. They have only a small number of fighting men; too few of them are well trained or well armed. If there is another raid, they will need our help once more."

"Is it time to renegotiate peace with the Uí Bairrche then," said the Rí. "And if they cannot be persuaded to stop their raiding and give us compensation for the cattle that were taken, we may have to take it up with the Rí Laighin." Cellach turned to Sinnach. "You're being thrown directly into the fire now I'm afraid. It would have been kinder to start your tenure with the settling of simpler matters, but I do not control such things. We will go as soon as we may to the edge of Mumu in the east."

Summer is the season of skirmish and cattle raid. As a warrior-chieftain, the Rí Mumhan must be prepared for both. So he rode with his champion, his fili, and a company of fighting men to the border between Mumu and Laigin. They rode for two days and came at last to the boundary stone. A dozen warriors from Osraige were waiting for them there.

"We will make camp here and await your return," said Cellach. He gazed into his fili's face with perfect trust.

Sinnach went rigid; his thoughts were flighty. *Gods, I hope my chieftain's faith is not wrongly placed.* He straightened his back, pretended an air of confidence, and crossed the border into Laigin with two servants in tow.

"Are you sure you don't want to send the fili with armed warriors? Are you so confident of his powers?" Búan asked her brother.

Cellach nodded. "The man may look mild, but I've seen him be deadly. And he came with the highest recommendation from the great fili of Géarán Tuathail, Ollamh Conall. No harm can come to him—there is no man of Ériu so vile, or so stupid, to attack a fili without provocation. Such an act would widely endanger order in Ériu, for the filid's ability to travel freely and negotiate between túatha is inviolable."

The host of the Érainn waited a day and a night at the border. As the sun rose to its zenith on the second day, the Rí Mumhan heard a sound in the distance. A pounding of hundreds of feet came swiftly towards the camp. Heartbeats quickened. Spears and shields were taken in arms. A hand was placed on the hilt of every sword.

Then Cellach breathed a sigh and relaxed his grip, for he heard above that thunder a lowing of cattle.

A herd of cows and bulls broke through the cover of the Laigin forest and tramped across the border. A red-haired man holding an ash-wood staff led the herd on foot. He gave no call nor gesture to the beasts and yet they followed behind him, deferential as ducklings. His attendants lagged behind, as glassy-eyed as the cows. Sinnach approached the Rí Mumhan and halted. The company of beasts behind him halted as well, swishing their tails and licking their pink noses with long wet tongues.

Cellach laughed in delight. "I have never before seen a single man herd so many. You must have enchanted them!"

Sinnach smiled with charm. "Well, one could say it like that. But I simply explained the situation to them and where we were headed. They were more than happy to oblige." He called then to the host of the Érainn: "Are you ready to receive them?"

The Rí Mumhan gave a command to his company and several horsemen surrounded the herd. Then Sinnach turned to the cattle and spoke several lines of poetry in a rhythmic meter. At once the beasts became less placid. They jostled and broke rank, their eyes drifting away from where they were fixed upon the shape of the red-haired man.

"The cattle can be guided home now," said the fili, "they will follow me no more." And with that the herdsmen of the Osraige took back their livestock gladly.

A warrior rode up to the Rí. "Cellach, there are fifty cattle here, far more than left Mumu. What shall we do with the extra head?"

"Divide them evenly between every cattlelord that had been robbed." Then he turned to Sinnach. "My friend, I had confidence in your success, but this... you've exceeded my expectations! How did you convince the rí Uí Bairrche to give us this compensation?"

"Not hard to say," said Sinnach proudly. "I called down from the sky a flock of birds as wide and dark as a stormcloud, and they set about destroying the chieftain's fields of grain. At once he begged me to let up, yet I would not until he promised peace and compensation to the Osraige. That he did, and I called the birds off. He returned the cattle to me, and wisely gave a few more as a token of commitment to his oath."

Búan looked down at the fili from atop her blue roan, and for the first time appreciated how his clever eyes twinkled in an attractive way.

Returning to Brugh Rí after this great feat, Sinnach gave more thought to the running of his household. Slowly, he was settling in to the pattern of his new life, growing more accustomed to the pleasures and obligations of a man of wealth. The Rí had given him a large house, twelve servants, eleven cows and a bull, a small flock of sheep, a herd of swine, a field of oats, a field of barley, and a share of the woodland that was tended communally for its timber and nut mast. All this provided food and fiber for the needs of his household.

Yet still, he felt it was more than he needed. The obligation to care for a dozen underlings was quite burdensome at times, and he longed for the days when the only person he was responsible to feed was himself. Some nights he lay awake and wondered if all this was just a distraction.

Why is society so unnecessarily complex? Why do we not just live by simple truths, in simple ways? Perhaps I am not suited for this life after all.

In spite of all these inconveniences, Sinnach could not deny there were a few luxuries he did enjoy: a warm bath whenever he wished; a meal of his own choosing at any time of the day; avoiding outdoor chores in dreary weather; and having all the cooking, cleaning, and upkeep of his home dispensed by capable and responsible householders. Best of all, he could be left alone in a house all his own with a simple command.

As Cellach had promised, Sinnach was allotted the time for his requisite solitude out of doors. The role of the fili was not as hectic as he had feared. The Rí even joined him on these walks occasionally, though Cellach was always flanked by several armed warriors; privacy was the only luxury the Rí Mumhan did not have.

Daily service to a chieftain was something else to adjust to. His days were shaped around the times of Cellach's open court where he always stood at the Rí's side to hear disputes and requests from all the free classes of society: fuidir, ócaire, bóaire, aire, craftsperson, scholar, and flaith. When the Rí received visiting dignitaries he was there as well to guide negotiations of trade and alliances. In his advice Sinnach gave his nuanced appraisal of a relevant law and reviewed the legal precedents of every case set before them. Sinnach found Cellach's judgments exceptionally fair and reasonable, and much of the time Cellach asked for his fili's advice simply to confirm his own intuition. The Rí was yet a young man and inexperienced in the giving of judgments, thus he was glad to rely upon the fili's wisdom—he had not yet sufficient confidence to do without it.

Sinnach served as druí as well when it was needed. He advised and prepared appropriate rituals, offerings, and divinations for harvests, healings, and protections from the weather, wild animals, and the Síd. This work Sinnach found the most enjoyable, for it required him to enhance his observations of the natural world. There was great joy in finding solutions of balance and beauty. To him, this was the highest use of his poetic art.

Yellow summer ripened to the red of autumn's fruits. Since the solstice there had been no serious skirmishes, and the Noí warriors did not rove for anything but the hunt. When the chieftain's sister was not off riding with her comrades, she sat beside Cellach in his councils. Búan rarely spoke there, but when she did she captured every eye and ear. She chose her words carefully and articulated with sharp wit and stone-hardness. Her counsel was shrewd, she never spoke thoughtlessly, and yet as a woman her opinions seemed to hold less weight in a council comprised solely of other men. She was often interrupted, and even when her positions were wise and well-reasoned she would receive little response from the men. Then another man in the council would repeat her words almost verbatim, as if they were his own, and all heads would nod to confirm the sagacity of the point.

It frustrated Sinnach very much to witness this, and he tried his best to uplift Búan's voice in the council. Yet his efforts seemed to have little effect on the habits of the other men; even Cellach took no notice of the inequity. Búan seemed unperturbed by this, or at least, she was well-practiced at hiding her feelings under a mask of serenity.

That Búan could keep her composure in the midst of this subtle, per-petual injustice caused Sinnach to admire her all the more. She was so unlike other women in the Brugh. She was not in the habit of smiling nor laughing at men's trite jokes or witty comments, nor was she not of a mind to validate any man's ideas unless they were of true and unequivo-cal wisdom. Most men, even those of high rank, gave her wide girth as if she were the court's monarchic mare. It was a kind of soft power she wielded over them, a power of quiet intimidation. Watching her wield it so deftly, Sinnach himself felt gripped by that power and yearned to earn her respect.

Yet with the Noí she was entirely different. She teased them, toyed with them, romped and rough-housed with them as if they were all her little brothers. In war she was of course their leader, but in play she was their equal. And when not adventuring with the Noí or sitting in the Rí's council, she was often trailed by a pack of young men pleading for her favor. Then an impish gleam would come into her eye, and she played with them as an otter plays with a school of beached eels.

Sinnach, too, allowed himself to be played with. On a whim, once day he invited Búan to walk with him, and she accepted. They strode along the river together, side by side, through the crunch of fallen leaves.

On that brisk day Búan was dressed elegantly. She wore a long woolen dress striped with many sanguine shades, low-cut above her bosom. A heavy crimson cloak was about her shoulders, fastened with a red-bronze brooch. Drops of gold hung from her ears, and her long tawny plait fell the length of her spine. Her fingernails and lips were painted with a cherry color. When not in fighting gear, the woman took great pleasure in her appearance. That day she was exquisite in her femininity, and it was this that so confused Sinnach. Her affect encompassed both extremes of gender—the warrior and the noblewoman both—and so, to sort out his bafflement, Sinnach ventured a question.

"Lady, you look lovely today, as you do on all other days. From every other woman in the Brugh you are distinguished; not just by your magnificent visage, but more so by the roles you play in your brother's court. Not only do you fight with the warriors, but you lead them. When you are on a campaign, you dress and act as any other man might. When you are in the Brugh, you dress in a lady's finery and mingle with the other flaith women. To which do you feel more drawn—to the life of a man, or the life of a woman?"

Búan looked at him coolly. Though her kinswomen often teased her of her love of manly activities, no man had ever inquired about it her forthright. She answered honestly: "I am drawn to them equally. Every noblewoman has the freedom to engage in any profession of her choosing, informed by her talents and attractions—her sex need not be a barrier. At an early age I showed interest and skill in the fighting arts, and so my father agreed to school me alongside my brother. My mother too, for you see, I come from a long line of women warriors. Such is not unusual in the flaith lineages of the Érainn. Some men, being ignorant of history, believe that warriorship is a profession exclusive to their sex. If they cared to consider the truth, they would see it has never been so."

"Of course. We have many tales of rígain and women warriors, to be sure. Rígain Medb and Rígain Flídais of Connacht. Rígain Macha of Ulaid. And the warrior Scáthach who tutored Cú Chulainn in the arts of combat."

"Yes. And yet combat was not the only art Scáthach tutored him in," Búan said. She lowered her lashes seductively.

She's just toying with me, as she does with the others. Sinnach tripped on a stone and stumbled. He caught himself, wiped his clammy palms on his trousers, and brought the conversation back to his original question.

"But have you ever felt you were..." he hesitated and started again. "Have you ever wanted to *be* a man... in the form of one?"

"Have I ever wanted to be a man?" Búan looked at the fili, perplexed. She burst our laughing. "Of course not! What a strange question! I am proud to be a woman. And yet..." Búan paused. She was unused to divulging her emotions to any man; but Sinnach's soft gaze made her feel safe to do so. "And yet, I will admit I do resent that my sex prevents me from having equal footing in the Rí's council. There is nothing besides the shape of my body that elicits their disrespect, for my ideas seem valuable enough to claim for their own. You have noticed this too, I think."

"I have. It vexes me so."

Búan smiled. "Does it now? You are unpracticed at withstanding it, I suppose. But I wonder why you can perceive it and find it loathsome when to the others it is invisible?"

Sinnach shrugged, careful to appear nonchalant. "It is an injustice. I abhor all injustice, to women and children especially for they are the least able to defend themselves."

"Oh?" Búan frowned. "Are you blind to whom you speak?" Perhaps he was less enlightened than she had thought.

"Oh... I meant... I apologize, lady. I could never be blind to you. I am witness to your power. I wish only that I may assist you in asserting it."

"For that I am grateful, ollamh. I do recognize your efforts in that regard, but so far we've made little progress."

"I will keep trying." Sinnach paused and nervously fingered the cloak pin at his shoulder. "So you then you... you don't mind the women's work?"

"I love gathering with my women and gossiping with them, weaving, singing with the children, and so on. It is a welcome reprieve from the gravity of my other roles. Though I will admit something to you now, since you asked." She leaned in close to whisper in his ear, as if to share a potent secret. Her breath was warm on his neck. "I am clumsy with the sewing and needlework. My hands are much too rough for it. And anyhow, I've always despised it."

Sinnach laughed nervously, acutely aware of her closeness. "I've never much liked it myself," he said.

Búan shot him a quizzical look. "What do you mean? Do they also teach tailoring at the school of the filid?"

Sinnach caught his breath, regretting his mistake. "Oh. No, of course not. I only meant that if I were made to do it, I'm sure I would detest it as much as you do."

The warrior looked away, seeming unassuaged. The two of them walked in silence for a moment, watching the rippling river.

"How are you adjusting to life at Brugh Rí?" asked Búan.

"I find myself enjoying it more and more, though it has taken much effort to grow used to living in my own household. I am unused to having such wealth, and now I feel that I have too much when so many others have too little."

"Are you not nemed born?"

Sinnach paused. Perhaps he should not have admitted this to her, but now he felt compelled to be honest. "No, lady."

"Then you must have worked very hard to achieve all that you've gained," replied Búan. "You've gained your status by your merit. Is that not fair?"

The fili sighed. "If it is fair, it is only because I was given a chance to prove my worth to the those above me. So many others of the lower classes may also have such talents, but may never be granted an opportunity to develop them."

"So then they become storytellers or harpers or bards in their villages," Búan replied. "Those are esteemed professions amongst the common folk. And anyway, most in the lower classes have not the intelligence required for the study of the higher arts."

Sinnach frowned. "How might we judge one's capacity for learning without first giving him the chance to seek proper education?" He said defensively. "I myself was born a fuidir. I was adopted by my foster-mother who is an ollamh fili at Géarán Tuathail. So, you see, it is not class that determines one's aptitude for the intellectual arts, but one's individual talents—and one's connection to the divine source of knowledge."

Búan raised her brows and walked several strides in silent contemplation. "I see now why you are so much more concerned with equality than other men. You and I both know how it feels to be made unequal by arbitrary social conventions." She paused. "But if you believe the lower classes are not given adequate opportunity to prove themselves, then why not do something about it? Why not take apprentices of your own? You could mentor children who might otherwise be overlooked because of their low status."

Sinnach's eyes brightened. The thought had never even occurred to him. "You're right, Búan! That is a wonderful idea. Thank you! I may not be ready at this moment to take on apprentices, since I am still getting settled in here at the Brugh, but I will certainly plan to make your idea manifest."

They came upon a grey heron fishing at the bank. They stood and watched it a while. At last it speared a perch and flew off to dine elsewhere. A cold breeze came from the north, so fili and warrior walked back to the Brugh speaking of little things.

Thereafter, Sinnach and Búan kept closer company, sharing their wishes and worries and stories of youth. Together they reflected upon the conduct of council and court, and developed together strategies to engender more equity in the discourse.

CHAPTER TWENTY ONE

The Plague of the Elder Tree

Bealtaine came, bejeweled with buttercups and brooklime blossoms. Calves were born, and foals, who soon frolicked in the fields with bouncing bliss. The sap of trees and the blood of man and beast quickened and caused flushing, passion, readiness for the mating.

No man was immune to the pull of the spring tide, not even a learned fili. Sinnach grew ever fonder of Búan, spending almost as much time with her as with Cellach. Sometimes they gathered altogether in the hall or ambled together in the hills, which delighted the fili most of all.

How blessed I am to have two close friends, and each of them close to each other. Every day he warmed a little more to humanity.

One day, he and Búan sat in the meadow beneath the shade of a rowan tree, hearing the skylark trill his cheery monologue. The two fell quiet to listen.

With a pounding heart, Sinnach ventured to touch Búan's hand. She smiled sweetly and leaned in close. Her face and breast nearly touched his own. The scent of her skin was like pine pins on the forest floor felled by a gentle rain. Her breath was hot upon his face.

The young man became abruptly aware of the shrinking space be-tween their two bodies, and balked. He withdrew his hand and pulled away from her.

Búan scowled at him, puzzled. "What? Do I insult you?"

"No, I..." He cut himself short, for he could find no words to explain.

"I've never met a man so timid of touch," she said in frustration. "You are indeed a queer one, Sinnach mac Lí Lon". She stood and traipsed alone across the meadow.

A week past Bealtaine there came to the court a bóaire from a village to the west. He was a wealthy man, having thirty head of cattle and a bull of his own. He came before Cellach in acute distress, wringing his hands, fidgeting his feet.

"Mo Rí," said the bóaire tensely. "I am afraid for the health of my herd. A plague has come upon them, and of the seventeen of my cows who have calved, all of their milk has dried up and three of their calves have died of starvation. The others will soon follow. My bull is lethargic and wants only to sleep in the pasture, hardly caring to stand or eat. And two of my horses have become lame. Just yesterday my closest neighbor reported his own stock are showing these signs as well. What shall I do?" he pleaded.

Sinnach spoke first. It was his role to diagnose the problem. "When did this all begin?"

"Three days after Bealtaine."

"And was there anything that occurred at that time which may have contributed to this situation?"

The bóaire ducked his head sheepishly. "Ollamh, there is only one thing that I can think of." The man hesitated, then continued. "I ex-panded my field of oats this year and an elder tree was in the way of it. So

I cut it down. I tried to burn the scrubby branches in the burn pile, as I usually do, but they would not light. Not at all. My father-in-law told me afterward that it was a bile. I hadn't known it at the time. I swear I hadn't."

Sinnach hissed and said admonishingly: "This is very serious. To cut down an elder tree is by itself a great risk, for they are favored by the Síd. But to cut down a bile, and one that is in full flower, as it would be at Bealtaine... this is a mortal danger to you and your herd. And I suspect your affliction will only get worse. It could spread farther afield."

The bóaire quivered. "What shall I do then, Ollamh? Is there anything I can give to quell the hatred of the Faeries?" The fili hissed again at the public use of that word. "I mean... the Good Folk."

Sinnach considered his question a moment, then turned to Cellach. "With the Rí Mumhan's permission I will go to the place and ask the Síd what compensation is needed to stop this plague."

Cellach nodded his approval, and Sinnach took a chariot to the place where the bóaire had cut down the elder tree. When they arrived there, the bóaire dismounted from his horse and pointed to the stump across the field, but would not go any nearer.

Stepping from the chariot, Sinnach left it in the care of his charioteer and approached the tree stump alone. As he drew close, a sudden tension seized his chest. It was as if he were being berated with hateful, malicious words, yet the air itself was silent. No bird nor beast would cross the field. The hair on the fili's neck stood on end. Frequently, he had an urge to look over his shoulder, but when he did, there was no one there. He felt a strong impulse to flee from the place, but he resisted.

Sinnach knelt down and placed his hand upon the open wound of the severed tree trunk. With a yelp he drew back his hand, for when he placed his palm there he felt a burning of his flesh. He looked at his hand; it was unharmed.

"The tree's spirit is haunting this place," Sinnach whispered. With his ash staff he drew a circle around himself and spoke an incantation of protection. Then, sitting down in the new-green stubble of the oat grass, he closed his eyes and entered a meditative trance.

Sinnach crossed a swift-flowing stream and entered a wood of green-glistening beauty. He walked a while, studying the path, very sure that he had not come this way before. In the distance he spied an open glade, and in that glade was a man bent double, planting saplings. The man placed each one in the earth with loving, tender words, as if speaking to a little child.

The fili approached the man and called to him cordially: "To you, peace and wealth."

The man stood and replied: "To you, luck and health." He was clad from head to toe in verdant green. His long hair was snow-white, and yet his face held the smoothness of youth. The man seemed at once ancient and ageless.

"What do you do here, sir?" asked Sinnach politely.

"I am planting trees, of course. Ash, rowan, and hazel today."

"And do you know of an elder tree, a bile, that was planted by your fair folk in the world of men, not far from here?"

The man nodded brightly. "Yes, I know of that bile. It is I who planted it."

"Then you must have heard of its death?" the fili asked cautiously.

The man became rigid as if he himself was made of wood. "No, I have not."

"Oh! Then I am truly sorry to be the one to tell you. A man of my world cut down that tree in his ignorance, and now his herd has been afflicted by a plague."

The Síd man knotted his brow in anger and said nothing. Grief was painted thickly on his face. A long moment elapsed in tense silence. At last he said: "That is fair punishment then." He bent back to the earth and continued working.

"Good sir, I wish to correct the man's mistake and compensate you for the offense so that we may turn back the tide of the plague."

The man growled. "Though I am insulted by the stupidity of your people, it was not I that caused the plague. You must appease the tree itself. Trees have loves and hatreds and revenges all of their own. Ask the elder what must be done to bring its spirit peace. With that I cannot help you."

Sinnach roused himself from his trance and inched closer to the stump of the hundred-ringed tree. Bowing his head in respect, he addressed its spirit.

"Elder, white blooming, black berried, shelter of wisdom, most dear to the Síd, I greet thee. Elder, bright blushing, reddening of faces, glow of anger, I beseech thee. Your life was taken wrongly, without just cause nor compensation. Tell me please, O venerable bile—what can I do to quell your fury? What can I do to turn back the plague that you have set upon the bóaire and his herd?"

Sitting in meditation, Sinnach waited, his only companion the silence. It was a hard task to keep his mind receptive in the midst of such dread. For a long while he received nothing, yet still, he waited.

The words of his master came to him from a conversation they had many years ago. *Trees move and think and speak more slowly than we human beings do, so the druí must have patience when conversing with the people of branch and bark.*

Gradually, he felt a softening of the energy about him, like a blossom beginning to unfurl. Images took shape in his mind, images that were not of his creation: a ring of five elder trees in full flower around a severed trunk. A full moon rising over the green meadow. The white milk of a ewe, a mare, and a heifer spilled upon the black earth at the roots of those five trees.

The image subsided and the fili's mind became clear once more.

"I've received your request, and upon my word, it will be done," Sinnach said resolutely. At the utterance of these words the tension in the air unknotted and was soothed. The fili respectfully stepped away from the elder stump and came to the bóaire.

While all this occurred the bóaire watched the fili fretfully. Sinnach relayed to him the tree's request of compensation for its murder. The man balked.

"Every month?" he whined.

Sinnach nodded. "What other choice do you have?"

After a moment's consideration, the bóaire gave his consent.

"And did you or your family harvest the bile's berries last year?" asked Sinnach.

"My wife did."

"Then bring to me five of those berries."

The man left and came back at a jog. He placed in Sinnach's hand five dried purple-black elderberries. "Stand back now," said the fili.

Sinnach planted the five berries in a ring around the stump of the elder tree. Then he stood beside the stump, closed his eyes, and chanted a rhythmic incantation.

The bóaire gasped and stumbled back, for five green sprouts sprang up from the ground at once. Those seedlings grew into saplings, the saplings grew into trees, and upon the boughs of those trees bloomed countless clusters of lacy flowers.

"It's... a miracle," gasped the bóaire.

When the trees were fully grown and in flower, the spell was done. Sinnach lowered his hands and opened his eyes. To the bóaire he said: "It is not all finished, my friend, for if you wish to remain safe from the wrath of the bile and the Síd who planted it, you must uphold your part of the obligation as I have instructed. Repeat to me what I told you."

The man obeyed. "Every full moon, from Bealtaine to Samhain, I will take the milk of a ewe, a mare, and a heifer and feed it to these five children of the elder bile."

"And?"

"And I and my descendants will be the faithful protectors of these trees for as long as my line persists."

The two men went back to the bóaire's farm and were gratified by what they saw. The cows' milk had been restored and their calves were once again suckling hungrily. The bull had returned to his regular obstinate humor, and the horses had been suddenly cured of their lameness.

"Thank you! Bless you, Ollamh Sinnach! You are indeed a great and powerful druí!" The farmer insisted on giving payment to the fili for saving his herd, and presented him with a white milch cow and her dun calf. Though Sinnach wished to refuse, for he had no need to take from the bóaire's wealth, he was obliged by custom to accept it. Tethering the cow to the cart of the chariot, he rode in his dignity back to the Brugh.

Thus began the enrichment of the fili's esteem, and his renown was spread across the province. Not a year had passed since the start of his tenure and already the flame-haired fili had performed two great feats. As was his aim, Sinnach's honor enhanced the people's faith in their chieftain, and so it was said throughout Mumu: "The reign of Cellach Érainn will indeed be prosperous."

And as they spoke it, so it was.

CHAPTER TWENTY TWO

The Óenach at Lugnasad

The summer was warm and mild, with long, clear days and calm, rainy nights. A summer so beneficent no elder could recall. Gladness was in every heart and thoughts of winter were put off for another day.

One bright morning Sinnach returned from his morning meditation in the forest to find a woman at his hearth. She sat in his own chair with a posture so perfect he knew her in an instant.

"Muimme!" he exclaimed, and came to kneel before her like a homesick child. Lí Lon beamed at him; the corners of her eyes wrinkled in a way that the young man had not remembered. She kissed him on the forehead and hugged him to her breast.

"I'm glad to see you, my son," she said fondly. She took his hands in her own. "News of your great deeds have reached us all the way in the mountains. Tell me more. I wish to hear everything."

Mother and son talked for many hours, exchanging news from across the province. Lí Lon stayed for several days, and so they walked together down Sinnach's favorite walking paths.

One evening, on the night of the Summer Solstice when the bonfires were lit on the hillsides and the folk danced and sang there under the starry sky, Lí Lon and Sinnach lit their own bonfire and sat together bathed in moonlight. Most folk had gone off to cavort in the outlands, and so the village was left quiet.

Lí Lon spoke above the crackling of the fire. "It is a year and a day since you came to Brugh Rí, my son. Máel Conall and I conspired to give you a gift, to mark this achievement." She called to one of her attendants. A serving woman came out from the roundhouse holding a bulky garment across her arms. Lí Lon took it and held it up to the firelight. It was a cloak made of a thousand feathers, having every color and hue of the sublunary world.

Sinnach gasped and was struck speechless. Lí Lon nodded and had him turn so she could place it upon his shoulders.

"Máel Conall and I agreed that you have come now to earn it. As you move about the worlds in your new role, this cloak, the tuigen, will assist you in your work—it will confer to you even greater respect. But it is fragile so use it sparingly—only for ceremonial occasions or negotiations which require a more commanding presence." Lí Lon regarded him with approval. "It suits you. I am proud of you, my son. It is as I said long ago: you have become a great and powerful fili. And you will become greater even still."

It was the last day of Lí Lon's visit. After breakfasting together, she made ready to depart. Sinnach had missed her dearly and enjoyed her visit very much, and now he was sad to see her go. He presented her with many gifts for herself and Máel Conall, so many that he insisted she take a pack horse to carry them all. Smiling, she accepted and said wryly, "Generosity is a virtue, Sinnach, but be sure to manage your wealth wisely. Keep enough for yourself and your household."

"Oh, never worry! I have much more than I need. Sometimes I feel burdened by it all; sometimes I wish for the simple, austere life of a scholar in the mountains once again." Sinnach paused. "Muimme, there is something in that regard that gives me concern. I often think of my past poverty in my childhood, and of the family I left behind. Though I have gained wealth, in all likelihood my family is still poor—perhaps even poorer than when I left, for my actions against the aire Talorc might have caused them a debt." His shoulders drooped with the heavy weight of those memories. "I feel a need to share my wealth with them somehow. Or at least, buy them out of whatever debt I might have caused. I fear they may have lost their freedom and become dóerfuidir. If this is true, and if I could free them and let them get away from that hateful tyrant, I would."

Lí Lon puckered her mouth in displeasure. "You owe them nothing, Sinnach—those people who so harmed you and caused you to flee for your life. And anyway, what would you give? How would you give it? Surely you would not return to them yourself?"

"No. No, I would not go back myself. I would need someone to go on my behalf. I had thought to give them two of my black heifers and the white cow with her dun calf who were given to me as payment for curing the plague of the elder tree. I don't need them. It would effect me very little not to have them, but it would surely lift my former family from their poverty."

Lí Lon stared into her son's face, her expression unreadable. At last she spoke with resolution. "It is noble of you to show them such charity, though I doubt I'd do the same if I were in your place. And yet, I do not know what this burden feels like in your soul. So I will go west and give your cows to the family that shunned you. I will take it upon myself, as a mother's duty to her son, to help heal an old wound in his heart."

"Oh, Muimme! You would do this for me?" He swallowed back grateful tears. Then he took pause, for there was an edge to her words. "And you will not... you will be kind to them, when you meet them?"

Lí Lon raised her slender eyebrows. "I will not display my prejudice, if that's what concerns you. But I *will* tell them how their *son* became the highest fili in Mumu. They will weep with pride, and they will weep with sorrow that they had treated you with such cruelty."

Sinnach shook his head. "That is in the past now—I wish to be done forever with the suffering between us. I hold onto that pain no longer. And you, Muimme, should not feel obliged to hold it for me."

With one last embrace, Lí Lon left for the western coast, trailed by her two servants, the packhorse, and the cows.

Soon after Lí Lon left, Sinnach sought out and accepted two young apprentices from nearby villages in Fellubair. They were each of low-status families: one a fuidir and one an ócaire. Lí Lon had endorsed the decision, deeming him ready to take students of his own. He found teaching them a delight, for he enjoyed inspiring in others a love of knowledge. Thus July passed quickly, busy with the care and education of two new wards.

On Lugnasad began the óenach which would last seven days and nights. It was an annual festival to celebrate the summer harvest, and for the Érainn it was held at Brugh Rí. In the day there would be races on foot, races on horseback and in chariots, feats of strength, hurling games, and many other contests. At night, folk from all around would gather in the Rí Mumhan's hall to feast and boast, sing and dance. The Rí would open his court to negotiate the year's payments and exchanges of land and livestock, and there he would also accept the annual dues of tribute and taxes from the túatha he governed. The óenach was the place to proclaim new laws and important legal judgments that were decided the previous year.

Cellach joined these contests with zeal and vigor; hardly any were the match of his strength and stamina. Búan competed too, and so it was revealed to Sinnach why she had been chosen as the Rí's champion. She was graceful and fierce, lithe and cunning. And though she was slighter than the men she came up against, she was faster and more agile. Búan won nearly as many contests as Cellach.

On the third day of the óenach were the horse races. Fáelán and Cúanu, two warriors of the Noí, teased Sinnach as he stood watching the Rí's sister from the sidelines.

"I'll give you some advice, Sinnach, of a thing I've seen more than once," said Cúanu, smirking. "Búan will take no man to her bed unless he can best her in a contest."

Fáelán sidled up close to Sinnach and draped his arm around the fili's shoulders, forgetting for a moment the proper distance owed to a nemed. "Hardly a man here has not strove for her favor, though most have failed. Why not try your hand at it, eh Ollamh? I say with surety that you'll get no further with all this eye-batting you do." Fáelán fluttered his lids in mockery.

Sinnach scowled and threw off Fáelán's arm. He was embarrassed that his feelings for Búan were obvious enough to attract these men's goading. And yet, despite himself, their teasing worked: he began to toy with the idea of joining a race. *Oh, but wouldn't those two find it amusing if I should be humiliated in public?* It was true, yet still he was tempted, for he had not lost his youthful love of contest.

With a sudden surge of virility, he set aside his staff and his mantle and stepped forward for the contest. Fáelán and Cúanu trilled with glee and pushed the fili towards his choice of racehorse.

The contestants mounted their steeds and held their horses behind a line made in the turf. They fidgeted, pranced, and jostled. Sinnach had chosen a muddy bay gelding who tossed his head again and again as the fili fumbled with the reins.

Búan came up beside him on her elegant blue roan, whose name was Búada: victory. "Are you sure you wish to race with us, Sinnach? Do you have much experience with horses?" she asked with concern.

"Em... well, not so much. But I'm sure I can handle myself," he said stubbornly.

Búan raised her eyebrows and shrugged. "Very well. But be careful. I suggest you stick to the outside. If you come off, try to land on your feet and roll. The head of a fili is too valuable to be broken." She walked Búada to the other end of the starting line and stood a stride from Cellach on Airgetmong, his grey. The stallion pawed the earth and chomped at the bit with a foaming mouth. Out of earshot Búan spoke to Cellach, and the two siblings shot Sinnach a worried glance.

"Riders at the ready!" called the marshal. A line of thirty riders stood side by side, pointing their horses down the length of a long, flat field freshly clipped by the mouths of sheep. They would race in a circuit around the field and end again in the place where they started.

All was quiet but for the huffing and stomping of horses impatient to stampede. A horse reared in his excitement and nipped at his neighbor. Hardly a one could stand still for the excitement coursing through them, ready to explode in a flurry of limbs.

"GO!" shouted the marshal, dropping his flag to the ground. And with that began a thundering of hooves that kicked up a great cloud of black soil in their wake.

With both hands Sinnach held to his gelding's mane as his steed leapt forward underneath him, carried away by the energy of the other galloping horses. Fáelán and Cúanu watched with delight as Sinnach's gelding drifted at a loping canter toward the shade of the forest beside the racing field. The fili bounced like a log in the saddle, lost his balance, and fell forward onto the horse's neck. The two of them were lost from sight under the cover of the trees.

The spectators roared with laughter. Fáelán and Cúanu held to each other's shoulders, wiping tears of laughter from their eyes.

But what they saw next shut them up completely. A streak shot out from the wood where Sinnach had disappeared. Two shapes emerged, not one horse, but two. There was the bay gelding without his rider, and beside him was a chestnut stallion. The two horses galloped away at top speed toward the pack that had outpaced them.

Cellach and Búan were at the lead. All they could hear was the roar of the wind in their ears and the pounding of hooves beneath them. Each sibling kicked their horse forward, one striving to outpace the other.

Suddenly, a figure came up beside them. Búan turned her head and was shocked by what she beheld. A glossy chestnut stallion without bridle, saddle, or rider was keeping pace beside her roan. She watched in confusion as the stallion tilted his head and caught her eye with his own eye of amber. She knew those eyes. Búan glanced behind her for the sight of Sinnach, but he was not to be seen. There were only the other contestants and with them a riderless bay gelding.

Búan turned back to the chestnut. "Sinnach?" she shouted against the wind. The stallion tossed his head and whinnied once. Then he sidled up close to the mare, bumping against Búan's leg. He tossed his head at her once more.

Finally, she took his meaning. With the greatest feat of horsemanship anyone there had ever seen, Búan dropped her reins, folded her legs, and placed her two feet on the seat of her saddle. She crouched there for one, two breaths, then leapt like a salmon onto the stallion's bare back. Instantly, they shot off ahead, easily outpacing the rest of the pack. They barreled across the finish line a good five paces ahead of Cellach and his grey.

As rider and stallion slowed to a walk, the crowd surged around them. Búan and the chestnut circled slowly to catch their breath. At last, Búan slid off the stallion's back and patted the crest of his arching neck. He bowed his head to her courteously and plunged back into the wood whence he had emerged.

Cellach dismounted and came to his sister utterly perplexed. "Was that... was that...?"

"Sinnach," she said, mystified. "Or at least, I think it was."

A cheer erupted from the crowd as a figure emerged from the trees. It was Sinnach, pulling his tunic down over his head and hastily wrapping his belt around his waist. He was panting and dripping with sweat, his long red hair fell unplaited about his shoulders.

Cellach laughed heartily and gripped the disheveled man by the shoulder. "Well now, if you were the horse upon whose back the race was won, then who is the winner: the rider or her steed?"

Sinnach smiled magnanimously. "The win belongs to Búan, for it was proven to us all by her salmon-leap that no rider in Mumu is the match of her horsemanship."

Búan reached forward and gently pulled her fingers through Sinnach's free-flowing chestnut hair. It was the exact color of the stallion's mane.

In the next moment she was lifted up and swept away by the current of the cheering crowd.

Every night of the óenach there was a sumptuous feast held in the Rí's hall, and this night was no different. Platters were piled with roasted meats and river fish, cheeses and breads, greens and fruits. Goblets were filled from heavy cauldrons of beer and mead. All shared in song and boastful storytelling. The dancing was merry, as was the conversation.

The Rí Mumhan sat at the center of the high table beside his sister, the royal parents, the Rí's líaig, the three aire who gave him closest council, and Sinnach as his fili. The Noí stood or lounged beside the high table, their weapons always at arm's reach should they need to protect their chieftain.

First the bards and harpers sang their tunes, then it was the turn of the Rí's fili to sing his praises. Sinnach had prepared a praise poem to sing to his chieftain that night. He went to the center of the hall and took the harp in his hands. Letting his eyes fall upon the face of the Rí Mumhan, he sang in clear, lilting timbre:

> Cellach Rí
> Righteous brilliance from his brow
> Beauteous beacon of men
> Might and wisdom have no match.
>
> Bright-headed fearsome and fair
> Grievous gifts are for his foes
> Perfect judgments passed in peace
> Right wrought his weapons, his words.
>
> His locks alight like sun rays
> Flowing flames lick the black earth
> There upon Áine's bride-bed
> Gently touched he germs the grain.
>
> As stag he leaps light of foot
> As boar he bellows hard-tusked rage
> As kite he scalds with shrewd eye
> As hound he guards the giving of oaths.
>
> Bronze breasted in battles won
> Games greeted with flashing grin
> Learned as Lug the Long Arm
> Every craft his cunning keeps.
>
> He makes our riches ripen
> He guides in glory our blades
> He buoys our happy hearts
> Rí Cellach!

Silence settled in the hall. Many cheeks were wet with adulatory tears. Cellach glowed as brightly as he had the day of his coronation. His golden hair rippled as the light that glints from the rolling sea; his shoulders spread as broad as an eagle's wings; his spine erect with the dignity of a seven-pronged stag.

Cellach must be the fairest Rí that has ever ruled Mumu, Sinnach thought to himself.

Then the fili's eyes strayed for a moment and were caught by the face beside the Rí; the face of a woman with hair the many shades of ripe barley, with eyes like the sea darkened by a storm, with lips the red of raspberries. Búan was to Sinnach as striking as her brother, and all in the court adored her as if she were herself a rígain.

The night progressed, the revelry persisted, and with the unceasing flow of drink the hall grew steadily louder. Sinnach never let a drop of mead nor beer touch his lips, but he watched the Rí Mumhan drain cup after cup of beer. The fools and the farters performed their tricks, and when the mood reached a level vulgarity not to his liking, Sinnach gave his excuses to leave.

As Sinnach got up from his chair, Cellach gripped his arm and pulled him back down. "Where are you going, Sinnach? Here, have one last drink with me." The chieftain thrust a goblet of beer in the fili's hand, spilling much of the liquid over the table. His speech was slurred. The Rí was drunk.

Cellach drained his own goblet and set it down on the table with a crack. He leaned forward to catch Búan's eye. "Sister!" he shouted. "All night I've watched the two of you making eyes at each other. Thinking of riding him for a second time tonight, perhaps?" An outbreak of chuckling came from the Noí behind the table. "But sister, you've not even kissed him yet! Here. Let me show you how it's done." And with that Cellach took Sinnach's face between his two strong hands and pulled the fili into a rough and passionate kiss on the mouth.

Sinnach flailed his arms and pushed the Rí away. His mouth and nostrils were filled with the stench of alcohol. Tearing himself free, Sinnach sputtered and wiped his lips in disgust. He got up and stormed out of the hall. All those in witness roared with drunken laughter, including Cellach, who was too intoxicated to note the fili's adverse reaction.

The revelry continued into the young hours before dawn. At last the hall fell quiet as the feasters staggered home to their beds.

For the remainder of the óenach Sinnach was nowhere to be found. He was not in the hall nor in his roundhouse. He was not within nor without the fort. Búan looked for him in all the places they usually walked together, and yet she could not find him.

Finally, a day past the last night of the óenach, a spearman on the rampart spied two figures approaching in the distance; each was of a bright, ruddy hue. The spearman pointed them out to his fellow. One of the men beheld two foxes; the other man beheld a fox and a man. As the figures came close, the spearmen recognized them: it was Sinnach accompanied by his familiar, the wild vixen.

"The Rí and Búan have been looking everywhere for you, Ollamh," said the guard at the gate.

Sinnach nodded stoically, his face inscrutable. "Tell the Rí I will speak with him now. I will wait here." No man besides the first fili of Mumu could dictate the time or place of a meeting with the Rí Mumhan. Sinnach was Cellach's equal in status and power; it was an appropriate moment to remind his friend of this fact, he thought. On a sun-warmed stone he sat with his back turned to the Brugh. The vixen sat quietly beside him, her lustrous tail curled daintily around her haunches.

Cellach met the fili outside the wall of the Brugh, and with some convincing dismissed his attendants upon Sinnach's request. "This must be a private conversation," Sinnach said sternly.

Cellach followed Sinnach and his familiar to a shady stand of silver birch trees, near enough to the Brugh but out of earshot. The Rí's gazed at the vixen warily. He had never come so close to the fili's familiar. She was powerfully timid, and had allowed herself to be seen by him only once or twice before.

There was a tension in the air between the two men. Cellach knew something was amiss, but thought to give the fili the chance to speak first.

They sat opposite each other on fallen logs. A long moment passed. Finally, the Rí could not bear the silence any longer. "Sinnach, I see that you're upset. Tell me, what is the matter?"

The fili's face was stormy. "Do you remember what happened four nights ago, at the feast after the horse race?"

Cellach scratched his head. "Oh. Em... I remember your praise poem. It was beautiful, of course. I am honored by your art. Then... well, I think I might have had a drop too many to drink. I was drunk—perhaps more drunk than I've ever been. I don't remember much of the rest of it." The Rí paused with concern on his face. "Why, Sinnach? Did I say something to offend you?"

The fili shook his head. "No, Cellach. You kissed me. You kissed me on the mouth in the middle of the hall." His voice grated with anger.

Cellach's cheeks reddened as if he had been slapped. "Oh. Oh! I'm sorry, Sinnach. I didn't... I wasn't in full control of myself." The Rí paused and took a shaking breath. "But perhaps... perhaps I'm glad the drink gave me boldness enough to divulge a secret I've kept hidden for so long. It's been like a leash around my neck which pulls tighter every time I look at you. Some days I feel I can hardly breath when you are near me."

Sinnach growled. "I am not a woman, Cellach!"

"What? N—no. Of course not. That's not what I..."

"Then what did you mean by it? I hope this is not like one of those boyish pranks that the Noí play on each other."

Cellach swallowed hard and spoke with voice aquiver. "It's not. I'm being honest with you now. You are my closest friend, Sinnach. I thought you to be the type of man who could listen to my truth and not think ill of me for it. Will you hear me, Sinnach? Will you suspend your judgments long enough to listen to your friend?"

The fili closed his eyes and inhaled deep to quiet the pounding in his ears. Cellach was right, he deserved to have his truth received graciously. *As my own secret had been by my masters.*

"I'm sorry, Cellach. I was just... surprised. Tell me then. I wish to hear it."

"What I tell you now... keep it between us. You will not share it with anyone."

"I swear it, Cellach."

"Good," Cellach replied. He wrung his hands, opened his mouth to speak, and closed it again. Away above the rushing river, an eagle called and was answered by another. At last he lifted his eyes, and the words so long held back came tumbling out.

"I love you, Sinnach. I love you like a brother... but more than that still. Ever since you found me in the wilds when we were boys, you've had my admiration. On that day, I was so struck by your wildness, your wit, your handsome face, and in the years we were apart I thought on you often... I dreamed that some day we would be together again. And now—oh, how the fates have blessed me! I have you always at my side; I can look upon your shining face whenever I wish. And yet... yet I cannot decide which is more painful: when you are far away and out of sight, or when you are near at hand but out of reach. So when you sung your praises that night just past, I thought... I thought that maybe, finally, you had come to return my attractions." Cellach sighed and dropped his eyes. "But I see now I was mistaken."

Sinnach sat rigid, stunned by the Rí Mumhan's words. Cellach loved him as a *man*? Could a man love another—as a lover?

I suppose it is not as strange as a girl growing up to become a man who is attracted to women, he admitted. In Nature animals occasionally pair up in couples of the same sex. *Then it must be a natural variation, like being Eclipsed.*

"So you love men, then? Do you take men to your bed?"

Cellach nodded.

"Ah, I understand now," said Sinnach with dawning comprehension. "This is why you ran away from home as a boy! And it's why you haven't yet taken a wife, though more than half the women in Ériu seek to be your consort." The fili paused, thinking. "The goddess Áine... when you mated with her was it difficult for you?"

Cellach paused and rubbed his face. "No, it wasn't difficult. I was afraid at first she might know my desires and reject me for it. But I was wrong: she knew them and indulged me. I am not the first Rí Mumhan to have such feelings, she said. And as a goddess she can take any form she wishes. So she took not the form of a woman, but a man."

Cellach's eyes widened and darted away. Sinnach intuited there was something else his friend had left unsaid. The fili guessed it and was grateful not to hear it spoken aloud.

Sinnach regained the use of his tongue. "I do not love you in that way, Cellach. I love you as a brother, not as a lover. I am attracted to women, not men."

Cellach sighed. "I know that now, Sinnach, and it pains me. When I watch you and Búan courting, I am awhirl with emotion. I have both jealousy and joy that my sister has so captured your affections."

"I'm sorry, Cellach. I'm sorry to cause you such sorrow. If it is better that Búan and I not—"

The Rí shook his head. "No, no. You and Búan... I am glad you two have become close. I don't want to get in the way of it. No other man is as worthy of her courtship. And it's not your fault that I feel this way. I've tried to be different. I've tried to be *normal*. I've tried to love women. But... it just feels wrong to me. It feels unnatural. I don't know how to explain it in a way that you might understand." Cellach hung his head in melancholy. "You must think me an abomination."

"No, Cellach! Not at all! How could I when the goddess Áine so clearly holds you in her favor and accepts you as you are?" Sinnach looked at his friend with compassion, finally ready to speak his own closely-guarded secret. "I understand your suffering better than you know, for I also have a secret; until now I've not had the courage to share it. But you inspire me, Cellach. It is time."

Sinnach breathed deep and continued. "I was not always a man, Cellach. When I first met you long ago in the mountains, I was in my original form—that of a female. You see, when I was a child I had to flee my home because my parents believed I was a Faery Changeling come to replace their little girl. When finally I could not withstand any more abuse, I fled into the mountains, to the place where we met. It was not until I had studied the draíochta druadh for nearly five years that I mastered the skill which allowed me to transform myself into a male. At last, my body took the shape that aligned with my soul. And there are others like me—there always have been. We are called the Áes Múchta. For generations immemorial we have served as filid and druíd."

It was Cellach who was now speechless. A thousand questions flooded through his mind—too many to know which should be asked first. Then he laughed and said: "What an odd pair we make, eh Sinnach? Fili and chieftain, both who are so queer!"

They laughed together, each relieved to have his honesty met with compassion.

"Let us be done with secrets, Sinnach," said Cellach. "Though we are not lovers, I wish for us to be close—like brothers still. We will share with each other our thoughts and our struggles. Won't we?"

Sinnach nodded.

"And if you pursue my sister's hand, I advise you to tell her what you have just told me. She must know this and she must know soon, before your courtship goes any further."

The fili nodded reluctantly. The Rí's council was sound, but it would not be an easy task. "Does Búan know? About you, I mean."

"I suspect that she does, though we've never spoken of it. In my youth I was nearly found out once or twice, but she helped me in ways that prevented my humiliation. She is a good woman, and fair, but she is not fond of surprises. I know this of her from our campaigns together: she is in her best form when the battle is known beforehand. Tell her gently and I think she will receive it well."

CHAPTER TWENTY THREE

Thine Enemy is Come

After the óenach, Sinnach became more aware of the space between himself and Cellach. It was difficult, for a time, to think how he might remain close to his friend, now knowing Cellach's feelings towards him. In the lulls amidst courtly business, their eyes often met awkwardly.

Is he looking at me as his friend or as his point of desire? Sinnach found himself asking too often. He forced the question from his mind and focused on the tasks at hand.

The weeks passed peacefully and Sinnach was reassured by Cellach's respectful manner. Outwardly, the Rí's actions towards him changed very little, and with time the tension between the two men eased. They spoke no further of those sensitive subjects. Yet some days Sinnach perceived a subtle pain in his friend's face, shading his bright eyes as a cloud passes across the cerulean sky.

In autumn Cellach took up the hunt with more vigor. Most mornings he cantered off on the back of Airgetmong accompanied by his hunting hounds and four of his men at arms. Búan never went with him.

"My brother requires the privacy of his own company sometimes, as do I," she said to Sinnach wisely. The fili looked at her sideways, wondering how much she meant by it.

Mending tears in the community cloth gave Sinnach great pleasure. As brithem and druí he judged legal cases and resolved many magical ills. It was an honor to meet the need of Mumu as its first fili, and by his judicious service his esteem continued to grow. *I am fulfilling my life's purpose here*, he reflected.

With all this his self-assurance grew, yet Búan never let him become prideful. Some days when he walked with his head held too high, her teasing brought him back down to his roots. At first it galled him to be the constant target of her fun, yet in time he hungered for it. Her jests were like the little stings that guard the hive's honey.

Yet in her smile Sinnach spied her ignorance of what he kept hidden: that he was once called a girl and a Changeling; of his transformation to become a man. *Would she smile at me so if she knew these things?* And it was for want of finding approval in those flashing eyes that he stayed his word, though it was against the advice of her brother.

The more frequently Sinnach was in Búan's company, the more acutely he perceived her unknowing. A fear then crept into his heart—a fear that intimacy without honesty was betrayal. *Surely Cellach knows her better than I. He was confident she could handle the truth.* For weeks he chewed on his indecision, and at last he resolved to tell her. Or at least, to attempt it.

On a mild day in early October, the two walked alone on the bank of the River Maigue as they had not done in many months. Sinnach spread his cloak upon the ground and there they sat together, eating of frost-sweetened sloes. The fruit's sweet juice dribbled down Búan's chin and made her laugh with embarrassment. She leaned over the bank to rinse her hands and mouth in the river, then sat up and flicked her fingers dry, spraying water in the fili's face. He smiled, and closing his eyes chanted the first transformation spell he had ever learned. Droplets of water froze upon his face. He peeled those pearls from his cheeks, now ice, and cast them at her.

Búan gasped in mock vexation, then reached up and plucked a crystalline tear from his skin, marveling at it.

"Búan," the fili said finally. "I've been meaning to tell you something... a truth of import." Her eyes locked onto his; her cherry lips parted just a little in her listening. Sinnach gulped down air nervously.

"I have something to admit to you, though it's hard for me to say," he continued. "I wish to do nothing in the world to displease you, Búan. I wish to have your favor, and as such, I must be honest with you."

The woman opened her eyes a little wider and leaned close. Her nearness strummed his nerves like a harp string, and yet he had sworn to recoil from her no more. "You once called me timid, and I confess it to be true. I wish I were braver with you, but there is good reason for my fear. You are... you are so precious to me, Búan. I fear I could say the wrong thing and send you away. And so I've waited... but I think I can wait no longer. I'm sorry you've had to exercise such patience with me. But if we—"

"I am no poet, Sinnach," Búan interjected. "Words are worth less to me than deeds. So if you love me, show me. I tire of all this talking." She tipped forward and pressed her soft lips to his.

By instinct he leapt back from her as if scalded by her kiss, then scolded himself. *Be a man, Sinnach! You shall shrink no more from this woman's touch!* Before she could respond with frustration, Sinnach touched his own lips to hers and tasted again that sloe-sweetened mouth. Her hand came to the back of his neck as they inhaled the same breath. A sudden blaze coursed through his body, catching like wildfire in dry grass. He had never felt such lust; it threatened to overwhelm him. He slid his hands down her back, wishing to touch every surface of her skin; her body as firm and smooth as a river stone. In the grip of his desire,

Sinnach was losing control. Would that he could surrender to the pull of her body—but still, he was afraid.

Búan pulled back then, rescuing him from this torment. She inhaled deeply, drinking in his scent, and smiled. "There. I hope that was better than the kiss of a drunken chieftain."

Sinnach blushed. "Verily," he panted. "Your lips do much to heal me from the rudeness that night."

Búan's eyes rested on the poet's face. "You are new to this, I can tell. So let us start slowly. Perhaps it's good for me to practice patience. I had forgotten until now how thrilling it is to be held in the waiting."

She touched her lips again to his quickly, like the nip of a puppy, then stood and held out her hand. Sinnach grasped it and was pulled to his feet. Taking up his cloak again, they continued their stroll, shoulders touching, arms entwined. So enamored was he of her beauty and the touch of her hand that all thought of his confession left his mind completely.

The feast at Samhain was fast approaching and preparations were made to mark the end of the year. This was the holy day to give thanks for the year's abundance, to remember and honor the dead, and to be wary of the veil's parting between the worlds.

The Brugh was all abuzz, for the Rí would be soon hosting a great number of guests. Servants bustled between the kitchens and outbuildings, baking and roasting and taking in goods for the feast that would begin in two days. Sinnach tried his best to stay out of the Brugh to avoid being bumped and rebuked by busy servants, yet the last of the year's legal cases had to be attended in the hall.

That afternoon the fili sat by Cellach in the hall to judge a dispute between two ócaire farmers.

"My neighbor owes me a portion of his honey," said a rotund brown-haired man. "My hive swarmed in the summer and he took them for his own."

"I didn't *take* them," said his black-haired neighbor, the younger of the two farmers. "My new beehouse was empty and it is the hive's choice to nest wherever they wish."

"But Brandubh built that house specifically to catch them!" said Cassán, the older man. He pointing accusatively.

"That's absurd! I built it not for your swarm particularly, but for any swarm that should seek it," said Brandubh.

Cellach interrupted this heated exchange. "Ócaire, please. Calm yourselves. Brandubh, is it true that you received the swarm that left your neighbor Cassán's land?"

"It is true, mo Rí."

"And is there any reason then why he is not owed the usual portion of honey due to him for his lost swarm?"

"Yes, mo Rí, there is. Cassán is neglectful of his bees. That is why they left. It was one of three hives he lost this year. His beehouses are unkempt and falling apart. And he found it convenient to wait until I'd harvested and filtered the last of the summer's honey to stake a claim in it, so that he might avoid the work himself."

"Cassán," said Cellach. "Is it true that you've lost three hives this year and that you've allowed your beehouses to fall into disrepair?"

"I had meant to build my bees new houses this summer, but then they swarmed so it was no use."

"Preparation for summer should be done in winter, Cassán," said the Rí Mumhan. "And it was ill-done to wait to bring a suit until now, at the very end of the year no less! When you believe a wrong has been done to you against the law, you must announce it to your túath immediately. It was inappropriate for you to delay the telling until the season ended and the bees had been put to bed."

Cellach pause and leaned towards Sinnach to whisper in his ear. The fili whispered back and the Rí nodded affirmatively.

"Then I make this judgment: Cassán shall be given a portion of the swarm's honey from this year. But as a result of his negligence of his hives, the payment will be docked in half. Brandubh will give Cassán not a third of the honey harvest, as it would have been under normal circumstances, but a sixth. And he will not be owned any portion of the honey harvest next year nor any year following." Cellach addressed Cassán directly. "From now on take better care of your hives so that this does not happen to you again."

The two ócaire bowed and gave their thanks for the balanced judgment. It had been the last judgment of the day and dark had already fallen. The door to the hall was closed. Sinnach stood from his seat, and flanked by his two young apprentices, made to leave for supper in his own home.

"Would you like to sup with me in my house, Búan?" said the fili to the Rí's champion. She had been sitting to the side of the court, watching the proceedings with her usual keenness.

"It would give me pleasure," replied Búan. Sinnach offered her his hand and she took it. Hand in hand, together they made for the door.

There was a sudden scratching at the door and when it was opened, a streak of red fur flew in yipping. It was the vixen, Sinnach's familiar. She came to him and barked in great agitation.

Sinnach went rigid as a stone. All color drained from his cheeks.

"Sinnach... you've gone pale. What is the matter? What does the fox say?" asked Búan.

Sinnach stammered: "She said... 'Thine enemy is come. Thine enemy is come'."

Cellach's eyes darted between the fox and the fili. The face of each reflected the other's fear. "But whose enemy... yours? Who is that, Sinnach?"

Before the fili could explain, a commotion was heard outside of the hall. A man's voice was raised in anger: "I've traveled two full days, by land and sea. I expect to be seen by the Rí Mumhan tonight!" There was further exchange of bitter words, and at last the door of the hall was opened. Cúanu came in with a spear in his hand and concern on his face.

"Mo Rí, an aire has come from Fír Lúachair to seek your council. I told him you've finished with court for the day and that he should come back tomorrow morning—but he insists to be seen tonight."

Cellach spoke sternly: "Dark has fallen and my court is closed. Let him in so that I may tell him myself to come back tomorrow. He will find lodging in my guesthouse for the night." The Rí gestured for the door to be opened.

The aire came into the hall flanked by two of his warriors, disarmed, and an attendant fili. Six of the Rí Mumhan's guards surrounded the strangers, holding their spearpoints upright.

The man was richly-dressed and broad-shouldered. Though his sallow face and dour expression made him unattractive, the man's presence was nevertheless formidable. Sinnach squeezed Búan's hand fretfully.

"Welcome to my hall, aire. I am sorry to inform you I have just finished hearing cases for the day. But you are welcome to bring your issue before me tomorrow morning. You may stay in my guesthouse for the—"

"I will not stay in your brugh at all," the aire interrupted. Many in the hall gasped at his rude demeanor. No one ought to interrupt the Rí Mumhan or address him so curtly. "I will be heard tonight and leave straight away. I wish not to linger here."

Cellach furrowed his brow. "And who are you to make such demands of me, your Rí?"

The sallow man puffed out his broad chest. "I am Talorc mac Iollan, aire of the Fír Lúachair, cousin to the rí Fír Lúachair. I have news of an imposter residing in your house." The man gazed about the hall and found the face of the red-haired fili. "There! There she is! That one is the imposter," he spat venomously, pointing directly at Sinnach. Sinnach stood paralyzed with fright, unable to speak.

"What do you mean by this?" asked Cellach. He could no longer conceal the anger in his voice. "This is my fili, the Ollamh Sinnach. He is not an imposter. He is my most trusted advisor."

"That... person... is not who she appears to be," said the aire. "I knew her as a child—a girl child. She is no man and certainly no fili. She is a woman and a fuidir, a fuidir that accosted me many years ago and fled my túath so as to avoid the fine."

The Rí Mumhan stood up from his chair, white-knuckled. He raised his voice menacingly. "You know little of what you speak. Sinnach is of course a man and a fili—the most esteemed fili in Mumu—no matter who he was before. Why come you now to my court to make such a dishonorable accusation?"

Talorc stepped forward, his body tense as a rutting bull. "Because the family that *she* left behind was indebted to me as a result of her crime and so were made dóer, unfree. For twelve years they were my dóerfuidir and would have remained so if it wasn't for a mysterious payment brought to them this spring. A strange woman, claiming to be a fili and foster-mother to the fili of this court, gave them three cows and a bull calf. She told my dóerfuidir that her foster-son was their lost child who had run away. It was only last week, after the last harvest of the season, that I discovered all this had occurred. My fuidir gave me those cows as payment to clear their debt. Now they are free, they have left my land, and I am unexpectedly lacking in labor for the winter. I came to you, Rí Cellach, to inform you of your fili's treachery. You should thank me for this warning, for she is a certain danger to you. I also come to be compensated for the unjust loss of my dóerfuidir. What was given to them should have, in propriety, come through me and not to the family directly. Dóerfuidir may not own property of their own."

In a passion, Cellach began to glow as if touched by the sun. His voice boomed like thunder across the hall. "I shall not thank you for telling me of things I already know. Your arrogance in coming here and speaking with such disrespect is intolerable. Know your place, aire—it is far below me.

"And as for your compensation, you shall have none. Sinnach's property may be given to whomever he chooses. And it seems to me amply just that those dóerfuidir should have gained their freedom from you, for I see you are the kind of man who is unrightly cruel to his tenants."

Talorc stood there red-faced with fury. "This is wrongful judgment, and I pray it will leave you marked."

All in the hall were shocked to hear those heinous words. The Rí's guards lowered their spearpoints and the Noí came at Talorc with their swords unsheathed.

"Hold!" Cellach called out to his warriors, and the men held. "Talorc, leave my hall at once and take your insolence with you. I wish never to lay eyes on your boorish face again. You are forever barred from entering the Fellubair túath."

The brazen aire bared his teeth and bellowed: "If we ever meet again there will be two blades between us." He turned and stormed out of the Brugh, consumed by the night.

The hall was perfectly silent; every face reflecting naked distress. Every eye turned to stare at the red-haired fili.

"Sinnach, is this true? What is the meaning of this?" Búan whispered. She dropped his hand and stepped away from him.

Sinnach could not speak; he quivered with fear and shame.

Búan glared at her brother. "You knew this? You knew and you didn't tell me?" She turned to Sinnach again with a look of disgust. "What are you even... a man or a woman?"

Sinnach reached out to her and croaked, "Búan, let me explain..."

"You led me on! You led me to believe a falsehood! Do you two conspire to shame me?" Búan pulled her arm away from Sinnach's reach. "No! Leave me be. I must... I cannot think with you near." Búan left in haste for the shelter of the women's house.

Watching Búan flee from him in such distress, Sinnach's will finally broke. Before all to see, he transformed himself into a fox and leapt out from the pile of his clothes on the floor. Darting between the legs of the men that tried to catch him, the fox galloped into the night with the vixen close behind.

CHAPTER TWENTY FOUR

The Hall of Joy and Pleasure

Sinnach sped on silent paws through the shadowed woodland. What direction he took he could not say, for all reason had left his mind. All that was left was pain: pain of loss, humiliation, and shame. He ran so long and so hard that he outpaced his familiar and sprinted alone through foreign glades.

For hours he raced headlong in no discernible direction, but eventually his strength began to wane. He slowed to a trot, then to a walk, and finally he halted, panting. Sinnach let his fox's shape fall away, and so became a man once more, naked and cold, shivering and weeping.

"All is lost," he sobbed. "All is lost."

He fell to his knees and wetted the ground with his tears. Covering his face, he wept with such agony that he took no notice of the mist that rose up around him.

"What is lost, dear Sinnach?" asked a soft voice beside him.

Sinnach started and looked up. A shape emerged from the mist: a woman with dark hair and skin that shone like seafoam in the moonlight. She knelt by him and peered into his eyes. Sinnach knew that face: it was Toltu, the Síd-chieftain's daughter.

"I was... I was shamed. They found out... she found out..." He was buffeted by another wave of sobbing and could say no more.

With a word Toltu conjured a cloak made of the soft pelts of white hares and wrapped it about him to cover his nakedness. Gently, she lifted his chin with her slender fingers and dried his cheeks with her sleeve.

"I knew this day would come," said Toltu. Her voice was soothing, as a breeze through birch leaves, and the sound of it made Sinnach's chest quiet its heaving. "Humanity is ignorant and cruel. They cannot understand you as I understand you. They cannot love you as I love you."

Sinnach stared at her then in wonder. This Síd-woman whom he hardy knew, this being of unearthly beauty, could love *him*? She knew his present; she knew his past. She knew him as fili and fuidir, man and Grían Múchta, and still, she wanted *him*? But he was so far beneath her: only a man, red-haired and of humble birth. How could he deserve the affections of one so perfect?

Toltu touched his face tenderly and stopped the tears from flowing. "Come now. Come with me to my ráth where I shall give you hospitality." She stood and pulled him to his feet. The woman held his hand as they traveled in the moonlight through the Otherworld wood to the gate of the Mór-rí's ráth.

In the hall Mór-rí Géarshúileach gave Sinnach a warm reception. "Welcome back, Sinnach. I knew you would return." The fili nodded his thanks, yet sorrow prevented him from saying any more.

Toltu guided him to the guesthouse, and bid him lay on a bed made of swan's down. The house was empty of other guests; he would sleep there alone in that strange empty space.

The woman covered him with silken sheets and stroked his long red mane. "You have such lovely hair," she said. Then she kissed him on each eye and said: "Sleep well, Sinnach. Here you shall have no worries. Leave every sorrow behind, for life in my ráth is free of all feelings but joy and pleasure."

She smiled and lithely stood. All that lit the chamber was a globe of glowing lichen which hung above the bed. Its soft light cast about her head a halo of green. Before she departed, Sinnach caught her hand.

"Please, Toltu. I wish... I ought not to be left alone with my thoughts this night. My mind will be my enemy here in the darkness."

Her smile brightened. It was the world's most perfect smile, and to see it made Sinnach's heart drum like the hooves of a bounding deer. She leaned over him, face shining like the moon under the liquid fall of her raven hair. She put her hand on his side and gently touched her lips to his. Sinnach returned her kiss with a passion doubled.

That was the first night Toltu and Sinnach spent in each other's arms, and every night thereafter they bedded down together. She tutored him in the arts of giving pleasure to a woman's body, showing him the full use of his masculine form. There was healing in her touch, in her soft eye, in her laughter, and in the joining of their two youthful bodies.

Every day Sinnach spent in the Otherworld was more joyful than the last. The mornings he spent with Toltu in her father's court, and in the afternoons he explored that strange and beautiful countryside. Many trees and flowers and grasses were new to him and so he studied their names and their natures. In the woodland he harkened many foreign birdsongs which he learned to sing.

Toltu and Géarshúileach were powerful druíd and skilled poets, and so they imparted to him knowledge unknown in the temporal world. They taught him many intricate poetic meters and songs of harmonic beauty. They taught him their ballads and epics: of hunting, of romance, of journeys, of betrayals, and of Síd battles. And they taught him skills of the draíochta druadh that had not been shared with a human being in many generations.

The Síd dressed their guest in fine clothes of linen and silk, and put about his shoulders a poppy-colored cloak trimmed with a ruddy fur like a fox's. Every day the sky was bright and warm, and every night at Géar-shúileach's table he ate of rich and delicate foods. In the Mór-rí's ráth, no bodily urge ever went unsatisfied.

Such luxury Sinnach enjoyed as if in a dream, for in truth he could hardly tell if all this was real or illusory, nor did he care to know. He indulged in all these pleasures without reflection. Yet as time passed, one day blending into another, Sinnach began to wonder how long he had been in this dream. With sudden concern, he realized he did not know how many days and nights had passed here. Had it been weeks? Months? The season of this world seemed always to be summer. But in a far distant memory of his life before the dreamtime, the days had been shortening and the wheel of the year had been approaching Samhain.

One day, as Sinnach and Toltu walked together in the orchard where they had first met, he asked how long he had been at her father's ráth.

She said only: "Oh, not long." Then she unpinned his cloak and laid it down in the meadow grass. There they made love in the golden glow of sunset's smolder.

Yet once it was asked, Sinnach could not get the question out of his mind. Some days later he asked her again and she said: "Oh, not long." But this time Sinnach watched her face more carefully. Though her expression was perfectly smooth, betraying nothing, her fingers grasped a little cloth talisman hung about her neck.

Many dawns born of mist and many dusks forged from bronze approached and departed. With every passing day Sinnach began to recollect pieces of a distant memory. He felt a desperate need to seize them and bind them together before they floated away; somehow he knew the memory was important. The memory was dull at first, foggy and frayed like the hem of an old cloak. Yet when he grasped for the ends of those tattered threads and traced them to where they merged, the memory grew more solid, more shapely.

At last, after many days of effort, he knew enough to make sense of its meaning. It was the memory of two faces, a woman's and a man's, and to both of them he had spoken these words: 'I sacrifice my solitude and my isolation.' He remembered something further: the people who wore those faces were his foster-mother, Lí Lon, and his other master, Máel Conall. To them he had spoken the nature of his geasa, that which he had sacrificed to transform himself into a man.

Am I at risk of breaking my geasa? Is this isolation, to be here in the Otherworld separated from my people?

Then, with a shock, Sinnach remembered why he had come to the Otherworld. He remembered Cellach and Búan. He remembered the anguish that Búan had last worn on her lovely face. He remembered his duty to serve the Rí Mumhan as his fili. And he remembered the oath he had sworn to Ériu.

"I must return," Sinnach whispered to himself, and resolved to tell Toltu straight away.

That night he shared these thoughts with Toltu. A spasm of sorrow crossed her face and she said, "You cannot go back, Sinnach. They know what you are and they spurn you for it. They do not love you as we love you here. Here you are cherished. Here you are wanted." She combed her fingers through his hair.

"But I have a duty to my people. I swore an oath to serve Ériu. And what's more, I have a geas on me. I fear I am at risk of violating it here."

Toltu turned her face away from him, fingering the talisman strung around her neck. "You need not go now. Stay a while longer. You have still time to take pleasure here." Striding across the room, Toltu picked up her harp and set it in her lap. She strummed those silver strings, and in an instant Sinnach was pulled into a deep and peaceful sleep.

Another day passed. And another. Sinnach struggled to hold onto the memory of that conversation. Then one night, before they laid together in their bed, Sinnach took the harp in his own hands and said to his lover: "I wish, tonight, to be the one to sing thee to sleep." Toltu smiled and agreed, and so he sang to her with a sweet and melodious tenor. When her chest rose and fell with the even breaths of slumber, Sinnach crept into bed beside her. Pulling back the sheets he exposed her lily-white breasts, and there between them was the cloth talisman. Carefully, he opened it. Inside was a lock of curling red hair—his own hair.

"What enchantment is this?" Sinnach whispered to himself. With his belt knife he cut a bit of ruddy fur from the neck of his cloak, and placed this fur inside the talisman in exchange for his own lock of hair. He closed up the talisman tightly, and with a whispered spell reattached the severed lock to his own head of hair.

Toltu's eyes fluttered open as if waking from a troublesome dream. "Sinnach?" she breathed.

"I am here, my love," he cooed. He brushed his lips against hers and encircled her in his arms.

CHAPTER TWENTY FIVE

The Prophecy

Since lifting his lock from Toltu's talisman, Sinnach had become more lucid. It was obvious to him now that he had been enchanted, though in the beginning he admitted the enchantment was welcome. As his memories returned, so did his suffering. He was harried once again by guilt: guilt for keeping the truth from Búan for too long; guilt for bringing such strife to Cellach's court; guilt for lingering in this luxurious dreamtime. No matter how pleasant it was here, the Otherworld was not his home. He had geasa to honor, obligations to fulfill, and wounds to heal in the temporal world. Now Sinnach was adamant to regain his freedom and return home, and yet he was wary of having to fight for it. Despite his lover's deceit, he still loved Toltu very much.

But how much of my love is genuine, and how much am I still seduced by her spell? he wondered.

One evening after feasting in the Mór-rí's hall, Sinnach spoke to the chieftain cogently. "I must return now to my own land, to my own people. I have duties to attend there; I have oaths there to uphold." Sinnach struggled to keep the quiver from his voice. He was nervous to speak so plainly to the Mór-rí, for the chieftain's druidic power more than doubled his own. "I will not be kept here any longer against my will."

Géarshúileach paused and set down his silver goblet. "If that is what you wish Sinnach, we shall not hold you here against your will. I cannot refuse your request if you wish to leave, though I am saddened that you do not appreciate what we give you here."

"No, Mór-rí. I could not be more grateful for the hospitality you have shown me. Your generosity has healed me of a great wound to my soul, and without it I might have been undone. But I must go now and mend what I have made a mess of."

"You are an honorable man, Sinnach," said Géarshúileach in his cavernous voice. "We will be sorry to see you go. Know that you are always welcome in my hall."

Sinnach stood up from the table, bowed to the Mór-rí and his wife, then left the hall with Toltu's hand in his own. In silence they walked by wooded paths through the rolling hills of that fair land, and in the pastel twilight they came to a glade Sinnach knew. It was through this very glade that Toltu had brought him into the Otherworld, naked and weeping, that fateful night so many moons ago.

Toltu turned to her lover, her crystalline eyes glistening. "I have two gifts to give you now, and one of them is an entreaty. The first is this..." She took his hand and placed it on her belly. Sinnach felt beneath his hand an unusual humming, a tiny vortex of energy, a growing locus of lifeforce inside her womb. Sinnach was speechless and searched her face.

"I carry our child," she said, answering his unspoken question. "And thus, I entreat you to come back to me when the child is ready to be born."

Sinnach looked down in wonder and caressed her belly. Her pregnancy had not yet begun to show. Pierced by polar emotions, his mind was aswirl: with pride and excitement, fear and resentment, and the heavy weight of an unwanted responsibility.

"The second gift I have to give you is a prophecy. And since you now have the power to withstand it, I shall not speak it. I will show you." Toltu touched the fingers of her right hand to his forehead between the eyes; her left hand she placed over his heart. At once he was submerged in a terrible vision:

Sinnach stood upon a plain looking towards Brugh Rí from a distance. Before him was a battlefield strewn with the bodies of men maimed and slain. Warriors engaged in a battle a thousand strong on either side. A clash of metal on metal. The screams of men in battle rage and bloodlust struck terror in his soul.

A sudden stroke of light caught his eye and he glanced back at the fort. With a wave horror, he watched as the wooden rampart caught flame and was consumed in a violent conflagration.

"No!" Sinnach shrieked, and the sound of his own voice released him from the vision.

Sinnach was alone, standing in the midst of a dark forest. It was an earthly forest, he was sure. As he stood there beneath an elder tree, the evening call of a long-eared owl sent a shiver down his spine. He was cold for the first time in many days; though how many days, he did not know.

Still reeling from the shock of his vision, Sinnach turned a circle, orienting himself to the directions. At last he found the rising moon and turned from her to face west.

"Brugh Rí!" he cried, and sprinted as swiftly as his human legs could carry.

Thus ends book one of the Tale of Sinnach the Seer.

Author's Note

The concept of time has fascinated me since I was very young. Although I am not a professional historian nor an archeologist, many years of diligent research informed this work. It was my aim that this story be both historically accurate and fantastical to reflect the character of the ancient Irish myths themselves. The expert eye may detect some inaccuracies, for which I do apologize.

Compared to the Bronze Age before it and to the medieval period after it, we know relatively little about the Iron Age in Ireland. The Irish Iron Age was prehistoric, meaning there are no written records of what occurred in this period. Therefore, our historical knowledge of this era comes from stories and myths passed down orally and recorded several hundred years later in the medieval period. There is no clear distinction between history and myth in the Iron Age and early medieval periods, thus I use the term mytho-history to refer to accounts of this era.

As a result of the Roman invasions of Gaul, Galicia, and Britain in the late Iron Age, there is plenty of (biased) documentation related to the so-called "Celts" of those regions. Not much of these accounts can be used to infer truths about the contemporary Irish Gaels, for according to the archeological record the Irish culture of the time was quite distinct from that of the "Celts" in Britain or Europe. Ireland was, as well, relatively isolated since the Irish Sea provided a formidable barrier to all but the most adventurous (or desperate) travelers.

In order to evoke the feeling of a world that has been lost by time and is now mysterious to us, I wove together my understandings of Irish mythology, archeology, folklore, linguistics, druidism, and early medieval Irish history. A review of the selected bibliography below should elucidate which elements of this story are rooted most firmly in scholarly research, and which elements are born of my own imagination.

Much of the information that I have gleaned is contradictory; there is a significant amount of disagreement in almost every line of inquiry I explored. However, as a writer of fiction, the enigmatic nature of the Irish Iron Age has presented me with an opportunity for creativity. Where there are holes in our understanding of the past, I have used my artistic license and my intuition to fill them in. I hope it was done tastefully and with enough historicity to satisfy readers more learned than I.

Bibliography

Bonwick, James. *Irish Druids and Old Irish Religions*. 1894.

Calder, George. *Auraicept Na n-Éces : the Scholars' Primer; Being the Texts of the Ogham Tract from the Book of Ballymote and the Yellow Book of Lecan, and the Text of the Trefhocul from the Book of Leinster*. 1917.

Carmichael, Alexander. *Carmina Gadelica: Hymns & Incantations*. 1900. Reprint: Floris Books, 1992.

Carmody, Isolde ÓBrolcháin, and Chris Thompson. *Story Archeology*, www.storyarchaeology.com.

Joyce, P.W. *A Smaller Social History of Ancient Ireland*. 1906. Reprint: Dodo Press.

Kelly, Fergus. *A Guide to Early Irish Law*. Volume III, Dublin Institute for Advanced Studies, 2016.

Mac Neill, Eóin John. "Early Irish population-groups: their nomenclature, classification, and chronology." *Proceedings of the Royal Irish Academy. Section C: Archaeology, Celtic Studies, History, Linguistics, Literature* 29 (1911): 59-114. https://celt.ucc.ie//published/E900000-003/index.html.

Meyer, Kuno. *A primer of Irish metrics*. AMS Press, 1909.

O'Curry, Eugene. *On the manners and customs of the ancient Irish*. Vol. 2. Williams and Norgate, 1873.

O'Brien, Kathleen M. "Index of Names in Irish Annals." *Medieval Scotland*, 21 May 2015, www.medievalscotland.org/kmo/AnnalsIndex/index.shtml.

Patterson, Nerys Thomas. *Cattle-Lords and Clansmen: The Social Structure of Early Ireland*. University of Notre Dame Press, 1994.

Raftery, Barry. *Pagan Celtic Ireland: the Enigma of the Irish Iron Age*. Thames & Hudson, 2000.

Westropp, Thomas Johnson. "On Certain Typical Earthworks and Ring-Walls in the County Limerick. Part II. The Royal Forts in Coshlea (Continued)." *Proceedings of the Royal Irish Academy. Section C: Archaeology, Celtic Studies, History, Linguistics, Literature* 33 (1916).

Acknowledgments

Firstly, I would like to thank Sinnach himself, for his story carried me through a very difficult time in my life. Secondly, I would like to express my deepest gratitude to two people in particular: my sister and my good friend Tom. Without their encouragement and early enthusiasm, this story may not have been published. Thanks also to my friends and family who gave me helpful feedback on the early drafts of this work: Janice, Story, Ana, Pan, Ben, Miel, Jason, Aylin, Tyler, Janine, and Victoria. Thank you to editor Kat Enright. I am eternally grateful to Isolde ÓBrolcháin Carmody and Chris Thompson of StoryArcheology.com, whose scholarship and storytelling inspired the creation of this new myth. Thank you to Bonnie Maslin, an extraordinary matron of the arts.

I give gratitude to this sacred land where I live, Wabanakik, and to the ancestors and deities who reside here. I give gratitude to the muses who visit me in that misty place between waking and dreaming, and to Imbas, the water of my creativity. I give gratitude to Ériu, the land of my ancestors, and to the Irish people for sharing their rich heritage with the world.

Go raibh maith agat agus beannacht.

ABOUT THE AUTHOR

M.Z. McDonnell is an ecologist, herbalist, and writer living in Vermont (Wabanakik). Their first novel, *Miach & Airmed,* was published in 2018.

To purchase books or to contact the author, please visit: www.mzmcdonnell.com

Every reader review helps get the word out. Please consider writing a review of this book at: www.goodreads.com

Ingram Content Group UK Ltd.
Milton Keynes UK
UKHW010649120323
418424UK00001B/357